Bet

Casey Gordon

Publisher: Casey Gordon

Saint Cloud, Minnesota

ISBN: 979-8-9862755-0-5 (Ebook)

ISBN: 979-8-9862755-1-2 (Paperback)

ISBN: 979-8-9862755-2-9 (Hardback)

Library of Congress Control Number: 2022911449

Cover design by: Casey Gordon

This book is a work of fiction. Names, characters, brands, organizations, media, places, events, storylines, and incidents are the product of the author's imagination or are used fictitiously. Any resemblance to any person, living or dead, business establishments, events, locales, or any events or occurrences is purely coincidental.

To my husband.
To my boys.
To my mom and dad.
To my sisters.
To my entire wonderful family.

For encouraging me to dream.
For being there for me.
For believing in me.
For loving me without limits.

I love you all, you bunch of a**holes.

Contents

Chapter 1

"I want to go on record that this is a terrible idea," Sunny Montgomery stated as she paced the bedroom of her best friend, Parker Crawford.

"Noted," Parker replied, head down, as he sat hunched over his laptop on his Jackson Pollock-inspired rug. Parker typically never stopped talking, so the simple fact that he was barely speaking demonstrated how focused he was on the task at hand.

Sunny, short for Addison, plopped herself cross-legged on the rug facing him. "Like, a straight-up terrible idea. Terrible AF. If you like a girl, you should just tell her. Playing games never ends well."

Parker remained silent.

"But you're going to do it, anyway?" Sunny prompted.

"Yup."

Sunny nodded and felt the ponytail on top of her head give a little bob. She had tossed her long, wavy blonde hair up into a high ponytail this morning because of the heat. Ninety degrees, rare for Minnesota in early June, but not unheard of. It was too hot to leave the heavy strands dangling down her back, and Sunny always went for function over form. A simple ponytail was perfect. No muss, no fuss.

"Why? Why go to all this work when you could just ask her out? That's way easier." Sunny asked.

"Two birds, one stone," Parker said. His eyes drifted up to gaze out of the wide bay window to his left as he mused, "Or is it really three birds, one stone in this case? Maybe four? I'm not sure. It's a lot of birds."

"Parker! Focus!"

Parker's eyes flew back to Sunny's face, and he blinked. "Sorry. What?"

"Dude!" Sunny was getting impatient. "You told me you have some weird plan to get Mika to fall in love with you. I asked you why you don't just ask her out like a normal human being."

"First of all, I did not call it a 'weird' plan. I think my exact words were 'genius' plan. And second, I already told you why!" Parker paused, taking a deep breath as though preparing for a dramatic monologue. "This will give me the perfect excuse to get closer to Mika, and it's the perfect summer activity to cap off our senior year before everyone leaves for college. It'll be totally sick. Oh, and did I mention this will totally get you into MIT? Admissions people love crap like this. But most importantly, and I cannot overemphasize this point, I'll get to spend hours with Mika working on this, and she won't be able to resist me!"

Mika Smith was Parker's dream girl. She was the class valedictorian. Tall and athletic, with long dark hair and huge brown eyes that crinkled at the corners when she laughed. Even Sunny had to admit, she was the total package; smart, funny, and beautiful. Parker had mooned over her for their entire senior year, but never found the courage to ask her out. Now that it was summer, he was determined to make his feelings known before everyone left for college. It struck Sunny as kind of pointless. Everyone was leaving. Why try to start a relationship now? But Parker did what Parker wanted, and Sunny had learned long ago that it was easier to just go with it.

"Okay. So you won't trick her or anything weird?"

"You keep using that word. I would never do anything weird! I'm just trying to spend some quality time with her. She's amazing, Sunny. I just know she's perfect for me."

Sunny took a breath. "Okay. I still need more details, but I guess if it's that important to you and you think it will help get me off the waitlist for MIT, I'm in," she stated with a hesitant nod of her head. "So, what's the plan, genius?"

Parker looked up from his laptop, and a grin spread across his face. "I never doubted you for a second, Sunshine," he said, motioning for her to look at his laptop. He had a document open with a list of items. "So, I've laid out a list of stuff we have to do, and I have the perfect job for you. It's one that only you can do." The smile on his face reminded Sunny of how handsome he was, a fact she frequently forgot because they were both firmly, happily, and permanently in the friend zone. Having met when they were just eleven years old, Parker had won Sunny over with his endless chatter and upbeat personality. Nothing ever seemed to get him down. They had been inseparable ever since. There was no romantic chemistry between them, and there never had been. Privately, Sunny was glad about that. Who needed romance complicating a friendship?

Sunny shook herself out of her reverie, swiped the laptop off of Parker's lap, and started reading the list he had created. The first item on the list read, "Convince Sunny to help." It looked like Parker was making progress on his goals.

"What do you need me to do?" Sunny inquired as she continued to read.

"You are going to take that little app that you made for us and make it work for everyone in our class."

Sunny's eyes flew up to meet Parker's. She closed his laptop with a thud and gently tossed it onto the rug. "Nope. Not gonna do that!" she barked, making Parker's orange cat, Sasquatch, jump with fright. The cat sat lounging in the over-sized window seat enjoying the sunshine. She glared at Sunny for daring to wake her from her afternoon nap, her ears flattened back to show her annoyance. They had a love-hate relationship. Sunny loved the fat cat, but Sassy did not return the sentiment. It had all started, Sunny believed, when Parker and his brother, Zeke, first adopted the cat six years ago. Sunny had wanted to name the tiny, orange kitten Marmalade and call her "Marmy" for short. The tiny kitten hissed and batted her paw at Sunny, seeming to take offense to the name. Meanwhile, the boys pretended to puke and declared the name "too girly" for a cat owned by two boys. They wanted a name that conveyed size and terror, and Parker suggested Sasquatch, having just watched *Harry and the Hendersons* a few weeks prior. Sunny remembered arguing about it for a long time, but Parker had insisted. Sasquatch, it was, and it turned out that the nickname "Sassy" suited the cat pretty well.

"Oh, calm down, Sassy. You're fine." Sunny said, as she gave the cat an apologetic smile. In reply, the cat stood up and turned around, showing Sunny her backside before plunking down and going back to sleep.

"Oh, come on! The betting app you made for us is amazing," Parker said, growing more animated as he explained. "It will be perfect for what I want to do. You know how it keeps track of who wins or loses each bet? Side note, did you know that, as of today, I've won 542 bets, which puts me in the lead ahead of your meager 478 wins?"

"Yes, I know what the app does, Parker. I designed it." Sunny rolled her eyes. "But I'm not gonna release it for everyone to use. Are you insane? It's not even good. It's just some dumb thing I threw together a few years ago for us to use. I never meant for anyone but us to use it." Sunny paused. "Also, FYI, you are only winning because you forced me to add in all of the old bets going all the way back to when we started keeping track in sixth grade. You may have won a lot back then, but I've won way more bets in the past two years. At this rate, I'll have you beat by next year. Easy-peasy lemon squeezy."

Parker snorted. "Never gonna happen, Montgomery. Keep dreaming. In fact," he said, opening up his laptop and placing it back on her lap, "keep dreaming while you go ahead and change that app."

Sunny shook her head. "I already told you! That's not gonna happen. The code is a mess! I wrote it years ago when I didn't know what I was doing. The whole thing would need a rewrite before I would even think of making it live. And I still don't even get what you are trying to do. How would it work? You want us to bet with the kids in our class? And how does this help you with your plan to win over Mika, who, might I remind you, barely even knows you exist, despite the fact that she's the so-called love of your life?"

"I'm glad you asked," Parker said, rising to his feet like he was about to give a speech in front of an audience. He spread his arms wide. "You see, we are going to plan a bet. One bet on an epic scale. Like nothing anyone has ever seen before! The bet to end all bets! This bet is going to be between me and our entire senior class. Winner gets $10,000. And I get Mika. And you get into MIT. Well, if everything goes according to plan."

After Parker's dramatic speech, Sunny convinced him to sit back down and outline his plan.

"Picture this," Parker said. "It'll be like a treasure hunt. I'll bet the entire class that they can't follow our clues all the way to the end. And some of the clues will be old-timey historical clues, giving me the perfect excuse to get close to Mika."

Mika's mother worked at the Cloud Lake Historical Society, and this summer, Mika was interning there before heading off to college.

"Parker," Sunny began suspiciously, "have you been watching *National Treasure* again?"

"Maybe..." Parker hedged. "And so what if I watched it again last night? It's an incredibly underrated movie. You know that. Everyone loves a good treasure hunt!"

Sunny had to admit that a treasure hunt did sound pretty fun.

"Okay. So you aren't really talking about our exact betting app. You're actually talking about a totally new thing that's way bigger, like multiple individual tasks inside one giant bet." The wheels began to turn in Sunny's mind, and she started ticking off items on her fingers. "We need accounts for everyone to track their progress. They'll need to be able to use the app to digitally check in at the places the clues send them to so that we know they solved the clue. Then we can send the next clue to their app. It would also be cool if everyone in the class could see everyone's progress, so you know who has been eliminated and who is still in it…"

She trailed off as her brain continued to spin with all the possibilities. Her hands itched to get started, but she wasn't going to design this app on Parker's laptop. For this job, she needed her own computer. Setting Parker's laptop aside, she reached for her fully-customized black laptop. She had lovingly decorated it with nerdy gaming stickers she'd bought online. She opened up a new document and started drafting an outline of what the app would need in order to function.

Sunny knew from the moment Parker had told her he had a scheme to win Mika that he was going to need her help. Parker was the creative type, very artistic, but he wasn't so great at actually buckling down and doing the work to make his ideas a reality. And in this case, app development was way out of his skill set. Sunny was logical, the perfect counter-balance for Parker. She had learned how to develop apps for mobile devices when she was just thirteen years old. Her dad sent her to a coding boot camp one summer. She had hated the camp but loved the programming. The camp directors had spent the entire time painstakingly walking the class through everything step by step, but that didn't work for Sunny. She wanted to learn faster. Tuning out the teacher, she'd followed the steps from the book on her own, finishing the project in just a few hours and using her spare time to write a script that made the computer make a farting noise every five minutes. The kids went into fits of giggles whenever the noise went off, but the teacher hadn't been so amused. When it was discovered that the noise was originating from Sunny's computer, she was taken aside and given a stern lecture about using her skills for good and not mischief.

What the teacher didn't realize was that Sunny hadn't been trying to cause trouble, exactly. She was actually a rule-follower. She was simply bored and looking for something to learn. Computer stuff just clicked for her. She understood it. Tell the computer to do something; it happens. Logical. Predictable. It just made sense.

When her dad picked her up from camp, she began begging for a computer of her own before they had even gotten to the car. It ended up being a surprisingly easy sell. She didn't even have to promise her dad good behavior in return. He was thrilled that Sunny wanted to work on something educational in her spare time. From that point on, she taught herself through experimentation, researching online, and watching YouTube videos.

Sunny's fingers flew over the keys while Parker hovered over her shoulder. She paused, fingers halting in midair, mildly annoyed. "You know this is going to take me a while, right?" Parker nodded, continuing to stare at the screen as though an app would magically appear at any second. She continued, "Meaning, could you, like, give me some space or something? This is going to take hours, weeks even, and I can't work with you breathing down my neck, taco-breath."

"That's cool," Parker said, not the least bit offended. He was accustomed to Sunny's somewhat affectionate name-calling. He stood up and flopped onto the bed, staring up at the ceiling, which was currently painted black with streaks of purple and neon green meant to replicate the look of the northern lights. "I'll just chill here while you work. Do you think I should repaint the ceiling in shades of blue so it looks like I'm sleeping underwater?"

"Sure," Sunny said absently as she continued thinking about how to make the app work. She had to admit, Parker's bedroom was pretty amazing. For starters, his dad let him do whatever he wanted with the room, so he was always changing the paint colors and rearranging furniture. Sunny's parents had painted her bedroom a soft gray color when her mom was pregnant with her eighteen years ago, and when they'd moved, her dad had painted her new bedroom that exact same shade. It was still that same color today. When she was younger, she often begged to paint it purple or pink or blue, but her dad always replied, "Your mother picked out that gray especially for you, sweetie. She loved that color." Subject closed. Eventually, Sunny just stopped asking.

Parker's room was massive, easily three times the size of Sunny's. It featured a king-sized bed on one side and an entire gaming area on the far side of the room by the bay window. Parker's dad was a successful lawyer, but even his salary couldn't afford this type of house. The Crawfords had family money. Not just a little money, serious money from a few generations back. And it showed. From the Olympic-sized pool in the backyard to the gourmet kitchen, their house was high end. Being Parker's friend certainly had its perks. They were both huge movie fans, and the movie theater in the basement was Sunny's favorite place to hang. Because of that and the pool, they ended up spending way more time at Parker's place than Sunny's completely normal, suburban house, which was located just a few blocks away.

"I don't hear typing..." Parker sang, his voice nudging Sunny back to work.

Sunny laughed, grabbed a throw pillow from the floor, and tossed it at him. "Yes, drill sergeant!"

Parker caught the pillow easily, stuffed it under his head, and closed his eyes with a contented sigh.

Head down, Sunny got back to work.

Sunny was deep into work mode. She holed up in her room all week, writing code, testing, and tweaking. She even ignored Parker's texts and video calls. Occasionally, she responded to his texts with "Busy" and a smiley face emoji so he knew she wasn't mad at him. Thank goodness they had already graduated last week, because Sunny definitely would have skipped school to finish this app. When she focused on a project, there wasn't room for anything else.

Mountain Dew was her drug of choice. As she cracked another one open and eyed the pile of empty cans on the floor next to her desk, she considered the fact that she may have a problem. She had gone through at least two cases this week alone. Her dad was going to kill her when he took out the recycling. Then she would have to endure a long lecture about sugar, proper nutrition, and heart attacks in young people caused by energy drinks. Insert eye roll. When Sunny was making progress, the last thing she wanted to do was stop and sleep. Even if she did take a break, her brain kept chugging through the lines of code in her head and she couldn't actually rest. Sometimes she even dreamed about writing code. When it was that intense, she preferred to just stay awake, using the sugar and caffeine from the Mountain Dew to keep her going. Sunny's dad, though proud of her computer expertise, didn't seem to understand that it was all part of her creative process.

At last, Sunny ran a quick test on the app simulator she had launched on her computer. Everything was looking good. She fixed a few typos and a link that wasn't loading correctly. Sitting back in her chair, she smiled as she thought about how much she had accomplished and how amped Parker was going to be when he saw it. Sunny was no graphic designer, but she had passable skills in making things user-friendly. The app was clean and easy to use.

It was designed so anyone could download the app, make an account, and create an unlimited number of bets. The person creating the bet could type in the terms of the bet, including setting a timeline for the bet and what the winner would receive at the end. They could invite participants and appoint someone as a judge to help verify the winner. The coolest feature, in Sunny's opinion, was the ability for all of the participants of the bet to see the progress of everyone else engaged in that same bet.

Sunny's stomach churned as she got everything ready to submit for review in the app store. Once it she submitted it, the company would review it to make sure it complied with their guidelines. She would have a chance to fix things before they would let her publish it. The review could take a day. It could take two weeks or more. There was no way to know. Sunny felt queasy when she thought about having an expert look at what she built. What if it wasn't good enough?

When Parker had first suggested that she take their fun betting app to the next level, Sunny freaked out inside. She and Parker had been using her app to track who won their bets for a few years now, but this was completely different. That was just the two of them. This new app would be released to the world. It was terrifying on another level completely. With all those eyes on it, people were bound to find problems and give negative reviews if they didn't like it.

To calm her nerves, Sunny picked up the phone and texted Parker.
Sunny: *Done.*
His reply came swiftly.
Parker: *For real sweet can I see it*
Parker never used punctuation for texts, much to Sunny's unending frustration. She tapped out her grammatically correct reply.
Sunny: *No. I'm chickening out. I haven't even submitted it yet.*
Parker: *Dude just nut up and do it*
Sunny: *That's gross, P.*
Parker: *What r u scared of*
Sunny set the phone aside and considered his question. What was she afraid of? No one would likely even see her app. Only the kids in their newly graduated class were going to download it, so this wasn't a big deal. Right? Sunny's eyes drew back to the submit button on her computer screen as she weighed the negative possibilities in her mind. This was so much bigger than anything she'd made in the past. Why was she even putting herself through all of this stress? Part of it was to help Parker, but that wasn't the only reason.

She closed her eyes and thought about MIT. She had been wait-listed back in January. It was already June, and she had heard nothing from them. She knew that the longer they remained silent, the less likely it was that she would get in. And she simply had to get in. Her mom and dad had both attended MIT. It was where they met. It was where they fell in love. "College was a transformational experience," her dad often said, smiling fondly. Now a college professor himself, there was nothing more important to him than education. For as long as she could remember, Sunny's attendance at MIT had been a given.

When Sunny was born, Frank and Sally Montgomery started setting aside money every month into her college savings account. When her mom died suddenly in a car accident the year Sunny turned ten, her dad had put the entire life insurance policy into that fund, ensuring that Sunny never had to worry about money while she attended. Frank had never questioned whether or not she would get in to MIT. They didn't even tour any other colleges. It had crushed him when she was waitlisted, and he had insisted on calling everyone he knew in the alumni office to argue her case. Sunny could only assume that all waitlisted parents likely did the same thing, because it yielded no results. Nearly every day, he asked Sunny if she'd gotten an email from MIT. The disappointment she felt from him each time she had to answer "no" was slowly crushing her soul.

However, there was something even worse than her father's disappointment. A few years ago, on her sixteenth birthday, her dad presented her with a diary written by her mother while she was pregnant with Sunny. After tearing off the wrapping paper, Sunny clutched the diary to her chest with a sense of nervous anticipation. That night, she jumped into bed and read the entire diary by flashlight late into the night. She could hear her mother's voice in her head as she read. After missing her for so long, it was like having her back. In those diary entries, Sally spoke of all the things she was going through during the pregnancy. She wrote about the aches and the pains, the size of the baby growing in her belly, and her doctor's appointments. But those weren't the words that still stuck with Sunny two years later. Scattered throughout the diary entries were the hopes and dreams of a mother for her baby.

I hope you always know how much I love you and that you can come to me with any problem you encounter.
I hope that you are brave and strong. If you talk back to me, I promise to remind myself that it's a good thing because you will be able to take care of yourself one day.
I hope you have your dad's smile. Your dad is one of the kindest men I've ever met, and every family needs more kindness and laughter in their heart.

But there was one diary entry in particular that haunted Sunny over the last six months.

I can't wait to see who you become when you grow up. When you are eighteen, your whole life is ahead of you, my little one. I have such big dreams for you. When I went to MIT, I was so young and naïve, but once I was there, my entire world opened up. I learned about things I never imagined. When you set off for MIT, I'm going to cry and kiss you goodbye, but I will know in my heart that it is the perfect place for you. You may feel overwhelmed by it all, you may change majors a time or two, and you may even get your heart broken. But I want you to experience all of it. The friendships, the laughter, the learning, the love, it's all there waiting for you.

When she'd received the letter informing her she was waitlisted, her mother's words echoed in her head. Her mother wanted all those things for her, and Sunny had failed. She felt tears spring to her eyes as she recalled her disappointment that day.

Sunny simply had to get into MIT. Her mother was gone, but when Sunny walked those halls to class, she knew she would feel close to her again. No backup plan would be sufficient. The clock was ticking. College was less than three months away. She needed something big to impress the Admissions department, so she let Parker talk her into his crazy plan. However, that didn't stop her stomach from feeling queasy the minute she thought about pushing the submit button.

Everything she had built in the past had only been for herself. This felt like baring her soul to the world. What if someone found a bug and exposed her as an amateur coder? She really didn't have any formal training. Who was she to think she could even do this? What if people hated it and the Admissions staff decided she didn't even deserve to be on their waiting list anymore?

Sunny pushed the negative thoughts away. She had promised Parker she would do this for him, and they never broke their promises to each other. And if this was the only way to achieve her mother's dream, she didn't really have a choice. This was her last shot.

Sunny took a deep breath and clicked the submit button.

Chapter 2

"Where's your brother?" Sunny asked, striving for a casual tone. It had been three days since she submitted the app for review, and she had busied herself by hanging out at Parker's house as much as possible. They were playing Mario Kart in Parker's room, and Sunny was winning as per usual. First-person shooters were Parker's jam, but Sunny thrived on puzzle and racing games.

She hadn't caught a single glimpse of Parker's older brother, Zeke, in the past three days, despite the fact that she was pretty sure he was at home. It was odd. But what was odder still was that she was a bit disappointed about that fact. Zeke and Sunny hadn't been on the best of terms before he'd left for college last fall, and she hadn't even seen him since Christmas. She wasn't sure why she was asking about him now, but she told herself it was because she needed a distraction from agonizing over the app.

Parker barked out a laugh in reply to her question. "Hiding. He's barely come out of his room in the last two weeks. Marta has been delivering food to his bedroom door like she's fricking Uber Eats." Marta was the family housekeeper. She'd been with the Crawford family since the boys were in diapers, long before their mother had passed away and she'd taken on the role of surrogate mother to the two boys. Sunny loved Marta dearly. She was warm and kind, with gray hair always swept up in a bun atop her head. Whenever the kids were sad, she baked a batch of German cookies just for them. Sunny loved them, but Marta always refused to share the recipe with her. Whenever Sunny would ask, Marta would reply in a deep, accented voice, "What do you need the recipe for? You have me!"

Parker continued, "I think he's embarrassed about everything that happened. You know what he's like. He isn't exactly social on a good day, but now he's gone full-on recluse. Just call him Howard Hughes."

At Parker's words, Sunny instantly pictured Leonardo DiCaprio in the movie based on Howard Hughes' life. Zeke didn't look much like the famous actor, but they did have one thing in common. Both of them were easy on the eyes.

Sunny knew exactly what Parker was referring to when he said Zeke was embarrassed. He was talking about the reason Zeke came home early from college. He had been kicked out a few weeks earlier, right before the end of his freshman year, for violating the ethics policy. Specifically, underage drinking and drunk driving. Well, actually drunk crashing into a tree at a frat house, to be even more specific. Parker was surprisingly tight-lipped about it all, but Sunny had poked and prodded until she'd gotten most of the story. The short version - Parker drove down to stay with Zeke for the weekend. Zeke got completely drunk at some house party and crashed his Camaro into a tree. Neither had been seriously injured, likely because they hadn't been going very fast. Parker had been knocked unconscious and taken to the hospital. Thankfully, it was only a mild concussion, and they released him the next day.

It made Sunny angry to even think about the fact that Zeke had driven drunk. One thing she had learned from losing her mom in a car accident when she was ten years old was that people were gone in a flash. Life was too precious to take risks like that.

Uncomfortable thinking about the horrible possibilities, Sunny struggled to change the subject. Glancing at the clock, she saw it was already noon. Sunny asked, "Wait, why are you here with me right now? I thought you were supposed to be meeting Mika today to work on the clues?"

Now that Sunny was done with the app, it was Parker's turn to work on his part of the plan. He needed to build the clues for the bet, and to do that, he needed Mika. Sunny had thought Parker was going to meet up with her last week and get started, but it never happened. Yesterday, when Parker finally texted Mika to tell her his idea and ask her to help to make up the clues, she was really excited about the idea. It turned out that Parker had been right. She was a total history nerd. Coming up with a bunch of historically based clues to lead their former classmates all over Cloud Lake this summer was clearly her idea of a good time.

"Well," said Parker, looking chagrined, "turns out, I should have explained myself better over text. Instead of asking her to help me write the clues, I think I may have maybe perhaps given her the impression I wanted her to write the clues by herself. I texted her to confirm meeting up today, but she told me that I didn't need to worry. She'd take care of it." Parker shrugged, looking forlorn.

"What?" asked Sunny, outraged. She stood and tossed her controller down onto the couch. "Are you kidding me, Parker? The whole point of this damn thing was so you could have an excuse to spend some time with her! This was all your idea!"

Parker threw his controller down onto the carpet and covered his face with his hands. "I know, I know! I'm gonna fix it. I swear!"

"How?"

"So I have a plan..."

Sunny groaned and spoke through clenched teeth. "No. More. Plans."

"No, for real. This is a good one. You'll like it."

"No. Just no. You have to go talk to the girl. Period."

"This is totally going to work, Sunny. It'll be fine! I'm going to call up Mika and tell her you broke your arm... or maybe your leg? Yeah, your leg. No, wait. I need something that heals fast in case she sees you walking around later. Maybe you pretend to have a concussion, and you can be all confused..."

As Parker continued rambling, Sunny gave him the side eye and picked up her cell phone.

Parker paused. "What are you doing?" he asked suspiciously.

She didn't answer. Her fingers furiously danced across the screen of the phone.

"Sunny! What are you doing? Who are you texting?" Concerned, Parker stood and tried to get a peek at her screen.

With one last furious jab of her finger, she threw her phone down and said, "There. Taken care of."

A look of terror crossed Parker's face. "What did you do?"

His phone dinged and his eyes got even bigger. "What did you do?" he asked again, scrambling to reach his phone. "It's Mika." He looked up at Sunny, panicked.

"I fixed it. With the truth. You're welcome." Sunny smiled smugly. She and Mika didn't run in the same social circles, but she had Mika's phone number from when they'd done a group project together in biology class a few years ago. She figured the simplest way to fix the situation was to text Mika directly.

Parker read his newest text message aloud.

Mika: *Hey! Sunny said you are bored and driving her nuts and you want to help. Want to come over to my house to work on the clues?*

Parker turned to Sunny and threw his arms around her as he proclaimed, "Sunny, you are a genius!"

Sunny relaxed on the over-sized lounge chair beside the Crawfords' pool, her eyes closed against the bright afternoon sun. Parker left less than an hour ago to visit Mika, and he'd told Sunny to stay and hang out as long as she wanted. Sunny briefly considered heading home, before discarding the idea when she thought about the empty house that awaited. Her dad was teaching today, and he had one class in the morning and another in the late afternoon. A long-time mathematics professor at the University of Minnesota, he often stayed on campus in between teaching classes rather than make the thirty-minute commute home and back again. It meant that Sunny was pretty much on her own during his teaching days. Sunny didn't mind the freedom. Since her mother's accident, her dad tended to be a bit overprotective. Actually, smothering might be a better term. But just because she liked the freedom didn't mean she wanted to go home to an empty house. At least here, Marta was bustling around the kitchen, Zeke was somewhere nearby, and she didn't feel quite so alone. Plus, she didn't have a pool at her house, so being able to stay and use Parker's was a bonus.

A low, quiet voice disturbed the peaceful relaxation time Sunny had been enjoying.

"Hello, Addison."

Sunny's heart jumped in her chest. She opened her eyes and looked up. Zeke stood before her with a smile. A smile that struck Sunny as very, very sexy, though she would die before admitting that to anyone, especially him. He loomed over her, blocking the afternoon sun as she lounged near the pool.

Sunny felt her face flush as he looked down at her. It had been five months since she had last seen Ezekiel Jefferson Crawford. Zeke for short. But the second she saw him, it was like no time had passed at all. All those complicated feelings were still there, the ones she didn't want to stop to consider.

Zeke had always confused her, but never more so than in the past few years as they all struggled into adulthood. He had always been mature, from the first moment she'd met him when he was just twelve years old and she was eleven. Sunny knew his maturity came from the fact that he'd had to grow up and take charge of Parker when the boys' mother had passed away from cancer. As he got older, Sunny came to learn other things about Zeke too. He was insanely talented, even though she hadn't seen him play the piano in a long time. Freakishly smart, although he always tried to hide it. And, oh yeah, did she mention hot? He was muscular, tall, with short, brown hair that sometimes spiked up in all directions when he ran his hands through it. But it was his eyes that always caught Sunny off guard. They were bright blue, and she sometimes felt like there was a sadness inside them that never went away, even when he was smiling or laughing. Zeke had always been a quiet kid. Quiet, not shy. Kind. Popular. He never seemed to care what other people thought of him, but everyone liked him anyway. Perhaps it was because he didn't care that they liked him. He got along with nearly everyone.

Everyone except Sunny. Oh, they'd gotten along great when they were kids. But in the last few years before he'd left for college, it seemed like they were always sniping at each other, always getting under each other's skin. It wasn't anything Sunny could put her finger on. It wasn't that she disliked Zeke. In fact, she'd spent most of her teenage years trying to hide exactly how much she liked him. Perhaps it was that Zeke was too overprotective. She already had one overprotective father, thank you very much, and she didn't need another one. Perhaps it was Sunny's own complicated feelings for Zeke that set her teeth on edge whenever he was around. Or maybe Zeke simply thought Sunny was just a dumb little kid, and he only tolerated her because she was Parker's friend. Whatever the reason, Sunny felt like she was walking a tightrope whenever he was in the room. It was exhausting. Though she'd missed him when he went to college, she had to admit that it had been nice being able to let down her guard when he wasn't there.

Laying in front of him with his blue eyes staring down at her, Sunny felt uncomfortable and gawky. Zeke, meanwhile, looked perfect. Perfectly tan skin, perfectly tousled dark hair. There even seemed to be more muscle definition in his arms under his plain black t-shirt. *Ugh, why is the world torturing me?* thought Sunny.

"Hi Ezekiel," Sunny said, hoping she annoyed him by using his full first name, as he had used hers. She nodded stiffly up at him. "You're blocking my sun." No welcome home friendliness from her. It pissed Sunny off that he was stupid enough to drive drunk and that he had gotten Parker hurt, but that wasn't why she was being cold. It was a defense mechanism. After all, what better way to hide her feelings for him than to act like a bitch? She knew he didn't deserve it, but it had been going on for so long like this, frankly, at this point, she didn't know how to stop.

"Where's your other half?" Zeke said, ignoring her frosty greeting and glancing around the empty pool area as though Parker would magically appear.

"Meeting a girl," Sunny said, leaning up on her elbows. As soon as she did that, she realized it made her chest stick out, and she immediately sank back down on the chair. She didn't want him to think she was trying to advertise her assets.

Zeke snorted with laughter. "No way. The only girl Parker talks to is you."

Sunny shrugged one shoulder.

"For real?" Zeke continued with an amazed look. He flopped down on his side in the lounge chair next to her and leaned up on his right elbow, his body turned to face her. "So, what's the story there?"

Something inside Sunny warmed at the casual way he spoke to her, like they were old friends again, even though they hadn't been that way in quite some time. Sunny turned over to face him, leaning up on her left elbow, mirroring his position. She looked down and picked some lint off the lounge chair cushion underneath her.

"You know Parker. It's just some girl he is in love with that he's never spoken to before," she said in a slightly bitter tone.

"Oh," Zeke said. "And do you not like her?"

She glanced up at Zeke. "No, no. It's not that. She's actually really nice. It's just..." Sunny blew out her breath. "Parker's just Parker, you know? Like, he just likes the idea of things. He doesn't even know her, but he loves her. And it's all he will talk about, but then he comes up with these crazy, elaborate plans, and when it all gets messed up,

I'm the one who has to clean up after him. I guess I'm just tired of cleaning up his messes. It's just...frustrating."

Zeke grimaced and nodded slowly. If anyone knew how frustrating Parker could be sometimes, it was Zeke. "I know exactly what you mean." He paused. "So you aren't, like, jealous?" he asked.

Sunny wrinkled her nose. "Jealous? Of what?"

"You know... Parker... and another girl." Zeke looked uncomfortable as he said the words aloud. He wouldn't quite meet her eyes.

Sunny huffed out an angry, "What?" and sat straight up, nearly bouncing out of her seat. "Of course not! You know we're just friends!"

Zeke sat up too. "Well, I know you guys always say that, but I guess I just thought... I mean, I think everyone just thought you two would eventually..." he trailed off again and looked away, embarrassed.

Sunny could feel her cheeks coloring. She knew what everyone thought. She wasn't stupid. But it just wasn't like that with her and Parker. She thought at least Zeke, who was the closest to the both of them, would have known that.

She stood up and decided to let her frustration out. "I thought you, of all people, would know there is nothing between Parker and I except friendship. Frankly, I'm sick of people not believing us! Guys and girls can be just friends, you know! It's possible without us losing our minds and throwing ourselves at each other. And besides, I'm seeing someone right now." She folded her arms defensively. It wasn't a lie exactly, but she omitted the fact that she was pretty sure she was going to break up with Graham. They'd only been on a few dates, and the truth was, she didn't think about Graham much at all. She hadn't even texted him the entire week she'd been working on the app. Graham hadn't texted her either, though, so she was pretty sure he wasn't going to be heartbroken when she broke things off between them.

Zeke nodded and looked up at her. He smiled, but it didn't quite reach his eyes.

"So, who's the guy?"

Sunny already regretted mentioning him. "His name is Graham. He's very nice, and I like him a lot. We're going out tomorrow." Lies. She didn't like him a lot, and they weren't going out tomorrow. She was grasping for evidence to prove to Zeke that she wasn't hung up on Parker. Desperate for a distraction, she grabbed her half-empty water bottle and chugged the rest.

"Where's he taking you? Mini golfing, so you can show him your expert skills?" he teased. From their years of golfing together, Zeke knew Sunny was horrible at putting, and he never passed up a chance to remind her. When they were younger, she had lost a lot of bets to Parker because of her lousy putting skills.

"Ugh," Sunny groaned, ignoring the question and throwing her empty water bottle at Zeke. He caught it easily. "Why'd you even come out here? Just to torture me? I was having a nice, relaxing afternoon before you showed up."

Zeke shrugged, turning serious. "Tell you the truth, I was going a little stir-crazy in the house." He looked down at the water bottle in his hands. "And I thought... Well, I mean, I hadn't seen you yet since I'd come home, so when I saw you sitting out here, I figured I should say hi."

"I just thought you were avoiding me on purpose," Sunny said dryly.

"No, not you specifically. Just... everyone." Zeke paused. "My dad, my friends. It's weird. Everyone is home for summer, and I'm just home. Like, for good. Period. With no future. Nowhere to go. Except my community service, of course." He tried to chuckle to lighten the mood, but his voice caught. Zeke's punishment for drunk driving could have been a lot worse, but his dad had been a lawyer for a long time. He had connections and knew just what to do. Zeke's license was suspended for thirty days, and he had to pay a fine. The judge also gave him a bunch of community service hours. All in all, Zeke was lucky he didn't have to serve jail time.

Zeke picked at the label of the water bottle as the silence stretched between them. Sunny had never seen him look so lost before. He was always in charge. The leader. The planner. The responsible one. Now here he was, like a boat adrift at sea. Seeing him like this tugged at Sunny's heart.

"I'm sorry," Sunny said, mostly because she didn't know what else to say, but also because she really was sorry for what he was going through. It was awful to think that his entire future was ruined because of one mistake, even though it was a big one.

Zeke stood up and nodded. "Yeah, well, thanks. Nothing to be done about it now. Just gotta deal with the consequences. I'll be fine."

The way he said it made Sunny wonder if he was trying to convince her or himself. *Deal with the consequences.* His words echoed in her head. Sunny had heard those words many times before from the boys' father, Alan Crawford. As a lawyer, he was obsessed with consequences, frequently lecturing them all about the ramifications of their actions. As the eldest, Zeke bore the brunt of it, and it always made Sunny sad to hear Mr. Crawford scolding him. Zeke was the most responsible out of all of them, and most of the time, he'd been the one cleaning up their messes. She'd never understood why his dad came down so hard on him.

Sighing, Zeke tossed the empty water bottle into the garbage and turned to head into the house. He paused, meeting Sunny's eyes with a sad look that stole her breath away. "Listen, have fun on your date. I hope he's good enough for you."

Her heart flipped over in her chest at his words. She was grateful he was walking away so he couldn't see that she was speechless.

Sunny didn't want to consider why Zeke was being so nice to her. She was worried if she started down that road, she would start hoping again. She sometimes felt like she'd spent her entire life wishing that Zeke would just love her, and she couldn't let herself do that again. It would hurt too much when he didn't love her back. No. It was better to keep her distance, build that wall back up again.

She pushed her concern about Zeke aside and picked up her phone to text Graham to set up a date.

Chapter 3

S unny stifled a yawn, her fifth one of the night. This date was not going well. Sunny was going to have to dump Graham. He was so very nice. And so very boring. Parker had told Sunny that fact weeks ago, but Sunny hadn't listened. There were few things she hated more than being wrong. She had been determined to give Graham a chance. Tonight, however, she had reached her breaking point.

Sunny and Graham were seated at an old-fashioned, Formica-topped booth in a cozy little diner. They hadn't even ordered yet, so it was pretty early in the night for Sunny to throw in the towel. Perhaps it was Graham's commentary on how the changes in the ocean currents were causing an unprecedented migration of ocean life (*yawn!*) that pushed Sunny over the edge. In the middle of Graham's speech, Sunny heard the welcome tones of her Indiana Jones theme song ringtone.

Yes, she thought, inwardly rejoicing at the interruption.

Sunny eagerly grabbed her cell phone from where it rested on the table and apologized to Graham, rising from the booth and making her escape to the back corner of the restaurant where no one was sitting. "I'll be right back," she called over her shoulder towards Graham without waiting for a reply.

"Hello?" she said without even glancing at the screen to see who was calling.

"Addison?"

Sunny knew that voice. *Crap.* Why hadn't she checked the Caller ID?

Caught off guard, Sunny rambled out a stilted greeting. "Why, hello, Ezekiel, fancy hearing from you. And a phone call, even? Funny, I always thought you were more of a text kind of guy."

There was a pause. She rolled her eyes towards the ceiling and grimaced at her own awkwardness.

"What's that supposed to mean?" Zeke asked. He sounded annoyed. Well, crap, she hadn't meant to insult him. It was just that no one really called anyone on the phone anymore. They texted all the time. Video chat too. But phone calls? That was rare.

"Nothing. Forget it. Just me being dumb." Scrambling to change the subject, Sunny added, "To what do I owe the pleasure of your call this fine evening?" Again, she cringed at her oddly formal greeting. What was wrong with her tonight? She took a deep breath, willing herself to calm down as she waited for his response. She didn't want to consider why she was stumbling over her words and why his voice sent little thrills of excitement down her spine. Sunny hated talking on the phone, and this was even more stressful than usual. She tended to think of herself as awkward in person, but when she was on the phone, her awkwardness grew exponentially. She wondered for the millionth time why they didn't make a calling plan that only allowed text messaging.

At least Zeke didn't seem to notice how strange she was acting as he answered hesitantly, "I'm... well, I need your help."

Sunny's heart gave a thump in her chest. Zeke never asked for help, and her brain went into overdrive. Something must be wrong. "Is it Parker? Is he okay? What happened?" she asked. The memory of getting the call from her dad that Parker had been hurt in the car accident was still stuck in her brain, and Zeke's words filled her with an immediate sense of dread.

"No. No one is hurt," he said quickly, reassuring her. "But I need you to come over to our house and help me figure something out. It will be easier if I explain in person, but it's important. I didn't want to bother you, but I really need your help. Can you come over?"

Curiosity piqued, she wanted to ask more questions, but she was so happy to have an excuse to bail out of her date that she didn't even hesitate. Sunny heard her voice say breathlessly, "I'll be there in ten minutes."

Zeke let out a sigh of relief. "Thanks."

It almost seemed like he expected her to refuse, a thought that struck Sunny as sad. Zeke didn't have a lot left in his life since getting kicked out of school. Sunny wondered how their relationship had gotten so bad that he didn't even know if she would help him when he needed it. She softly answered, "You're welcome."

"Oh, and Addison?"

"Yes?"

"It was a pleasure speaking with you this fine evening." *Click.*

Feeling her face turn red, Sunny realized he had definitely noticed her weirdness at the beginning of the call. Just great. On the positive side, she had an out from her date with Graham tonight. She would figure out how to break up with him later. For now, Zeke needed her. Shaking off her embarrassment from the phone call, Sunny turned and walked back to the table where Graham was patiently waiting, the perfect boyfriend that she didn't even want.

Sunny reached the booth and leaned down to grab her coat off of the seat. "I'm so sorry, Graham, but I have to go. That was an emergency."

She started backing away from the table as Graham made a move to rise. "I hope everything is okay! Do you want me to give you a ride?"

"No, no," Sunny waved her arms dismissively. "You stay. Order a milkshake, or a burger, or both! I'm so sorry to ruin our date." By this time, she had reached the door and didn't even give Graham time to respond.

"I'll call you!" Sunny called as she hurried out the door, tossing her jacket on as she practically ran to the safety of her car. Thank goodness she'd insisted on meeting Graham at the restaurant tonight. He protested, of course, in true gentlemanly fashion, but she held firm. Sunny thought some part of her must have wanted an escape route at the ready because she knew this relationship just wasn't a good fit. Funny how Parker always seemed to know her better than she knew herself. Best friends were helpful and annoying like that sometimes.

As Sunny backed out of the parking lot and turned towards Zeke's house, a kitschy old phrase floated through her head...

Out of the frying pan and into the fire.

Zeke looked frazzled as he opened the door and ushered Sunny inside. His hair stuck up in different directions as though he had been running his hands through it.

Sunny knew from experience that he did that whenever he was agitated. She thought briefly of smoothing it down and then quickly checked herself, knowing that would be too intimate. Busying her hands with taking off her coat, she hung it on the coat rack in the corner of the foyer. She noticed Parker's hoodie was missing from the rack, no doubt because he wore it to the baseball game he was at tonight with Mr. Crawford. It could get chilly at Target Field in the early summer evenings. This was the first game Parker had gotten to go to with his dad in years, and he had been so excited.

"Thanks for coming so quickly," Zeke said. "I hope you weren't doing something important."

"Nope, not at all," Sunny said, feeling slightly guilty at dismissing Graham so callously. She could have rubbed the date in Zeke's face, but that just didn't seem right when he looked so upset. "You said it was urgent. What's up?"

Zeke motioned for her to follow him, and they walked down the marble-tiled hallway into the office. The room was Sunny's least favorite in the entire house. It was dark, filled with wood paneling, an enormous stone fireplace, and shelves of legal books. There was a stiff-looking leather sofa and a matching leather armchair on one side. An over-sized mahogany desk dominated the opposite side of the room. Sunny imagined the room was designed to be cozy and welcoming, but she had always thought the space was cold and uninviting, a fitting analogy for Mr. Crawford himself. He had always seemed so unapproachable and distant to Sunny, despite the fact that his house was basically her second home.

Zeke motioned Sunny over to the desk. There was an open laptop resting on top. "I'm making something for Parker's birthday. A photo album. It's supposed to be a surprise. Tonight is the last night I can place the order and still get it in time for his birthday, and everything is a mess. But that's not even the worst part. I was selecting pictures to upload, and I clicked something and they were just gone. I think I accidentally deleted the photos of us with Mom. A lot of them, Sunny. Just gone. I can't lose those photos." His voice cracked, but he continued, "Parker and Dad will kill me. Those are the only copies we have. It's all we have left. When the pics disappeared, I just stopped touching anything and called you. Can you get them back?"

Zeke looked desperate. Sunny didn't need convincing. She knew exactly how important those photos were to the whole family. She'd lost her mother too, after all, and she couldn't imagine what she would do if she could never look at her photo again.

Sunny attempted a reassuring smile, even though there was a pit of dread in her stomach at the possibility that she might not be able to get them back. "I can't make any promises, but I can try. Usually things aren't really gone, so I'll see what I can do. I might have to buy some recovery software or something. We'll find a way."

"Anything. I'll pay anything," Zeke said.

Several hours later, Sunny and Zeke sat hunched over the laptop together. After she had inspected the situation, she'd quickly discovered that Mr. Crawford had used a service to back up all of their family photos, so it was a quick fix to recover all of them. Zeke had been really grateful, but Sunny shrugged his thanks off, feeling embarrassed. She really hadn't done much of anything, but Zeke acted like it was a miracle. His whole attitude had changed after he'd seen the photos reappear on the computer, like a weight had dropped off of his shoulders, and Sunny asked if she could sneak a peek at the album.

"That's the other problem," he said sheepishly. "I might be in over my head with this whole thing. I feel like I'm normally a pretty smart person, but when it comes to photo albums, I don't have a clue."

"I can stay and help," offered Sunny. She told herself that it was only because she had nothing else to do tonight, but she knew that wasn't the real reason. She wasn't ready to leave yet.

They'd been working together for the past few hours, Zeke describing the vision for what he wanted the album to look like and Sunny working her magic on the computer. They were almost done, and Sunny knew Parker was going to love the album. It had pictures of the family, starting when Parker was a baby, snuggled up in his mother's arms. It highlighted all of the major events going up through his graduation just a few short weeks ago. There were photos of Mr. Crawford, his hands resting stiffly on Parker's shoulder, looking proud.

As they put the finishing touches on the album, Sunny thought about Zeke. He was smart, and he had an amazing eye for what he wanted this album to look like. When they were growing up, her dad had always said Zeke had potential. He'd worked hard in high school and gotten into Notre Dame. He had a lot of friends, but he wasn't a partier and had never gotten into trouble like some of the other kids in high school. So what had changed? What made him throw it all away by drinking and driving?

Sunny had questioned Parker pretty hard about that night and what happened. Had they gotten into a fight? Had Zeke been depressed or upset? Parker said no to all those questions, but he also remembered nothing after his first few shots, so he wasn't exactly a wealth of information. Parker woke up in a hospital bed the next morning to an array of cuts, bumps, and bruises, a concussion, and a very pissed-off father. Mr. Crawford had taken most of his anger out on Zeke, partly because he had been driving but also because he was the oldest and supposed to be taking care of Parker. Parker and Mr. Crawford's relationship appeared to be back to normal, as evidenced by their outing to the baseball game tonight. But Zeke was still on thin ice.

Zeke's knee bumped Sunny's as he reached to point at a picture, startling Sunny and making her jump.

"Sorry," Zeke said.

"It's fine," answered Sunny.

"I was thinking we finish the book with this photo here of me and Parker, but maybe we should find one that has all three of us now. I couldn't have finished the book without you, so it's only fair you get credit too. The present can be from both of us."

Sunny nodded, smiling. "That's nice of you."

Zeke was always thinking about others. She didn't understand what had happened between the two of them. When they'd first met, Zeke had always been kind to her. At first, she had thought he was just being nice because both of their mothers had died and they had that in common. But as she got to know him, she realized Zeke was simply a really kind person. After being alone with only her dad to hang out with, Sunny relished having two new friends who treated her like family.

And it was great at first. She'd never had close friends like Parker and Zeke before. But as they grew older, something changed. Not with Parker. Just with Zeke. Suddenly, the times when he was giving her advice or trying to help chafed. She didn't like being told what to do or treated like a child. Sunny really couldn't pinpoint a day when they started to butt heads, but during the last few years, whenever they were in a room together, it seemed like a fight was brewing. Parker was the mediator, and his constant talking often worked to ease the tension between the two of them. They survived. They tolerated each other. But they weren't as close as they had been before. There was a wall between them. Sunny missed how easy it had been before. And sitting here with Zeke now, getting along so well, she didn't feel a wall at all. It was hard to admit to herself, but she was beginning to wonder if maybe the reason she and Zeke hadn't been getting along all this time was her own fault.

For the past few years, Sunny had been wearing armor whenever she was around Zeke. The mental kind. She always had her guard up, kept her distance, and tried to maintain a constant appearance of not giving a crap about him. Zeke had plenty of female admirers, and Sunny didn't think he needed one more. He was kind, athletic, and gorgeous. He even played piano like a pro. What girl wouldn't swoon at his feet?

Determined not to be one of those girls throwing herself at him, Sunny had decided when she was fifteen years old that she would not let her feelings show. Had that been when this had all started? She wasn't sure, but she remembered that day vividly. Back then, they had all played soccer together pretty regularly in the field behind the school. It was a mix of people from Zeke's grade and from Parker and Sunny's grade. One particularly hot day, Sunny headed to the side-line to take a water break while the other kids practiced passing. Sarah Holmes was sitting in the bleachers with her best friend, Victoria Dickinson. They often came by to watch, but neither played. They were in Sunny's grade, and Sunny doubted they had ever participated in anything that might cause them to break a nail or a sweat. As Sunny gulped down water from her Gatorade bottle, not caring about the droplets that were sloshing down her chin, she overheard their nasty giggles.

"She's so obvious," Sarah said in a mock whisper.

"I know. It's so embarrassing how she throws herself at him," Victoria snickered.

Oh, god, who were they talking about? *Please don't be me, please don't be me,* Sunny thought.

She tried to sneak a glance to see who they were looking at, but they were facing each other. She saw Sarah nod. "You know, Zeke told me that she's not really his friend. She's just his brother's friend. She's so annoying, but I think he basically has to let her hang with them." Sunny's heart sank. They were definitely talking about her. She bent down, adjusting her shin guard, listening while Sarah continued, "Did you know his dad makes him be nice to her because her mother died?" Sarah sighed longingly, and Victoria echoed her sigh with one of her own. "Isn't he just the sweetest guy you've ever met in real life?" She paused. "William told me that Zeke is planning to ask me to the dance next week. Can you believe it? Older guys are so much better than boys our age, you know. Much more mature."

She felt her chest tighten at Victoria's words, and hot tears threatened to spill down her cheeks. She swiped at her eyes angrily. Grabbing her backpack, she ducked her head so that the girls couldn't see her face and ran from the field all the way home. Thankfully, it was only a few blocks. The truth was, she did have feelings for Zeke. And she felt like an idiot for thinking maybe he might like her back.

Later on, when Parker asked where she'd gone, she told him she got her period and had to leave. It was embarrassing, but it wasn't as embarrassing as the truth. Plus, she knew if she blamed her period, he wouldn't say one more word about it. And he didn't.

After that day, she fought to wear a mask whenever Zeke walked in the room. She didn't want anyone to think she was pining away for him. She tried to be indifferent, cold even. She wasn't going to let anyone laugh at her like that ever again. Her goal was to never let anyone see that she cared, most of all him. She pushed her complicated feelings for Zeke way down deep, so far down that even Parker had no idea how she really felt. And if Sunny had anything to say about it, he never would.

"Sunny?" Zeke said, waving a hand in front of her face.

She blinked, having not heard a word he just said. "Huh?"

"I asked if you had any ideas for what photo of us three we could use for the last page."

"Oh, yeah." She halted, casting her thoughts back across all the photos she could remember of the three of them together. "How about that one from the day Parker beat me on the trampoline flip challenge? I think that was around his fourteenth birthday, right? I remember we didn't have driver's licenses yet because we spent all summer hanging out here talking about where we would go if we could drive."

"That's a great one," Zeke said, his face lighting up at the memory. "Man, he was so happy when he beat you."

"I know. He still rubs it in my face whenever he gets the chance. I had to eat fish sticks every day for a week when I lost that bet. Blech. I still can't even smell a fish stick without wanting to throw up." Sunny shuddered and Zeke laughed. She flipped back through the photos on the computer until she found the one she was looking for. All three of them were lined up in front of the trampoline with big smiles plastered on their faces. Their arms were slung around each other.

Sunny clicked the button to add it to the album. Then she saved the album and sent it to preview mode so they could give it one final look before submitting it to the company to print. As she waited, she thought about that photo and how happy all three of them were. It was so much simpler back then, before she had to worry about getting into college and what she was going to do with her life.

"Do you ever wish we could go back?" she asked Zeke, swiveling her chair to face him. He swiveled his chair to face her as well.

"Back to what?"

"Back to the age we were in that photo," Sunny explained. "Back when things were just... I don't know, easier. I miss just hanging out, doing nothing, not worrying about anything. You know?"

Zeke leaned in, holding her gaze. "Not a chance."

Sunny was curious and found herself leaning in towards him as well. "Why not?"

"Do you even know how much I worried back then? Nothing was easy for me. Dad shut down after Mom died. We were on our own, and I worried about Parker all the time. I worried about whether he was gonna pass chemistry. Remember how horrible he was in Chem?"

Sunny nodded, and Zeke continued. "I worried about my dad and if he would show up at our school Christmas concert and what I would say to Parker if he didn't. Would he remember to buy birthday presents for Parker? Did he sign the permission slip for the field trip? Would he remember to take us to Mom's grave on the anniversary of her death? I literally never stopped worrying. So, no, I wouldn't go back to that age even if you paid me. As hard as it is now, at least I'm old enough to be in control of things instead of just a helpless kid trying to act like an adult."

"I never realized...You never said anything..." Sunny trailed off, her brow furrowing as she thought about all the responsibilities that Zeke carried alone all those years. She'd never thought about how hard it had been for him.

Zeke's eyes met hers. "I even worried about you, you know," he said softly.

Sunny's eyes widened a bit, and her heart thumped in her chest. "You did? But why?"

"Stupid things, mostly. Every time you got in a fight with Parker, I worried that you'd stop coming over to visit. When you and Parker used to dive into the pool, I worried you'd break your neck trying to keep up with him." He lifted a hand and brushed a strand of hair away from her face, tucking it behind her ear. Sunny held her breath.

"I worried that you'd go off to college and forget all about me and Parker, and I'd never see you again."

Sunny was frozen in place while her mind whirled. Zeke had never spoken to her like this before, and she wasn't sure what was happening. Was he worried about their friendship? Or something more?

Suddenly, a door slammed. Sunny and Zeke jumped. "Parker!" Sunny yelped. "We've got to finish the album!"

Zeke jumped up and shut the office door quietly to keep them hidden from view. "Just order it!" he whispered.

"But we didn't proofread it yet," Sunny protested.

"We don't have time. I'm sure it's fine. Finish the order, quick!"

At Zeke's urging, Sunny clicked the button to order the album from the printing company. Then she looked at Zeke. "Now what? How do we explain why I'm here with you?"

Zeke opened the door and listened. They could hear voices approach from the garage and then fade away. Zeke whispered, "We don't. It sounds like they both went into the kitchen. I think we can make it to the front door if we're quiet."

They snuck out of the office and padded to the front door. Zeke opened the door slowly and mouthed "thank you" to Sunny. She nodded, smiled, and headed to the car, mulling over Zeke's words on the drive home.

Chapter 4

Spending time at Zeke's looking through old photos had gotten Sunny thinking a lot about the past. After she arrived home, she said goodnight to her dad and headed upstairs where she dug out an old box of family photos from the hallway closet. She sat on her pink and gray bedspread and sifted through them. She focused on a photo of her mom and dad laughing together. Frank and Sally Montgomery. The photo was taken at her tenth birthday party, just a few months before her mom died. Sunny felt the tears slip down her cheeks as she thought of how happy they had been that day and how quickly it had all changed.

The accident happened out of nowhere. Her mom had been driving home from work, just as she always did. She collided with another car that ran a stoplight, and bam. She was gone.

When Sunny's mom died, her dad became her whole world. She was ten years old when it happened, and she remembered how confusing it all was. It didn't seem real. She kept walking into the kitchen expecting to see her mom, but she wasn't there. When her dad would pull up at school to pick her up, it surprised her to see his black SUV instead of her mom's white one. In the beginning, she cried a lot. She remembered feeling afraid when her dad cried because she'd never seen that before. She hadn't understood, until years later, what her father was going through.

A short time after her mom died, her dad started getting her grandma to come and stay with her on Saturday nights. At the time, Sunny hadn't known where her dad went on those nights. Her grandma just said he was visiting some friends. Later, Sunny learned that it was a widower's support group, a place for her father to talk about his loss with other people who understood.

Things got better after that, though she still missed her mom every day. Little by little, her dad seemed happier. When Sunny was eleven years old, something happened. It seemed small, but it ended up being one of the most significant events of her entire life. One day, her dad announced they were going golfing with a friend he had just met at his support group. Sunny had never been golfing before, and it always excited her to try something new. Her dad informed her that there would be two little boys for her to play with and that they went to Sunny's new school. That only heightened Sunny's excitement. They had just moved, having downsized to a smaller house for just the two of them, and she didn't have any friends in her new neighborhood. It was summer, so she hadn't met any school friends either yet. That Sunday morning, Sunny hoisted her brand-new golf clubs into the back of her dad's SUV, eager to meet some new friends.

When they arrived at the golf course, her dad stopped the car next to a man and two little boys who looked about her own age. Her dad introduced the man, Alan Crawford, and his two sons, Zeke and Parker. The older boy, Zeke, kicked at the rocks in the parking lot with the toe of his shoe, not meeting Sunny's eyes. The younger boy, Parker, rushed up to her, grabbed her hand and pumped it up and down in an excited handshake that left Sunny's arm feeling like jelly. Sunny liked him immediately, and she hooked her left arm through his as she hefted her golf clubs over her right arm.

Sunny didn't remember everything about that golf outing, but she remembered two things. She remembered her first impressions of meeting the boys, and she remembered the bet.

Sunny was still young and didn't understand the rules of golf until much later in her life, so she didn't know that normally there were only four people allowed to golf together in a group. However, Alan was a well-respected member of the country club and he was on the board, so that meant he didn't have to follow the same rules as other members. All five of them traipsed down to the tee and prepared to golf. They had rented a golf cart for the kids, while Alan and Frank had caddies carrying their bags. Sunny and Parker sat beside each other on the seat of the cart, Parker in the driver's seat, waiting for their turn to hit the ball. Zeke stood quietly behind the cart.

Parker nudged Sunny's arm. "Bet I can hit the ball farther than you can."

Sunny had never golfed before, but she knew she didn't like the challenging tone in Parker's voice. She stuck her chin out and replied, "I doubt it. I'm very good at sports, you know." She wasn't, but she wasn't going to let him know that.

"What should we bet?" Parker asked.

Sunny considered that. She'd never bet anyone anything before.

"A dollar?" she suggested, uncertainty in her voice.

"Nah," answered Parker. "That's no good. Don't you know anything about bets? Its gotta be something the winner wants and the loser doesn't want. A dollar's nothin'. We need something better."

Sunny remained silent, thinking.

Parker snapped his fingers, something Sunny couldn't do yet, making her instantly envious. "I've got it! Winner gets to pick the loser's flavor of ice cream."

"What ice cream?" Sunny asked.

Parker smiled. "Dad always buys us ice cream in the clubhouse after we get done golfing. They have tons of flavors. Some of them are awesome, like chocolate or orange, and some of them are awful, like pistachio or butter pecan or licorice. They used to have a pizza flavored ice cream, and it was the worst of them all. They got rid of that, though, and replaced it with bacon flavored ice cream that sounds good but is actually..." Parker made a face like he was throwing up. Sunny guessed he wasn't a fan of the bacon flavor. "So here's the bet. The winner gets to choose the flavor that the loser has to eat. And the loser has to eat the whole thing. That's the punishment for losing." He said this last part very dramatically. Sunny was learning that Parker liked to talk, but she didn't mind. She'd never met anyone like him before.

Parker looked at her expectantly and said, "You in?"

Sunny hesitated and then nodded. Licorice ice cream sounded horrible, but she wanted Parker to like her, so she didn't stop to consider that she wasn't likely to win, having never golfed before.

Parker turned to his older brother. "You in too, Zeke?"

"No thanks, Parker," Zeke replied.

It was the first time Sunny had heard Zeke say anything at all. She turned to look at him. His voice was soft and kind, not at all what she'd expected from his grumpy exterior.

"Why not?" Parker whined.

Zeke smiled, his entire face lighting up as he looked down at his brother. "It wouldn't be fair, Parker. I'm older than you, and I've had a lot more practice. It's better if you two just do it, since you're the same age. I don't mind not playing. I'll still let you pick my flavor of ice cream. Don't worry."

That brought a smile back to Parker's face.

Sunny thought that was rather nice of Zeke. She'd never had a sibling, and she experienced a moment of jealousy, looking at the two of them smiling at each other. They had lost their mother too, just like her, but they had each other. She wondered what it would be like to not feel so alone.

Predictably, Sunny did not win. In fact, her ball never made it off the tee, as she swung with all her might and missed the ball completely. She learned that was called a "whiff" in golf. She also learned that it was embarrassing. Parker and Zeke, to their credit, did not laugh. Parker simply threw his arm around her shoulders and said, "I hope you like rum raisin," with a cheeky grin.

Sunny found out an hour later that she did not like rum raisin. Not one bit. But she ate the entire ice cream cone anyway, determined not to let Parker down. It may have been her first betting experience, but she got the distinct impression that it was unforgivable for the loser not to follow through on their punishment. Zeke sat nearby, and he ate his pistachio ice cream silently, without a single complaint.

As Sunny continued thumbing through pictures, she found some shots of her with Zeke and Parker on the golf course. They were older in these photos, in their teens. After that first golf game, it became a Sunday ritual, with the fathers breaking into a twosome and golfing ahead with their caddies. The threesome of Sunny, Parker, and Zeke always trailed behind, riding their golf cart and sometimes spending more time laughing than golfing. During the winter months, golfing was replaced with brunch in the clubhouse every Sunday. However, everyone looked forward to the first days in May when they could get back out onto the course.

Zeke and Parker, who had been golfing their whole lives, gave Sunny tips. Soon she improved so much that she was capable of out-driving the boys from the women's tee.

Sunny caught sight of a picture of her and Parker sitting on a golf cart, her cheeks pink from the sun. Zeke leaned in towards the camera, an arm lazily leaning on the golf cart. She remembered that day. It was late August. Sunny and Parker were seventeen, and Zeke was just preparing to leave for college. Her dad had taken the photo, saying something about how this might be the last time they were all together until the next summer. Everyone headed out for their usual round of golf, but there was a sadness to it. Summer was almost over, and things were changing.

Sunny stood at the women's tee, taking her turn to drive down the first fairway. Zeke leaned an arm on the golf cart, patiently waiting and calling out a few corrections on her form. Sunny couldn't help but notice the way his shirt stretched across his tan, muscular arm as he leaned on the cart. She was immediately irritated at herself for noticing, and Zeke's instructions grated on her nerves. She was finding it harder and harder to ignore the growing attraction she felt towards Zeke with each passing day.

"Tighten up that back arm, Sunny," Zeke called.

"I know!"

"Your stance is too tense. Bend those knees."

"Stop talking in my backswing!" Sunny yelled, head down, eye on the ball.

Zeke threw his arms up defensively and went silent.

Sunny gritted her teeth, tightened up her arm, and swung hard. Her swing felt horrible, and she knew the second she connected with the ball that it was bad.

The ball sliced way to the right and into the rough.

Damn it, Sunny thought, her face flushing red. The last thing she wanted to do was look incompetent in front of Zeke. She stomped over to the cart and slammed her club down into her bag.

As she hopped into the passenger side of the cart next to Parker, she growled, "Don't say a word."

Parker ignored her, per usual.

"I wasn't going to say anything," he began, just getting started. "If I was going to say anything, though, it would have been to ask what's wrong because that was a horrible shot. I mean, just terrible. You are so much better than that. So something must be bothering you, because that was just... awful."

Sunny heaved out a breath. Normally, she found herself strangely calmed by Parker's incessant chatter. The nice thing about Parker is that he didn't expect an answer, so in many ways, it took the pressure off of her and gave her mind a chance to reset. Today, however, it set her teeth on edge.

"Thanks for the pep talk, coach," Sunny said as Parker started up the cart. He didn't seem to notice her irritation and kept on chattering as they headed towards her ball. Zeke walked along behind, carrying his clubs, silent as usual. Sometimes Sunny thought the reason Zeke was so quiet was because Parker never let him get a word in edgewise. Or perhaps Parker talked so much to fill the silence. Either way, the brothers complimented each other nicely and always seemed to argue less than other siblings.

Sunny's mind snapped back to the golf game as Parker stopped the cart a few feet away from her ball. She headed to the back of her cart and chose a seven iron that should get her ball out of the rough. She looked to her left, and Zeke was patiently waiting for her to hit before he went to find his ball, which was yards ahead on the fairway. He was perfectly positioned to get the ball up to the green in one more hit. Sunny, much to her frustration, was going to need at least two more strokes to get up to the green.

The sun was high in the sky, and it was a hot, humid day. Sunny was already starting to feel the sweat prickle on her skin as she leaned down to line up her shot. She could feel Zeke's eyes on her, and she was acutely aware of every movement of her body as she adjusted and lined up the shot.

Smack.

This one wasn't great, but it wasn't terrible. It put her back on the fairway where she needed to be. Sunny trudged back to the cart, still disheartened.

On the next hole, her drive off the tee was just as bad as the first one. As Sunny sullenly took her seat on the golf cart, Parker rambled, "Wow. I mean. Wow. You are really off today. Were you snatched by aliens last..." Parker trailed off as Zeke looked at him and pointed his thumb towards the fairway, silently indicating that Parker should get off the cart and walk.

"Ooookay. I'm gonna walk for a while, I think," Parker said, and hopped off the cart, unstrapping his clubs and hefting them over his shoulder.

Zeke set his clubs in Parker's spot and strapped them down. Meanwhile, Sunny stared down at her hands, her nerves building. It was bad enough trying to focus with Zeke standing across the fairway. How was she going to focus with him sitting next to her?

Zeke slid into the driver's seat and took off without a word. The silence stretched between them as they headed towards her ball, far on the right in the rough again.

Sunny couldn't take it anymore and burst out, "You didn't have to kick Parker off the cart. I'm fine. It was just a couple of bad shots. I'll warm up soon."

Zeke glanced over at her, expression neutral. "What, this? Oh, this wasn't about you. I just wanted to sit for a while. My knee has been bothering me a bit today. Old soccer injury."

Chastened, Sunny mumbled, "Oh, sorry," and stepped off the cart to hit her ball. Of course, everything wasn't about her. Zeke stayed on the cart and leaned back like he was resting, eyes closed.

As she approached her ball, feeling no eyes on her, Sunny felt the tension ease from her shoulders. She focused on the quiet sounds of the birds chirping, the wind brushing against her face.

Whack.

A beautiful shot back up onto the fairway and in perfect chipping distance from the green. Sunny's mood lifted.

The rest of the game went smoothly, with Zeke and Sunny riding silently next to each other and Parker walking, chattering here and there. There were a few times she swore that Zeke purposely parked the cart farther away from Parker, as though he sensed that she needed some space today. Maybe it was just a coincidence, but either way, Sunny was grateful for the peace.

At the clubhouse, Parker broke off to return the cart, leaving Zeke and Sunny standing by their clubs waiting for him. Their dads were already inside the clubhouse getting something to drink. Sunny, feeling grateful to Zeke for having given her a bit of peace and quiet that morning, impulsively threw her arms around him in a hug.

Instead of hugging her back, Zeke stiffened, pushing her away and exclaiming, "What the hell?"

Embarrassed, Sunny stammered, "I... I'm sorry. I just wanted to say thank you."

"For what?" Zeke said, taking a step away from her like she had the plague and he didn't want to catch it.

Suddenly unsure and feeling foolish, Sunny answered, "For riding with me today? I had fun. I'm gonna miss this when you leave."

"Whatever," Zeke said, his face stony as he dismissed her thanks. "I told you, it wasn't about you. My knee just hurt today." He picked up his clubs and turned away from Sunny.

"I'll see you and Parker back at the car," he tossed over his shoulder as he walked away.

"What about the ice cream?" Sunny called after him.

"Not hungry," he called back.

Sunny huffed out a breath. They had been getting along so well all day and that hadn't happened in a long time. She had ruined it, but she wasn't quite sure how.

It was nearly a year later, and she still didn't understand. She thought about it as she looked at the photo of the three of them and recalled Zeke's words about how he worried about her. Was it possible that he cared about her more than she realized?

Chapter 5

S unny sighed in relief as she hung up the phone. Calling Graham to officially break things off with him had been weighing on her mind ever since she'd left Zeke's side last night. Even before that, actually. She had originally wanted to just text Graham. It was so much easier! She video chatted with Parker as soon as she woke up and told him about her idea to break things off via text, but Parker called her a coward. Well, what he'd actually said was, "'The Lord hates a coward,'" while holding his hand over his heart and hanging his head low.

Having no idea which movie Parker was referencing, Sunny searched her memory. It had that old-timey feel, but she was coming up empty. She guessed, "*The Good, the Bad and the Ugly?*"

"Nope," Parker had replied. "*The Untouchables.* You are really terrible at all the old movie quotes, aren't you?"

Parker's quote had resonated in her head after she ended the video call with him. She didn't like being accused of cowardice. Her skin itched at the thought that maybe her mom was looking down on her from heaven, if there was a heaven. She imagined sending a text to Graham and her mom shaking her head in disappointment, her short blond hair swaying from side to side. No. Her mom would have wanted her to do this the right way. So she did, and luckily Graham, being the nice guy that he was, said he understood and hoped they could still be friends. Sunny assured him they could be, and that was that.

Sunny's heart felt lighter with that task out of the way. She flopped back onto her bed, thinking over Zeke's words from last night for the millionth time. Could she dare to hope that maybe he felt something more than friendship for her?

A ding from her phone interrupted her thoughts, and she snatched it up eagerly. As soon as she read the words, her brain jumped into overdrive. It was an email alert that the app had passed review and was ready to go live. Her heart thumped. Today was the day. They didn't even list any changes she needed to make. Both excited and nervous, she jumped up, throwing off her pajamas and tossing on a pale blue t-shirt and a pair of well-loved jean shorts. She pretty much lived in shorts and a t-shirt all summer long. As she brushed her teeth and added some mascara to her lashes, she texted Parker to let him know she was coming over. The truth was, even though she still worried about what would happen when she released the app, this was a welcome distraction from thinking about Zeke. She was eager to get to Parker's house and talk about the next phase in his plan. Her deadline for submitting extra materials to MIT was looming, and she needed to produce something that would make them take notice.

Sunny headed downstairs, laptop in hand, to grab a banana for the walk to Parker's house. She was never big on breakfast, preferring a simple snack like a granola bar or some fruit. She read the note her dad had left on the counter before he headed to work, telling her he loved her. If her dad had been home, he would have forced her to sit down and eat a balanced meal before she left. Protein, carbs, fat, all perfectly portioned out. Plenty of fruits and veggies. Her dad wasn't a health nut or anything. He never even watched what he ate himself. But ever since her mom passed away, he had made it his personal mission to make sure that Sunny started her day with a nutritious meal. Most of the time Sunny didn't mind too much, but she certainly looked forward to the days when she had the freedom to choose her breakfast for herself.

As Sunny walked the few blocks to Parker's house, she thought about her relationship with her dad. She loved him so much, and she was grateful that he was always there for her. He went to every concert when she was in the middle school choir. He helped her with her homework every evening. He even looked up makeup tutorials on the Internet when she had turned twelve and asked for makeup for her birthday. She didn't really have any friends who were girls that she could turn to, and Parker was no help with makeup questions. So her dad stepped up, and he never complained.

Sunny knew how lucky she was. Even though she would miss her dad terribly when she went to college, part of her was eager for more freedom. Eating what she wanted, going where she wanted, doing what she wanted, it sounded amazing to her. She had some of that now whenever her dad was working, but when he was home, it was a different story.

She was beginning to chafe a bit under his close watch, like wearing a shirt that was too tight. Whenever she felt like that, she tried not to snap at him. She knew why her father hovered so much. It was a normal reaction to losing someone so suddenly. When her mother's car accident had happened, Sunny had been ten years old, too young to really remember everything, but she remembered snippets here and there. Waking up to find her grandma at the kitchen table in the morning and her dad gone to the hospital. Her dad hugging her close and telling her that her mother was in heaven. Standing beside the casket with a single red rose in her hand. Laying in bed wishing her mom could come in and read her a bedtime story like she used to.

For Mr. Montgomery, his wife was there one day and gone the next. He clung to Sunny like a life raft, but it wasn't just because caring for his daughter gave his life purpose in a time when he felt lost. It was also fear that drove him, fear that Sunny could be taken away as quickly as Sally had been. Even now, years later, that fear remained. Sunny could hear it in his voice when he called to ask where she was or what time she'd be home. She could see it when he greeted her at the door if she was even a minute late for curfew. Most of their classmates didn't even have a curfew anymore, but Sunny still did. Having a daughter who planned to move from Minnesota to Massachusetts for college must be eating her dad up inside, but if it was, he never let it show. He knew how important it had been to Sunny's mother, and outwardly, he was nothing but supportive of the move.

Sunny thought about Massachusetts and how far away she would be from her family and friends. The idea still wasn't completely real in her mind. Having spent so much of her life depending on Parker, Zeke, and her dad, she couldn't imagine leaving them all behind. Her shoulders slouched a little as she thought about being all alone. But she had arrived at Parker's door, and there was no time for sadness. She shook the feeling off and squared her shoulders as she knocked on the door. There would never be a move to Massachusetts if she didn't impress MIT first.

"Do it, do it, do it!" Parker chanted. They were seated at the wide granite-topped island in the Crawford kitchen, Sunny's laptop open in front of them. The kitchen was gigantic, like everything in the Crawford house. It had tons of white cabinets, a massive double refrigerator, and a fancy stove with so many buttons and dials that Sunny was afraid to even touch it. Marta was off grocery shopping right now, so they had the kitchen to themselves.

"Wait," Sunny said, putting up her hand. "I need to go over the plan one more time before I publish the app."

Parker groaned. "'You're killin' me, smalls!'"

This quote, Sunny knew instantly. Zeke and Parker had made her watch the movie over and over when they were younger. "Easy. *The Sandlot.*"

"Ding, ding, ding! That is correct."

Sunny shook her head, getting back to the topic at hand. "Tell me what you and Mika figured out."

"I already told you." Parker sounded a bit like a whiny child, but he must have heard it in his voice because he checked himself. "Okay, okay. So Mika and I came up with ten clues. They are absolute fire. Seriously, Sun, you are gonna love them. She had this idea that we should save the best clue for last, but the other clues can really go in any order. It's not like a scavenger hunt, where one clue leads to the next. These are each stand-alone clues that point people to a location. We are basically betting the entire class that they can't solve our clues. Solve each one, show up at that location to prove you solved it, and boom. You are eligible to get the next clue whenever we release it. But you have to have solved every single clue to win the bet and the money. The best part is Mika and I will go to each location together to see who shows up. That's like ten dates, Sunny. Ten dates with Mika! This couldn't have worked out any better." Parker folded his arms behind his head and leaned back in his chair, looking proud.

"But what if a ton of people work together and share the solution? Or post the location online and everyone shows up?"

Parker released his hands from behind his head and smiled at Sunny. "Well, they'd be stupid to do that because then they'd have to split the prize. It's going to be in everyone's best interest to work alone, or at least in very small groups. Whoever makes it to the end splits the $10,000. If they help other people and two hundred people show up, that's only fifty dollars per person. People are greedy, Sunny. They won't want to share with too many people."

Sunny thought about that. It was sad, but Parker was right. She could already envision people sneaking to the various clue locations or trying to distract other players with false leads. It was exciting to think about what might happen. She had gotten sucked in by Parker's enthusiasm, but it wasn't just that. There was a certain joy in solving a good puzzle. When she was younger, she'd always enjoyed playing problem-solving games like Clue. She wasn't participating in the class bet. Since she had made the app, people might think she was cheating. But she was still excited to see other people play. One thought gave her pause. The prize money.

"Does your dad know you are doing this?" Sunny asked.

Parker barked out a laugh. "Are you kidding? No way. Does yours?"

"Not a chance. Dad is still completely confident that MIT will take me off the waitlist. He said something about calling another friend who knows somebody that works there. I don't know. I just know that I can't sit here and do nothing while someone else decides my fate."

Taking a deep breath, Sunny grabbed Parker's hands. She looked into his eyes. "Okay, Parker, this is a big responsibility. I built the app, but running the bet is your territory. From here on out, I'm depending on you." Parker rolled his eyes, but Sunny pressed on. "This app. It's my ticket to MIT. It has to go well."

Nodding, Parker shook off Sunny's hands and patted her on the head as though she were a small child having a meltdown. "I got it. Just trust me, Sunshine. We will both get what we want if we just stick to the plan."

Sunny blew out a breath. "Stick to the plan," she repeated. The words sounded hollow to her. Despite her fears, she clicked the button to release the app.

Oh crap, she thought. *What have I done?*

Bet was live.

Parker rubbed his hands together and picked up his phone. He was ready to work. It had taken the app about eight hours to appear in the app store after Sunny published it. Parker knew because he'd been checking every hour since Sunny had pushed the button. It was evening now, and Sunny had gone home to have supper with her dad. Parker was perched in the window seat in his bedroom, Sassy nestled between his legs. Every time he moved, she let out an annoyed meow.

He downloaded the app to his phone and opened it up. Sunny always complained that she wasn't good at making graphics, but the app looked professional to Parker. He knew MIT was going to be impressed and all Sunny's worrying would be for nothing.

Now that the app was live, it was Parker's turn to do his part. He needed to log into the app and actually start the bet for the entire class. When he opened the app, the first field said "Name your bet." He mused aloud, "What to call it? What to call it?" as he looked around the room for inspiration. His mind immediately turned to movies where people had to solve clues or a puzzle. *National Treasure? Clue? Now You See Me?*

If Sunny was here, she would be upset that Parker hadn't already considered all of the details before, but that just wasn't his style. He liked to deal with problems as they came up, and he always thought the best solutions came to him under pressure. He found it exhausting to worry about everything ahead of time like Sunny and his brother did. Why worry about something if it was never even going to happen?

He spotted *The Goonies* poster on his wall. An all-time classic. Aha! He typed, "Goonies Never Say Die," in the box. His favorite quote from the movie. He thought it was a fitting title since this was the last hurrah for the senior class before leaving for college or wherever, just like all the Goonies banded together one last time to find the treasure before Mikey and his brother had to move away.

Next, Parker added a short description. He typed, "Cloud Lake Senior Class - I bet you can't make it to the end! Solve all ten clues and winner gets $10,000."

When that was done, Parker quickly outlined the rules in the next text box.

The plan was that Parker and Mika would release clues randomly throughout the summer. As soon as they released the clue, the players would get notified via the app. Each player had one hour to solve the clue and get to the location. The player would remain in the game as long as they got to the correct location and hit the button on their app to check in before the clock expired. If the player didn't get there on time or didn't click the button, they were out of the game. If they were out, the app wouldn't let them see future clues nor check in at future locations.

If they made it to the end and solved all ten clues, they would take home the $10,000 grand prize. If there was more than one winner, they would have to split the prize evenly.

Parker already had the money withdrawn from his bank account and sitting in an envelope in his desk drawer. He shook off the guilty feeling that arose as he thought about the money. Having grown up wealthy, Parker wasn't worried about giving away the money. He had a lot more than that tucked away in his trust fund. What made him feel guilty was what his dad would say if he knew Parker had used some of his money to fund a game. He could already hear his dad in his head, bellowing words like "irresponsible" and "immature."

Parker told himself that it didn't really matter what he did anyway. His dad was hardly ever around. As a high-powered attorney in the Twin Cities, he worked long hours, away from home six days a week. Even when he was home, he was constantly on the phone. Really, the only time they spent together anymore was on Sundays when they had brunch or went golfing with Sunny and her dad. And even that was only because Sunny's dad practically forced Parker's dad into it. One time, Mr. Crawford had tried to cancel. Mr. Montgomery had shown up at their house, bellowing about the importance of family and how it could all be taken away from them in a minute. Parker didn't exactly understand the friendship between the two fathers. They were such different people. But for whatever reason, Mr. Montgomery seemed to be the only person who could get through to Parker's dad these days.

It hadn't always been that way. Parker remembered a time, before their mother had passed away, when they had gone places together as a family. Restaurants, movies, baseball games. He even remembered going to an indoor water park and Disney World for vacation. All that ended when his mom got sick. She'd been diagnosed with stage

IV pancreatic cancer when Parker was ten, and she'd fought hard for a year. But in the end, she just couldn't beat it. After she passed, no one in the family was the same. They couldn't go back to who they'd been before. Their lives had been on hold for a year, and they had all three emerged different people. Parker's dad focused on his work, disconnecting from his family as much as he could without actually leaving.

Parker really missed his dad sometimes, but he pushed those thoughts out of his mind. He didn't like to dwell too much on his mom or how their family used to be before she died. It hurt too much. He told himself that his dad would likely never even find out about the bet and turned his attention back to the task at hand. He wanted to finish setting it up tonight.

Adding everyone's names and contact info was easy. Their senior class president had already compiled a list of email addresses and cell phone numbers so that everyone could keep in touch after graduation. It still took Parker a painstakingly long time to enter each one into the app. With 247 students in their graduating class, it was no small task. Parker worked as quickly as he could.

The bet was due to start in two days. Everyone would need to click the link to download the app and agree to the terms of the bet. Then they were officially in. Anyone not logged into the app by the time the bet started would be excluded. Parker wasn't worried about the tight timeline. If he just texted a couple of kids to let them know about it, he was confident that they would hear rumblings on Snapchat and Twitter quickly after that. Pretty soon, everyone would have the app downloaded. FOMO was real, and he knew people wouldn't want to miss out, especially with a $10,000 prize on the line.

Because they already knew all the answers, Parker and Mika couldn't actually be players in the game, but Parker didn't mind. It had always been his intention to give up the $10,000. This was one bet he didn't want to win. Parker simply wanted to spend time with Mika. He knew it was silly, going to all this work just to get a girl to notice him. But in his mind, it was money well spent. And if it also helped his best friend in the whole world get into MIT, then that was win-win as far as he was concerned.

After all, he had nothing else to do this summer before he headed off to college. He didn't have rock star grades like Zeke, but he had somehow managed to get admitted to the exclusive New York University's Tisch School of the Arts as a film major. He wasn't sure exactly what he was going to do in the film industry, but he knew he loved movies and telling stories. Tisch had a great program where he would get to learn all aspects of film-making, and he had never felt more certain that it was the right place for him.

Parker finished up and quickly sent the message to notify the entire senior class of the bet. Then he texted Mika and Sunny to let them know. They were probably asleep because it was after midnight, but they'd see his message in the morning.

He smiled to himself as he got ready for bed. He thought about all the time he would get to spend with Mika this summer. It had been sort of hard to connect with her when they'd met to go over all the clues earlier this week. She didn't get any of his movie references, for starters. She actually said she preferred reading to movies. Parker couldn't imagine. She kept talking about the settlers who had founded the town hundreds of years ago, and Parker found it hard to keep focused on her words. He had never been a huge fan of history, unless it was wrapped neatly inside of a storyline like *Saving Private Ryan* or *Braveheart*. But Parker wasn't worried. With all the time they'd be spending together in the coming weeks, they'd find their groove eventually.

As he lay in bed about to fall asleep, his thoughts turned to his brother. Now that he had a plan to help himself and Sunny, maybe it was time he helped his brother out too. Zeke was clearly stuck in a rut since coming home from college. Parker knew that with a little ingenuity, he could come up with something that would fix everything for Zeke too.

Chapter 6

Zeke was sprawled on the rug on his bedroom floor, staring up at the ceiling. In stark contrast to Parker's colorful, ever-changing room, Zeke's room was outfitted in colors of navy and white. It had been that way as long as he could remember. Sassy bumped her head against his cheek before turning around and settling against him, her tail draped across his face. Zeke pushed it out of his way, and she swished it back.

"Come on, Sassy." He sighed and gently turned her body so her tail went the opposite direction.

He was feeling sorry for himself, and he knew it. His life was at a dead stop. No future, no plans, nothing. Still, he tended to stack all problems up against the tragedy of his mom's illness and death. Nothing measured up. This was bad, but it wasn't as bad as that. Zeke knew he would be fine eventually. But for now, he was hunkered down, taking a time-out, regrouping. He knew it was silly, but he felt a little bit like a caterpillar in a cocoon. Something was coming, but he didn't know what.

Hearing a knock at his door, Zeke responded, "Come in," without moving from his position on the floor. Parker barreled into the room and flopped on Zeke's bed, looking down at him from the edge.

"What's with you?" Parker blurted.

"What do you mean, what's with me?"

"You're like, extra mopey today. Still in your pajama pants at three in the afternoon? You gotta get outta this funk. You can't live like this, dude."

"Maybe I'm just taking some time to figure things out. It's not like I've got anything else to do right now," Zeke said dryly.

Parker threw a pillow directly at Zeke's face. Zeke let it hit him and roll off to the side, but Sassy jumped up and glared at Parker before stalking out of the room. "Snap out of it! I've never seen you feel so sorry for yourself before. This isn't you. Listen, there's a party tonight at Victoria's house. Her parents are gone. It's gonna be sick. You gotta go. Say hi to people. Talk. Be social. You know, things normal human people do!"

Zeke sat up and swiveled to face Parker. There was surprise and fury building on his face. They had both gotten in trouble for partying, and here was Parker, suggesting another party, like that would fix anything at all.

"I wouldn't have gone to Victoria's party before. What makes you think I'm going to go now? And wait a minute. You aren't going, are you? Dad would lose it. Neither of us should be anywhere near a party, probably ever."

"Nah, I'm not going. But Sunny is."

"Sunny's going alone?" Zeke's eyebrows rose.

"Wrong again, dude. She's got a date. Nathan Davis. You know him?"

Inwardly, Zeke felt a stab of jealousy that Sunny had yet another date, but he didn't let that show on his face. "Davis? That guy's a total douche. Why is she even going out with him? What happened to Graham?"

Parker shook his head in mock sadness. "He's old news, bro. She dumped him. For real though, that dude was booooring. I'm glad she said 'adios' to him."

"Boring is way better than Nathan Davis, though. Aren't you going to go with her in case he, like, tries something?"

Parker turned to Zeke with an incredulous look on his face. "Go with her, like on her date with the two of them? This isn't *Pride and Prejudice*, man. She doesn't need a chaperone to be alone with a guy." He narrowed his eyes at Zeke. "Why are you being so weird?"

"I'm not being weird. That guy is no good. Haven't you heard the stories he tells at school? I mean, I was a grade above you all, and I still heard the stories. He laughed when that girl was super drunk at Max's party and he got her to go upstairs with him."

"Listen, Sunny's a big girl. She'll be fine. And I highly doubt she's going to get drunk or go upstairs with anybody. Have you met her?"

"I can't believe you. Some best friend you are!"

"Hey! Get off my back! She's an adult, and it's not my job to be her parent. I have my own stuff going on too, you know. I saw Mika's Snapchat, and she's hitting up Cherry Berry later with some friends. I'm going to intercept them."

"I can't believe how selfish you're being. If you won't go help her, I will."

Parker tossed his phone down, stood up, and walked over to Zeke's closet, pawing through the hanging shirts. "Excellent! Knock yourself out. She'll just tell you to buzz off anyway. No way she wants you crashing her date. But I am glad you took my advice about going to Victoria's party. It'll be good for you." He paused his perusal of Zeke's clothes and turned back to Zeke. "Do you think I should wear my black v-neck sweater or my Pink Floyd t-shirt? Do I want to look fancy or chill? What speaks to girls more?"

Zeke shook his head and headed for the bathroom door. "I'm going to shower. Don't you ever think about anybody but yourself?" he asked bitterly as he walked out the door. Parker was right about one thing. Zeke had been down for far too long, and he was finally ready to do something about it.

Parker turned to study himself in the mirror and frowned. He spoke to an empty room. "I don't just think about myself. Do I?"

Sunny had been sitting on the love seat for over a half hour, trolling Instagram out of sheer boredom. She hated Insta on sheer principle, all the fake poses, the fake smiles, the fake people. Sure, the pictures were pretty. But none of it was real. Tonight, however, she was desperate. Nathan was late, and he wasn't answering her texts. Sunny didn't run with the crowd at this particular party, so she needed something to do to fend off the feeling of self-consciousness. Her skin crawled with the certainty that people were staring at her, probably wondering what on earth she was doing here, sitting alone like a social pariah. She saw Victoria glancing in her direction and then whispering to her friends. They all giggled.

I should just leave, Sunny thought. She was never really into Nathan in the first place. She'd awakened this morning to a text from Parker telling her that the bet would officially start in two days. Well, one day now. Trying to ignore the knots in her stomach, she headed to Starbucks to distract herself. She was standing in line waiting for her coffee when she spotted Nathan. They'd chatted a bit about how summer was going, and it had surprised her when he asked her out. She was so caught off guard that she didn't stop to consider if she really wanted to go. She just said yes. He was hot, with wavy blond hair and an athletic body, but she didn't really know him at all. He wasn't even here yet, and she was already regretting her decision.

Maybe he got a flat tire or something. *Five more minutes*, she told herself. Then she was leaving.

Sunny heard the clump of boots approaching behind her and forced herself to keep her eyes on her screen, double-tapping on a photo of some random, adorable kitten. Kitten pictures, those were an appropriate use of Instagram.

"I never knew you were such a cat lover," a deep voice behind her said, chuckling. "You and Sassy never seemed to see eye to eye."

Sunny's skin flushed instantly. Zeke. Of course, he would be here to witness her sitting alone at a party like a total loser. She was too mortified to turn around and face him. She felt the wall that had been coming down between them slide right back up into position.

Dropping her phone onto her lap, she stared straight ahead and replied, "Maybe you don't know me as well as you think you do."

Zeke leaned down, and his hot breath tickled her neck as he murmured, "I wouldn't say that, exactly."

He moved out from behind the couch and plopped himself down next to her. She shivered and wasn't sure if it was because she could no longer feel his breath on her neck or because the entire right side of her body was pressed up against him on the suddenly too-small couch. She glanced over at him. He was wearing a plain gray t-shirt, dark jeans, and black motorcycle boots. It wasn't exactly party attire, but on him, it worked. Sunny, meanwhile, had spent hours this evening artfully curling her long blonde hair into beach waves and applying makeup. She was even wearing a new black sequined top paired with black jeans and white Keds. Even on a date, she wasn't crazy enough to force her feet into uncomfortable heels like all the girls giggling across the room, but it was still way more effort than she usually put into her looks. She wasn't even sure why she'd done it. Boredom, perhaps? However, sitting here with Zeke so close, she was grateful she didn't look like a total slob.

"Make yourself at home," she said sarcastically, gesturing to the couch.

"Thanks," he said with a crooked smile. "I already did."

That damn cocky grin.

Zeke draped an arm on the back of the couch, making Sunny feel as though he had put his arm around her. She refused to admit how much she wanted to lean into that arm.

"So, come here often?"

Sunny grimaced at his terrible joke. "Ha, ha, very funny. You know this isn't my crowd."

"Then what are you doing here?"

Was it just her imagination, or did he seem genuinely interested?

Sunny frowned and narrowed her eyes. He was probably just making conversation. But she wasn't interested in revealing that she'd been stood up. Neatly avoiding his question, she countered, "What are you doing here? You've been cloistered in your room for weeks, and this is where you choose to go on your first outing? This isn't exactly your crowd, either." She chose not to mention the fact that he had just gotten into trouble for drinking and probably shouldn't be here at all.

One quick glance around the room and Sunny saw several sets of female eyes, including Victoria's, currently shooting daggers at her. She shifted uncomfortably in her seat, trying to put a little space between herself and Zeke. "And could you give me some room here?"

"Why? Am I making you uncomfortable?" Zeke asked, and she swore he actually leaned a bit closer.

"No," Sunny said through clenched teeth, unwilling to give him the satisfaction of letting him know that he had an effect on her. She smiled tightly. "But your gaggle of infatuated women are ready to do me bodily harm, and I'd prefer to get out of here with all my limbs intact."

"Hmmm," he paused, glancing around. "I have a gaggle? I hadn't noticed."

Sunny snorted. There had always been a parade of women tagging along wherever he went, a variety of shapes and sizes, and his statement was accurate. He never noticed. All women just seemed to love him, and he was adorably clueless about it all. "Of course you didn't notice. Women have been falling at your feet for as long as I can remember."

"Not all women. Not the right woman," he said thoughtfully, turning to stare into her eyes.

Sunny couldn't look away. Could he be talking about her? Her heart hammered in her chest as she forced herself not to break eye contact. She would not let him intimidate her. She wasn't a child anymore, and this was her chance to prove it to him.

Sunny took a deep breath.

"What the hell, Montgomery?"

Shit. Nathan. She'd forgotten all about Nathan, which was actually kind of funny since he'd basically left her sitting there alone for nearly an hour.

Sunny was about to shoot to her feet when Zeke's arm, previously draped casually on the back of the couch, drifted down to rest on her shoulders, effectively holding her in place.

Sunny gave him a confused glance before turning her attention back to Nathan. He looked seriously pissed, standing there in his crisp blue polo shirt and khakis, arms folded like an angry parent yelling at their misbehaving toddler.

"I show up for our date and find you plastered onto this dude? Who the hell do you think you are?"

Sunny's face flushed with anger at his words. How dare he accuse her of doing anything wrong when he'd been late without even a text message?

Sunny glared at Nathan. "Who do I think I am?" Her voice was getting louder with each word she spoke, and the room was getting quieter as everyone stopped to watch the drama unfold. Sunny found that she didn't particularly care. "You're a fucking hour late, Nathan. And you didn't even text me to let me know. As far as I'm concerned, our date never happened and it never will. So I'm free to plaster myself all over anyone I want, and it's none of your business."

Zeke snorted.

Nathan puffed up his chest and took a step forward. "You got something to say, Crawford?"

Zeke shrugged lazily. "Nope."

Sunny gave Zeke a half-smile. She was impressed that he hadn't tried to get involved or stand up for her. It made her feel a little proud that he knew she could handle this on her own.

Nathan turned his attention back to Sunny, looking slightly chastened. "Listen, can we go upstairs and talk about this privately?" Nathan said, holding out a hand to Sunny.

Sunny's expression turned stony.

"No thanks. Bye, Felicia," Sunny said, turning back towards Zeke and effectively ending the conversation with Nathan.

Sunny heard a chorus of laughter spread across the room as Nate's face flushed with anger.

"Whatever, bitch," he muttered under his breath as he pushed his way through the crowd and out the front door. Drama ended, everyone lost interest and returned to their partying.

Zeke looked into Sunny's eyes. "Wanna get outta here?"

"For sure," she breathed. "I could use some fresh air."

Out on the porch, Zeke and Sunny stood side by side facing the street, hands on the white railing in front of them. They were alone on the porch, but they could still hear the thump of the bass from the party music and the occasional burst of laughter from the drunken partiers inside. Sunny turned towards Zeke, but he continued to stare out into the night.

"You never told me what you were doing here tonight," Sunny stated, narrowing her eyes at him.

"That is correct. I did not."

"Are you going to tell me now?"

Zeke turned to face Sunny. He leaned in. Sunny imagined closing the distance between them, rising up on her tiptoes to gently brush her lips against his. She felt frozen in place, that if she so much as blinked, she would break whatever stretched between them.

"Nope," he said, his voice nearly a whisper.

She heard her phone ding in her pocket, and the mood was broken. It dinged again. She thought about ignoring it, but the damage was already done. She took a step back and pulled out her phone, swiping up to read the text message.

Parker: *Sorry just read txts. Hes a jerk*

Parker: *U ok?*

"Parker?" Zeke asked.

Sunny looked up. "How'd you know?"

"It's always Parker."

Sunny wasn't sure if it was her imagination, but she thought Zeke's voice had a slight edge to it. She cocked her head to the side and studied Zeke's face.

Feeling a little reckless, she tossed out, "Jealous?" Then she held her breath as she wished she could take it back. It revealed too much.

Zeke leaned his hip on the railing, angling his body to face her, and shrugged. Sunny got the distinct impression that he was not as relaxed as he was trying to appear. "What if I said yes?"

Sunny stopped breathing for a second. This was dangerous territory. There was no way she could let herself believe that Zeke actually liked her, not after what he'd said about her so many years ago. She was just a stupid kid. Wasn't she? She weighed her options. If she admitted that the thought of him being jealous sent a thrill through her and he was just joking around, he would never let her live it down. She'd already been brave once tonight and didn't think she had it in her again. Better to play it safe.

"Yeah, right," Sunny said, rolling her eyes and choosing to lighten the mood. "I'm sure you are super jealous of your baby brother texting his bratty best friend. Look, I know you just feel bad for me because Nathan stood me up, but I honestly don't give a shit about that guy. I don't need your pity."

Zeke gave her a half-smile, looking surprised. "I don't feel sorry for you, Addison."

"You don't?"

"No. I can't believe you thought that. That guy didn't deserve you. Hell, no one at this party is good enough for you."

Sunny's heart warmed at his words.

Zeke stood and took a step towards her.

This time, it was the sound of his phone ringing that broke through the silence. Zeke swore under his breath and pulled out his phone.

"I gotta take this," he said, moving to the other side of the porch for more privacy.

Sunny replied to Parker's texts in an effort to pretend like she wasn't listening, not that she could make any sense of Zeke's terse one-word responses to the caller on the phone. From the tone of Zeke's voice and his clipped responses, she guessed it was his dad. She had just clicked send after texting Parker that she was fine when she saw Zeke approaching.

"I'm sorry. I gotta go. You need a ride?" he asked. Sunny considered asking about his phone call, but Zeke looked angry. She decided against it. It wasn't her business.

"No, but thanks for the offer. I'm parked down the street. I'll walk with you, though, if you're headed that way," Sunny said, waving a hand in the general direction of her car.

"Yeah, I'm parked over there too."

They both headed down the stairs, down the driveway, and out onto the street without saying a word. As the sounds of the party faded, it became quiet enough that they could hear the crickets chirping. A companionable silence fell between them.

"Well, that party was a bust," Sunny said as they reached her car.

"I wouldn't call it a total bust," Zeke said smoothly. He opened her car door and motioned for her to get inside. "Drive safe, Addison."

She answered, "You too, Ezekiel," as she shut her car door and started the engine. As she pulled out of her parking spot, she saw him watching her drive away. She had an unsatisfied feeling that she couldn't shake. It was like she'd just missed something, as though something was just out of her reach, but she wasn't sure what.

Chapter 7

The next morning, Sunny did something she rarely did. She rolled out of bed and texted Zeke. Not Parker. Zeke. She didn't know what came over her. Parker was nearly always her first text in the morning. But this morning felt different. She awoke thinking not of the bet that was launching soon, not of what Parker was up to, but instead of what Zeke was doing. Perhaps it was because they seemed to be getting along so much better lately. She tapped her fingers against her lips as she contemplated what to say. Best to keep it simple, she decided. She reached for the phone and tapped out a text to Zeke that she hoped seemed completely casual.

Sunny: *Hey.*

She didn't have to wait more than a few seconds for a reply.

Zeke: *Hey! What u doing?*

Sunny inwardly rejoiced both at the fact that he texted back and that he was using punctuation.

Sunny: *Nothing much. Heading to your house to swim with P. You around?*

Zeke: *I wish.*

Zeke: *Community service this morning.*

Sunny's heart sank both at the reminder of Zeke's drunk driving and the fact that he wouldn't be around today. After last night, she couldn't shake the notion of wanting to see him. Sunny wasn't normally one of those girls who cared a lot about clothes or looks, but she had bought a brand-new bikini before school got out. She hadn't bought it with Zeke in mind, exactly. But now that she was seeing more of him, she was secretly hoping that when Zeke saw it, maybe he would confess his undying love for her. A girl could dream. She wasn't going to show him how disappointed she was, though.

Sunny: *K. Maybe next time!*

Sunny tried not to feel too disheartened. She busied herself by texting Parker that she was on her way and packing her bag with her swimsuit and other essentials. Before she left her room, she ran a quick check to see how many people had downloaded her app. Parker would want to know since he was supposed to release the first clue tomorrow morning.

158.

Sunny's heart skipped a beat. 158 out of 247 students was a pretty good number of participants in the bet. Her surprise outweighed her nervousness about so many people seeing something she developed. Parker had only sent one initial invitation email to students. Sunny hadn't been sure if any of the kids in her class would even care about the bet at all. Apparently, a $10,000 prize was a better incentive than she'd anticipated.

Sunny mulled this over as she exited her room. The smell of frying bacon wafted up the stairs, and she headed down to the kitchen. Her dad was home, having no classes to teach that day. That meant family breakfast.

"Hi, Dad," Sunny said, gliding over to snatch a piece of bacon from the plate her dad was carrying. A small kitchen table sat in a cozy breakfast nook attached to their modest-sized kitchen. Their house wasn't tiny by any means, but it was no mansion like the Crawford house. Her dad had always said it was the perfect size for two people.

Frank Montgomery answered with his typical morning greeting, "Good morning, Sunshine." He leaned over to give her a hug with his free arm. Her dad was tall, so his chin rested on her head when he hugged her. Ever since she was a little girl, Sunny had loved how she felt completely safe when his strong arms surrounded her. Dressed in his typical day-off attire, a polo shirt and khaki shorts, he looked like he was ready for the day. Her dad was a handsome older man, and it surprised her that he'd never dated after her mother passed away. Silver hair, neatly trimmed beard, warm smile, intelligent, with a well-paying job. Sunny was sure he could have dated if he'd wanted to. But she was his entire world, and he didn't seem to need anything else.

Setting the bacon on the table, he asked, "How are you this morning?"

"Doing good," she answered.

They both sat down at the kitchen table. Frank had prepared a feast, as usual. Eggs, bacon, sausage, pancakes, and fruit. It was more food than two people could eat, and Sunny wasn't even that hungry. But she scooped a little of everything onto her plate, not wanting to disappoint her father.

"And what's on the agenda today?"

Sunny answered with a mouthful of bacon. "Headed to Parker's," she garbled. She swallowed. "We're just gonna hang and swim. Nothing too exciting."

Frank scooped some eggs into his mouth, nodding. "Oh," he said in between bites, "I almost forgot. I've got a call with my contact at MIT today. I'm making headway in getting you off that waitlist."

Sunny lowered her eyes to her plate. She could hear the disappointment in his voice whenever he talked about the waitlist. She reminded herself that she had a plan now, and it wouldn't hurt to share a bit with him. Not the whole thing. He wouldn't approve of it any more than Mr. Crawford would. And he would definitely tell Mr. Crawford, and that would just get Parker in trouble. But she could talk about her app without disclosing the entire plan.

Twisting her fingers in her napkin, she met her father's eyes and said, "Dad, I wanted to tell you something. I've been working really hard on an app, and I finished it. The Admissions person said I could contact her if I had anything additional that I wanted to share with them about my qualifications. I'm thinking if I write her a letter and talk about the app I developed, maybe that would help change their minds about me? It can't hurt, right?"

"That's brilliant, Sunny!" Her dad leaned over and kissed the top of her head. Sunny felt his pride glide over her like a warm blanket, and she smiled in relief. He continued, "You are always thinking. Your mom would be so proud of you." Her dad's eyes misted over, and he dabbed at them with a napkin. He cleared his throat. "This is exactly the type of initiative that MIT likes to see in their students. You are going to fit in perfectly there."

Sunny's smile wavered, but she forced it to remain in place, determined not to dampen her dad's joy. His words echoed in her head. *You're going to fit in perfectly there.* How did he know that? MIT was almost within reach. The goal had always been getting in. She just hadn't spent a lot of time thinking about what it would be like once she was actually there. As she finished her food, her dad chattered on about college. She nodded and murmured "uh-huh" in the right places, but her mind was elsewhere. She tried to envision herself sitting in the classroom listening to teachers drone on about various subjects. She thought about what it would be like in her dorm room, studying late into the night. The images eluded her.

Her breakfast done, Sunny cleared her plate, but her mind was still cluttered. She hugged her dad goodbye, promised to text, and headed to Parker's house. As she walked, a question flitted at the edges of her brain. MIT had been the perfect fit for her mom and her dad. What if it wasn't the perfect fit for her?

"Cannonball!"

The splash from Parker's leap into the pool didn't even reach Sunny's toes. She lay on a giant pink flamingo air mattress on the far side of the pool, having learned her lesson years ago. Zeke and Parker loved diving into the pool, splashing any unsuspecting person in close proximity. She carved out a no-splash zone for herself at the far end. That's where she stayed whenever she didn't want to get drenched.

"Weak," Sunny critiqued his form. "Your legs weren't tucked in tight enough. I expected way better from you, P."

He sent a spray of water towards her with his hands, laughing. The spray sprinkled her from her head to her teal-painted toes. Sunny realized she wasn't as safe as she'd previously thought, but she didn't mind. It was over ninety degrees today, and the water felt like a magnificent relief in the sweltering humidity. This was shaping up to be the hottest June she could remember.

"Let's see you do better," Parker challenged.

"Bet?" Sunny challenged back.

"Bet," Parker confirmed.

Well, Sunny shrugged, why not? She was already wet. Rolling off of her air mattress and into the cool water, she thought about her app again. When she'd told Parker how many people had downloaded it, he hadn't seemed surprised. Apparently, his phone had been blowing up with texts from classmates. They were trying to coerce him into giving hints, so he already knew word was out. Parker was the kind of guy that everyone in their grade knew and liked. He was good-natured and funny, friends with everyone. Not close friends, but friendly. Sunny was content to let Parker be the social butterfly. She grilled Parker about the texts, asking if anyone had reported any problems with the app, but none had. All seemed to be well, much to Sunny's relief.

As her arms expertly stroked through the water towards the pool ladder, demonstrating the fruition of years of swimming lessons, Sunny planned her strategy to win the bet she'd just made with Parker. A cannonball? Or something more creative? The deep thump of bass resonated in the water as music poured from the outdoor speakers that surrounded the pool. Someone inside the house had turned on the sound system and put on a classic rock song Sunny vaguely recognized as from the '80s or '90s.

Sunny pulled herself out of the water just as Zeke emerged through the open patio doors. She was already self-conscious about her new bikini, and seeing him unexpectedly made it even worse. The bikini was modest and black. When Sunny decided she wanted to stretch out of her comfort zone and look for something other than the one-piece that was her usual summer attire, she knew she didn't want to be subjected to Parker's endless ridicule. So basic black, it was. The bikini was more skimpy than anything she'd worn in public before. Sunny had finally gained the curves to fill it out. Even though her brain recognized that she looked fine, in her heart, she still felt flat-chested and gawky.

Sunny watched Zeke freeze as soon as he spotted her. His eyes trailed down her body in what she gathered was an appreciative gaze. Warmth spread throughout her stomach, and her cheeks heated. Hmmmm. Maybe there *was* something there. It seemed like maybe Zeke liked what he saw. Then again, maybe he was just looking because he was a guy. Best not to let her head get too big.

"Hey!" Parker yelled at Zeke. "Eyes on me, dork face."

Zeke's eyes snapped over to Parker treading water in the middle of the pool. He gave Parker a smirk as he strode past Sunny towards the lounge chairs along the side of the pool. "Dork face? Is that the best you can do? Addison needs to give you some vocabulary lessons, or you'll never hack it in college."

"Says the guy who got kicked out of college," Parker taunted.

Zeke faltered and his eyes trained on the ground, but he continued walking. Sunny didn't think Parker noticed the slight movement, but she had. The comment was harsh, even for brothers who were used to ribbing each other. She could tell from the way Zeke had ducked his head that Parker hit a nerve. But Parker seemed oblivious. She was tempted to remain silent, but she just couldn't hold it in.

"Rude, Parker," she scolded. Zeke glanced over at her, but he didn't seem exactly pleased that she'd jumped to his defense.

"Sorry, my bad," Parker said sheepishly. The thing about Parker was that he might say the wrong thing at the wrong time, but he was always ready to admit when he crossed a line.

Zeke nodded his acceptance of the apology. "Thanks."

As Zeke reached the lounge chairs, he peeled his shirt off, exposing a tan stomach rippled with muscles. He clearly hadn't been skipping his workouts all year. Sunny's mouth went dry, but she didn't let herself swallow. If she did, she knew it would be a sure sign that he affected her. She looked away and busied herself lining up her jump. She thought about a dive, but discarded that idea when she remembered Zeke's words about how he worried about her. In the end, she opted for a simple cannonball. She knew she could beat Parker's form.

Sunny paused, her body ready to launch into the water. She looked at Parker. "Terms?"

Parker immediately proclaimed, "Loser has to make chocolate ice cream shakes for everyone."

"Deal," she agreed.

"Show me what you're working with!" Parker yelled, egging Sunny on.

It was all the encouragement Sunny needed. She took a few running steps and leapt into the air. She executed a perfect cannonball, legs tucked in tight, spine in a curve. Sunny may not have been an Olympic swimmer, but she had great cannonball skills, perfected over years spent in this pool. She thought she heard Parker swear loudly as she crashed into the water, knowing he'd been beaten.

The cool water surrounded Sunny, quieting the noise in her head. Her thoughts had been so full of Zeke. Too full. She needed to forget about him. She used her arms to propel her body up to the surface and took a deep, cleansing breath as she broke through. In with the fresh air, out with the thoughts of Zeke. She opened her eyes to the bright sunshine. And stared directly into Zeke's beautiful blue eyes.

Well, crap. *So much for putting him out of my mind*, thought Sunny. How had he gotten into the pool so quickly? He was too close for comfort, only inches away from her, and she immediately went on the defensive. Her brain warned her not to show him how much of an effect he had on her. Sunny felt as though, for most of her life, she had been trying to prove to him and everyone else that she wasn't in love with him.

"What?" Sunny said irritably, shooting him a glare.

"What?" he echoed back, good-natured and even-tempered as usual. It usually took a lot to make Zeke irritated. That alone was enough to aggravate Sunny even more.

Out of the corner of her eye, Sunny saw Parker use the ladder to hoist himself out of the pool. He headed towards the outdoor bar area, no doubt to start making the chocolate shakes. He had clearly lost the bet, no judge needed. She returned her attention to Zeke.

Sunny tread water, waving her arms to keep afloat. "You're just swimming here, staring at me like a creeper. What do you want?" she asked.

He smiled and leaned back, relaxing into a back float, kicking away from Sunny leisurely, his muscular arms stretched out wide on either side of him. "I wasn't staring at you. I was looking at you. Totally different and not creepy at all, I promise," he said with a chuckle as he floated away.

Sunny laughed uncomfortably as she swam back over to her air mattress on the far side of the pool. "Oh, I see. Just admiring my cannonball perfection?" she joked. She had launched herself up as she spoke and was now busy arranging herself comfortably atop the floaty. "And what are you even doing here—" she began.

Sunny never saw it coming. One second she was lying on top of her floaty, feeling smug. The next moment she was upside down, underwater, with powerful arms locked around her waist, making sure she didn't drown. Tugged up to the surface, she found herself treading water, chest to rock-hard chest, with Zeke. As she sputtered and coughed, she had to admit that being cushioned by his arms didn't feel bad at all. Not one little bit.

"No," he said quietly as Sunny swiped the water out of her eyes with a free hand. Zeke's fingers brushed her chin, lifting her face up to look into his own. "I wasn't admiring your cannonball. I was admiring how brave you are."

Heat spread across Sunny's shoulders and cheeks, and she knew she was blushing. That was the thing about fair skin; Sunny didn't just blush on her cheeks. When she was embarrassed, it was like her entire upper body blushed. It was her lifelong sorrow, to have her emotions on full display for everyone to see. There was nothing that scared Sunny more than people knowing how she felt.

"Hands to yourself, Handsy McHanderson!" Parker yelled good-naturedly from across the pool behind the bar. "There are children present!"

Sunny and Zeke sprang apart, partly from the surprise of Parker's barked order and partly from something else. Sunny thought perhaps she had been enjoying that embrace a little too much, and she felt guilty, as though she had done something forbidden. Parker pointed a long skinny arm at Zeke, and he jovially shouted, "You can do what you want in private, but my eyes are virgin! I don't want to see any of that monkey business!" With that, Parker mashed his palm down on the blender's controls, drowning both of them in the grinding noise of the machine. And just like that, whatever magic had just existed between Sunny and Zeke was washed away. Again.

Sunny cleared her throat and headed back towards her air mattress. "Before I was so rudely interrupted," she said, sweeping her wet hair out of her eyes, "I was asking what you are doing here? I thought you had community service?" She had to speak loudly to be understood over the blender.

"I did," Zeke answered, his voice not quite a yell. "We were cleaning up a road ditch, and we finished the stretch of highway we were supposed to be working on, so they said we were done for the day.

He still signed our slips for the full eight hours, though, so that was cool."

"Cool," Sunny echoed, picturing Zeke in a neon vest, with one of those trash picker sticks in his hand.

The blender stopped, and they heard the clink of glasses as Parker got the shakes ready. Sunny kicked backwards across the pool, enjoying the silence and sunshine while she waited.

Parker carried their drinks over and sat down at the edge of the pool at the shallow end, legs dangling into the water. "Come and get it!" he announced.

Sunny changed direction and swam to the side of the pool before climbing up to perch beside Parker. Zeke swam over next to Sunny but stayed in the water. It was only about three feet deep, so Sunny had to avert her eyes to make sure she wasn't caught staring at his chest.

Parker's phone dinged, and he got up to check his text messages.

"Who is it?" asked Sunny, knowing that Parker wouldn't mind her nosy question.

"Becca," he answered. "She wants to know when the first clue will be released."

Zeke's ears perked up at that. "Clue?"

Parker nodded. "Yeah, it's this thing we are doing with our senior class. Kind of a last hurrah. Sunny made an app, and it's legit. Over a hundred of our classmates already downloaded it. I'm sending people on a treasure hunt with clues about the town. Sick, huh?"

"Treasure hunt, huh? What's the prize at the end?" Zeke asked, his gaze razor sharp.

Parker hesitated, and Sunny busied herself with slurping her shake.

Zeke frowned and glanced back and forth between the two of them, his eyes finally narrowing at Parker. "Parker, what's the prize?"

Parker laughed nervously. "Nothing to worry about, bro. Just a little monetary reward at the end to incentivize people. 'What's worth doing is worth doing for money.'"

"*Risky Business*?" Sunny guessed. She wasn't certain where she'd heard the quote before.

Parker shook his head. "*Wall Street.*"

Zeke interrupted. "How much money are we talking, Parker?"

Avoiding Zeke's piercing gaze, Parker mumbled something unintelligible.

"How. Much. Money," Zeke bit out.

"$10,000," Parker admitted reluctantly.

"What? Are you insane?" Zeke shouted.

"'Money isn't everything, Mortimer,'" Parker replied calmly. He took a sip of his shake.

"*Trading Places!*" Sunny shouted triumphantly. She loved that movie. Zeke turned his glare in her direction.

"Hey, stop stink-eyeing me. I'm not the one giving away my money."

Zeke pointed a finger at her. "You could have stopped him."

"No one can stop Parker, and you know it," Sunny replied indignantly.

Parker waved his arms. "Hey. Standing right here! In charge of my own life. An actual adult now."

"Shut it down," Zeke commanded.

Parker folded his arms across his chest. "No. It's too late. It's already out there. People have downloaded the app. I can't back out now. I won't."

Zeke let out a frustrated growl. "You're an adult," he scoffed. "Clearly not! Adults don't throw their money away on a game, Parker. Do you know who dad's going to blame for this when he finds out? Me!"

"So we make sure he doesn't find out, capisce?" Parker looked hopeful.

Zeke looked at Sunny, resigned. "This is a horrible idea. You know that, don't you?"

Sunny nodded and patted his shoulder sympathetically. "I've been saying that from the beginning."

Chapter 8

"What's your partner-in-crime up to tonight?" Zeke asked, flopping onto Parker's bed and smashing a pillow under his head. It was evening. Sunny had gone home for supper with her dad after they finished swimming. Meanwhile, Zeke and Parker showered and devoured the roast beef and potatoes Marta had cooked for them. Their dad was still at work, a fact that didn't surprise either of them.

Parker sat on the window seat, engrossed in his phone. He answered absently, "On the way over. Movie night."

"Ha, what's new?" Zeke laughed. Parker and Sunny spent a lot of time watching movies. Sometimes Zeke joined them. After all, their movie theater room in the basement was pretty spectacular. He liked movies too, but he didn't have the obsession that Parker seemed to have.

They heard a door slam downstairs. A voice called up the stairs, "Boys, I'm home!"

"Great," Zeke muttered.

"Hi, Dad," yelled Parker. Then he put his phone down on the window seat and turned towards Zeke. He leaned forward and rested his elbows on his knees. "Dad still laying into you about the... you know?"

Zeke understood exactly what Parker was referring to. He sighed and sat up, swiveling to face Parker. "It'll be fine, Parker. Dad will get over it eventually. You know him."

Parker nodded. "So what's your plan now?" he asked.

"My plan?"

"Yeah, you know. Like, how are you going to get back into college?"

Shaking his head, Zeke replied, "I don't know if I am, Parks. Dad said he was working on it. I think he's trying to donate a ton of money to bribe my way in or something. But what if I never get a school to accept me? I'm starting to think maybe I need to give up on college and go get a job. It's not like I had a major picked out anyway. There's a big demand for electricians and plumbers. I could learn a trade, something with on-the-job training, you know? I can't just hang around here the rest of my life doing nothing."

"No way." Parker stood up and began pacing. "Not that you wouldn't make a great electrician or whatever. You'd be great at it. But you were, like, born for college." He ticked off reasons on his hands while he paced. "You love to read. You love studying. You actually enjoy going to the library. You even love math. I mean, who loves math? It's unhealthy; that's what it is. But it's you. You need to go to college."

"Don't get me wrong. I'd give anything to undo what happened. I just think it's time I faced reality."

"Reality shmeality," Parker rhymed, waving his hand dismissively. "Just don't give up on your dream yet, okay? Dad will get you back in. He's the best at arguing with people and getting what he wants."

"Truth," Zeke said, nodding. "Okay. I won't give up just yet."

Parker sat back down and picked up his phone. Zeke took his silence as an opportunity to change the subject.

"Still not going to give up on this whole bet thing, huh?"

"Nope," Parker said. "First clue gets sent in the morning. So save your breath. You can't talk me out of it."

"Parker, when dad finds out—"

Parker groaned. "I said, save your breath! I'm not going to change my mind. Get off my back already!"

Standing up, Zeke crossed over to where Parker sat. "Well, excuse me for trying to help when I see a disaster coming. You can't keep screwing up and expecting me to clean up your mess, Parker. I won't always be there to fix things for you."

"No one asked you to fix things for me! I'm not a baby anymore."

"Could have fooled me," Zeke said, folding his arms across his chest and frowning down at him.

"Real mature. Insulting me just because I won't do what you want. You're not the boss of me, you know!" Parker stuck his tongue out at Zeke and flipped him off at the same time.

"Oh, now who's being mature?" Zeke shook his head, his eyes narrowing in annoyance. "Listen, I know you didn't ask for my help, but it's not like Dad's ever around. And Mom isn't here to take care of you anymore. That just leaves me."

"You're not Mom."

Zeke stilled. He felt a pinch in his chest. Of course he wasn't their mother. He ran a hand over his face. "Do you think I don't know that? I've made a complete mess of everything. If Mom were here, things would be so different..." Zeke's voice trailed off as he thought about how much better their lives would have been if their mom was still alive.

"Yeah, well, she's not," Parker said.

"No, she's not. And I'm sorry you're stuck with me." Feeling defeated, Zeke strode to the door. He was angry and sad, but he tried to calm himself down. They were getting nowhere by insulting each other and yelling. He turned around at the doorway. "Listen, you may think I'm just being bossy, but I really am trying to help."

Parker sighed and flopped back against the pillows on the window seat. "I know. But it's my life. Go figure out your own life."

Zeke took a deep breath and left without another word. His brother was right. It was his life, not Zeke's. But after years of taking care of Parker, Zeke wasn't ready to let go quite yet.

"Wow. Are you never not hungry?" Zeke asked, startling Sunny into dropping an opened bag of pretzels, which thankfully landed upright without spilling all over the pantry floor. "Not that I'm judging," he continued. "I'm just impressed."

Sunny reached down, picked the pretzel bag up, and swiveled around to face Zeke, who stood at the pantry door. She'd been on the hunt for movie snacks. He leaned towards her, both arms braced against the door frame. Sunny took a step back, his presence filling the small space. Trying to shake off the feeling, she purposely shoved a handful of pretzels into her mouth and replied, "I have a very fast metabolism." Her words were a little garbled, but he understood.

"I can see that," he said, looking her up and down with a wink.

The pretzels turned to sawdust in Sunny's mouth as her face heated under his scrutiny. Sunny swallowed the dry pretzels and wished for a glass of water to wash it down, but Zeke still stood blocking the doorway. She set the pretzels on the shelf and grabbed a nearby bottle of Gatorade, which earned her a raised eyebrow from Zeke. Accepting the unspoken challenge, she twisted the cap and chugged half the bottle.

Zeke chuckled and shook his head. Desperate to take the focus off of herself, Sunny asked, "Are you following me?"

Zeke shot her a wry smile. "Paranoid much?"

"Stalker much?"

"Can't a guy get a snack in his own house without getting hassled?"

"Why do you always answer a question with a question?"

Zeke threw up his hands. "Okay. Okay. I surrender. No more questions."

Just then, Zeke heard a noise behind him and glanced back toward the kitchen.

"Oh shit," he said, shoving Sunny farther into the pantry and quietly shutting the door behind him, closing them both in the small, dark room.

"What the hell are you..." Zeke's hand clamped over Sunny's mouth, cutting off the rest of her question. His other hand wrapped around her waist, drawing her in close to his chest.

Zeke's warm breath tickled her ear as he whispered, "Shhhhh. It's my dad. I can't deal with him right now." He removed his hand from her mouth, but kept his other arm around her waist. She had to admit she liked the feeling of being nestled against him.

"But why do I have to hide from him?" Sunny whispered back. She tried to convey as much outrage as she could in a whisper, even though she didn't feel very outraged at all.

Zeke paused, considering her point. "Sorry," he said, "You were already in here, and I needed a place to hide. Collateral damage."

Sunny could barely make out his features in the darkened room, but he didn't sound very sorry to her. In fact, she thought he might even be smiling. Though she didn't like being pushed into hiding, being wrapped in Zeke's arms certainly didn't feel too bad. His arms were steady and firm, wrapped around her in the small space. Her traitorous body wanted to melt into his and snuggle closer.

Mr. Crawford's footsteps drew nearer, and Sunny gave in to her temptation to move closer to Zeke. Though she told herself that she was only holding onto him because she couldn't see anything else, she knew that wasn't true. Her hands were resting on his forearms, and as she focused solely on him, her heartbeat increased. Was it just her imagination, or was he drawing closer to her too? She thought she felt his hands tighten at her waist. They were so close that if she tilted her head up, their lips would meet. She considered closing that small remaining distance between them, but fear kept her frozen. Reminding herself that Zeke didn't think of her like that, she stood rooted in place. She was just his younger brother's friend. And if she tried to kiss him and he rejected her, she would never recover from the humiliation. She would be stuck avoiding him for the rest of their lives.

Suddenly, there was a loud clattering noise. They both jumped. It sounded like Mr. Crawford was putting some dishes in the sink. The heated moment was lost, and Sunny mentally breathed a sigh of relief that she hadn't actually been foolish enough to try to kiss Zeke. They stayed silent for a few moments until they heard Mr. Crawford's footsteps recede.

Zeke said softly, "I think he's gone now," and his arms loosened slightly, though he didn't let go.

Sunny let out a breath she didn't know she'd been holding. She wasn't even the one who was avoiding Mr. Crawford, but she certainly hadn't wanted him to walk in and discover them in the closet alone together. That would have been difficult to explain. Even though Mr. Crawford was gone, Sunny was in no hurry to move out of Zeke's embrace. It appeared that Zeke was in no hurry either. The silence stretched between them, neither moving, even though there was no reason to stay in the pantry any longer.

Suddenly the door swung open, and they found themselves staring into the face of Parker.

Everyone froze. Zeke's arms were still wrapped around Sunny, and her face heated. Again. Parker's face remained blank as he stood there for a beat, reached into the pantry, grabbed a bag of chips, and said, "Carry on," shutting the pantry door.

"Well, he's certainly silent like a ninja," Zeke said wryly.

"I know, right?" Sunny said, reluctantly extricating herself from Zeke's arms and opening the pantry door. "Now he's going to think there's something going on between us, which is ridiculous." She laughed, but it sounded hollow to her ears.

Zeke remained silent as he followed her over to the kitchen island.

Desperate for something to do with her hands, Sunny grabbed a clean glass off the drying rack and poured herself a glass of water. As she poured, she asked, "So why are you ducking your dad?"

Zeke sighed and leaned down, resting his elbows on the granite countertop. "Oh, you know, trying to avoid the usual lectures on how I've screwed up my whole life with my poor choices."

"Really? That's all? You seemed more desperate than usual to avoid him. I mean, I've never seen you hide in a closet to get away from him before."

Zeke studied his hands and didn't reply.

Something wasn't right. Even though she told herself it was none of her business, she couldn't stop herself from pressing, "Zeke?"

Zeke stood and shoved a hand through his hair, making it stick straight up in the air. "Uh, yeah, so, you can't tell Parker this. Okay?" Sunny nodded and Zeke continued, "So I overheard my dad talking to my uncle on the phone a few minutes ago, and he's planning to ship me off somewhere. I was eavesdropping because I thought he was trying to get me back into college, but I guess he must've given up on that. I didn't catch the whole conversation, but I can't deal with it right now. If I just avoid him for a while, he can't kick me out yet," Zeke frowned. "I don't know where he's sending me, but I know I don't want to go."

Sunny's stomach tightened at the thought of Zeke leaving. "What do you mean, ship you off? He can't just kick you out of the house! He's your dad."

"You do know my dad, right? He doesn't just change his mind. If he says I'm out, I'm already gone. My best bet is just to avoid him as long as I can."

"But you're an adult," Sunny protested. "He can't make you go somewhere you don't want to go."

"Yeah, right, Addison," Zeke said with a roll of his eyes. "I'm an adult with no money. I've never held down a job. I have zero skills. Even if I can get a job quick, a minimum wage job wouldn't even pay the rent in an apartment, much less food, utilities. And my dad still controls my trust fund until I'm twenty-five. All my money is his. I'm pretty much under his thumb until then."

"Oh," Sunny said dumbly, looking down at the untouched glass of water in her hands. "I'm sorry." He was right. He couldn't keep living here if Mr. Crawford kicked him out. She wasn't sure how to help. He'd done something incredibly stupid, and he was paying the price. She'd never asked him about that night, why he'd been drinking, why he'd gotten behind the wheel when he was so incredibly drunk. It was unlike him to be so reckless. When she first heard about it, she thought maybe he'd changed when he went away to college. But now he was home, and he still seemed like the same Zeke to her, responsible and caring. It didn't make sense.

"Well, I better go explain to Parker that nothing was going on between us in the pantry," Sunny said, backing away from the counter.

Zeke grabbed her hand, his voice urgent. "Wait, you can't!"

Sunny's heart leapt in her chest. Maybe it hadn't been her imagination that he had been moving closer to her. "What do you mean?" Sunny asked tentatively.

"I mean, you can't tell him what I just told you. I don't want him to know Dad is sending me away, at least not quite yet. How are you going to explain us being in there without telling him that?"

"Oh," Sunny said, nodding as comprehension dawned. Her face hardened into a mask as she pushed the hope back down, chiding herself for being sucked back in again. She shook her hand out of his grip and said coolly, "You don't have to worry. Your secret is safe. I'll just tell him you were avoiding another lecture from your dad and I got stuck in there with you. You know Parker," she said, waving her hand dismissively, "he won't even question it."

Sunny walked out of the room without a backward glance.

As Sunny headed downstairs to the movie theater, she prepared herself to be inundated with questions about what she and Zeke had been doing in the pantry. It was Parker, after all.

Pushing open the swinging oak door, she marveled at the room, just as she always did when she entered. Lovingly dubbed "The Cave," it was a large, square room with no windows, black-painted walls, and dark gray carpet. Parker had deemed it perfect for movie watching because of the lack of outside lighting. According to Parker, movies must be watched in pitch black darkness with sound so deafening that Sunny was quite sure it would permanently damage her hearing. She complained loudly and frequently about the noise level, but secretly, she loved it. It made her feel like she was really inside the movie. Parker's dad had let him install surround sound speakers, a ninety-inch television, and two rows of super comfy black leather reclining seats. They were the kind of theater seats that could be used as one long couch or individual seats, depending on whether the arm rests were up or down. No movie theater was complete without a bar area and a fully stocked refrigerator. Mr. Crawford had even bought Parker a gourmet movie theater popcorn popper for his birthday. The smell of buttery popcorn lingered in the air. Marta made sure that the cupboards were always stocked with popcorn, butter, and salt. His dad never did anything halfway, and this theater was a testament to that.

Dropping the bag of pretzels onto the bar, Sunny steeled herself for a barrage of questions.

"So you wanna watch *Raiders of the Lost Ark*? I'm in the mood for some treasure hunting," he said as he shoved a handful of chips into his mouth.

"Um," Sunny said, surprised. "Sure?"

Parker tossed the remote to Sunny. "Cool, cool," he said. "I'll make the popcorn while you get the movie ready to go."

"But we already have pretzels and chips!" Sunny said.

"So?" Parker said with a grin.

"Fair point," Sunny answered with a smile. "Now I remember why I'm friends with you. It's all about the popcorn."

Well, that was easier than she'd thought.

"So what movie are we watching?" Zeke asked jovially, as he sat down next to Sunny on the couch, close enough to cause a tiny flutter inside her stomach. Zeke didn't always join them for movies, and she hadn't realized he was planning to watch with them tonight.

Parker was the first to reply to Zeke's question. "*Raiders of the Lost Ark.*"

"Again?" Zeke's voice had an exasperated edge to it, no doubt because they had all watched this movie a dozen times over the years.

"It's a classic!" Parker and Sunny exclaimed together. They then turned to each other and yelled, "Jinx!" at the same time.

Zeke smiled. "Sweet. Now it will be nice and quiet for the movie, since I have no intention of saying your names anytime soon."

Sunny and Parker both scowled, which earned a bark of laughter from Zeke in reply.

Parker started the movie and plopped down on the couch next to Sunny. He reclined his seat and handed her a tub of fresh popcorn. He knew that the popcorn was almost more important to Sunny than the movie itself. She took the tub from him, but didn't dig in like she normally would.

Parker was seated on Sunny's right, Zeke on her left. However, while the armrest was down between Sunny and Parker, there was no armrest separating her and Zeke. Zeke hadn't pulled it down, and Sunny wasn't about to either. She was incredibly aware of every part of him that brushed up against her. His thigh, clad in well-worn jeans. His muscular arm, partially bare because he had thrown on a faded old Metallica t-shirt after his shower. She was laser-focused on every area their bodies touched. Popcorn was the furthest thing from her mind, until Parker nudged her with his elbow.

"Something wrong with the popcorn?" he asked, nodding to the still-full bucket.

Before Sunny could respond, Zeke leaned forward and threw a pillow at Parker, almost knocking the soda out of his hand. "Hey! You are jinxed," Zeke reprimanded him. "No talking."

When Zeke reclined back on the sofa again, it seemed like he'd moved closer to Sunny. Yes, he definitely had. Full arm to arm contact this time, elbow to shoulder. Heat radiated down the side of Sunny's arm, and she swore the temperature rose in the room. She was suddenly aware of every breath she took. Did he realize how affected she was by his nearness? God, she hoped not. If he noticed, he certainly didn't show it. Zeke looked relaxed, with that same 'cool guy' vibe that Sunny so admired. Always comfortable in any situation. Did anything ever ruffle him?

Zeke reached his left arm in towards the popcorn bucket in Sunny's lap. It was like a blast of cold water. The top layer of popcorn was sacred to her. The first few bites out of a fresh bucket of popcorn were her favorite. No one came between Sunny and those perfect, buttery, salty bites. She smacked his hand away and grunted at him angrily, screwing up her face into a snarl so he understood that her popcorn was off-limits.

Undeterred, Zeke just laughed and asked, "Anyone want a blanket? Just grunt if you do. Apparently, Addison thinks grunting is acceptable when you are jinxed, and I'm willing to let it slide this time."

Neither Parker nor Sunny said anything, but both shook their heads, declining a blanket. Zeke hopped up and strode over to the basket piled high with fluffy blankets in the corner of the room. He grabbed an over-sized, brown blanket, returned to the couch, kicked up his feet on the recliner, and covered his legs with the blanket. Was it possible he was even closer now? A small bit of the blanket was draped over part of her lap. Lord, she could barely breathe. And he was just sitting there, completely unaffected.

This was going to be the longest movie of Sunny's life.

An hour into the movie, Parker let out a gigantic snore. Sunny was so on edge from sitting close to Zeke that she jumped sharply, spilling a few kernels of popcorn onto her lap. She popped the spilled pieces into her mouth and set the tub on the floor, leaning back and glancing over at Zeke, who was chuckling. Whether he was laughing at Sunny or at Parker's snoring, she wasn't sure, but she gave him an answering smile that she hoped looked fairly normal.

Zeke raised his arm, laying it on the back of the couch behind her. Then he leaned over and whispered in her ear. "Sunny," he said, officially unjinxing her, "what do you say we have a little fun?"

His breath tickled her ear, and she couldn't decide whether it was his words or his nearness that sent the tingle down her spine. She threw caution to the wind and decided she didn't care. Either way, she was in for whatever Zeke was going to suggest next.

"What did you have in mind?" Sunny replied as coolly as she could manage.

He nodded towards Parker. "Marker on the face? A hand in a bowl of warm water? A recording of his snoring so we can blackmail him later? What do you think?"

Sunny tried not to let her disappointment show on her face. What was she doing getting her hopes up? She was supposed to be cold and indifferent. He had been talking about playing a trick on Parker. Stupid. Of course, he wasn't interested in her. She was just his kid brother's friend. Sunny felt her bubble of hope burst again, and she wasn't feeling very playful anymore.

Sunny shook her head. "Nah, let him be," she said stiffly. "He was up late last night. Besides, my favorite part is coming up." Sunny nodded her head towards the TV.

Zeke looked slightly disappointed, and Sunny tried not to be encouraged by the fact that he left his arm on the back of the sofa. It was touching her shoulders, and it felt a great deal like he had his arm around her.

Towards the end of the movie, Sunny stifled a yawn. Zeke glanced her direction. She felt his right hand on her shoulder, nudging her to lean into the crook of his arm as he used his left arm to throw the rest of his blanket onto her lap, effectively cocooning her with him on the couch.

"You look tired too. Feel free to fall asleep on me. I make a great pillow. And I promise not to marker on your face." He grinned.

Sunny murmured, "Gee, thanks." Her heart skittered a little in her chest. Sleep. Ha. She would never be able to sleep this close to him, breathing in his cologne, feeling his rock-hard muscles so close to her.

Eventually, Sunny relaxed into him, leaning her head a bit more onto his chest, letting his warmth seep into her. He was like a furnace, and she liked it. She was perpetually cold, and it felt nice being warm for a change. Sunny realized this was the first time she had ever snuggled with someone while watching a movie. She had gone to movies with guys before, but they always sat stiffly, nervously holding clammy hands, if anything. This felt comfortable, cozy, and natural.

Zeke shifted on the couch, and her arm tingled as his left hand brushed her arm. She froze, unsure if it was an accident or one of those signs a boy gives a girl when he wants to hold her hand. A few seconds passed, and she felt his fingers, trailing down her arm, drawing lazy circles up and down.

Maybe, Sunny thought, just maybe he really did feel something for her. This was definitely a sign, wasn't it? She couldn't take the anticipation anymore. She had to know. Did he like her? Did he want her as much as she wanted him? It was now or never. Sunny took a deep breath and craned her neck upwards to look directly at him.

"Zeke, can I ask you something?"

Suddenly Parker snorted loudly and jerked awake, flailing a bit like he was falling. Zeke and Sunny shot apart like they'd been caught making out, even though they hadn't done anything wrong. Sunny huffed out a breath in irritation.

"Just when things were getting interesting," Zeke said wryly, shaking his head.

Parker shook his head. "Ahh, I slept through almost the whole movie!" he complained groggily.

Sunny gave him a shove with her elbow, trying to act normal even though her heart was racing. Her mind was a jumble of questions. She smiled at him. "Don't worry, P. It's not like you don't already know what happens."

Yawning loudly, Parker protested. "Yeah, but just because you already know what happens doesn't mean it isn't fun to watch."

Sunny and Zeke nodded their agreement, and they all watched the closing scenes of the movie together. When the credits rolled, Sunny cleaned up the popcorn bowls and gathered her things. Her dad would be waiting up for her at home. Parker and Zeke walked her to the door, debating the best villain from all of the Indiana Jones movies.

Interrupting the guys, Sunny waved goodbye, one hand on the doorknob. She said, "See you tomorrow morning, Parker. I'll meet you at the location for clue number one. Blackwater Creek Pavilion, right?"

"Shhhhhhh!" said Parker, putting his finger to his lips. "It's supposed to be a secret!"

"From who?" Sunny said, glancing around the empty foyer. "Your brother can't play, and there's no one else here."

"We have to be careful," Parker said seriously.

Sunny rolled her eyes. "Okay. Fine. I'll see you tomorrow. At the secret location. At eleven a.m." She winked dramatically.

Parker winked back. "Exactly," he answered.

Pausing, Sunny looked over at Zeke. "Are you coming too?" She tried to act casual, as though she didn't care about the answer.

Zeke shrugged and shoved his hands into the front pockets of his jeans. "Hadn't thought about it. I don't have any community service tomorrow, so I might tag along."

"Cool," Sunny said with a soft smile.

"Cool," Zeke answered.

Parker looked back and forth between the two of them. "You guys are weird."

Zeke grabbed Parker around the neck, bringing his head down for a noogie, and said, "You're weird."

"No, you are!" yelled Parker, as he tried to get out of the headlock while simultaneously trying to sweep Zeke's legs out from under him.

"You're both weird! G'nite!" Sunny yelled as she opened the door and fled the chaos.

Chapter 9

"We're famous!" Parker shouted into the phone.

"Dude. Why are you calling me so early? In fact, why are you calling me at all? You never call."

Parker laughed and ignored Sunny's question.

"Didn't you hear me? We're famous! Our app, I mean, your app. It's on the news!"

Sunny shot up in bed. "Wait, no way. What are you talking about?"

Parker kept going. "Well, it's only the local news, but it's still out there for the world to see! Tons more people will download it now."

"What? The actual news? Like on the TV? You don't even watch the news!"

"I know! Mika texted me. Apparently, she watches the news every morning with her mom. She's really into, like, important world stuff. Isn't she the best?" Parker's dreamy sigh echoed over the phone.

Ignoring his question, Sunny continued her interrogation. "What are they saying about it? Is it good or bad?"

"Of course it's good! One of the news anchors heard about it from her daughter, so they decided to feature it on their tech segment this morning."

"Did they talk about your bet with the senior class?"

"Nah," Parker said, "but that's good. I didn't want my dad to find out, anyway. But this is great for you. MIT will love the fact that you are getting attention from the media!"

While Parker spoke, Sunny grabbed her laptop from her night-stand. She flipped it on and immediately opened two windows, one to stream the local news and another to check how many people had installed the app.

4,191.

Wait. What?

"Parker, there's been over four thousand downloads. How is that possible? There's only 247 kids in our class!"

Parker laughed. "Apparently, more people like to bet than we thought! These are real actual people. Like out in the world, Sunny. People are using your app for their own bets!"

Sunny felt like everything was moving in slow motion, and her brain wasn't quite connecting the dots. Other people? Sure, she knew anyone could download it, but she never actually expected that to happen.

The news had already moved on from talking about her app by the time the stream picked up, so Sunny slammed her laptop shut and flung herself back onto her pillows, still on the phone.

"I am shook." Sunny wasn't sure if she wanted to shout for joy or puke.

He laughed. "I know! Now, get showered up and don't be late. Eleven a.m. sharp. Today is the day!"

Click. Parker ended the call.

Now that Sunny was fully awake, her brain swirled with questions, both about the app and about Zeke. Her app had been on the news. This was huge. She could mention the news segment and include the installation totals in her letter to MIT as proof that her app was working, proof that she was worthy. She had planned on starting the letter yesterday, but had opted to hang out with Parker instead. It was on her agenda to start today, and it looked like she had even more things to write about. She should be thrilled. This was everything she'd wanted. But her stomach churned.

She was glad that she'd agreed to meet Parker and Mika at the clue location. It was a pleasant distraction, and she wanted to be there to make sure the geolocation feature of her app worked well. She and Parker had tested it before launch and it worked flawlessly, but she was still nervous. When people arrived, they would click a button on the app. It would save their location, and that was how Parker could validate who was eligible to remain in the bet.

As she got dressed, her mind turned to Zeke. She had been so close to asking him how he felt about her last night. As she slipped on her flats, she wavered between sheer terror at the idea of asking him today and disappointment when she thought about letting the opportunity slip through her fingers. She considered her options. Option A, she could pretend like nothing had happened. That felt like the coward's way, but it certainly was the most comfortable option. Option B, she could wait for a moment alone and ask him if he liked her. That option terrified her beyond belief. She would be so vulnerable, and she wasn't sure she was ready to take that leap. Option C, she could wait for him to make some kind of move. But she might be waiting forever. And if he really liked her, why wasn't he making a move?

Parker hopped from foot to foot, a bundle of nervous energy. Mika had texted him right before she left home, so he knew she was about five minutes away by now. His plan was coming together. Sunny was getting what she wanted, and soon Mika would fall for him. They hadn't really clicked yet, but he knew it was just a matter of time.

They'd only hung out while developing the clues. While it hadn't been disastrous, it certainly hadn't been amazing either. She'd texted Parker her address, and he headed over there in his dad's white metallic Porsche Cayman. Mr. Crawford drove a black Porsche Cayenne to work, but he kept the Cayman just for fun. To Parker's complete amazement, he allowed the boys to drive it. But only after forcing them to read and sign a two-page document outlining the rules, of course. No food or beverages, no giving rides to friends, always park with no cars around to prevent door dings. The list of rules went on and on. But Parker happily read and signed. Who wouldn't? The car was totally sick.

When he rolled up to Mika's, she was sitting on her front porch waiting for him. She lived in an older neighborhood with small yards and even smaller houses. But the blue split-level was clean and well-kept. Parker had expected her to say something about his car when he pulled up. Most people commented on it, after all. But she didn't say a word. She was all business, showing him the history books about the town that she'd checked out from the library.

Once, she referred to how the townsfolk had tried again and again to convince the Northern Pacific Railway to build a train station at Cloud Lake before finally succeeding in 1905.

"'Do, or do not. There is no try,'" Parker quoted, but Mika had just wrinkled her nose, confused.

"Don't tell me you've never seen the *Star Wars* movies?" asked Parker, flabbergasted.

Mika shrugged. "I'm not really into movies."

"Not into movies? How can you not be into movies? That's like not being into walking... or... or breathing!"

"I don't know. I guess I never got the fascination with wasting two hours of your life staring at a screen. I'd rather be learning about something or doing something. You know what I mean?"

Parker did not know what she meant, but he nodded anyway. After that, they'd spent their remaining time picking out locations around the town where they could send their classmates. Then they looked up historical facts and tested out different angles for how they could frame the clues. It took several hours, but Mika was a hard worker and a fast researcher. It would have taken much longer without her help, and Parker was grateful. He knew the clues wouldn't have been even half as good without her.

He needed to remember to tell her that when she arrived. Parker waited for Mika just inside the pavilion that rested along the banks of Blackwater Creek. The pavilion was stained a dark mahogany, octagonal, with a roof and no sides. There were a series of large square columns all around the edges holding up the roof. There were a few dozen wooden picnic tables lined up in rows, with long wooden benches on either side for seating. It was normally reserved for weddings, graduation parties, and other celebrations. Parker had decided this was the perfect first clue location. It was big enough to house everyone who solved it. To commemorate the release of the first clue, Parker wanted this to be an epic celebration, and this place was perfect for a party. Why do something at all if you couldn't have fun doing it? With Marta's help, Parker had purchased all kinds of party supplies. He had cheesy decorations, yard games, and a variety of sodas and snacks set up on a few of the picnic tables.

The plan was to release the clue at eleven a.m. exactly. Participants would have until noon to arrive at the pavilion and use their app to check in.

Parker already had the first clue ready to go on his phone, and his finger was itching to hit send.

> *I always run but never walk.*
> *I have a bed but never sleep.*
> *Makadewaagami is my name.*
> *Jiikakamigad is my game.*

> *Since this is the first clue, let's make sure everyone is clear on the rules. All clues will point to a location within a twenty-mile radius of the center of Cloud Lake. Get there. Check in. You have one hour.*
> *I bet you can't find me.*

The addition of the Ojibwe language was Mika's idea, and Parker thought it was brilliant. She was full of all kinds of trivia about the town. Some of it was because her family had lived there for years. Her ancestors were Indigenous. The rest of her knowledge was because of her obsession with reading about history. Mika told Parker that the Indigenous people who lived in there had originally called the area "Makadewaagami," meaning black or dark water because the sediment in the creek bed made it look as though the water was almost black. Many years later, the town had been renamed Cloud Lake. Mika felt as though it was fitting to honor the origins of the land to use Ojibwe words in the clues. Parker thought they should include the word for wedding or party too, since the creek was long and winding, and they needed people to come to the pavilion specifically. Mika suggested the word "jiikakamigad," meaning celebration.

Parker saw Mika's red Chevy Malibu pull into the parking lot and bounded out to greet her.

"Hey!" Parker yelled as he approached.

"Hey," answered Mika with a warm smile as she exited the car. Her long, dark hair was pulled into a simple but elegant braid. She wore cut-off jeans and a yellow tank top. Parker found himself a little tongue-tied at the sight of her. That was rare for him.

"Hey…" he began and then stopped when he realized he'd already said that. "How are you?" he finished quickly.

"Great! Well, other than the fact that I had three cups of coffee this morning because I was so excited about everything, and now I'm low-key shaking." She gave Parker a rueful grin and threaded her arm through his as she drug him over to the pavilion.

"Wow," she marveled, dropping his arm and spinning around to look at all the food. "This is impressive," she said, picking up a cracker from a nearby tray and munching on it.

Parker blushed and stammered. "Yeah, well… I… I wanted this to be a big celebration, the first clue and all that."

Nodding, Mika said, "I get it. I barely slept last night. Hence, the coffee today." She smiled. "Anything you need help with?"

"Nope," Parker said, turning his attention to his phone. "It's 10:58 now. Two more minutes and I can hit send! Sunny should be here any minute now."

"Great! Let's do this!" Mika exclaimed.

Just then, they heard the rumble of Sunny's car pulling in the parking lot. Sunny hopped out of her blue Nissan Versa. She was wearing gray shorts with a mint-colored t-shirt, dressed for what the news had predicted would be another scorching June day. Her laptop was by her side, ready to troubleshoot if anything should go wrong. She smiled as she greeted Mika and Parker with hugs.

Parker checked his phone again. Eleven a.m. on the dot. "I'm doing it," he announced, and clicked the button to send the first clue. He felt a skitter of panic, but it was gone before he even had time to think about it, replaced by excitement over the party that was to come.

"I wonder how many people will figure it out," he said, turning to Mika.

She shrugged. "Well, it was one of the easier clues, I thought. If they search the words on the Internet, they should all be able to get here. It will get a lot tougher after this!" She rubbed her hands together in anticipation.

"Yeah. I hope so. I mean, I...I hope people solve it," Parker stammered. "Like, not everyone, because that would mean our clues were too easy, but... well, we want plenty of people to stay in the game, at least for a while..." He fell silent.

The silence stretched awkwardly between the three of them. Parker started re-arranging the food on the table, mostly so he would have something to do with his hands. He switched two bowls around. He paused. Then he switched them back again. He looked up. Sunny was staring at him with a questioning look on her face.

Parker laughed nervously. Sunny frowned at him. When Mika turned away and headed over to the wall to drop her purse, Sunny leaned close to Parker and whispered, "You're acting super sus. What is going on?"

Holding up his hands innocently, Parker protested quietly. "Nothing. I swear."

"Then why are you being so weird?"

"I'm not weird. You're weird."

Sunny shook her head. "I'm having déjà vu. Didn't we just have this argument last night?"

Grabbing a soda out of the cooler, Mika headed back their direction. Worried that Mika would get the wrong impression about his relationship with Sunny, Parker tried to surreptitiously shove Sunny away from him, but her knee knocked into the bench and she tripped, upending a bowl of chips as she fell down.

"Parker!" Sunny scolded.

"Oh, are you okay?" Mika asked, running the last few steps to reach them.

Parker forced a laugh, eyes on Mika, who looked worried. "Oh, Sunny. Such a klutz. Here, let me help you. Mika, could you grab some ice out of the cooler for her knee?" He grabbed Sunny's arm and hoisted her to her feet, his eyes shooting daggers at her.

"Don't ruin this for me," he muttered under his breath.

Sunny whispered back, "Ruin what, Parker? I didn't even recognize whoever that was talking to Mika. It definitely wasn't my best friend."

Parker grimaced. "I don't know what to say to her. I get so nervous. I want her to like me so much."

Sunny softened. "You are a great guy, dude. Relax. The only person you need to be is yourself."

Parker thought about what Sunny had said. Maybe she was right. He kept trying to be what he thought Mika wanted, and he was no closer to her than before he started this entire scheme. Maybe he would try being himself and see where that got him.

As Mika carried a paper towel filled with ice over to them, Parker resolved to show Mika the real Parker Crawford.

Chapter 10

"There's 197 of you still in the bet!" announced Parker at five minutes past noon, yelling to be heard over the blaring music. A giant roar went up as everyone cheered. The party was in full swing.

After Parker released the clue, it had taken fifteen minutes for the first participant to arrive. People arrived slowly at first, walking up to check in, bumping fists with their friends that were already there. Then a crush of people all arrived together, a caravan of cars pulling into the parking lot. It wasn't a race, but many of them acted like it was as they ran up to the pavilion. Cheers went up each time someone new arrived. Lastly came the stragglers, the few at the very end who tore into the parking lot kicking up gravel and dust. Some hooted in triumph when their app checked in. Others experienced the crush of defeat when they realized they'd missed the deadline by just a few minutes.

It was after one p.m. by the time Zeke arrived. Sunny spotted him the moment he pulled up. Since he'd wrecked his car, he'd been driving an old red and white Chevy pickup truck. Sunny thought his dad had given him the oldest pickup truck he could as punishment, but he didn't even know his son well enough to realize that Zeke didn't care what kind of vehicle he drove. Zeke looked unhappy when he saw the crowd of people, and his face turned downright thunderous when he saw that many of them were drinking. Zeke wasn't normally opposed to underage drinking, per se. After all, it was pretty common around their town, and they had been to lots of parties throughout high school. What really upset him this time was that Parker was throwing this party. How could he be so reckless after the accident?

Zeke stomped over to Parker, who was chatting with a couple of guys. Zeke grabbed his arm and pulled him to the side. Parker tossed the guys an apologetic look and let himself be dragged away.

"Parker, what are you doing?"

Per usual, Parker didn't rise to Zeke's anger. "It's a party, man! There's still almost two hundred people in the bet. Isn't that awesome?"

"Parker, you've got to shut this party down. Where'd you even get the alcohol?"

"Relax, relax," Parker placated Zeke. "I didn't bring the booze. They must have brought their own. I promise, I just brought soda and stuff." He gestured to the tables laden with food and beverages.

Zeke softened slightly at that, but continued his protest. "You think the cops are going to care about that when they bust you? You could lose Tisch, Parker. Listen to me."

"You worry too much, bruh." Parker patted Zeke's shoulder.

"And you don't worry enough." Zeke shook his head, disappointment clear upon his face.

"Why should I worry when I have you around to do it for me?" Parker smiled congenially. Though he was joking, there was a truth to his words that stung.

Zeke was at a loss. He wasn't sure how to make Parker take this more seriously.

Sunny watched from across the pavilion, but as she noticed Zeke's frown deepen, she decided to intervene. She knew from experience that when Parker and Zeke faced off against each other, it could escalate quickly. She approached, grabbed Zeke's hand, and tugged.

Zeke barely acknowledged her presence, so she tugged again more forcefully.

"Zeke, can I talk with you for a minute?" she asked insistently. She motioned for him to come with her. To her surprise, he did.

Sunny drug Zeke out of the pavilion and behind the first row of cars to get some privacy. Suddenly conscious of the fact that they were still holding hands, she dropped his hand like a hot potato.

"He's throwing his life away! Over and over, it's always the same."

"Calm down, Ezekiel," she said, using his full name, hoping it would distract him from his tirade. "I get that you're mad, but you need to calm down so we can talk about this."

"Calm down? He never learns! I feel like I'm in the movie *Groundhog Day,* except there's no way to magically fix this in the end."

Sunny placed her hand on Zeke's arm. "Why are you freaking out about this? It's just a party. And it's Parker's life, not yours!"

"Parker's life, huh? Don't act so high and mighty, like you don't tell him when to jump and how high. You basically run his life for him. You should be telling him this party is a mistake too!"

His words fueled her anger. "I run his life? What about you? Don't you bring me into your fight with Parker! I told him this whole thing was a bad idea. He's doing it anyway, but that's his choice! This isn't about me. This is about you and Parker. You've got to back off. He's not your responsibility!"

Zeke's blue eyes darkened as he scowled down at Sunny. "See, that's what you don't understand. You don't have any siblings! He *is* my responsibility! He will always be my responsibility!"

"I just don't understand what you're so worried about. It's not like Parker has made that many bad decisions in the past. I mean, yeah, we've all cleaned up his little messes. But there's never been anything that's been catastrophic. Why are you so worked up about this?"

Zeke shook his head, dropped his eyes to the ground, and stuffed his hands into his pockets. He kicked at the dirt with the toe of his worn, black leather motorcycle boots, remaining silent.

Sunny paused, thinking. Suddenly, it clicked in her mind.

"Oh my god. There has been something catastrophic, hasn't there? Parker... Parker was driving the night of the accident. He was, wasn't he? I knew something was off about that night! You weren't driving at all." It wasn't even a question, because Sunny already knew the answer.

Zeke looked up, surprise written on his face. Quickly, the surprise was replaced by fear.

He came towards her, hand outstretched, grabbing her arm gently, imploringly. "You can't tell anyone, not ever."

"Why did you take the fall for him? You ruined your life! College, everything!" The words burst from Sunny's lips.

Sunny's mind sputtered backwards as she tried to piece together what had happened. How was Zeke the one arrested? Why didn't Parker tell her that he was driving that night?

Looking around a bit frantically, Zeke shushed Sunny and guided her over to his truck. He opened the driver's side door and waved her inside. Eager to hear more about what had happened, Sunny willingly jumped in and slid to the middle of the long bench seat. Zeke followed her and slammed the door, shutting out the cheers from her classmates, who were clearly fully invested in the second phase of Parker's plan, the partying. But the party was the last thing on Sunny's mind.

Zeke turned the truck on, twisting the dials to get the air conditioning running. He sighed, turning towards Sunny and running a hand through his hair, making it spike up at odd angles.

"Dammit," he muttered. "You can't tell anyone," he repeated.

"But why?"

He said quietly, "Parker would be in serious trouble. And so would I. And maybe even my dad if they thought he knew and covered it up."

"No. I don't mean that. I meant, why did you lie? Why would you throw your life away?"

Zeke didn't answer right away. Sunny waited.

"It was my fault. I took him to that party. I wasn't watching him closely enough. I had let him drive my Camaro to the party," Zeke explained. "He was so excited to be at college and to drive the car and to go to a party with me. I didn't even want to go to the damn party in the first place. I just... I wanted him to have a good time. Just once, I wanted to be the cool older brother, to show him how fun college is, how fun I am. I didn't want to be the one telling him 'no' and enforcing the rules. I just wanted to relax. We were both drinking, but I only had a couple. Honestly, I wasn't paying attention to how much Parker had. I should have been. But I never thought..."

He trailed off and turned away from Sunny, looking out the front windshield, which was steaming up at the edges from the humidity. Sunny still didn't understand what he was telling her, how the police could have blamed Zeke if Parker was actually behind the wheel. She stayed silent, waiting for him to explain.

"I was inside the house talking to some friends, and he'd been out on the porch with a couple of guys I knew. I went out, and that's when I realized how much he'd had to drink. He was slurring his words, practically falling over himself as he laughed like a hyena. He was a total mess. I tried to cut him off, to take him home. We argued about it, and he took off... He had the keys because I'd let him drive to the party," he said, shaking his head. The guilt he felt made his shoulders slump in defeat.

Zeke turned to Sunny again, his eyes imploring her to understand. "It was my fault. That's why I took the blame. He still had the keys because I let him drive there. I wasn't watching him. He drank way more than I realized. I wasn't there for him that night. If I had been paying attention, I would have been able to stop him. I'm bigger and stronger than him. It just...it all happened so fast. He was in the car and tearing away before I could even get to him."

"But how did no one know who was driving?"

Zeke shrugged and sighed. "I don't know. It was a college house party. There were a lot of minors there. When people realized police were coming, everyone ran. I chased after Parker as he drove away, and it was just a couple of blocks before he crashed into the tree. I saw it all happen. I've never run so fast in all my life. When I pulled open the car door and saw all the blood, I yelled for someone to call 911. Parker was completely passed out. I didn't know if he was dead or alive. Thankfully, someone actually did call 911. I pulled Parker out of the car. When the police came, everyone else was gone except me and Parker. One cop started helping Parker, and the other one pulled me aside. I just told him I had been driving and that Parker was in the passenger seat. No one even questioned me. I don't think they cared since I had confessed. They never spoke to anyone else, as far as I know. I mean, how often does someone admit to drunk driving if they didn't actually do it? The ambulance took Parker to the hospital, and they wouldn't even let me go with. They gave me one of those breath tests. I failed, of course. And that was that."

Questions swirled in Sunny's head, and she struggled to pick just one. In the end, she spit them all out at once. "Why didn't Parker say something when he woke up? I can't believe he's never told me this! How could he just let you take the blame like that? And didn't your dad question any of this?"

Zeke barked out a sarcastic laugh. He waved his hand dismissively.

"Dad? Are you kidding? The guy who always believes the worst about me? He was so mad, yelling and slamming doors. He still won't look me in the eye when we talk. I don't think he'll ever forgive me."

The last words came out in a bitter tone.

"But what about Parker?" Sunny insisted. "Why didn't he tell your dad the truth? Or me?" Selfishly, it hurt that Parker had kept this from her. They never kept secrets from each other, at least not about really big things like this.

Zeke looked at her sadly. "Parker isn't lying. He really doesn't remember a thing about that night. He only knows what I told him."

Relieved to learn that her best friend wasn't lying to her, Sunny asked, "But don't you think he'd feel differently if he knew the truth?"

Zeke blew out a breath and turned to look at Sunny again. "Honestly?" he asked. "I don't know. Maybe he'd still blame me for not taking care of him. I still blame me! Why shouldn't he? It doesn't matter who was driving. It was still my fault!"

He looked like he was in so much pain, and Sunny's heart ached for him. She leaned forward and enveloped him in a hug. His arms wrapped around her, and he clung to her.

"Zeke, this is not your fault! You have to believe that. Parker's mistakes aren't yours. He's an adult now. You've got to stop protecting him. You've got to let him stand on his own two feet."

Sunny felt Zeke's body shake as he chuckled sadly. "How can I do that? He's still my little brother. Without Mom here... he doesn't have anyone to take care of him. Dad's not exactly good at that sort of thing. You know that Parker has always needed me."

Zeke pulled back from the hug, but he kept his arms around Sunny. She didn't move away.

Sunny looked up into Zeke's eyes, willing him to believe her as she said, "He will always need you. But to support him when he makes mistakes, not to protect him from them. You've got to stop living his life for him. He will never learn if you don't let him face the consequences of his actions."

"You're wrong. He'll never make it without me. How can I stop protecting him when he has proven over and over that he can't make the right choices?"

Sunny's face took on a determined look, and she narrowed her gaze. "You start by telling him the truth."

"No way," Zeke shook his head. "I'm not telling him. This mess is over and done with. We're all moving on with our lives. There's no need to dredge it all back up!"

"It isn't over and done with," Sunny insisted. "You aren't moving on. You got kicked out of college for something you didn't do. If you admit it now, you get your life back!"

"It doesn't work that way, Sunny. They don't just say 'thanks for telling us the truth' and now we'll let you back into school and erase your permanent record. It's a crime to lie to the police too, you know. I'd just be trading one crime for another. And taking Parker down with me."

"Then we talk to your dad! Tell him the truth, and let him help you."

"You're cracked if you think he's going to help me now, especially when it means Parker will get in trouble. You know what he'll say? He will say that it's too late to fix this, and we just have to move forward. And he'll say I already ruined my life and that it doesn't make sense to ruin Parker's too. Parker would lose Tisch, and you know how much he wants to go there. It's everything to him."

Sunny wanted to protest, but she knew Zeke was probably right about his dad. Mr. Crawford was very practical, and his reputation took a hit when his son was arrested for drunk driving. He wouldn't want to dredge everything back up again. One thing Zeke had said was niggling at the back of her mind. "Zeke, wait a minute... I still don't understand. I get that you felt guilty and you wanted to take care of Parker and all that. But you were at Notre Dame. Notre freaking Dame. Why would you give all that up just so Parker could still go to Tisch? You loved it there," Sunny paused as Zeke remained silent, thinking back and questioning herself. "Wait. You did love it there... didn't you?"

He met her question with silence.

"Zeke? Talk to me." Sunny insisted.

"Listen," he said, avoiding her question. "Life hasn't been easy for Parker since Mom died, and it's my job to take care of him. You know it's true," he said as he saw Sunny begin to shake her head. "Parker was always the baby of the family. When things went bad, I fixed things for him, even before Mom died. But you don't know what it was like with her in those last few weeks. She knew her time was almost up, and she made me talk with her about all the things she wanted for us. She made me promise..." Zeke paused, his eyes welling up. But he didn't let the tears fall. "She made me promise to look after him. And I'm good at it. There was..." he paused again, searching for the right words. "I like being who she wanted me to be. Sometimes it feels like she's still here with me somehow, watching over me, guiding me, happy that I'm taking care of him."

Sunny felt her heart breaking for the young boy Zeke had been. Feeling like he had to be both mother and father to his younger brother couldn't have been easy. "Zeke, you were just a kid. You shouldn't have had that kind of responsibility put on your shoulders. It wasn't fair, and it doesn't mean you have to carry that weight forever."

"Sure, it does. Family doesn't stop being family when they turn eighteen," He laughed wryly. "Did you know, no one even questioned me when I said I was driving? There I was, sitting there talking to the police, completely coherent, not a scratch on me, and there was Parker, bloody and bruised and smelling like a distillery. And I said I was driving, and they all nodded, like they knew I was the bad one." He laughed again, but it came out wrong, almost like a sob. "Dad was the worst of them all. He started yelling at me the minute he got to the hospital about how irresponsible I was and how I'd endangered Parker's life."

Zeke cocked his head to the side, and his hair flopped into his eyes in that way that made Sunny's stomach dip like she was on a roller coaster. "How did you figure it out?"

"I don't know. I guess something had always been bothering me about it. It wasn't like you at all. Things didn't really add up. And Parker wasn't talking about it much, which was super sus. He talks about everything. It just didn't make sense to me. And I suddenly just realized that you would never do something like that."

Zeke leaned towards Sunny. "How do you…" he stopped, and looked at her so intensely she felt like he must be able to see into her soul. "You are the only person who questioned me. You know that? You might be the one person in my life who actually sees me."

His words sent a warm shiver down her spine, but she frowned, thinking about how sad it was that Zeke felt so alone. "I do know you. You're the person who stood up for me when Billy the Bully stole my lunch in elementary school. You're the one who helped me up when I fell off my brand-new, pink Power Ranger bike. You're the one who held my hand the night Parker was in the hospital getting his appendix out, and I was so scared he would die like our moms. Growing up, you were my hero. That's why I've been so confused lately. Nothing added up to the Zeke that I know. I just knew it wasn't you."

Zeke leaned in closer, placing his forehead against Sunny's and smiled wryly. "It's kind of nice," he said quietly, "to have someone think I'm the hero instead of the villain."

Sunny's breath caught at his closeness. His lips were just inches from hers, and her gaze dropped to them. They were together, all alone, sharing secrets in his truck. It felt so intimate. *I could kiss him right now,* she thought. It would be so easy. He was right there.

Before Sunny could make a decision, he made it for both of them. He backed away, letting out a ragged breath. Immediately, she realized she was too late, and a pang of regret shot through her.

Zeke drew a hand through his hair roughly. "You shouldn't be here. You shouldn't be with me. It's too easy for me to…" he trailed off.

"To what?" Sunny prompted eagerly, hungry to hear what he was going to say next. Too easy for him to kiss her? To love her? What was he trying to hold back?

He looked away, out the window towards the other cars in the parking lot, and his face settled into a mask as he distanced himself from Sunny. "It's too easy for me to think about things I have no business thinking about." Her hopes lifted at his words. He continued, "You've got your whole life ahead of you. I just... I want to protect you."

"You've always been protecting people," Sunny insisted. "You don't have to do it anymore. I know you. You'd never do anything to hurt me. "

"Not intentionally, no. But all I seem to do lately is mess things up. And I'm not going to be the one who hurts you."

"Then don't be," Sunny said, sliding closer to him.

A mighty roar went up outside, and Sunny looked out the window to see people throwing beanbags and cheering.

"I won't tell anyone your secret." Sunny said, as Zeke turned back to look at her, "And I won't let you push me away." With that, she leaned forward and, before she could overthink it, she pressed a feather-light kiss to his lips. The kiss was as fleeting as a snowflake landing on warm skin in a snowstorm. It was there, and then it was gone.

Sunny pulled back and studied her hands. Zeke sat frozen, immobile. She couldn't raise her eyes to look up at him. She was terrified of the rejection she might see revealed on his face.

The truck filled with silence. Sunny's heart sank. She'd just made the first move, and...nothing.

She couldn't bear it. Mustering up the courage to speak, Sunny said quickly, "I've got to get going. Parker will be looking for me."

In a smooth motion, she opened the passenger side door and jumped down from the truck. Slamming the door, Sunny forced herself not to look back as she headed towards the crowd of people in the pavilion.

Despite all the noise, Sunny thought she heard Zeke's truck door creak open and heard him yell her name.

She didn't look back.

Chapter 11

I knew it, Sunny thought to herself. *How could I be so stupid?* This was the exact reason she had never told a single soul about her feelings for Zeke. She knew this would happen. If she exposed her heart, it would get trampled on somehow. She'd kissed him, and he'd just sat there. He had probably been trying to figure out how to break the news that he didn't think of her that way. It was mortifying.

She recalled her words, telling him that she wouldn't let him push her away. Brave words. But she didn't feel brave anymore. Not at all. She felt young and naïve. And she didn't like how that felt.

Sunny paced back and forth in her bedroom. It was late afternoon. After she left Zeke at his truck, she headed over to the crowd in search of Parker. She found him chatting up Mika. He was acting relatively normal, thankfully. They seemed to be having a good time. Her heart just wasn't into small talk, so she quickly said her goodbyes and headed home to wallow in her embarrassment alone.

She plunked down on her comforter and contemplated her options. She could move to Switzerland so she never had to see him again. Nope, too expensive. She could fake being sick the rest of the summer and hide in her bedroom. Nope, her dad would drag her to the doctor if she even so much as hinted that she was feeling under the weather. She could pretend like nothing had ever happened.

Wait, that might work... or better yet, she could pretend like the kiss meant nothing. Just a little peck between friends. Europeans did that all the time, didn't they? That could actually work.

As she considered how she could recover the situation with her dignity intact, she heard the ding of her phone's text message alert. She plucked it off of her nightstand and saw it was a message from Zeke. Holding her breath, she read his words.

Zeke: *Hey. You disappeared today.*

She exhaled. Okay. At least he hadn't said, "You are a total weirdo for kissing me," so that was a good sign. Maybe he just wanted to forget the whole thing had happened. He had certainly looked uncomfortable in the truck. If he was going to ignore it, she would too. Sunny told herself to play it cool as she tapped out a reply.

Sunny: *Sorry. Went to help Parker with some party stuff. Then headed home.*

Zeke: *You didn't tell Parker, did you?*

At first, Sunny thought he was talking about the kiss. Of course she didn't tell Parker that she'd kissed Zeke! She didn't really discuss things like that with Parker. TMI. Then she felt a flutter of annoyance when she realized he was talking about the accident.

Sunny: *No. I promised you I wouldn't.*

Zeke: *Thanks.*

Here's my opening, thought Sunny. *I can make him think the kiss meant nothing to me.* She typed her reply. She liked to think it was the perfect message to show him that he didn't affect her at all. Short and sweet.

Sunny: *What are friends for?*

Sunny clutched her phone in her hands as she waited. After a few minutes, there was still no reply from Zeke, so she hugged the phone to her chest and flopped backwards onto her pillows. Her heart clenched. Friends. So, that was it. She supposed she should be relieved. This was her opportunity to be casual, and she used it to make him think that friendship was all that she felt for him. She should be grateful that he seemed normal in the text messages.

At least he wasn't making fun of her for kissing him. She cringed as she relived the memory again for the thousandth time today. Yet she didn't feel relieved. She felt disappointed. When she saw his text message, for an instant, she hoped he was texting to tell her it was all a misunderstanding, that he shouldn't have let her walk away today, that he was crazy about her. But things like that didn't happen in real life. His silence today made it clear he wasn't interested. She could take a hint. She wasn't stupid.

Sunny sighed and hopped off of her bed, suddenly filled with nervous energy. She checked her phone again, but still no reply. She composed a quick text to Parker, asking what he was up to tonight.

Seconds later, Sunny's phone buzzed with Parker's reply.

Parker: *With Mika ttyl*

She was both glad and disappointed at the same time. Parker's incessant chatter would have been an excellent distraction from her thoughts about Zeke, but she also wasn't sure she could handle seeing him and knowing this giant secret about the accident. It had only been a few hours since she found out, and it was already eating away at her. Not to mention, she definitely did not want to chance going over to the Crawford house and running into Zeke. She wasn't sure she could face him anytime soon. Her feelings were still too close to the surface.

Still restless, Sunny padded over to her desk and opened up her laptop. She logged in and loaded her dashboard to check her app's progress. Her mouth gaped open when she saw the number. To her surprise, she saw 11,892 total installations. How had she gained over seven thousand downloads since this morning? Her mind whirled. Quite a few people watching the news must have downloaded her app right away. Sunny was amazed. And terrified.

She flipped over to read the reviews, her stomach clenching in fear. This was what she was most afraid of, people looking over her app and finding it lacking. What bugs and problems would they report? What would they complain about? If Parker had been there, she would have made him read the reviews for her. But since she was alone, no help was forthcoming. She took a deep breath and dove in, her body tensing as she braced for the worst.

There weren't many reviews yet, which was understandable since many of the downloads had only happened that day. But it surprised her to see that the ones she read were positive. She had 4.7 out of 5 stars. 4.7 stars! That far exceeded her expectations when she'd created the app. Some said they loved her clean and uncluttered design. Others raved about the idea and how no one had ever thought of a betting app before. One person mentioned they wished the app would allow them to exchange money through the app at the completion of the bet. Sunny quickly discarded that idea because there was no way she was going to mess with all the regulations surrounding handling money in apps. The tension in Sunny's shoulders eased as she realized she had nothing to worry about so far. She smiled as she continued reading the last of the reviews. People liked something she made. It was an amazing feeling.

Sunny's phone dinged again. She glanced at the screen and saw it was from Zeke. The smiled faded from her face. She chewed on her bottom lip. How would he react to her last text?

Zeke: *See you tomorrow.*

See you tomorrow? That's it? And what did he mean, tomorrow? Sunny's worry grew as she realized exactly what he meant. Tomorrow. Sunday. Golfing.

Crap.

Parker's foot tapped a relentless beat on Mika's front porch steps. About an hour ago, just after dark, they left the still-raging party by the creek and headed to Mika's house to strategize. They needed a plan for which clue to release next, when to release it, and what to do when everyone gathered together. Neither Parker nor Mika had been drinking, so they each drove their cars to Mika's house and hung out on the porch talking through the plan.

"Parker, you okay?" Mika's dark brown eyes looked up at him, the moonlight glinting off of her face.

"Yeah, yeah, of course! Why wouldn't I be?" He gave a nervous laugh, fingers playing with the strings of his favorite black hoodie he'd thrown on to stave off the chilly nighttime air. It had a white Punisher skull on the back, and Parker always thought it made him look badass. Maybe a slightly nerdy badass, but still badass.

Mika shrugged. "I don't know. You seem...kinda high-key right now." She gestured to his foot, still furiously tapping away.

Not having realized that his foot had a mind of its own, he immediately froze. All day, he tried to take Sunny's advice and be real with Mika. They'd had a great time today, and she'd even laughed at some of his jokes. But now that he was alone with her, he was finding it difficult to control his nerves. "I guess I'm just a little nervous around you," he admitted. He let out a whoosh of breath, relieved to get the truth off his chest.

"Me?" Mika seemed surprised. She smiled, the corners of her eyes crinkling. "That's funny. I'm usually the one who's nervous. I guess I spend so much time around books, I forget how to talk to people. But for some reason, I don't feel nervous around you. You're easy to talk to, Parker."

Parker ducked his head, his hair falling into his eyes. He felt warmth spread over him at her words. "Thanks. You are too," he replied, even though nothing could have been further from the truth. He felt like he never knew what to say around Mika.

A comfortable silence fell between them. Mika stared up at the moon, and Parker continued twiddling the strings of his hoodie as he thought about what to say next.

Mika was the first to break the silence. "So," she began, "we already agreed we are releasing the next clue in a few days, but we haven't decided which one. Got any ideas?"

It didn't really matter to Parker. What did matter to him was making Mika happy. "Which clue do you want to pick?" he asked.

Pausing, Mika mulled over his words. "I guess, if I had to pick, I would do the one that leads them to the old mill out on Danvers Road. I think that's another easier clue, so it might be a good way to keep more people in the game longer. And it's outside, so it can fit a lot of people. But it's okay if you have a different idea. It really doesn't matter to me, Parker. It's your bet. I'm just here to help."

"Okay." Parker paused, considering the rest of the clues. He nodded. "Yeah, I like that idea. It will be more fun to keep more people in the game for longer. Plus, I love Captain Marvel!" He gave a chuckle.

"Huh?" Mika frowned at Parker, her nose wrinkling in confusion.

"You know, Captain Marvel, the superhero? Real name, Carol Danvers? Danvers Road? 'Higher, further, faster, baby.' You know what I mean?" Parker practically bounced in his seat with excitement as he quoted the Marvel movie. It wasn't one of his top favorites, but he'd never met a Marvel movie he didn't like.

Meanwhile, Mika looked lost. "Not really," she said with a half-hearted smile. "I don't read comics."

"Well, there's the movie too! It's, like, super popular. How can you not have heard of *Captain Marvel*?"

"I mean, I've heard of it, but I don't know anything about it, really. Like, I didn't know her name or anything. Remember, I told you I don't watch movies?"

Parker deflated a bit. "Yeah, I remember. I just figured maybe you'd watched it, since it was new and everything."

Sensing his disappointment, Mika placed a hand on his arm. "You can tell me about it if you want?" she offered.

Even through the sleeve of his hoodie, he felt warmth bloom where her hand rested. Shaking his head, Parker replied, "That's okay. You really have to see it to make it come alive. Maybe we can watch it together sometime?"

"Maybe." Mika said, non-committal, removing her hand. "Back to the next clue. Okay. Danvers Road. What's the plan when they get there? Do we want to just have people check in and then leave?

Or should there be some kind of speech about the number of people still in the game? Or a party like today? What do you think?"

Before Mika even stopped talking, Parker was answering, "Another party. Definitely." He nodded firmly, jumping up from the steps and turning to face Mika. "Let's do it later in the day, like five p.m. This time, I could get it catered. Maybe some chicken or steak or something..."

He trailed off, thinking. Then he suddenly snapped his fingers. Mika jumped at the abrupt noise. "Tacos! Everyone loves Mexican food. I could call the guy who drives around with that taco truck and have him come out! Taco Loco, I think it's called?" Parker loved any chance for a party.

Mika looked mildly alarmed. She held up her hands to slow Parker down. "Okay, but this is going to get kind of expensive, Parker. You know, the food and drinks and party supplies. Are you sure you can afford all that? It's also going to be a lot of work if we throw a party for every clue."

Parker shrugged, seemingly unworried, but he considered her words. She was right. His dad wouldn't even blink when he saw the credit card charge for the party supplies for today, but if Parker rented out an entire taco truck, his dad was sure to take notice. But he really wanted this bet to be a success. It wasn't even just about spending time with Mika anymore. People were texting him all the time now, telling him how awesome the bet is, trying to get hints to win the money. He was caught up in the excitement of it all.

Things would change in just a few months. Sunny would head off to college, and they would be so far apart. And everyone else from their class had plans too. College or a gap year abroad or an internship or a job. Everyone would leave. This was the last time they would all be together. He was determined to make sure this was the most epic summer anyone ever had. A summer to remember.

But how would he pay for all this epicness? He pushed the niggling question away. Confident that he would find a solution given enough time, Parker told Mika, "It's no problem. I got this." Inside, he wasn't so sure, but he pressed onward.

Mika shrugged. "If you say so." She paused. "You know, you're an interesting guy, Parker. You set this whole bet thing up, and it's a ton of work. And you're giving away all this money. And you aren't even getting anything in return. I don't understand. Why are you even doing all of this?"

Be honest, thought Parker. *Tell her you are doing it for her!* But he didn't want her to think he was a stalker, and there was something a little stalker-y about going to these lengths just to spend time with a girl. He settled on something truth-adjacent. "What if I said I didn't mind all the work because it means I get to spend more time with you?" He smiled a cheeky grin to lighten the statement, even though inside he tensed, awaiting her response.

Mika rolled her eyes, laughing. "Well, that's very sweet and very cheesy. And you avoided my question. But I suppose, if you don't want to tell me why you are doing it, you don't have to." She was still smiling as she said it, and Parker got the impression that she really didn't mind. Mika seemed to be one of those people who just took people as they were, without judging. Parker liked that about her.

He decided to play it safe a little while longer until he could figure out if she just liked him as a friend or maybe as something more. He answered, "Well, no matter what my reasons are, I really have had fun planning this with you."

Mika stood, dusting off the back of her shorts. "Me too, Parker. It's been fun getting to know you better. I can't believe we didn't hang out in high school. I didn't even know what I was missing out on." She smiled up at him.

Feeling encouraged by her words, Parker got an idea. "Listen, every Sunday, my family goes golfing over at Stone Mountain Golf Course. It's just me and my brother and Sunny, usually. Our dads golf together ahead of us, and us three lag behind. Would you wanna come with tomorrow? You could be our fourth."

Mika wrinkled her nose, but the smile still hovered around her mouth. "Golfing? I'm not really very good at sports." She looked uncertain.

"Oh, golfing isn't like other sports. You'll like it, I promise! Plus, we play a really chill game. Super chill. It's a lot slower pace, and you really don't have to have any skill to just whack the ball. No one even keeps score. It'll be fun." He paused and cleared his throat, trying not to seem too eager. "But no worries if you aren't interested. It's cool." He gave what he hoped was a chill-looking bob of his chin.

Giving in to Parker's enthusiasm, Mika gave an excited nod. "I guess I'll give it a try. Text me the info, and I'll meet you there."

"Sick!" Parker gave Mika a wide grin. Sunny's advice had worked. After a day of just being himself, he already had a date with Mika. Well, not a date, exactly. Maybe it was a date? Maybe it was just a group hang?

Whatever it was, Parker couldn't stop thinking about it the entire way home. He was already making plans. Zeke and Sunny were going to have to ride together on a cart so he could share a cart with Mika. Lately, they'd all been walking and carrying their clubs, but that wouldn't work for what Parker had planned. When they walked during golf, everyone went their separate ways, chasing their own ball. Great for solitude. Not great for socializing. Parker wanted to spend as much time with Mika as possible. Sharing a cart was the best way to get as much one-on-one time as possible.

If all went well tomorrow, his maybe-date could turn into an actual date.

Chapter 12

"Parker!" hissed Sunny. "I am not sharing a cart with Zeke." Sunny had just arrived at the golf course with her dad and had barely set her clubs down on the paved parking lot when she was accosted by Parker, dressed in crisp khaki shorts and a blue polo, not a wrinkle in sight. *Marta must have ironed it for him,* Sunny thought. She felt slightly jealous. Her own white polo and gray shorts were clean but wrinkled. A perpetual state for Sunny. Neither Sunny nor her dad liked to iron, so they both avoided it at all costs. Parker had grabbed her by the elbow, pulled her towards the clubhouse, and told her his plan. Sunny had emphatically disagreed, but Parker was insistent.

"Um, yes, you are." Parker's eyes were pleading, but his tone was definitive.

"I. Am. Not." She bit out the words.

"Are." Parker retorted, undeterred. Sunny began to protest again, but Parker interrupted. "Listen. I know something's going on with you guys, but I don't give a crap. Suck it up and do this for me because you love me. You know how much I like Mika. This is my shot!"

"Fine," Sunny grumbled, giving in. Parker was hard to resist. She side-eyed Zeke as she spotted him pull up in an immaculate green and cream golf cart. Sunny watched as he loaded their clubs into the back cart and strapped them down. Stone Mountain was very high-end so the entire course was pristine. Sunny and her dad could never afford to golf there on their own every week, but being friends with the Crawfords had its perks.

"You owe me," Sunny muttered to Parker, turning and trudging over towards Zeke.

"Put it on my tab," Parker yelled after her.

Sunny turned around and stuck out her tongue at him, still walking away.

By the time she reached the cart, Zeke was already loaded and ready to go.

"Hop in," he said, slinging an arm along the top of the cart seat. He smiled easily at Sunny, the picture of relaxation. His breezy attitude made Sunny's foul mood even fouler. Her plan was to act normal, to act like nothing happened between them in that pickup truck, but she didn't know how to do that. Constantly pretending like he didn't affect her was wearing her down. And seeing him so calm and collected when she felt so off-kilter was grating on her nerves. Somehow, she'd drifted away from unaffected all the way into angry territory. She needed to get herself together.

"I'm gonna grab a water in the clubhouse," she said. She realized she sounded grumpy and begrudgingly added, "Need anything?"

Zeke shook his head, but his eyes focused on hers, laser sharp. He studied her like she was a puzzle he couldn't figure out. Uncomfortable, she spun away and headed inside to escape his scrutiny.

Sunny had been gone for nearly ten minutes when Zeke went looking for her. They were going to miss their tee time if she didn't get her butt outside. How long did it take to get a water anyway?

Zeke's frustration turned to a simmering anger when he opened the clubhouse door and saw Sunny cozied up to Duncan at the counter. Duncan had graduated the year before Zeke, and he was pre-med at the U of M. He worked summers at the golf course to help pay the bills. Dark hair, tan, athletic. Duncan had always been surrounded by girls in high school. He'd seemed so arrogant to Zeke, always bragging about his latest win on the golf team or something like that. Although he didn't like him, Duncan didn't strike Zeke as a horrible human being. The sight of Sunny chatting him up shouldn't have made Zeke's blood boil. Yet it did.

Sunny had a bottle of water in one hand, and her other hand was on Duncan's arm. When she laughed, her head tipped back and her blonde hair spilled down her back. She looked so free. Zeke couldn't remember the last time he saw her look like that. Happy and relaxed. Lately, it seemed like she was so tense all the time.

And yesterday hadn't helped anything. Now she knew everything about the accident. She knew he was a failure. He'd failed to protect his brother from getting hurt, and he was failing Parker again because he was all caught up in this bet nonsense. And when Sunny kissed him, he'd been so caught off guard. It was all he could do not to bury himself in her arms and never let go. He'd loved her for as long as he could remember. To think there was a chance she returned his feelings was almost more than he could stand. But he held himself back. He was no good for her. No college, no future. He was nothing, a failure. Sunny deserved better.

When she texted him yesterday, he was relieved she hadn't seemed upset at all. It was like nothing had even happened between them. Maybe he'd misread her kiss. But then she seemed so grouchy this morning. Was it possible she was more upset than she was letting on? He just couldn't get a read on her. And now here she was, flirting it up with Duncan without a care in the world. What was going on with her? Zeke had never been more confused in his life.

Wanting to yank Sunny away from Duncan, he curbed his impulse as he realized he had no justifiable reason to do so. He settled for clearing his throat to interrupt them. "We're going to miss our tee time, Sunny."

She turned to look at him, her smile dimming slightly. It felt like a punch to his gut. He didn't want to admit to himself how much he wanted her to smile at him like she'd been smiling at Duncan. "Oh." She looked back at Duncan, and the wattage of her smile increased again. Another gut punch. "See you later?"

"Definitely," Duncan said, returning her smile and adding a little wink.

An arrogant little wink that made Zeke see red.

Walking toward Zeke, Sunny frowned at the expression on his face. "What's up with you?" Whatever bad mood she'd been in before seemed to have melted away during her conversation with Duncan. Now she just looked confused. Zeke felt his annoyance grow.

"Nothing," Zeke ground out through clenched teeth. He opened the door and waved a hand to usher her outside. She walked over to the cart, eyeing him suspiciously.

"Are you sure nothing's up? You look off right now," she said. She pulled the hair tie off her wrist, shook out her hair, and drew it up into her signature ponytail on top of her head. Zeke knew that Sunny never wore her hair down when it was this hot out.

Zeke shook his head and took a calming breath. "Nothing's up, I swear. Just didn't want to miss our tee time." He didn't want to admit that seeing her with Duncan bothered him, especially because he had no right to be bothered by it. She wasn't his girlfriend. And even if she had been his girlfriend, she wasn't doing anything wrong by talking with Duncan. But he couldn't use logic to fend off the jealously creeping around inside him right now.

"Okay," she said, unconvinced, and plopped into the passenger seat.

Zeke dropped into the driver's seat, making sure not to brush up against Sunny in the process. The more space between them, the better he could think. And he needed to think in order to remind himself that he was not good enough for her. He stepped on the gas and tore off to meet up with Mika and Parker. Parker was already warming up on the men's tee box when Zeke drove over the hill. He was taking practice swings, nice and steady. His form looked great, and Zeke felt a burst of pride. Parker loved to golf, and he'd spent hours perfecting his swing. It proved to Zeke that Parker knew how to work hard when he wanted something. That was the kind of thing that made Zeke think Parker really could handle being on his own when he got to college.

Mika pulled out an iron from her rental bag and inspected it like it was a foreign object. She looked unsure and a little out of place. Zeke stopped the cart right next to her.

Sunny said helpfully, "You'll want to tee off with a wood, not an iron. One of the big giant ones. I'd go with the one that has a number 1 on it. We call that the 'Big Dog' around here." She smiled kindly at Mika. Zeke remembered how intimidated Sunny had been when she had to learn all the new lingo. But she'd been a trooper, never complaining, always trying to keep up with him and Parker.

Zeke added, "And you won't tee off from here. You and Sunny will tee off from the women's tee over there." He extended an arm, pointing to a small mound of grass nearby, closer to the fairway. "Don't worry. We'll help you every step of the way."

Mika turned to see where he was pointing. She turned back and smiled gratefully at both of them. "This is like a whole different world," she said almost reverently, gesturing out to the fairway where Mr. Crawford and Mr. Montgomery were hitting. They were nearly up to the green, which meant it was almost time for Parker and Zeke to hit from the men's tee.

Zeke nodded, understanding what Mika meant. "It's a lot to learn at first, but you'll catch on quick. Parker's an outstanding teacher."

True to Zeke's words, Parker was a great teacher. He was patient. He showed Mika how to hit, which clubs to use, and how to follow through with her swing for better accuracy. By hole five, Mika was walking up to the tee confidently and hitting the ball a fair distance for a beginner.

Zeke and Sunny mostly ignored each other. Their conversation, when they had any, was almost exclusively about where their ball was or whose turn it was to hit. They both took great care not to touch each other getting on and off the cart. For much of the game, it was almost like two strangers who just happened to be playing together for the day.

At hole seven, Duncan puttered by on a golf cart, waving like crazy at Sunny. Sunny laughed and returned the wave. Zeke's icy mask cracked as he stopped alongside Sunny's ball on the fairway.

"So, are you going out with Duncan now?" Zeke asked before he could stop himself. It was the first question he'd asked her all day that wasn't specifically related to golf.

A look of surprise came over Sunny's face. "What?"

Zeke swallowed. Now he was in it. He couldn't stop. He had to know. "In the clubhouse, you said you'd see him later. Are you going out or something?"

"Oh my god, no. I'm not interested in him. Why would you think that?" She wrinkled her nose at Zeke, looking confused.

"Well, you were sure acting like you were interested in him in the clubhouse," he said, sliding off the golf cart and walking around back to get a club out of his bag. As soon as the words left his mouth, Zeke wanted to take them back. But it was too late.

"What are you even saying right now?" Sunny retorted, hopping off the cart and coming around back to meet him.

Zeke knew he'd crossed a line, but he couldn't think fast enough to back out of the situation, so he turned to face her and stalled with a "What?"

"What yourself! You're acting ridiculous," Sunny said, her voice rising.

Feathers ruffled over being called ridiculous, Zeke replied, "Well, if you aren't interested in him, you are sure sending him the wrong message by hanging all over him." Oof, once again, he wished he could take his words back, but his brain was not in control right now.

"Hanging all over him? Are you serious? I was not hanging all over him! And even if I was, that's none of your business!" Sunny was outright yelling now.

"Listen," Zeke said, trying to de-escalate the situation. He placed his hands lightly on Sunny's forearms. "All I'm saying is that if you aren't interested in him, you are leading him on. It's not very nice to play with people's emotions like that." Something in his words stuck in his head. Was he talking about Duncan right now? Or was he talking about himself?

Sunny had never really stopped to consider chemistry before. What created sparks between two specific people? What was it exactly? Was it physical? Simply being attracted to each other's appearances? Or was there more under the surface, a recognition of one soul seeing something within another soul?

Whatever it was, Zeke and Sunny had it.

As Sunny stood facing off against Zeke behind the cart, she found her whole body on high alert. She was aware of her flushed cheeks, the prickle of sweat down her back, the way the hair that had escaped her ponytail brushed against the sides of her face. But she wasn't just aware of herself. She also noted Zeke's labored breath, his penetrating gaze fixed on her face, and his warm fingertips lightly holding her forearms.

"Well?" Zeke said angrily.

Sunny felt uncomfortably pressured. "Well, what?"

Zeke let out a frustrated growl.

"I'm not leading him on. If he's interested in me, it's not my problem." She shrugged a shoulder to show her lack of concern. Sunny was not normally so cavalier about people's feelings, but in this case, she was well aware of the fact that Duncan was not remotely interested in her. Duncan was gay, and he had been telling her all about his new boyfriend at college. He was completely head over heels for him. So she felt perfectly comfortable omitting that fact in order to push Zeke's buttons. He had no right to act like an overbearing father.

Zeke scoffed, his loose grip on her arms tightening slightly as he felt her try to back away. It wasn't uncomfortable, but Sunny felt like Zeke was too near. He was all she could see, all she could think of.

"Not your problem? Then whose problem is it?"

"Listen, I'm not even convinced there *is* a problem," she said defensively.

Zeke shook his head. "How can you not care about his feelings? It's cruel. And you aren't a cruel person. I feel like I don't even know you anymore. You're making him think you like him."

"No way! He is not even low-key interested in me." Sunny thought it might be time to enlighten Zeke about Duncan's love life. She opened her mouth to spill the tea when Zeke interrupted.

"Bet?" Zeke asked.

Mouth gaping open, Sunny paused, flustered. "What?"

"Bet," Zeke reiterated. "I'll prove it to you. I bet you that Duncan likes you. If he does, I win. If he doesn't, you win."

Sunny paused, angling her face up towards Zeke. "What do you get if you win?" Sunny was curious what he wanted out of the bet.

"You tell Duncan you aren't interested in him." Zeke's answer was instantaneous.

"Okay," Sunny said, considering his words, "and what do I get if I win?"

"The satisfaction of being right?" Zeke asked hopefully.

Sunny rolled her eyes. "Puh-lease," she said, a bit more sarcastically than was necessary. "I already have that because I know I'm right. Give me something I actually want."

Zeke folded his arms across his chest, practically glowering down at Sunny. Then his expression turned smug. "Okay. I'll teach you how to bake Marta's special cookies."

Sunny's eyes widened. "Wait, for real? I've been begging her for that recipe for years, and she won't budge. How did you get it?"

Zeke smirked. "Guess she just loves me most of all."

"Won't she be mad at you for giving it to me?"

Zeke shook his head. "You aren't going to win anyway, so I won't have to divulge her secret."

Chapter 13

"Your crush detector is legit terrible," Sunny said, laughing as she measured two and a half cups of flour into a sifter. She felt a little guilty about not letting Zeke know Duncan was gay before she accepted the terms of his bet. It felt a bit too close to cheating. But he'd been acting like such a jerk that she figured it was payback. And she had warned him that Duncan wasn't interested!

Zeke smiled easily as he grabbed baking soda and other dry ingredients out of the cupboard. One thing Sunny appreciated about Zeke was that he was not a sore loser.

"What can I say? I let my jealousy get the better of me." Zeke smiled at Sunny as he plopped the dry ingredients on the island countertop. He seemed to be in a much better mood this afternoon.

Sunny felt her cheeks heat at his words and focused her attention on sifting the flour into the big bowl. She stood at the giant island in the boys' kitchen, reaping the rewards of having won the bet about Duncan's affections. After they concluded their game, she'd marched Zeke right into the clubhouse and struck up a casual conversation with Duncan about his boyfriend. As she had known, Duncan's eyes lit up, and he talked about their upcoming date. Zeke had nearly choked on his water when he realized he'd lost the bet. But he hadn't seemed too upset.

She cleared her throat. "Jealousy?" she questioned with a cavalier tone, trying to convey she didn't care about the answer.

"Sure," said Zeke, smiling easily. "No one is good enough for my brother's best friend!"

Sunny's heart sank, but she wouldn't let that show on her face. She cocked an eyebrow at him. "No one? You do know I'm going to date eventually, right?"

Zeke shrugged. "Yeah, of course. I just... like, can you just make sure you pick someone better than Duncan?"

Sunny picked up an oven mitt from the counter and threw it at Zeke. "I never picked Duncan in the first place, you fool! I told you he didn't like me, but you didn't listen. He's not even my type, even if he was straight."

Tossing the oven mitt back on the counter, Zeke continued measuring out ingredients into a mixing bowl. "So what exactly is your type, then?"

"Why do you care?" Sunny questioned, turning towards Zeke.

"I don't. Just making conversation." Zeke said casually.

Sunny cleared off a spot on the counter next to Zeke and jumped up to sit beside him while he continued measuring. She held up a hand and ticked her list off on her fingers. "Well, he has to be smart. That's number one for me. And kind of athletic. Not super athletic, like he's working out all the time, but just athletic enough that he's healthy, you know? I don't want him to have all the same interests as me, so he doesn't have to be into computers or anything like that. But we should share something in common that we like to do together. He has to be honest and kind and trustworthy. He has to just be a really good guy, you know?"

Sunny felt uncomfortable as she realized she had just described Zeke nearly exactly. She sent up a quick prayer that he wouldn't notice.

Zeke added the eggs into the dry ingredients and washed his hands, silent. He returned to the counter and stirred the batter furiously.

After a moment, he asked with a sarcastic edge to his voice, "Gee, wherever will you find such a perfect guy?"

Sunny shrugged, suddenly embarrassed about everything she had shared. She also wasn't sure why Zeke seemed so angry. "I mean, he doesn't have to be perfect. You just asked what I was looking for," she said defensively.

"Be careful you don't set yourself up for disappointment. No one can live up to what you just described."

"I don't know. There are nice guys everywhere. I mean, you're a nice guy."

Zeke barked out a sarcastic laugh. "I'm not nice, Addison. I ruin everything. Look what I did to my own life this year."

Frowning, Sunny put a hand on Zeke's arm, halting his furious stirring. "You didn't really do anything wrong. So some people think you made a mistake. Big deal."

"A mistake is putting salt in the batter instead of sugar. What they think I did was so much worse. I have a record. I can't get into college."

"It doesn't make you an evil person. It doesn't have to define who you are."

"Tell that to my dad."

Sunny shook her head. "No. You tell that to your dad."

"What?"

"I've seen the way he talks to you lately. He's rude and demeaning, and you just sit there and take it. Tell him the truth. Tell him it was Parker driving, not you. Tell him you are sorry you lied but that you are still a good person. Stand up for yourself!"

"Easy for you to say! Your dad is amazing. He's supportive and encouraging. He loves you no matter what you do. One mistake in my house and Dad's shipping me off to live with my uncle in London."

Sunny gasped. "That's where he's sending you? Did you finally talk to him?"

"Yeah. A real heart-to-heart," Zeke said dryly, his anger giving way to resignation. "He basically told me I'm an embarrassment and if I want any hope of seeing my trust fund in a few years, I'll go live with Uncle Mark and behave myself until he can figure out a way to get me back into college."

"When?"

"I leave next week."

Her heart felt like it was ripped wide open at the thought of Zeke leaving. Resolute, she crossed her arms across her chest. "No, you don't."

"What do you mean?"

"We're going to figure this out. You aren't going anywhere."

"You can't change my dad's mind, Addison. He's immovable. He's more stubborn than anyone in the world."

"That's actually not true. Lucky for you, I'm even more stubborn than he is," she smiled, and there was a wicked glint to her eye. "You'll see."

"Talking to him will never work. Telling him I lied will only make things worse." Zeke paused. "It doesn't really matter where I am, anyway. I can't stay here forever with nothing to do. And honestly, why do you even care? You'll be gone to college soon."

Sunny's eyes slid away from Zeke's, and she lifted one shoulder noncommittally. "Because you don't want to go. I can tell."

"Is that the only reason?"

"Well," said Sunny, pausing, "that, and who would I hang out with now that Parker is obsessed with Mika? He's over at her house again right now!"

"He really is obsessed with her, isn't he?"

"Yes! That's what I've been saying all along!" Sunny and Zeke laughed together.

Zeke turned serious. "I appreciate the help, Sunny, but I can't let you fight my battles for me."

Sunny smiled sweetly at Zeke. "Oh, don't worry, you aren't. I'm only here to help. You're the one that's going to convince your dad to let you stay."

As the cookies finished baking, Zeke and Sunny sat at the kitchen island patiently waiting.

Zeke absently tore the label off of his water bottle and asked, "You know, since I got kicked out of Notre Dame, I've been thinking a lot about why people choose certain colleges. Like, why do you want to go to MIT so much?"

Sunny frowned, the corners of her mouth crinkling down. Zeke knew this already. "Because my mom went there."

Zeke nodded. "Right. But why do *you* want to go there?"

Sunny bristled at his probing question. "That's a silly question. It's an amazing school. I've wanted to go there ever since I was a little kid."

"Have you?" Zeke continued questioning. Sunny squirmed in her seat. "I remember you talking about it a lot, like how your mom and dad wanted you to go there. I just don't remember you talking about what you wanted to do there."

Sunny was emphatic. "Of course I want to go there. It's my dream school! It's the only place I want to go."

Zeke was undeterred. "But why MIT? Or, even better, why even college at all? Say you get in. You're there. Picture yourself at MIT. What are you doing there? What classes are you in? What activities? What excites you?"

The questions hit Sunny like paint balls, one after another. Bap, bap, bap. The pressure squeezed down on her, making it difficult to think. "Well, computer stuff, obviously," Sunny huffed.

Now it was Zeke's turn to frown. "Really? But you hate taking computer classes. Every computer class you ever took, you bitched about how slow the professor was going. Remember that programming class with Mr. Freedmont? For an entire trimester, Parker and I had to hear about how there was a YouTuber that taught you all that stuff in an hour."

Sunny was silent. She didn't have an answer.

Zeke continued, "I'm just surprised, is all. College just doesn't seem like it fits you." Zeke held up his hands. "Not that you aren't smart or wouldn't do well. I just always pictured something different for you."

"Really?" asked Sunny. "Like what?"

"I don't know...I guess I always just saw you building something of your own. Like the app you just built. I guess I pictured you doing that, but for a living. Seeing a problem out in the world and then fixing it with something you made yourself. You know?"

Sunny couldn't contain the excitement his words sparked. "Well, I do have another idea for an app... I thought of it earlier today when Mika was talking." She stopped, suddenly shy about sharing her idea.

"That's cool. What is it?" Zeke looked so interested that Sunny tossed her embarrassment aside and told him.

"Well, Mika told me she didn't get as much financial aid as she needs for college. She can't go if she doesn't find another option."

Zeke nodded.

Sunny continued, her voice growing more animated as she described her vision. "Well, it got me thinking. What if there was a way, through an app, that you could connect donors to students in need? Directly. Without going through the school. Students could post a funding request. Like, for example, I'm Sunny and I'm going to MIT. I could post that I need five thousand dollars because I didn't get enough loan money or whatever. And then donors could contribute to my tuition. So it's like a scholarship, but the donors get to choose exactly who they donate to."

"Wow. I'm seriously impressed. That's an amazing idea." Sunny felt warmed by Zeke's praise.

Zeke continued, "But how would you know that the money actually went to someone in school? Like, how would you prevent someone from just lying and saying they were going to school but then just taking the money and spending it on a new car or something?"

Zeke's questions were good ones, and Sunny didn't have a solution.

"I'm not sure yet. I have to think about it. But I'm positive there's a need for something like this out there. It's just going to take me some time to figure it out."

Later that night, after the dough was baked and Sunny's stomach was full of too many cookies, she headed home. Her dad greeted her in the kitchen and tried to force-feed her steak and potatoes. She just groaned and hugged her belly.

"Too. Many. Cookies," she moaned.

Her dad laughed, chucked her on the chin, and said, "I'll put the leftovers in the fridge for you when you want a midnight snack."

Sunny gave him a grateful smile and headed up to her room before he could pepper her with questions about where she'd been all afternoon. He knew she was at the Crawford house, but he undoubtedly thought she was with Parker. She wasn't quite sure what he would say if he knew she'd been with Zeke. Her dad had always liked Zeke, but she knew he'd been really upset when he heard about the accident. She didn't like the fact that her dad thought Zeke had driven drunk and endangered Parker's life. How could Zeke stand everyone thinking he'd done that? Sunny didn't understand it at all. But, then, she'd never had a sibling herself, so maybe it just wasn't something she was capable of understanding.

She sat in the tiny window seat in her bedroom, looking out at the night sky as she considered Zeke's words to her. He was right. She couldn't admit it to him at the time, but she did hate sitting in a classroom learning about technology. Ever since that boot camp so long ago, she'd known that she preferred learning at her own pace, on her own. Could she really imagine four years of sitting in a classroom? She would have access to some of the greatest technology minds in the nation, and she would no doubt learn a great deal. But what if she hated it there?

The thought of the new app she'd told Zeke about was still running around inside her brain. She could feel her fingers itching to sketch out what it might look like on paper. What if this was her real dream? Seeing problems and trying to find solutions. Using her technology skills to help people.

Sunny had never allowed herself to consider anything other than MIT. She was still on the waitlist, and she needed to write the letter telling the Admissions counselor about the app she'd developed. After all, that was the whole point of making the app, wasn't it? To get her into MIT. But she hadn't even started to write it yet. There was nothing holding her back. The app was done. It was working. So why couldn't she just sit down and do it? MIT had been the plan for so long that the line had blurred between what was her dream and what was her parent's dream.

And did it really even matter whose dream it was? The fact remained, it was the last thing Sunny had left to hold onto, the only way she could honor her mother. It wasn't like she could talk to her mom right now, ask her advice, tell her what she was thinking or feeling. She desperately wished she could. Because the more she thought about actually leaving for college, the more confused she became. Zeke's questions about what she wanted to do left her flustered and uneasy. It would be easier to stop thinking about it all and just follow in her mom and dad's footsteps like they wanted.

But what if college wasn't really Sunny's dream after all?

Chapter 14

"What is all this?" Zeke gestured to the papers scattered around Sunny as she sat cross-legged on the floor of her bedroom. A pillow rested on the ground beside her, indented as though she'd been laying on it earlier. Zeke stood in her doorway, having let himself in the front door and made his way upstairs to Sunny's room. He looked freshly showered, his hair still damp. He had dressed comfortably in forest green athletic shorts and a white t-shirt. His plain t-shirt stretched nicely across his chest and biceps in a way that made Sunny avert her eyes. She licked her lips self-consciously before answering.

"My three-pronged plan," Sunny said.

"Huh?"

"My three-pronged plan to change your dad's mind," Sunny said proudly. It was Monday morning. As soon as her dad had left for work, she'd texted Zeke, telling him to come over. Well, after she'd showered and changed into cute jean shorts and a heather-gray tank top with a delicate pink stripe across the chest. She had promised yesterday that she would help Zeke convince his dad to let him stay, and she meant it.

Taking a deep breath, she dove into an explanation, turning the paper in her hands around to face Zeke. He squinted at it from across the room. "So, I drew up this plan while my dad was force-feeding me breakfast this morning."

"He still doing that?" Zeke laughed. "Hasn't he realized you aren't a little kid anymore?"

"Nope. It seems like there are lots of people who haven't realized that yet," Sunny said pointedly. She didn't stop to check Zeke's reaction before continuing. "Anyway, so here's the plan. Step one, we launch a guerrilla marketing campaign to remind him of how much he loves you and all the good things you've done in your life." She used her yellow highlighter to point to the first box on the paper.

Zeke's confusion was apparent on his face. "Oooookay, not sure what that means."

Sunny continued, undeterred. She pointed to another box on the paper. "Step two, we develop an amazing proposal for how you are going to get yourself back into college. Step three, we set up a meeting with him at his office and lay out your proposal for him. He won't be able to say no."

"I understand nothing about your three-pronged plan," Zeke said, looking lost.

"It's simple," said Sunny, dropping the paper and holding up two fingers. "Your dad loves two things. His kids and his job." Zeke started to interrupt, no doubt to argue about whether his dad actually loved him. Sunny knew Zeke didn't feel particularly loved right now. But she waved his interruption away. "He may not know how to show it right now, but he loves you. Deep down." She paused. "Way deep down. Trust me. We are going to use those weaknesses to our advantage. First, we remind him that he loves you. It will soften him up. Then, we are going to play to his lawyer-ness with business lingo and convince him why you should stay. Every lawyer loves a solid argument."

Appearing to warm up to the idea, Zeke entered the room and plopped down next to Sunny. "First of all, I don't think lawyer-ness is a word. Second, I don't think loving his kids and his job are technically weaknesses."

"You know what I mean!" Sunny blew a lock of hair out of her face with an exasperated breath.

Zeke shrugged and replied, "I really don't, but I'm willing to roll with it for now because I really don't want to move to London." He gave her a lopsided smile, leaning back on his arms. Her stomach did a little back-flip.

Sunny shoved the wayward clump of hair behind her ear and paused. She didn't want to pry, but she suddenly needed to know why Zeke wanted to stay and if it had anything to do with her. "You know, I never asked you... I could see why you might not totally love your life right now. Between community service and avoiding your dad, it's not exactly a barrel of fun around here. So why don't you want to go to London and get a fresh start? Seems like it might be the kind of thing someone might want to do to escape... everything. Start over somewhere new, you know?"

Nodding, Zeke answered, "I know things are kind of miserable right now, but that doesn't mean I want to pick up and leave. Yeah, this summer kind of sucked... I mean, in the beginning, it definitely did. But my community service will be done soon. And I kind of like hanging out here with you and Parker before you leave for college. There's not a lot of time left before you're both gone. I mean, I don't like that my dad is mad at me all the time. But everything else is... good." He grinned sheepishly, and Sunny found herself smiling back. Even though it was so much harder when Zeke was around, she had to admit that she didn't want him to leave.

After their argument yesterday and then baking cookies together, they seemed to have reached a new equilibrium. And by equilibrium, that meant avoiding prolonged eye contact and not talking about what happened over the weekend. For Sunny's part, it was a tenuous arrangement, and she felt like her emotions might get the better of her at any moment. But it was working.

Parker walked in and froze, seeing the two of them sitting side by side on the floor.

"Uh," he said hesitantly. "Is it safe to enter, or are you two still..." He paused and made a hissing sound, raising his hands like cat claws scratching the air. Parker had seen their argument at the golf course, but he'd pretty much been with Mika ever since, so he wasn't clear on where everyone stood today.

Sunny rolled her eyes. "We're fine. Sit down, P." She shoved away the immediate feeling of guilt that shot through her every time she saw Parker lately. It was awful knowing the truth about the accident when he didn't. She suddenly remembered that Parker also didn't know that their dad was forcing Zeke to move to London. As surreptitiously as she could, she gathered up her notes on her three-pronged plan and shoved them under the pillow beside her. Luckily, Parker didn't notice.

Folding his long legs into a cross-legged position across from Sunny and Zeke, Parker sat.

"What are you doing here?" Sunny asked.

"Straight-up chillin'," he answered casually. "Didn't have anything to do today, so I figured I'd see if you wanted to hang." He nodded a chin towards Zeke. "Didn't know you'd be here too."

Zeke shrugged. "Yeah, I didn't have anything to do before my community service hours today."

There was an awkward pause in the conversation. Parker never could stand silence, so he quickly inserted, "So, what's new?"

Sunny widened her eyes dramatically and smacked Parker's arm. "What's new? That's all you have to say? I don't know. What's up with you, Parker? You've been with Mika nearly nonstop since yesterday. Deets. Now."

Parker smiled slyly. "Oh, you noticed that, huh? Let's just say I'm making significant progress on my goals this summer." He gave a forced laugh and offered up a high-five to Zeke. Zeke made no move to meet his hand. Instead, he raised an eyebrow at Parker.

"What does that even mean, Parker? Did you ask her out finally?" Zeke questioned.

"Well, not exactly."

Sunny and Zeke groaned in unison and then exchanged a glance. Sunny felt a warmth spread from her head to her toes. They both understood how Parker operated. There was something intimate in sharing that knowledge, being united in their exasperation. She forced her gaze back to Parker as he continued.

"Listen, I'm super close," Parker said. "She's just real hard to figure out. Like, we'll get really close to talking about going out, and then she'll tell me what a great friend I am. Or I'll try to talk to her about something I love, like movies, and she tells me how not interested she is in that exact thing. How can someone not like movies? I just don't understand her. It's like she's hot one minute and then cold the next. Well, maybe not hot. Just like lukewarm, and then cold. I just feel like we can't seem to get it right."

Something about that statement hit too close to home for Sunny. Doing everything in her power to avoid Zeke's eyes, she said, "I'm sorry, Parker." She patted his shoulder in sympathy. "You know, it's not supposed to be this hard. When two people like each other, it should be easy. Maybe you guys just aren't meant to be."

Zeke interrupted, an incredulous look on his face. "Not meant to be? What kind of crap advice is that?" He didn't sound angry, just frustrated.

"Excuse me?" Sunny's eyes shot to Zeke's face, but he wasn't looking at her. He was focused on Parker.

"Parker, listen," Zeke ran a hand through his hair. "This isn't a movie. In real life, relationships aren't easy. They take work. And honesty. If you want to date this girl, you need to tell her how you feel."

"Well, maybe that's a two-way street," Sunny retorted. Her hand found the pillow beside her, and she clenched it in her fist. She resisted the urge to throw it right at Zeke's face. Sitting there, preaching about honesty when she had no idea how he felt about her. Zeke finally turned to look at her. She continued, "Maybe it's not just on Parker to speak up. Maybe Mika needs to be honest about how she feels!"

"I couldn't agree more," answered Zeke smugly.

Sunny gave in to the overwhelming urge and threw the pillow directly at Zeke's head. He cackled in surprise and caught it cleanly, giving her a wide smile. Still smug. Sunny wrinkled her nose at him, annoyed at how she'd played right into his argument.

Confusion was evident on Parker's face, but he pressed onward. "I know you guys are right. I just feel so dumb when I think about saying the words out loud. But fine. I'll ask her out for real next time I see her." He sighed. "Look at me. Growing as a person. How fun," he deadpanned.

Sunny turned her attention back to Parker and smiled at him. "Good job, Parker!" She patted him on the head with a smile. "You're like a real adult. Well, almost. I don't think adults eat an entire container of cheese balls in one sitting. But other than that..."

He stuck his tongue out at her. "I only did it that one time. And it was only because you bet me I couldn't."

Nodding, Sunny agreed. "I know, I know."

"And I won that bet, you know."

Sunny cocked her head. "Is it really winning when you vomit orange a few hours later?"

Parker groaned and doubled over, clutching his stomach. "Uhhh, don't remind me."

Zeke stood. "Well, as much fun as this is, I gotta run. Community service awaits."

"Wait up! I'll walk you out." Sunny scrambled to her feet and followed Zeke out into the hallway and down the stairs. When they reached the bottom, she halted him with a hand on his arm. It felt hot under her touch. She said quietly, "Call me after you're done, okay? I'll come over, and we can start the first part of my plan."

Hesitantly, Zeke replied, "Okay. I don't think it's going to work, but okay."

Sunny dropped her hand from his arm, trying to mask her hurt. She'd put a lot of thought into the plan, but if it was going to work, he needed to be on board. "It can't hurt to try, right?"

Zeke nodded and turned away. He paused and turned back, looking down into Sunny's eyes. "It means a lot to me, that you'd try to help. Thank you."

"Of course," Sunny said with a soft smile.

Out of the corner of her eye, she saw Parker jog down the stairs, a bundle of papers in his hands. "Hey guys?" he said, confusion clear on his face. "What's this?"

Sunny felt the color drain from her face as she recognized the notes of her three-pronged plan clutched in Parker's hands.

After Parker discovered Sunny's notes, they'd been forced to tell him about Mr. Crawford sending Zeke to live in London. They gave him a quick rundown. Zeke omitted any mention of the truth about who was driving, giving Sunny a warning look. She felt disappointed that she still had to keep that one secret from Parker, but relieved that at least the London issue was out in the open. As Sunny had expected, Parker was livid about Zeke leaving and completely on board with helping execute the three-pronged plan. After all, there was nothing Parker loved more than a scheme.

Zeke had to run to make it to community service on time, so after he left, Parker and Sunny headed over to the Crawford house and up to Parker's room to brainstorm. By the time Marta called them down for lunch, the two co-conspirators had decided on a list of the things they needed to do in the next few days to remind Mr. Crawford of all the good things Zeke had done and of the importance of family. Parker took notes.

1. Get the old photo albums out of the office and place happy family photos strategically all over the house. (Parker)
2. Get out Zeke's box of old awards and leave them some-

where Dad can't miss them. (Parker)
3. Enlist Marta's help to make Dad's favorite meal. Host
a family dinner. (Zeke)
4. Get the community service supervisor to email Dad
about how good a job Zeke is doing. (Zeke)
5. Convince Sunny's dad to talk to our dad. (Sunny)

That last item was the hardest. It meant telling Sunny's dad about their plan and enlisting his help. Sunny and Parker had argued over that for an hour, with Parker coming out in favor and Sunny ruling against. She wasn't sure how her dad felt about Zeke lately. He'd always loved Zeke, but she knew he was really upset after the accident. Since her mom had died in a car accident, her dad was sensitive to people taking unnecessary risks with cars. If he was mad at Zeke, she wasn't certain he would help. What if he agreed with Mr. Crawford? Or worse, what if he exposed their plan? It could ruin everything.

In the end, Parker won by sheer force of will, per usual. Sunny had to admit that her dad could be a powerful ally. All she had to do now was get him on their side.

Chapter 15

"It's here!" Zeke said to Sunny, waving an arm that held a square object covered in bubble wrap.

"What's here?" Sunny said, sliding into a chair at the kitchen island. She unscrewed the cap from her bottle of water and took a drink. After lunch, Parker had headed out to shop for supplies for the next clue party. Sunny had so much going on, she barely even had time to think about Parker's bet. Her part was pretty much done, so she was leaving the party planning and clue stuff completely in Parker's hands. After all, he had Mika to help. So she had stayed behind at the Crawford house and started on the business proposal for her plan to help Zeke.

"Parker's photo album!" Zeke answered. He carefully unwrapped the album from its protective bubble wrap and laid it open on the table.

"It looks amazing," said Sunny, running a hand over the glossy cover with a giant photo of Parker's smiling face. "You did such a good job of finding pictures. Parker's gonna go nuts over it."

Shaking his head, Zeke refused to take all the credit. "We made a great team. It wasn't just me."

They shared a smile and went back to paging through the completed album. Sunny laughed when they came across the photo of the three of them all dressed up for Halloween. It had been only a year or so after they'd met, so they were young. Parker was dressed up as Iron Man because he'd been obsessed with superheroes, and the new *Iron Man* movie had come out that year. He had asked Sunny to dress up as Rhodey and be his sidekick, but Sunny refused. She had been fixated on *The Hunger Games* that year. She'd gone as Katniss, complete with a bow and arrow that she still had tucked away in the attic, mainly because her dad never threw anything away that had even remote sentimental value. Zeke had gone as Wolverine, and his hair was spiked up on the sides. She remembered using a whole tub of gel to get his hair to stand up like that.

When they got to the last page of the album, Sunny noticed right away something was wrong.

"Oh no!" she exclaimed when she saw the last picture. "It's the wrong photo!"

It was supposed to be all three of them on the trampoline, laughing with their arms around each other. But that wasn't the photo she was looking at. She must have selected the wrong one in the rush when Parker and his dad came home. They hadn't had time to proofread the album before they sent it to print. It was a different photo, but still in front of the trampoline. In this one, Parker was missing. This photo was just Zeke and Sunny. Sunny was looking at the camera, laughing at whoever was behind the camera lens, presumably Parker. And Zeke, well... Zeke was staring at Sunny. The way he was gazing down at her made her heart clench. He was smiling at her as she laughed, his arm wrapped loosely around her waist. He looked like a boy in love with a girl. In love with Sunny.

Sunny's eyes flew to Zeke's face.

Zeke glanced over at her before slamming the album shut. "No worries. It's still a nice picture of the two of us," he said. Was there a hint of embarrassment in his voice, or was that just Sunny's wishful thinking? He cleared his throat. "The album is great."

He was right. It would be fine. The album was from Zeke and Sunny to Parker, so it was perfectly acceptable that it was just a picture of the two of them. Likely, no one else would even notice. But Sunny noticed. She looked over at Zeke. "I'm sorry I messed up the photo."

Shaking his head, he waved off her apology. "It's fine. It's still amazing," he replied. He carefully wrapped it back up in bubble wrap and tucked it back into the gift box it had arrived in. He turned to face Sunny. "I really couldn't have gotten it done without you. Thank you for your help with it."

"You're welcome," Sunny answered, turning to face him. "It's a nice photo of the two of us."

"Yeah, it is," Zeke said. "I remember..." His voice faded as he hesitated.

"What?" Sunny prompted.

Zeke sighed and shoved a hand through his hair. "So many things... but I remember how much fun we used to have together. Do you remember that?"

"I do." She waited. He seemed like there was more he wanted to say.

"I know we don't always get along lately. And I'm starting to think that's my fault."

"That's funny," Sunny said with a wry twist of her mouth. "I was thinking it was my fault."

Zeke gave her an answering smile. "I think there are two sides to every story."

"I'm beginning to realize that," Sunny answered softly.

Silence. Neither of them seemed in any hurry to say anything. Sunny's eyes searched Zeke's for some hint as to how he felt about her. She silently begged for even one sign that he felt the same way. But he was as reserved as ever, never giving even a single hint of what was happening inside his head. Perhaps he needed a little nudge.

"Zeke?" Sunny began.

"Hmmm?" He answered.

"You know I'm not that little girl anymore, right? The one in that photo album?"

Reaching a hand up, Zeke tucked a few stray strands of hair behind Sunny's ear. "I'm beginning to realize that." He echoed her earlier statement.

The door slammed, causing them both to jump. Parker yelled, "Honey, I'm home!" as he barreled into the kitchen, dropping bags from Party City onto the counter.

Zeke neatly scooped up Parker's present from the counter and tucked it behind his back before Parker could see it. Sunny saw what he was doing and immediately tried to distract Parker.

"Hey Parker, check this out." She practically ran over to the refrigerator and tossed the door open, drawing Parker's eyes away from Zeke.

"What am I looking at, kid?" Parker said, peering over her shoulder into the fridge.

Sunny scrambled for something interesting to point out. Finally, her eyes landed on a new twelve-pack of sparkling water. "Marta found that new flavor of sparkling water you wanted to try!"

Parker was unimpressed. "Cool," he said dryly. When they both turned away from the fridge, Zeke was already gone. Sunny released a breath. She wasn't exactly sure what had just happened in the kitchen, but she knew something she hadn't known before. Zeke wasn't as immune to her as she'd always thought.

When Zeke was younger, he sometimes needed to go somewhere to think. His brother was a bit of a motor-mouth, and there was never any peace when he was around. And he was always around. Most of the time, Zeke didn't mind. Indeed, he appreciated the times Parker filled the silence in the house. After their mother had died, the silence was achingly painful at times. Their mother had always been singing or playing music or laughing. She had filled the giant house with life and vibrancy. Once she was gone, it was different. No singing. No music.

But there was still laughter. Parker's laughter. And Zeke welcomed it. Most of the time. Not all the time. All siblings need a break from each other once in a while, and Zeke was no exception. There were two places to which he would retreat when he wanted privacy from Parker's incessant chatter; the music room or the attic.

When Zeke left Parker and Sunny in the kitchen, he knew this was one of those times when he needed to be alone to think. His first thought was to head to the music room. It used to be one of his favorite spots in the house and had a giant Steinway grand piano planted squarely in the middle. It was painted a soft dove gray, with yellow accent chairs placed in a half-circle around the piano. Thanks to his dad's unlimited budget, the room had the best soundproofing and acoustic treatments that money could buy.

His mother had begun teaching him to play piano when he was just four years old. She and his dad had often tossed around the words "child prodigy," but all Zeke heard when he played were his mistakes, so he never took them seriously. When his mom had first gotten sick, she'd found him a classically trained piano teacher from Italy. His name was Alessandro, and Zeke's dad had gladly forked over the money to pay for lessons four days a week in order to make his wife happy. Zeke carried on lessons for the first few years after his mom passed away. But without his mother there, the thought of playing no longer sparked joy. He was still progressing technically, but Alessandro critiqued him constantly, saying his playing "lacked passion." Zeke grew frustrated, unable to access whatever emotion Alessandro expected out of him. When he was fourteen, he started making up excuses to skip lessons. Growing angry with Zeke's lack of focus, Alessandro eventually quit. Zeke told his dad not to hire a new teacher, and that was that. Zeke rarely played anymore, and the music room sat empty.

Zeke considered heading there now. Perhaps he would see if he could remember his mom's favorite piece, Tchaikovsky's Swan Lake. Knowing she couldn't hear him play it anyway, his feet wouldn't move that direction. Instead, they took him to his other favorite spot in the house. The attic.

There was no particular reason the attic should be a favorite of Zeke's, other than the fact that Parker never went there, so it was private. Parker had been so scared of the attic when he was younger. Too many horror movies, Zeke surmised. And Zeke had to give him credit. The attic was creepy. It wasn't dark like most attics. It was actually pretty bright because of the giant dormer windows that lined the two sides of the large open space. But depending on the time of day, light shone in and shadows fell in odd, ominous patterns across the walls, boxes, and floor. It smelled of old clothes and mothballs. Occasionally, mice skittered across the floor. Mr. Crawford said they couldn't put out poison because Sassy might get into it. Instead, the mice became skilled at eating peanut butter from the mousetraps and lived happily on. Their mother's old clothing and jewelry was relegated to a corner, packed into clear plastic tubs, looking dusty and forlorn. It was a visible reminder of the hole she'd left in their lives when she died. Zeke never went over to that corner of the attic.

For all those reasons, Zeke had known the attic was the perfect place to get some privacy and be assured his little brother wouldn't bug him. But what Parker didn't know is that if you walked all the way through the attic to the far side, Zeke had created a little oasis. Long ago, Zeke had dragged a long antique couch and a plush rug in front of one of the giant dormer windows. It created a cozy little nook where bright sunshine streamed in. He'd brought up a little end table, a couple of old blankets, and even a handful of books. This was his spot. The one place that was his alone.

Zeke sprawled out on the couch, throwing an arm over his face and closing his eyes. All he'd been thinking about lately was Sunny. He felt like his insides were all twisted up. Nothing felt right. The arguing. The effort it took to keep his feelings under wraps. It was exhausting. The only time things felt right was when he was being honest with her, like when he finally told her about the accident or about his dad sending him to London. It felt good sharing those things with her, not carrying the burden alone. He'd been alone for so long.

Her reaction to all of it had surprised him. She hadn't been afraid or angry or disappointed in him. She'd been strong, unshakably certain that he was a good person. He appreciated her advice. In fact, she had actually wanted to fix things for him. She was trying to take care of him. It had been so long since anyone had done that. He wanted to lean into her and let himself drown in that feeling. He wondered what it would feel like to depend on someone other than himself for a change.

As Zeke lay on the couch thinking, he considered Sunny's words in the kitchen. She was an adult. But he hadn't been treating her like one. She was capable of a lot more than he'd given her credit for.

He realized he'd been thinking about it all wrong. He'd been trying to stay away from Sunny to protect her, to stop her from getting hurt. But what he hadn't seen was how strong she was.

What if the reason things were so difficult between them was precisely because he was fighting his feelings for her? And what if he just let go of all of that worry? What if he just trusted her?

Chapter 16

Sunny was head down, digging on the bottom shelf of the kitchen freezer for her and Parker's favorite chocolate fudge ice cream. Marta had left out fruit and veggies on the counter when she'd gone home for the night, but it was almost ten p.m. now. And ten p.m. was no time for healthy food, according to Sunny. It was ice cream time. She had just spotted the familiar brown container and wrapped her hand around it when she heard a low whistle behind her.

Sunny quickly straightened up and whipped around, clutching the ice cream to her chest defensively. She found herself staring into the smiling face of Zeke.

A shirtless Zeke.

A very muscled, shirtless Zeke. He stood next to the counter wearing red gym shorts slung low on his hips. He looked like he had just come from lifting weights in their basement fitness room. Even in the dark, Sunny could see the defined muscles on his stomach and arms. Her heart gave a tiny flutter in her chest. She swallowed and tried to cover up the effect he was having on her with anger at his chauvinistic whistle.

"What the hell?" Sunny said accusingly.

"I was just admiring the view."

Me too, Sunny thought. But she wasn't about to tell him that. "Yeah, right," she scoffed. "Since when?"

"Oh, I've been admiring the view for quite some time now."

Sunny's mind raced at the idea that maybe he was serious, but she narrowed her eyes at him. She couldn't tell if he was joking or not. A week ago, she would have assumed he was, but now... she wasn't so sure. Even so, she wasn't about to let him know how much she wished his words were true. Not until she was certain. To hope would give him power over her, and there was no way she was going to let him lord this over her every time she saw him for the rest of their lives. She had to know for sure before she would risk it.

"Whatever," she said. "What are you even doing skulking around? I thought you were gone."

"Nope, I've been here. Just taking some quiet time to think, and then I was working out downstairs. Had some energy to burn off. What are you and Parker doing?"

"'The same thing we do every night, Pinky,'" she said, quoting *Pinky and the Brain.* "Watching movies downstairs."

Sunny advanced toward the counter with the ice cream container clutched in her hand like a lifeline. She pulled the lid off, snagged a spoon from a nearby drawer, and stabbed it into the gooey chocolate.

As she got closer to him, Zeke deftly snatched the container of ice cream from Sunny's hands.

"Hey," she yelled, grabbing at the container but failing to get a hold of it as Zeke held it just out of her reach over her head. "You know that's my favorite. You don't even like chocolate. Give it back!"

"Make me," he said with a giant grin on his face. Still holding the container aloft, he grabbed the spoon, now full of ice cream, and shoveled it into his mouth. Sunny was riveted, watching his tongue dart out to lick his lips. He moved the container behind his back and smiled smugly at her.

Comprehension dawned. Sunny stopped trying to grab for the container. This was a game. She didn't know how to play exactly, but she wasn't a total fool. She wasn't going to be able to take back the container by force. He was too strong. He wasn't going to give it to her willingly, either. And she certainly wasn't the kind of girl to beg. She had read enough books and watched enough movies to know that if she wanted to win, she needed to use her assets. Her decidedly female assets. She quickly switched tactics.

"Zeke," Sunny said breathlessly. She leaned forward, making sure to let her tank top gap open a tiny bit to show a bit more of her cleavage. Raising her hands, she ran her fingertips lightly down his chest as she looked up into his eyes with what she hoped was a seductive half-smile. She tried to widen her eyes in an innocent manner.

He blinked.

She let her fingertips drift down his chest, moving silently against his skin. She slowly meandered her fingers down and around until her arms encircled his waist.

She watched his Adam's apple bob as he swallowed. His body stilled. He watched her, eyes wary. She leaned closer until there was almost no space between them.

And snatched the ice cream container right out of his hands.

Ha! Victory! Sunny thought the words but refrained from yelling them out loud.

"Hey!" Zeke yelled with a smile. "No fair!"

Then the tide turned. Zeke's gaze turned calculating. But he didn't attempt to take the container back. Instead, he leaned toward Sunny, backing her up until her backside bumped against the counter. His arms surrounded her, and he placed his hands behind her, effectively pinning her between him and the counter.

Oh crap.

The mood shifted. It was no longer joking, playful. Zeke's eyes were filled with heat as he stared into Sunny's. She imagined leaning forward and kissing him right now. The sweetness of the chocolate, his soft lips pressed against hers.

"This is a dangerous game you're playing, Addison. Are you sure you're ready for the consequences?"

Zeke's body pressed against Sunny's, and she felt warm all over. Was she ready? She wasn't sure. For a long time, she had wanted this. She was still scared that he would reject her, but for the first time, her desire overwhelmed her fear. She didn't know if he truly wanted her or if he was just playing her. But she did know one thing. If this was going to happen, Sunny was going to be in control. She dropped the ice cream container onto the counter, leaned into his embrace, and placed her hands firmly on his chest.

"The question isn't whether I'm ready, Zeke," Sunny said softly. "The question is, are you certain you are?"

Zeke ran his hands up Sunny's arms and threaded his fingers into her hair, dislodging her ponytail. Her hair tumbled free, cascading down her back. She wanted to close her eyes and revel in the feeling of his hands on her, but she forced herself to keep her eyes focused on Zeke's. "I'd wager I'm more ready for this than you are," he answered, a wry smile twisting his lips.

"Oh, really? Wanna bet?" Sunny angled her face up towards his.

Zeke's blue eyes darkened. Sunny felt a moment of panic that she'd gone too far. But before she could dwell on it, Zeke's head dipped down. His mouth inched closer to hers. He murmured, "Bet."

And then their mouths collided.

Sunny had kissed a few boys before. A few. Not many. But nothing in her previous romantic life had prepared her for this. The heat. The all-consuming need to be closer to Zeke. The indescribable feeling of his body pressed against hers. The sheer joy that after all this time of wishing, wanting, Zeke was actually kissing her. It was more than she'd ever imagined.

Everywhere their bodies touched was on fire. Zeke's mouth moved against hers like he was drinking her in. He groaned. His arms encircled her, drawing her closer. She was barely conscious of her own arms as they wrapped themselves around him. Her whole body was moving on instinct.

Tearing his mouth from hers, he rained kisses down the side of her neck and into the hollow of her throat. She luxuriated in the feel of his mouth on her body. Her lips cried out of their own volition. "Zeke," she said breathlessly. His mouth returned to hers. Her hands made their way to the back of his head and buried themselves in his soft hair, drawing him closer.

Pausing, Zeke opened his eyes to gaze down at Sunny. She opened her eyes lazily to meet his gaze. His hands traveled down her body, sweeping under her legs and lifting her up onto the counter. Sunny gasped softly with surprise, and her mouth curved in a smile. He lifted her as though she weighed nothing, and something inside her loved the feel of him taking control. He stepped between her legs and pulled her closer, covering her mouth with his.

His fingers kneaded the sides of her hips as his lips continued their onslaught. Sunny matched Zeke in intensity, her hands moving down to explore the curves of his abs. His fingers danced upwards, lifting the hem of her shirt to dive inside, creating a trail of fire on her midriff.

Sunny never wanted this feeling to end.

As one of his hands crept higher and brushed the underside of her breast through her cotton bralette, she felt a jolt of panic. Things were moving quickly, and she still didn't really know how he felt about her. Her brain kicked into high gear. Was this just a game that had gotten out of hand? Or did he really care about her? Almost as though Zeke sensed her hesitation, his hands stilled, and he pulled back a little. He looked down at her, rested his forehead against hers, and whispered "Addison."

And she was lost again.

Ding.

Zeke and Sunny jumped apart at the chime announcing the house-wide intercom system had been activated.

"Sun, get down here!" Parker's voice reverberated in the kitchen, laced with incredulity. "You gotta see this. You'll never believe it."

Sunny and Zeke faced each other, both breathing hard. The air was charged. Sunny raised a hand to cover her heart as it thumped in her chest. Her lips felt tender, hot. She was certain if she had a mirror she would look flushed, her cheeks splashed with color. Zeke, for his part, looked equally flushed. His hair was disheveled, his body tense. He looked shell-shocked. Sunny wondered if he was as surprised as she was that things had escalated so quickly.

"Sunny?" Parker insisted, interrupting Sunny's thoughts. The line stayed open on the intercom until Parker chose to turn it off from the wall-mounted console down in the movie room.

"Yeah," Sunny croaked out before clearing her throat. "Yes. I'll be right down."

Ding.

The chime sounded again. Parker had turned off the intercom. Zeke and Sunny were alone again.

"I suppose I should..." Sunny said, gesturing towards the hallway leading out of the kitchen. Her words were tentative. She reached down to straighten her shirt which was hiked up around her midriff from Zeke's exploring hands. She was hoping Zeke would say something, anything, about what had just happened. But as much as she hoped he would, she was afraid too. Afraid he might say something that would cement what just happened and change their friendship forever.

But he didn't say a word about it.

"After you," Zeke said, sweeping an arm in the same direction.

Disappointed but determined not to let it show, Sunny bit her lip and led the way out of the kitchen, head held high. She shook her hair out as she walked, remembering how his hands had buried themselves in it. Her ponytail holder lay somewhere in the kitchen, forgotten, and she longed for it now. It would have been a comfort to put her hair back up and get herself back to normal. Right now, with it hanging down, she felt different, exposed, vulnerable. Perhaps it wasn't Zeke's words that would change their relationship forever. Perhaps their actions had already changed everything.

When they arrived downstairs, Sunny saw Parker sprawled in one of the chairs, the giant television paused. He looked past her toward Zeke.

"Oh, hey, Zeke, didn't know you were home. You gotta see this, man." He turned and pressed the button to start the TV again. "I rewound it for you, Sunny."

On the screen was a male news anchor, and at the bottom of the screen, the headline read "Bet: A new kind of game."

The news anchor spoke solemnly. "Have you ever made a bet with a friend? If so, our next story is for you. A new kind of app has taken the technology world by storm this week. Our own Della Thomas has the details."

The news anchor didn't look familiar to Sunny. The screen flashed over to a woman holding a smartphone. As she held it up, Sunny could see her app displayed on the woman's phone. She felt her mouth gape open. She couldn't place the station.

"Parker," Sunny said, blinking slowly. "Which local station is this? I've never seen these reporters before."

"That's the amazing thing, Sunny." Parker grinned. "It's not local at all. It's national! Your app is on the national news."

Chapter 17

542,681.

Sunny blinked in shock as she stared at the number on her computer screen. Over five hundred thousand people had installed her app. The story on the national news last night had sparked a flurry of downloads, and the number continued to grow every hour.

She flipped over to check out the reviews. Her overall rating had dropped to 4.2 out of 5.0. She was disappointed, but she tried to remind herself that was to be expected with hundreds of thousands of eyes scrutinizing her app. Over half a million. Sunny marveled at the number. It was hard to believe. But with that many downloads, people were bound to be critical, find issues, and want unique features. 4.2 was still a good rating. She spent the morning combing through reviews, making a list of bugs she needed to fix and features she wanted to add.

Truth be told, Sunny was happy for the distraction. After watching the rest of the news story with Parker and Zeke last night, she'd been shell-shocked. Thankfully, everything the reporter had said was positive, and they hadn't mentioned her by name. But it was still too much to take in. The app. Zeke. As the news reporter finished the story, Zeke and Parker turned to look at Sunny expectantly, waiting for her reaction. Panic had risen, making her chest tighten and her mind go blank. Like a zombie, she'd mumbled some excuse about needing to go home. She didn't even wait for them to respond before she fled, practically running back to her house. Her dad had been waiting up for her. As usual. He had peppered her with questions about her day, and she effectively dodged them, answering with vague platitudes that told him nothing. All the while, she was biding her time so she could slip away to the quiet comfort of her bedroom.

"Did you have a good day?"

"Yep."

"What did you do?"

"The usual. Movies."

"What is Parker up to lately?"

"Nothing much. Just hanging out."

"Did you have anything to eat? Are you hungry?"

"No thanks. I'm good."

She could sense her dad's frustration with her distance, but he didn't call her on it. As quick as she could, she made her excuses and headed to bed, feeling both relieved and guilty the entire time. She hadn't spent much time with her dad this summer, and he had to be lonely without her. But she couldn't think about that right now on top of everything else. As she fell into bed, she promised herself she would reserve some time to hang out with her dad soon. And she still needed to talk with him about Zeke's situation. Sleep was elusive, and the morning had come too quickly. She awoke feeling tired, cranky, and apprehensive about what was to come. But she pushed that aside and pulled up her dashboard to check her installation totals.

And that's when she saw the number. 542,681.

As she sat at her desk reading through the reviews, she realized that people really seemed to like the app. That felt good. Sunny had always wanted to help people. Originally, she had been so scared to release her app. Her baby. But with each review she read, she grew braver, more sure that this was what she was meant to do with her life. She was good at this, and she enjoyed it. What more could someone ask for out of life?

Sunny's phone dinged with a text message notification. She reached over, picked up her phone, and saw Zeke's name flash across the screen. Her stomach leaped.

Zeke: *We need to talk. Pick you up at 5?*

The breath whooshed out of Sunny's lungs. He was right. They did need to talk. A feeling of dread and excitement settled on her shoulders. Her fingers hovered over the keyboard for a second before tapping out a quick reply.

Sunny: *Parker's releasing another clue tonight. I want to go so I can make sure the app works. Can we meet after? 7pm?*

Zeke: *Sure. Pick you up there or at your house?*

Worrying her bottom lip, Sunny considered her options. If he picked her up at Parker's party, she would have to get ready ahead of time. And what if she got all hot and sweaty and gross at Parker's party? It was already eighty-five degrees outside, and she didn't want to have to worry about being gross when Zeke picked her up. But if he picked her up at home, she would need to explain to her dad why Zeke was there. *Wait a minute*, she thought, remembering something her dad had said to her before he left for work this morning. She flipped over to the family calendar app on her phone to double-check. Yes! Her dad had a faculty dinner tonight, so he wouldn't be home until after eight p.m. Perfect.

Sunny: *My house.*

Zeke: *Sounds good.*

Sunny: *Where are we going?*

Zeke: *Can't tell. It's a surprise.*

Sunny: *Very mysterious. Should I be worried?*

Zeke: *Nothing scary, I promise.*

Sunny: *Ok, then. See you at 7.*

Zeke: *See you.*

Sunny's stomach did somersaults thinking about being alone with Zeke that night. What should she wear? Where were they going?

Feeling her anxiety rise the more she thought about it, she instead turned her attention back to the app reviews. She diligently worked on fixing some of the suggestions and bugs people had pointed out in their reviews. It needed to be done, and she found the work calming. She knew she could take their feedback and make the app even better than before. It was just what she needed to take her mind off of tonight. And Zeke.

Thumbing through his unread texts, Parker shook his head. He had gotten nearly fifty texts that morning from classmates. Though the texts ranged in variety, it was clear everyone wanted one thing. Information about the next clue.

Some texts were casual.

Flower McAvery: *Whatchu up to?*

Mooch (real name: Michael Drum): *Wanna hang?*

Callie Jacobson: *HMU on snapchat?*

Others were more pointed.

Brandyn Meyers: *Dude, u gotta give me a hint. I'll cut you in!!! 50/50 split.*

Summer Andrews: *New clue coming out 2day?*

Demetrius Tyrone: *What's the next location bro?*

What these texters had in common is that they had never messaged Parker before. They were friends in the sense that they all knew each other from school and hung out at the same places, same parties. But they weren't real friends, at least not the kind that regularly texted each other or made plans together. So it was clear what they were after.

Rolling out of bed, Parker decided he better get going. Zeke was gone at community service, and his dad was at work like always, so he was on his own. And he had a lot to do today. Not only did he need to get ready for his party, he needed to help Sunny and Zeke with the three-pronged plan. He shook his head as he thought about it. Sunny could have at least come up with a better name for it. Every good scheme needed a name. Movie titles were the perfect inspiration. Saving Private Zeke. No, that wasn't very respectful of the military. Zeke Actually. A little better, with a slight nod to the fact that their dad was shipping Zeke off to the UK. Parker snapped his fingers. He had it! Ezekiel Crawford and the Holy Grail. Only Zeke's holy grail wasn't an actual holy grail. His holy grail was being able to stay home. It was perfect. If only Sunny had asked Parker to work on the plan earlier.

Parker wasn't mad that Sunny had kept this a secret from him. She'd explained how Zeke had asked her not to tell him. And Parker wasn't always the most intuitive guy on the planet, but he wasn't stupid. He knew Sunny had been in love with Zeke for a long time. He also knew his brother was equally hung up on her. But it was none of his business, so he stayed out of it. He had to admit he was a little upset with Zeke, though. Not over Sunny. He was upset about Zeke not telling him about their dad's plan. They were brothers. And not just regular brothers. They were the kind of brothers that liked each other. They were actually friends. He didn't understand why Zeke felt like he couldn't tell him about this. Did he think he was just a kid? That he couldn't handle it? Parker wasn't sure, but it dug under his skin and stuck there, like a sliver that he just couldn't get out.

Pushing it out of his mind, Parker spent the morning doing three very important tasks. He replied to his classmates' texts with vague non-answers, readied the supplies for the upcoming party at the old mill, and finished his assigned items from the three-pronged plan.

As soon as he'd completed his items, he texted Sunny to let her know. Prong one of her three-pronged plan was almost complete. At least Parker's parts. He'd placed family photos all over their nor-mally stark and utilitarian house. They stuck out like sore thumbs, and there was no way their dad could miss seeing them all when he came home. There were baby photos stuck with magnets to the refrigerator and a couple of framed photos of Zeke and Parker from elementary school on their dad's desk. Zeke's graduation photo was framed and placed on the foyer side table. But the living room was a true masterpiece, in Parker's humble opinion. In the living room, Parker had nearly covered an entire wall with photos from their lives, stuck with pushpins into the drywall. Parker knew his dad would be mad about the holes in the wall, but he did it anyway. He had painted his own bedroom enough times that he wasn't worried. He'd fix the holes and repaint it later, good as new.

But in true Parker fashion, he didn't stop there. The photos were just the beginning. After getting the box of awards out from under Zeke's bed, Parker had made a veritable shrine to Zeke in the dining room. He slid all the china and glassware in the china hutch off to the sides. Crystal champagne glasses clinked dangerously against each other. Wine glasses crowded up against white china daintily outlined in gold leaf. With all of those dishes pushed aside, right in the middle behind the glass, Parker placed Zeke's trophies and awards. There was a blue ribbon from when Zeke had gotten first place in a spelling bee. There was a series of trophies from soccer wins. He'd even been awarded an MVP trophy one year. The largest array of awards came from Zeke's piano competition days. It included framed certificates, engraved glass awards and plaques, even one shaped like a glass grand piano. Parker artfully arranged them all and stepped back to admire his work. His dad was sure to notice this. Parker hoped it was enough. He wanted his dad to fondly remember all the good days and soften his heart enough to let Zeke stay.

After he texted Sunny to let her know that he was done with his parts of the plan, he shot off a text to Mika.

Parker: *leaving now 2 set up*

Mika: *Meet you there!*

Grabbing the party supplies from the counter, Parker headed out to the garage and loaded them into his car. The taco truck was bringing all the food and supplies to go with it. They even agreed to haul out picnic tables for an extra fee. But Parker had still bought decorations. He had strands of color-changing lights, tablecloths, and centerpieces for the tables. The centerpieces had been Mika's idea. He was just going to buy streamers and balloons, but she'd wrinkled her nose at that suggestion, saying those seemed too much like a kid's birthday party. She seemed concerned with how much he was spending on the party, but that didn't stop her from giving him advice. Parker was a little uneasy about the cost himself, but he was in too far to back out now. He still wasn't sure what he was going to tell his dad when the credit card bill came. Promising himself he would scale back for the next clue, Parker checked his watch.

It was nearly time to get out to the mill, set up, and release the clue. He suspected that people might be tracking his movements, watching out for his vehicle, and trying to get a head start on the next clue's location. He couldn't be certain, but he even thought someone had followed him home the other day from Mika's house. Out of an abundance of caution, Parker took a weird, winding route to get to the mill today. He took back roads as much as he could, turning whenever he encountered a vehicle he thought looked suspicious. He knew he might look a little crazy if anyone could see him right now, but he couldn't be too careful.

Finally confident that he hadn't been followed, he pulled down the narrow dirt road and parked in a clearing alongside the pond. He could see the old mill, dilapidated and rotting at the far end of the pond. It hadn't been working in years, before Parker was even born. The structure itself wasn't even safe to be inside, with half of the boards falling down and the roof partially caved in. But the pond was still beautiful, crystal blue against the green grass and evergreen trees surrounding it. There was a short dock in the clearing. Occasionally, kids would come down here and fish off of it in the summer.

Mika wasn't there yet, but he knew she would be soon. After they released the clue, they'd have a little time alone together before people started arriving. He planned to tell her how he felt then. No more waiting, wondering. This was it. He channeled his nervous energy into unloading the supplies and tried not to think about Mika at all.

As Parker was getting all the supplies unloaded, the taco truck pulled up, followed by a truck and trailer filled with the picnic tables. He had needed to give the chef the location, but he hadn't used his real name, nor told him what the party was for, so he figured it was safe. The crew hopped out, and under Parker's direction, they set the tables up in no time.

A few minutes later, Mika pulled in, looking calm and cool in a light pink crop top and yellow shorts. She looked amazing. Parker swallowed, feeling the nerves creep into his throat again.

"Hey, Parker," Mika greeted him.

He bobbed his head, returning the greeting. "Hey!" Inside, he still felt awkward around her, but he forced himself to act normal.

"Are you ready to release the next clue? It's almost time!" She rubbed her hands together in excitement.

Parker's stomach gave a little jump.

Today was a big day for two reasons. They were releasing the second clue. And it was the day Parker was finally going to tell Mika how he felt about her.

Parker was ready. He grabbed his phone and opened up Sunny's app. Swiping over to where he'd preloaded the clue that would point everyone towards the old mill, he pushed the button to send it to the players. Then he turned to Mika and said, "Can I talk to you about something?"

"I like you. A lot. As more than a friend. Man, that sounds so stupid when I say it out loud, but it's true. And I've wanted to tell you for a while, but I just didn't know how. So now I'm telling you. I like you." Parker forced his mouth to close so he couldn't babble out any more words. Why was he talking so much? And why were his palms sweating so badly? He tried to wipe them on his shorts surreptitiously.

"You do?" Mika's eyebrows raised in a look of surprise.

Parker nodded and swallowed. She didn't look pleased, but she also didn't look upset, so he didn't know where he stood yet. His nerves jangled, and he tried to quell the urge to shuffle from foot to foot.

Mika's expression turned into a look of skepticism. "Are you sure you like me? I mean, Parker, what do you actually know about me?"

"Huh?"

Mika sat down at the nearest picnic table and patted the seat beside her. "What do you know about me?" Mika insisted.

Parker sat down on the spot she'd patted. "Uh…" He thought for a moment. "You like history."

"Yeah?" she prompted. "What else?"

"I don't really know," Parker said dumbly. He thought for a moment. "Oh wait, you don't like movies!"

"That's true too. But that's partly my point, Parker. We don't have a lot in common. You know what I mean? We don't actually like a lot of the same things. You like movies and comics and superheroes and golfing. I don't like any of those things. I'm into history and books and horses."

Now it was Parker's turn to look surprised. "Wait, you like horses?"

"Yes," Mika laughed. "See what I mean? I've been riding since I was five years old. I actually have a horse of my own. We don't have a barn, so I board him at a stable. He's wildly expensive, which is why I have to work all summer long. To help pay for his food and upkeep and everything."

This new side of Mika was not what Parker had expected. "What's his name?" Parker asked.

Mika smiled at the question. "Moonlight. He has a streak of white running down his nose, and I always thought it looked like a streak of moonlight shining across the yard on a dark night. I love him so much. Not just riding him. I love taking care of him. I think I might want to be a large animal vet one day, but I don't know…" She paused and shook her head. "Maybe I want to be something completely different, like a historian. Whatever. But my point is, you don't know anything about all that because you don't really know me."

"But we don't have to like the same things to like each other."

"No," she said slowly, "but having some things in common is the basis for a relationship."

"Lots of people in relationships are total opposites. Gwen Stefani and Blake Shelton." Putting a hand under his chin, Parker racked his brain before snapping his fingers. "Courtney Cox and David Arquette!" he yelled triumphantly.

"Parker, no. It's more than just that." Mika sighed. She waved a hand, gesturing between him and herself. "Don't you feel it? There's no... spark."

"Ouch," Parker said, pantomiming a dagger to the heart. It was a joke, but Parker actually felt a tightening in his chest as he realized she was telling him she wasn't attracted to him at all.

Mika shook her head. "I don't mean to be cruel. And it's not that you aren't good looking. You totally are. But when we hang out, it just feels easy, comfortable. Admit it! It's like hanging out with a good friend."

"But aren't the best relationships based on friendship?"

"I don't know," Mika shrugged. "I guess? But they also need something more."

Parker looked down at the ground, embarrassed. He knew he shouldn't have told her. If he'd just kept his mouth shut and spent more time with her, she would have fallen for him, eventually. He was certain of it. He felt so stupid.

Mika put her hand on his shoulder. "Parker, I'm so sorry. I never meant to hurt you. If it's any consolation, I don't think it's actually me you like," Mika said gently. "I think you have some idea of me built up in your head. I think the person you like doesn't really exist. Or maybe you just haven't met her yet."

Thinking about what she said, Parker looked out across the pond. He could definitely see her point. He had decided he liked her before he really knew anything about her. And when he thought about hanging out with a girlfriend someday in the future, he'd always imagined taking her to movies. Afterward, they would laugh and argue about whether the actors were any good and if the director could have done things better. He would never have that with Mika. After hearing her lay things out so clearly, he was beginning to wonder if he'd been living in a fantasy, chasing a girl that didn't exist.

Parker stood, and Mika's hand dropped to her lap. Even if she wasn't his destiny, he'd still enjoyed hanging out with her these last few weeks. He kicked a rock with his toe. "Maybe you're right," he said. He looked up at her earnestly. "We can still be friends, though, right?"

"Of course we can," Mika assured him, smiling warmly, her brown eyes shining kindly up at him. "You can't get rid of me that easily."

Chapter 18

"This is nuts," Sunny said, shaking her head in disbelief. She didn't know how it was possible, but this party was even bigger than the last one. There were people here she didn't even recognize. Did they even go to their school? There were 131 people who had deciphered the second clue and made it to the old mill in time. They were still in the bet. Eight clues to go. But there were far more people standing on the banks of the lake. Sunny guessed there were closer to three hundred. Some were swimming, some were eating, all were in serious party mode. It was clear that it was summertime in Minnesota, and they were going to enjoy it.

Marcus Anthony ran by, arms in the air, yelling, "Parker is the GOAT!" before catapulting himself off the dock and into the pond with a splash that soaked the crowd of classmates standing on the dock. Including Victoria Dickenson. Sunny wasn't normally a vengeful person, but she found herself smiling as Victoria sputtered, glowered, and tried to wring out her soaked shirt. Marcus emerged from the water, looked back at the people on the dock, and shrugged sheepishly. "Sorry," he declared, his cheeks dimpling as he smiled his apology. Everyone would forgive him, because everyone forgave Marcus for everything. If Sunny was forced to say who was the most popular kid in their entire class, she would name Marcus. He was sort of like the sun. For their entire high school lives, everyone gravitated around him. Athletic, smart, kind, and handsome. Sunny had often drooled over his smooth brown skin, his kind smile, his killer abs. For Sunny, he didn't compare to Zeke. But that didn't stop her from admiring him from afar.

And the fact that he had declared Parker the "greatest of all time," well, Sunny knew that meant something to Parker. Sunny looked over at Parker, standing nearby the shoreline, grinning from ear to ear. It's not that Parker and Sunny were unpopular. In fact, they were well-liked by nearly everyone in their class. But they kept to themselves a lot of the time. No one gravitated around them like people gravitated around Marcus and Victoria and the other popular kids. Sunny and Parker went to the parties. They didn't throw them. But this summer was different. Parker had made it different. And for better or worse, things would never be the same.

Mika bumped her shoulder against Sunny's. "You seem kinda far away. Everything all right?"

Turning away from the water to face Mika, Sunny answered, "Yeah, I'm good. Just a lot on my mind."

"I'm here if you want to talk, you know. I know we weren't super close in school or anything, but, you know, school's over now. It's a clean slate." She laced her arm through Sunny's and drug her towards the taco truck. "We're adults now, ikwe. We can be whoever we want to be, eat as many tacos as we want, stay out as late as we want. The world is ours for the taking!"

Her excitement was infectious, and Sunny couldn't help but laugh. "Well, when you put it that way..." she said, approaching the vendor. "Two chicken tacos, please," she said, holding up two fingers. Mika ordered, and the chef handed them their plates, laden down with tacos and fixings.

They each grabbed a soda from a cooler and sat down at an empty picnic table to eat. Sunny took a bite, swallowed, and asked Mika, "You called me 'ikwe.' What does that mean?" Sunny pronounced the word as Mika had, "ick-way."

Mika smiled and explained, "It means 'woman' in Ojibwe. My mother always used to call me 'niniijaanis' growing up. It means 'my child.' When I turned eighteen in April, she started calling me 'ikwe.' I love it. It's like she finally sees me as a grown-up. I mean, I'll always be her little girl, but it feels amazing to be an adult, finally." She smiled proudly.

Sunny sighed. What Mika described sounded heavenly. "I don't think my dad will ever see me as a grown woman."

"He's pretty protective?"

"That's the understatement of the year." Sunny paused, not sure how much to share. In the end, she looked at Mika's open and trusting gaze and decided to tell her. "My mom died when I was young, in a car accident." Mika nodded, her brow furrowing sympathetically. Sunny continued, "It was really sudden, and my dad, he just got so worried about me. How I was coping with things, if I would get hurt, if he would lose me, everything. He's been like that ever since. I don't think he'll ever change. Most of the time, I don't mind...it's sweet and I understand why. But every once in a while, it would be really nice to be treated like an adult, you know? Like your mom treats you."

"Have you ever told him how you feel?"

"Oh, god, no. Are you nuts?" Sunny laughed to take the edge off of her words. The smile died on her face. "I just...I don't want to hurt him. I get why he's so protective. He's scared of losing me...like he lost my mom."

Mika nodded in understanding. "Well, you maybe don't know this about me yet, but I'm pretty much an 'honesty is the best policy' kind of person. I think there's got to be a way you can talk to him honestly without hurting him. I mean..." she hesitated and glanced over towards the pond. Sunny followed her gaze and saw that she was looking directly at Parker. "You're Parker's best friend, so you probably know this already, but he kind of told me he likes me tonight." Sunny nodded but remained silent. "And I had to be really honest with him that I'm just not feeling it. And it sucked, and I probably did hurt him a little bit. But I know he'll be just fine. I really think you have to be honest about how you feel, no matter what. If you tell your dad the truth, even if he's a little hurt, it will be better for you both in the end. But that's just my opinion. You gotta decide for yourself." With that, she finished the last bite of her taco, stood, and tossed her plate into the trash can at the end of the table.

"Maybe," Sunny said. Her tone was noncommittal. She was preoccupied, worried about Parker. He'd put all his hopes and dreams into things working out with Mika. He must be crushed. Before she left to meet Zeke, she had to check on him. She suddenly realized she sounded a little dismissive of Mika's advice, so she smiled at Mika kindly. "I appreciate your advice. I really will think about it." She stood and tossed her garbage in the trash. "Well, thanks for the chat. I better go say goodbye to Parker before I head out."

"You're not staying?"

"Nope," Sunny said. As she thought about Zeke, she felt her smile widen and bit her lip to keep it from growing too big.

Mika saw right away that Sunny was trying to play it cool. "Ooooh, spill. Where are you going?"

"I'm meeting someone."

"A special someone?"

"Maybe." Sunny paused, "I mean, yes, a special someone. I'm just not sure if he's my special someone."

Grinning wickedly, Mika gave an excited little shimmy. "Maybe not yet, but it looks like he might be soon, ikwe."

"We'll see," Sunny said, but she could no longer stop the burgeoning hope she felt growing in her chest. Ever since last night, she'd felt that wall she'd built up come crumbling down. It was too late.

There was no protecting her heart now.

Approaching the dock, Sunny glimpsed Parker hanging out at the end, legs dangling off the edge. His feet were submerged, and the water went all the way up to his shins. It had been a wet spring, so the water level was pretty good despite the abnormally hot temperature.

"Parker!" Sunny yelled, waving Parker over to her side. He glanced back at her, a wide grin crossing his face. He hopped up and brushed himself off. Saying his goodbyes to the rest of their friends on the dock, Parker loped over to where Sunny stood at the edge of the water.

"Hey, Sun, what's up?" He stopped in front of her and brushed his hair out of his eyes with a hand.

"I'm heading out, Parks. Just wanted to make sure you're okay." She gave him a sympathetic look.

Parker ducked his head, embarrassed. "You heard, huh?"

Sunny nodded.

"Mika tell you?"

Sunny nodded again. Parker breathed a sigh of relief.

"Well, I guess I'm glad you heard it from her and not from someone else from school. I was low-key worried other people would hear about it. I don't really want anyone else to find out that she basically swiped left on my heart, you know?"

Shaking her head, Sunny assured him, "Mika wouldn't tell anyone. She wouldn't do that. I think she only talked about it to me because she figured I already knew and she wanted to make sure you were okay."

"Yeah." Parker was still looking at the ground, scuffing the dirt and creating mud with his wet, bare feet. "I should be glad, I guess. I mean, now I know. Right? But somehow this is worse." He shrugged, shoving his hands into his pockets. "At least before I asked her, I had hope. Like, I could dream about her. Think about what it might be like to have a girlfriend. But now that I know, it's just done. She doesn't like me. Period."

Sunny reached up and patted Parker's arm. "That's true," she said slowly, trying to come up with the right words to comfort him. "But look at it this way. It's over. Like officially." Her tone was bright and chipper, a stark contrast to the somber words.

Parker gave her a side eye. "Um, harsh, Sun. Jeez. Twist the dagger in my heart a bit more, why don't ya?"

Giving him a playful shove, Sunny laughed and offered an explanation. "No, I mean, it's over," she repeated. She spread her arms wide. "You're free! You won't waste any more of your time on her. Listen, do you remember the movie *500 Days of Summer*?"

Parker nodded. "I hated that movie. It was depressing," he said bluntly.

"Yeah, yeah, I know. But it's like in that movie, where the main character only saw the good things about his relationship with Summer and not the times they didn't work. Maybe you are only seeing things the way you want to see them, not the way they actually are. She clearly wasn't the one for you. Maybe now that you know that, you can be open to finding someone who is right for you."

Sunny could almost see the wheels turning in Parker's head. The movie reference seemed to have clicked for him, and he brightened a little. "I guess you're right. Mika kind of said the same thing, like I just liked the idea of her and not the actual her. I don't know. It kind of makes sense, I guess."

He leaned in and gave her a quick hug. "Thanks for listening. I'll be okay. I promise."

"Of course you'll be okay," Sunny said, stepping back and smiling up at him. Parker never had been one to dwell when things didn't go his way. Even when they were younger, if he didn't get what he wanted, he didn't pout or whine. He was a lot like Zeke that way. They both sort of accepted things and moved on. Sunny had always admired that about both of them.

With a questioning look, Parker asked, "Hey, I never asked where you were going tonight. Hot date?"

"Something like that," she said cryptically, turning to head for her car.

Parker returned her grin. "'Don't do anything I would do, and definitely don't do anything I wouldn't do. There's a little gray area in there and that's where you operate,'" he quoted.

Sunny recognized the line immediately. It was one of her favorite movies. "Easy-peasy. *Spider-Man: Homecoming*," she tossed over her shoulder as she sauntered away. Parker gave her a double thumbs-up.

Now that she knew Parker was going to be all right, her nerves returned. She needed to hurry home and get ready for Zeke to pick her up.

Chapter 19

"What?" Zeke said as he glanced over at Sunny.

Sunny had been furtively sneaking glances at him since they'd gotten on the road for three reasons. One, she wasn't sure where he was taking her. Two, he was looking really good this evening in his gray v-neck t-shirt and jeans. Really good. *How do guys do that?* Sunny mused. They just throw on a regular old t-shirt and look fantastic. Meanwhile, girls had to spend hours primping and plucking and curling in order to achieve a "I just woke up this way" natural look. Sunny had stared at her closet for at least thirty minutes tonight before deciding on a short periwinkle blue skirt with delicate dark blue flowers. She'd paired it with a flowy white blouse that fell off one shoulder and dark blue ballet flats. Her goal had been to look both effortlessly casual and dressy at the same time because she didn't know where he was taking her. It wasn't fair that guys had it so easy when it came to picking out clothes. *Harrumph.* And reason number three, Sunny felt weird being alone in an enclosed space with him. She had spent so much time at his house, around him, but mostly with others, usually Parker. Parker had been a buffer between them for as long as they had known each other. It was strange to have that barrier removed. She found herself feeling nervous and jittery but also kind of exhilarated and alive.

Sunny hadn't thought Zeke had noticed all of her sidelong glances. Apparently, she wasn't as sneaky as she thought. Hmmm, maybe she should rethink her possible career option of international spy.

"Nothing," Sunny said quickly and turned her face towards the window to stare at the fields passing by.

"Then why do you keep looking at me?"

"I'm not!" Sunny insisted.

"You are."

Sunny decided right there that she was going to die on this hill. He could not think that she was sitting here ogling him. She turned to face him again, defiantly. "I'm not," she said through clenched teeth, making a cross-her-heart motion with her hand.

The words burst out of Zeke. "I'm not blind!" he practically shouted, then stopped himself and took a deep breath. "Okay. Fine. You weren't looking at me. But then why is it so god-damned uncomfortable in here?"

Sunny admitted guilt without admitting a thing. "It's just weird. You and I... we don't really hang out alone. Parker is usually there. I can't even remember the last time you and I actually went somewhere together without Parker."

"I remember," he admitted quietly.

Sunny cocked her head to the side in curiosity. "You do? When was it?"

"It was right before I left for college." Zeke cleared his throat and adjusted his hands on the steering wheel. He hesitated, and she got the sense that he was reluctant to speak.

"Where?" Sunny prompted.

Zeke's eyes flashed to her quickly before returning to the road, and he continued. "I stopped home to grab something from my bedroom before I went out. I don't remember what it was even, but I know I was late to meet Eddie, and I was running upstairs. You were running downstairs, and we crashed into each other. It was warm outside, and you were wearing that worn-out 'Save the Earth' tank top you got a few years earlier at summer camp. Remember?"

"I do remember that," Sunny gasped in surprise. "I had a bruise on my shin for a week from where your knee hit me! And my elbow still gets sore every once in a while from hitting the wall." She rubbed her elbow in remembrance of the pain while she paused, thinking about what he'd said. She turned in her seat to face him more fully, as much as her seatbelt would allow. "You got me some ice and drove me home so I didn't have to walk. And then you made me hot chocolate to make me feel better. But that doesn't count. We didn't really go anywhere. And it wasn't really like this. That wasn't us hanging out. It was just a moment."

Zeke's eyes drifted over to meet Sunny's for a second before returning to the road again. He ran a hand through his hair and let loose a sigh that sounded wistful to her ears. "Life is just a collection of moments."

"That's poetic," Sunny said with a smile. Zeke didn't reply.

Sunny mulled his comments over as he signaled and turned off the main road to a narrow gravel road. It was not well-kept. There were dips, holes, and ruts that made the old truck bounce and groan. Zeke recalled that moment so vividly, and she hadn't even really thought about it at all. Did it mean something, the fact that he'd remembered it? Or did he just have an exceptional memory?

The truck hit a deep dip, and Sunny bounced uncomfortably in the seat. As she heard the rocks hit the undercarriage of the truck with constant little pinging noises, she wondered aloud, "Aren't you worried about the rocks wrecking your truck?"

Zeke shrugged. "Nah," he said, and patted the dashboard affectionately. He smiled at her. "This truck was my grandpa's. He always told me that life was made to be lived, enjoyed. I think the old guy would get some satisfaction up in heaven if he knew I was out on some gravel road with a beautiful girl, taking her to see something I loved. He'd be proud. He wouldn't mind the rocks one bit."

Sunny's stomach dipped, and it wasn't because of the bumps in the road. He'd called her beautiful, and she couldn't help but smile at both that and at hearing the memory of his grandpa Jake. She had only met the elderly man once before he passed away, and he'd seemed so kind and jovial. His weathered hands were warm as they clasped hers. His eyes sparkled, demonstrating he was sharp as a tack despite his advanced age, and she remembered thinking that Zeke and Parker both had his blue eyes. "I met your grandpa when Parker and I went to his ninetieth birthday party. He was really nice to me," Sunny chuckled as she remembered how embarrassed she'd been when he asked her when Parker was going to marry her. "He thought Parker and I were dating, and he told him to marry me before he lost me to someone else." She tossed her hair over her shoulder with a fake air of haughtiness, and continued jokingly, "So clearly your grandpa had good taste."

Zeke laughed and answered easily, "He certainly did," as he stopped the car. Apparently, they were at their destination. Sunny looked around but she couldn't see anything at all out of the ordinary. Zeke had parked right on the grass, under a small copse of trees. There were rolling hills speckled with groups of trees as far as the eye could see, and, in fact, she couldn't see any houses from here. He turned off the truck, unbuckled his seat belt, and turned towards her. "All roads end here, as my grandpa used to say."

"You're very profound today."

Zeke nodded with a smile. "I'm always profound. You just never noticed me before," he said quietly.

Does he really think I didn't notice him? Sunny pondered Zeke's comment as she unbuckled her seat belt.

Sunny swallowed and turned to face him. She'd promised herself she would be brave tonight. "I think you already know that's not exactly true. I noticed you, Zeke."

"I'm realizing that," he replied, cocking his head to the side and giving her a half-smile.

A nervous flutter bloomed in Sunny's belly. Her bravery wavered. She looked away. "So you brought me here to talk...where is here exactly?"

Zeke glanced out the windshield at the field in front of them. "Well, that's a bit of a story. Mind if we step outside? I brought some supplies. I know you already ate, but I thought we could have a little dessert."

Sunny felt her heart melt at his thoughtfulness. It was sweet that he had planned a dessert for her. But when he opened up the back of the truck, she saw he'd thought of so much more. He had a stack of fuzzy plaid blankets, a picnic basket, a cooler, a lantern, and even an electronic mosquito repellent device and some citronella candles. Mosquitoes were thick in Minnesota in the summer. The little bloodsuckers usually came out just after dusk. She was glad he'd thought of bringing something to protect them or they would have never survived being outside after dark.

Zeke spread out the soft blankets, and they unloaded the truck together in companionable silence. Sunny sat down and tried to peek inside the picnic basket, but Zeke plunked down next to her and slapped her hand away playfully.

"Ah, ah, ah," he said.

"What is it?" Sunny wasn't starving yet, just curious about what Zeke had packed for them.

"Are you hungry yet?"

"Well, not yet."

"Then you can wait! Good things come to those who wait."

They both gazed out towards the fields in front of them.

"So..." Sunny said awkwardly.

"So," echoed Zeke.

She looked out at the golden sun, low in the sky, then back at Zeke. "You were going to tell me where we are?"

"Oh, yeah. That." Zeke smiled. "This was my grandpa's land. As far as the eye can see. A long time ago, he bought up tons of property around the town. Not just this one, but all over. My dad said that any time a property would go up for sale," Zeke snapped his fingers, "Grandpa would snatch it up. I don't even know why. For the investment, maybe? But this spot..." he patted the ground beside him. "This spot was special."

Zeke stood and walked over to the trees, growing more animated as he spoke. "My mom and dad used to bring Parker and me out here. It seems like forever ago. Mom would walk around and..." Zeke turned back to Sunny, a wide grin stretching across his face. "See, it was always her dream to build a house here, out in the country. She never enjoyed living in that big house in town. She said she wanted to live where you couldn't hear anything but the rustle of the leaves through the trees."

"She would come out here and walk off the feet of the house. It was supposed to be small, simple, with a giant porch. She would walk off the length of a room, like fifteen feet or so, and then plop Parker down, telling him that was his bedroom. Then she would walk a little more and yell to me to come stand in my bedroom. Every time we came out here, the layout was a little different. She kept tweaking it, making improvements. And my dad would laugh and jot notes down on his notepad, telling her he would give the architect the updates. I don't know if he ever did. I never saw any floor plans myself. But she was so happy planning for her house in the country."

Zeke paused, his voice laced with emotion. "Then she got sick. And the planning stopped. And then she got really sick, and we knew it was the end..." Zeke trailed off.

Sunny rose and placed her hand on Zeke's arm, comforting him. She remained silent. "We came out here. At the end. They stopped the treatment, and she actually felt pretty good for a little while. So Marta packed us a lunch, and we headed out here, all four of us. We talked about everything that day, Sunny. Her life, how proud she was of me and Parker, old stories about when we were babies, everything. And we laughed. We laughed so hard our stomachs hurt. It was one of the best days of my entire life."

As much as she knew it was wrong, Sunny couldn't help but feel a little jealous. Zeke had this amazing memory of his last genuine conversation with his mom. Sunny had been robbed of all of that. One day, her mom was there. The next, she was gone. No goodbye. No words of wisdom for Sunny. Just nothing. Immediately, Sunny felt sick to her stomach over her envy. It was horrible to lose a mother, no matter how they die. To watch the person you loved fade away, it had to be torture. They had all suffered. There was no point in feeling jealous. It all sucked.

Shaking off her guilt, she said, "I would have loved to have met her."

Zeke smiled, "She would have loved you. I guess that's why I brought you out here. I come out here sometimes when I need to remember her. It reminds me of the good times. And it seemed like a good place to talk."

Sunny nodded, understanding.

"Should we get some of that dessert?" Zeke said, gesturing to the picnic basket.

"Yes," Sunny said, exhaling to clear out all the emotions that swamped her as she thought about their mothers. "Definitely."

"Oh, my," Sunny sighed, flopping backwards to lie on the blanket. "That was heavenly." An empty bowl sat beside her, and Zeke had one to match.

Zeke smiled. "I knew you'd like it!"

"How did you know? I don't think we've ever talked about banana splits before."

"I know that, but I know you love ice cream. I know you love bananas. And I know you love chocolate." He ticked each of them off on his fingers. "So I figured, how could I go wrong?"

She looked over at him and cocked an eyebrow skeptically. "Did you pack all this stuff? Or did Marta?" She gestured to the empty dishes, the three tubs of ice cream, vanilla, chocolate, and strawberry, now nearly empty. He'd packed the traditional banana split topping flavors of pineapple, strawberries, and chocolate syrup. He'd even remembered the whipped cream and maraschino cherries. Sunny was impressed. And seriously stuffed.

Zeke gave her a mock wounded look. "I'm hurt, Addison. Hurt," he continued dramatically. "I packed all of this myself."

"Well, I'm sorry I doubted you. It was wonderful. Thank you," she said, sitting up again. Zeke tossed the dishes and toppings back into the picnic basket, while Sunny loaded what was left of the ice cream back into the cooler.

"You are welcome," Zeke answered, beaming. He looked proud, and Sunny found herself smiling in return.

Neither spoke for a moment. Sunny wondered what Zeke was thinking. She'd always found him so hard to read. Unlike Parker. With Parker, when a thought entered his head, she pretty much heard about it right away. But with Zeke, everything was so closed up. She felt like she never really knew what was going on inside.

The sun was red on the edge of the horizon. Zeke turned on the mosquito device. As he produced a lighter from his pocket and started lighting the citronella candles, he said hesitantly, "Okay, so I think we've avoided the topic long enough. Do you want to talk about what happened last night?"

Images filled Sunny's mind. Zeke's face, the intensity as he leaned in to kiss her. Her legs wrapped around his waist. Her fingers running down his chest. Her cheeks flooded with heat, and she knew immediately she was blushing. Zeke's eyes darkened as though he could read her thoughts.

Annoyed at her own embarrassment, Sunny stuck out her chin defiantly. There had been two people kissing in that kitchen, after all. "Sure. You go first."

Zeke nodded. He turned to stare out at the setting sun and thought for a minute. Sunny was anxious to hear what he would say. Would he tell her it was a mistake? That he liked her? *What are you thinking?* she wondered. Those words were about to burst forth from her lips when he finally spoke.

"You know how sometimes your foot will fall asleep. And before that, you didn't even realize your foot was there. It just always was. And then it falls asleep, and suddenly you move it, and it's awake again, and you can feel every tingling part of it, and it's all you can think about."

Zeke angled his face towards Sunny. "You're like that for me. You were always there, a part of the family. And then something changed, and I can't...you're all I can think about."

Sunny resisted the urge to giggle at the absurdity of Zeke's metaphor. He was pouring his heart out to her, but all she could think of was that he'd just compared her to a foot. *Don't say it, don't say it,* she thought. Her brain lost the battle, and the words popped out of her mouth. "Sooo, I'm a foot in this scenario..." Sunny trailed off, already regretting her words.

"Yes. No. I mean, you're not a foot. You're *my* foot. You know what I mean."

"I think I might," she answered.

"You're a part of me, Addison. And I'm a part of you. Whether you want to admit it or not, you know it's true."

Sunny's heart sang at his words. Her skin, her hair, her entire body felt lighter than air. It's what she'd always longed to hear, but never thought she would. Nothing felt real for a moment. It was almost too much, this realization that he liked her, that he felt like she was a part of him. She felt giddy and off-kilter. Overwhelmed, a giggle bubbled up in her throat and burst out. "Did you just rhyme?"

Throwing up his hands, Zeke's expression turned furious. He practically growled, "Argh! Fine. Make jokes if you want to, but you're just too scared to admit that you have feelings for me too. I know it."

At his frustration, Sunny tamped down the nervous giggles still trapped in her throat. She swallowed, knowing that her next words would be important. It was time for complete honesty. She needed to be brave enough to lay her feelings bare to Zeke. He deserved that after all he'd done for her.

She took his hand. He looked surprised at the gesture. And she didn't blame him. She'd given him little reason to think she was going to take this seriously.

Sunny began, "You're right, I'm sorry. I'm just a little surprised. I never expected..." she paused, trailing off and reframing her thoughts. She took a breath. "Zeke, you're the first thing I think about when I wake up in the morning and the last thing I think about before I fall asleep. When I'm not with you, I wish I was. I have loved you for so long, I don't even know how to do anything else. You don't just have a part of me. I am one hundred percent, completely, utterly yours."

"Thank god," Zeke breathed as he leaned in, buried his hands in her hair, and kissed her.

Chapter 20

Oh no. Oh no, oh no, oh no. What had she done?

Sunny lay nestled in a cocoon of blankets and man arms, stretched out in the grass beside Zeke's pickup truck. It was morning, and her dad was going to kill her.

The sun was beating down on them, and there were blankets everywhere. Everything felt damp with morning dew. Sunny tried to untangle herself from Zeke's arms without awakening him. That was all she needed, for him to wake up. She couldn't deal with figuring out what to say to him yet. Sunny covered her face with her hands as she thought back to the things she'd confessed last night. The days of acting cold and indifferent were clearly over. And miraculously, somehow he returned her feelings. But that didn't stop her from feeling shy in the harsh light of day.

However, underneath her layer of embarrassment, Sunny was unbelievably happy. They had kissed and talked long into the night, and she replayed parts of their conversation over in her head. She bit her lip, smiling to herself. She wanted to lie back in his arms, snuggle in, and relish this feeling. But she knew her dad was probably panicked right now, so she sat up and reached for her phone instead.

As she lifted the phone, the screen lit up. Twenty-four missed texts and eleven missed calls.

Oh, she was in serious trouble.

Five texts were from Parker. The remaining texts and calls were from her dad. Yikes. When her dad had given her the cell phone at age fifteen, they had made a pact. Sunny agreed she would always answer when he called or texted. No matter what. This was the first time she had broken the pact. Biting her lip, she read Parker's texts first, not ready to face her dad's wrath yet.

Parker: *Hey, u home yet*

Parker: *U asleep? HMU in AM*

Parker: *Ur dad just called my dad Where are u?*

Parker: *Ok, now am worried. Text me back NOW*

Parker: *R u with zeke??? Hes not home either. CALL ME!!! Ur dad calling cops??!!*

Sunny's pulse began to pound. She quickly flipped to her dad's text thread and scrolled up to read all his texts. They were not as pleasant as Parker's. Sunny was in big trouble. She needed to get home quickly.

"Zeke," Sunny said, nudging him with her elbow. His face looked so peaceful as he slept, and she couldn't help feel guilty about having to wake him up. He moaned and threw an arm over his face. "Zeke, I gotta go. Wake up. You need to drive me home."

Zeke's arm stayed over his face, but his free hand patted the blankets until he found her arm. When he did, he latched on and tugged her back down to his chest. She resisted at first and then gave in to the delicious feeling of being cradled against him. "Just a little longer," he whispered, wrapping his arm around her and rubbing his hand up and down her back, creating a path of warmth in its wake.

Despite the fact that it felt absolutely amazing, it was too late for Sunny to relax. The real world had already crept into their little bubble, and there was currently a pit of dread the size of Texas growing in her stomach. She needed to get home fast before it got any worse.

Using every ounce of her mental fortitude, Sunny pushed away from his arms and forced his arm off his face. "I think my dad has the police out looking for me," she said in a panicky voice.

He groaned like he was in pain and sat up. "Okay. Shit," he said, running a hand over his face and through his hair. Despite Sunny's current freak-out, she couldn't help but notice how handsome he looked in the morning, all rumpled from sleep. His brown hair was messy and sticking up in every direction, but in an endearing way. She stared at his chiseled jawline and full lips. Those lips that reminded Sunny of a night full of kissing. She felt a blush creep up her cheeks, but luckily, Zeke didn't seem to notice.

He looked at Sunny with a serious expression, his deep blue eyes laser-focused on hers. "You better call him now. I don't know if he has the police out looking for us."

The gravity of their situation hit Sunny all at once. She felt her throat close up, and she had to force her words out. "Parker asked if you were with me, so they must know you're not home either. They could be looking for your truck. Check your phone."

"I don't have mine," Zeke answered, rising to his feet and folding up the blankets that surrounded them. "I forgot it at home yesterday, and I didn't bother going back for it because I didn't want to be late to pick you up. You better call your dad now."

Sunny hesitated, tapping her phone against her palm. "Can't I just text him instead?" Sunny asked hopefully, simultaneously knowing that was just the chicken's way out.

Zeke was all business, having snapped into his natural responsible mode. He motioned for her to get up so he could fold the blanket she was still sitting on. Sunny scrambled out of his way as Zeke answered, "No way. He'll just be more upset if you do that. Call him. Tell him it's my fault that I kept you out too late. Apologize. Tell him I'm bringing you home now. We'll see him in fifteen minutes."

Sunny's heart leapt at his words. "Wait, we?"

"Well, I'm not gonna make you face him alone. What kind of monster do you think I am?" He tossed a blanket in the back of the truck and walked over to Sunny. He grinned, brushing a strand of hair out of her eyes tenderly and pulling her towards him to plant a soft kiss on her forehead. "Besides, as soon as he sees me, he won't be so mad at you anymore. He'll be mad at me instead. Trust me. It'll be okay."

Sunny frowned, but she didn't argue as she unlocked her phone to call her dad. The way Zeke was trying to take responsibility for her mistake didn't exactly sit well with her. It was sweet, but she could take care of herself.

The phone only rang once before her dad answered.

"Thank god. Sunny?" Her dad's voice sounded exhausted and panicked.

"I'm okay, Dad. I'm so sorry. I fell asleep. My phone was on silent. I never saw your texts or calls."

"Thank god," he said again. "Where are you? Where have you been? I've been up all night worried about you!"

"I'm fine, Dad. We just fell asleep. We'll be home in fifteen minutes. I'm so sorry." Sunny cringed as she waited for his next tirade.

"We? Are you with Zeke? I called Alan, and you weren't with Parker, and Zeke wasn't home. Parker texted a bunch of your friends. No one had any idea where you were. I've been so worried about you. I called the hospital. I thought..." his voice cracked and faded away. Sunny felt her heart clench as she understood exactly how worried her dad had been. She knew he'd been remembering the call he'd gotten about her mom's car accident. She felt awful for putting him through all of that pain and fear.

Sunny took a deep breath. "Yes, I'm with Zeke." Sunny heard her dad's sharp intake of breath when she said Zeke's name, so she continued quickly. "We weren't drinking, and we didn't do anything wrong. I promise. We were talking, and we both just fell asleep. It was an accident."

"Addison Rose Montgomery. I raised you to be more responsible than this. There are people that were worried about both of you." Her father's disapproval seeped into every single word. Now that he knew she was safe, it was clear that his fear was being replaced with anger. And Sunny knew she deserved it. She'd never stayed out past midnight without calling her dad before, so he was right to have been so concerned.

Zeke was still loading up the back of the pickup nearby, so Sunny lowered her voice.

"I know. I'm sorry. I made a mistake. One mistake. Please don't make this a big deal."

She turned around and saw Zeke had finished. He leaned against the truck, waiting patiently for her. She gave him a weak smile and held up her pointer finger to let him know she just needed one more minute. He straightened up and slid into the truck, starting it up with a roar.

"Don't you tell me that this isn't a big deal, young lady. You left me here all night, thinking that maybe you were…" his voice caught, and he broke off. "You don't understand what it's like to sit here, worried that I might never see you again. And what's that noise?"

"That noise is the truck. We're heading home. We can talk more when I get there."

"You bet we will." His voice held a threat, although Sunny thought she still heard a hint of relief in his voice.

"Bye, Dad," Sunny said quickly. She hung up the phone before he could say anything else, feeling sick inside. He was right. She had been irresponsible. She felt the guilt weighing on her shoulders.

Heading over to the truck, Sunny slid in quietly. Zeke reached over and squeezed her hand encouragingly. "Your dad will forgive you." Sunny nodded, not so sure.

On the drive back, Sunny and Zeke were silent. She texted Parker quickly to let him know she was okay, she was with Zeke, and she would call him later. She asked Zeke if he wanted to use her phone to call his dad, but he just shook his head. Sunny couldn't speak as she mulled over all the ways she could try to explain to her dad what had happened last night. But no amount of explanations could take away what she had put him through. And once he saw Zeke, she didn't know how he was going to react.

"You know, I don't think you should stay. Just drop me off and drive away. It'll be easier that way," Sunny said.

Zeke shook his head immediately, a frown evident on his face. "No way. This is my fault."

Sunny shook her head right back at him. "No, it's not. It's no one's fault. We just fell asleep. It was an accident. And I actually think it might be worse if you are there," Sunny argued.

Zeke snorted in derision and muttered something under his breath that Sunny couldn't make out.

"What did you say?"

"Nothing. It's nothing. Just forget it. I'm going with you, and that's that."

"That's that? Oh, you get to decide for me how I'll handle my dad?" Sunny's voice was rising in volume. "No. It was my choice to go with you last night. I knew I was falling asleep as we were talking, and I just didn't want to leave. So I made a choice not to ask you to take me home. It was my mistake. This is MY life. You don't get to protect me like you protect Parker! I'm not your responsibility!"

Zeke pulled the truck over to the side of the road with a spray of gravel. The motion was so quick that Sunny clung to the door.

"Are you nuts?" she shouted.

Zeke faced Sunny squarely, a murderous expression on his face. When he spoke, his voice was low and calm.

"Let me be perfectly clear with you, Addison. I am well aware that you are not my responsibility. You've spent the last few years making it perfectly clear that you do not need me in any way, shape, or form. I'm not trying to protect you. I'm trying to do the right thing here. I'm trying to be a good person. I'm trying to be the kind of guy that your dad would let you date."

Sunny's anger drained away at his words. He wanted to date her. Though they'd spent all of last night talking, they'd never once spoken about the future and what came next for the two of them. She took a deep breath, choosing her words carefully. "My dad doesn't decide who I date, Zeke. I decide. And we're dating, whether you like it or not." Sunny smiled boldly, taking Zeke's hand.

Zeke squeezed her hand. "Oh, is that so?" he said, a cocky grin alighting on his face.

"It is." Sunny reached over and planted a kiss on Zeke's lips, marveling at the fact that she could kiss him any time she wanted to. "Zeke, you don't have to try to impress my dad. You don't have to be anyone other than who you are."

When Zeke's truck rolled up to the curb at Sunny's house, her dad practically flew out of the house and down the sidewalk to greet them. His arms wrapped around Sunny as soon as she'd gotten out of the vehicle, squeezing around her like a vise.

"I'm really sorry, Dad." Sunny returned his hug before pulling back and looking up at him. "It was an accident. It won't happen again. I promise."

"I was worried sick. I've never felt so scared. You don't know what I..." he trailed off. Tears filled her dad's eyes, but he didn't let them fall.

She shook her head, her own eyes welling up with tears to match his. "I do know. I know how worried you were, and I really am sorry. I don't know what else I can say."

Zeke got out of the truck and came around the front to stand next to Sunny.

"I'm sorry too, sir," he said, addressing Sunny's dad. "I should have been more responsible last night."

Sunny gave him a side-eye.

He cleared his throat. "We both should have been," he correct himself. Sunny felt a warmth spread over her at his words. She understood why he wanted to take responsibility for his own mistake, but she appreciated that he finally understood that she didn't want him to take responsibility for hers. Her choices were her own, and the consequences were hers to deal with.

Mr. Montgomery looked from Sunny to Zeke and back again. "Thank you for apologizing, but I'm still disappointed in you both. It'll take some time to rebuild our trust here. Sunny, you and I need to have a talk. Zeke, it's best you head home. Your dad will want to speak with you. He was just as worried as I was last night when we couldn't reach either of you. I called him after I got off the phone with Sunny, and he's expecting you home right now."

Sunny's eyes flew to Zeke's, panicked. Her three-prong plan. They hadn't even had a chance to finish it, and it was already ruined. After keeping both of their parents up all night worried about them, there's no way Mr. Crawford was going to change his mind about sending Zeke to London next week. He was certain to blame Zeke for all of this. And Sunny couldn't lose Zeke now. Not after waiting so long and finally finding out that he had feelings for her.

Zeke nodded and turned away. His shoulders drooped a little, realizing, as Sunny had, that hope was probably gone.

Sunny's heart began to pound. She couldn't let this happen. Even though this was the worst possible time to ask for her dad's help, she knew he was her only hope, her only chance of changing Mr. Crawford's mind.

Reaching for Zeke's hand, Sunny stopped him from leaving. He turned back, surprised. Sunny turned and addressed her dad, "Dad, I know this is bad timing, but can Zeke and I come in and talk to you about something? We need your help."

Her dad, who had always been there for Sunny, answered just as she hoped he would. He looked back and forth between the two of them, worried and confused. "Of course. You know I'm always here for you. Let's go inside."

After Sunny explained Zeke's situation to her dad, she told him about her three-pronged plan and how she intended to convince Mr. Crawford to let Zeke stay. She gave Zeke a pointed glance at one point, hoping he would take the hint and tell her dad that he wasn't actually driving the car, that Parker was the one who crashed. But his lips pressed into a firm line and he gave a nearly imperceptible shake of his head. She frowned and continued talking, keeping Zeke's secret despite her wish to be fully honest with her dad.

After she finished her story, Mr. Montgomery sighed and rubbed a hand across his short beard. Was it Sunny's imagination or was it slightly more gray than it had been yesterday? He looked from Sunny to Zeke and back to Sunny again. "You've put a lot of thought into this plan of yours."

It wasn't a question, but Sunny answered anyway. "Yes," she said emphatically.

Zeke finally opened his mouth. "I know what I did was irresponsible, Mr. Montgomery. The drunk driving," his mouth twisted over the words, forcing out the lie, "and staying out last night without calling. I'm willing to work to rebuild your trust. I know I need to rebuild my dad's trust too. But I can't do that from London. Sending me away won't solve anything. I need to be here. With my family. With the people that I care about." He looked over at Sunny as he said the words. She felt her face heat under his gaze and her whole body felt a warm glow, despite being in trouble.

Nodding, Mr. Montgomery's face cleared. Sunny recognized it as the signal that he had made a decision. He slapped his hands against his knees and stood. "Well, that makes a lot of sense, Zeke. In my opinion, problems never get solved by dividing a family. You gotta stick it out and push through the hard times together. I'll talk to your dad. I can't promise anything. He's a stubborn guy. But I'll talk to him." He held out his hand.

Zeke stood and shook it, letting out a relieved, "Thank you, sir."

"Now if you'll excuse us," Mr. Montgomery said, gesturing towards the front door, "I need to talk with my daughter alone."

All three of them headed for the door. Sunny gave Zeke an awkward wave goodbye, which he returned before loping down the sidewalk towards his truck.

After the door closed, Sunny's dad stopped her with a hand on her arm. "This is important to you, isn't it, Sunny? Zeke is important to you?"

"Yes," she breathed, praying that he wouldn't change his mind about helping them. If he didn't want them to be together, would he want Zeke to leave? She hoped not.

"I know it's none of my business. I know you're an adult, but... are you two... dating, or whatever kids call it these days?"

"We are." She swallowed. Having never talked to her dad about boyfriends before, this was unfamiliar territory for them both. Her dad looked as uncomfortable as she felt.

He paused, choosing his words carefully. "You know you are going to have to say goodbye eventually, don't you? Even if I can get Alan to change his plans for Zeke, you're leaving for MIT in just a few months. The goodbye is coming. And goodbyes...well, they're hard. Really hard." His voice grew thick with emotion. "I don't want you to get hurt."

His words sank like rocks deep into Sunny's chest. She knew he was right. She was going to have to say goodbye to Zeke at some point. But she didn't want to. Not when they were so close to... something. She wasn't sure what yet. But she wanted time to figure it out. She'd spent so much time being afraid of Zeke hurting her. She finally felt like she'd had the courage to take a risk, and it had paid off. Zeke liked her. And she wasn't ready to give that up yet. Besides, her dad was worrying about something that hadn't even happened yet.

"Dad, I haven't even gotten in to MIT yet."

Crooking a finger, he motioned for her to follow him into the kitchen. There, on the counter, lay a thin white envelope with the distinctive MIT logo on the left side. The letter was addressed to

Addison Montgomery. Her heart lurched. Whether it was in fear or excitement, she couldn't tell. Perhaps it was both.

A complete change had overcome her father by the time they got to the kitchen. Gone was the sadness from before. He practically bounced with excitement as she picked up the envelope. He grabbed his cell phone off of the counter and fumbled to open up the camera app to take a video. As he began recording, she took a deep breath and slid her finger under the seal, hearing the satisfying rip as it tore open. Taking out the letter, she read aloud, her brain barely processing the words, "Dear Addison, on behalf of the Admissions Committee, it is my pleasure to offer you admission to the MIT class of 2023."

She froze, her gaze flying up to meet her father's eyes. They were bright and filled with joyful tears. Her own eyes were filled with shock, wide and uncertain.

"Your mother would be so proud of you! I knew you could do it!" he whooped, picking her up and swinging her in a circle, just like he used to do when she was a little girl.

She couldn't help but let out a laugh as he spun her around once more before setting her back down on the ground and finally turning off the video that he'd forgotten he was taking. He swiped at his eyes. "I'm so proud of you," he said, smiling down at her. "You did it. I knew you would get in."

"Thanks, Dad," she answered numbly.

Her father had finally noticed her lack of enthusiasm. "You don't seem too excited," he said, a question in his voice and a concerned look on his face.

She fumbled to give him a reason why she wasn't jumping for joy. She wasn't even sure she could explain it herself. This was what she'd been waiting for, wasn't it?

"I'm just...shocked. I never thought it would actually happen."

Her dad nodded. "It will sink in soon. Listen, do you want some breakfast and we can talk about what classes you want to take this fall?" He looked eager, like a young child about to go to a carnival.

She hated disappointing him, but she shook her head. Her heart just wasn't in it yet. Even though she'd just gotten into her dream school, her mind was filled with worry that Zeke was in trouble. "I'm not really hungry, Dad. I think I just need to get some sleep."

He nodded in understanding. "Me too, me too. I'm exhausted. Let's get some rest, and I'll make us lunch later. Then we can start talking about classes and making your packing list for your dorm room, okay?" He rubbed his hands together in anticipation.

She nodded absently. "Dad, you'll still talk to Mr. Crawford, right? Today?"

He patted her arm. "Of course, honey. I'll call him after I wake up. I know it's important to you."

She couldn't read his expression. She was dying to ask what he thought about her and Zeke dating, but she was afraid she wouldn't like the answer. So instead, she asked, "Will you try, like really try to convince him to let Zeke stay? No matter how much he argues with you?"

Her father knew what she meant. He was well familiar with Mr. Crawford's penchant for arguing, being a lawyer. Smiling sadly at Sunny, her dad nodded again. "You know I will."

And she realized he was right. She had known it all along. If there was one constant in her life, it was her father. She gave him another hug as she realized how lucky she was to have him. "I love you, Dad," she said. She reached for him.

As he returned her hug, he answered, "I love you too, Addison Rose." He paused, pulling back from the hug to look down at her with a warm, but stern look. "You know we aren't done talking about last night, though, right?"

Sunny rolled her eyes and smiled. "I know, Dad."

Chapter 21

"**I** knew you'd get in!" Parker declared triumphantly. Sunny had texted him after her dad had gone upstairs to nap, and he came over right away. Her dad hadn't technically grounded her or given her any kind of punishment yet. She wasn't sure if he would even try. After all, she was an adult. And he was so happy about MIT that it overshadowed everything that had happened last night. She knew they would still have to talk about it, but for now, she was grateful for the temporary reprieve.

Before texting Parker, Sunny had texted Zeke to see if he was okay, but he replied that he would call her later. She'd questioned Parker about it as soon as he arrived.

He just shrugged and said, "I dunno. They've been hermetically sealed up in Dad's office for the last hour. I listened at the door for a minute, but I couldn't hear anything."

Sunny felt her stomach tighten, wondering what they were discussing in his office, hoping that Zeke's dad wasn't too mad. Zeke was an adult, after all. He was even older than her. His dad couldn't be too upset, right?

She had quickly updated Parker about MIT, and he'd been as thrilled for her as she should have been for herself. While he was busy celebrating, Sunny's mind spun.

"I don't understand," Sunny said, looking at Parker with a frown. "I never told them about the app. How did I get off the waiting list?"

Parker shrugged, avoiding her eyes. "Maybe a spot just opened up..." his voice trailed off. He grew quiet.

His demeanor threw up a red flag for Sunny. Parker was rarely quiet. "Parker," she said, a warning in her voice. "What did you do?"

This time, he met her eyes with a pleading look. "Don't get mad, okay?" She folded her arms across her chest. "I might have pretended to be you and written to the Admissions office to tell them all about the app and ask them to reconsider your application."

"Parker!" Sunny barked as she glowered at him. "You had no right to do that!"

"I know, I know. I just knew that the app was going to be awesome, and you were amazing. And I knew how much this meant to you. I figured if you weren't going to brag about yourself, I'd do it for you."

"What did you say in the letter, Parker?"

"Does it really matter, Sun? It worked."

She let out a groan that nearly turned into a growl.

"Okay," he said, putting his hands out defensively. "I'll email it to you so you can read it. But I swear it was all good. I just talked about how great the app was going to be, how you had plans to build more apps, and how MIT was so important to you because of your parents. I even had my dad's assistant proofread it, so I promise it was good."

Sunny paused, "How great the app was going to be?" She repeated his words back to him, confused. "Parker, when did you write the letter?"

"Remember that week you were holed up in your room building it? I wrote it back then."

The outrage Sunny felt grew stronger. She felt heat rise to her face and didn't even attempt to keep her anger in check. "Before it was even done? What if I hadn't been able to get it to work? Or what if it was terrible? It wasn't even ready yet!"

Parker laughed off her questions. "Sunny, you've got to have more faith in yourself. I knew it was going to be great. You've never failed at anything in your life."

"You had no right, Parker. This isn't your life. It's mine. This was a major overstep."

Parker looked confused. "But it turned out okay. You got in!"

He was right. It had all worked out, so why was she so upset? Sure, he shouldn't have pretended to be her. But she got in. She should be happy, shouldn't she? So why did her heart feel like it was being squeezed in a vise?

Sunny's anger melted away, and she sank down on to the bed like a deflated balloon.

"Sunny?" Parker said, concern in his voice as he bounded over to her and sat next to her on the bed. He put his arm around her as she remained silent. "Are you okay?"

Tears dripped down her cheeks, splashing onto her hands, which were folded on her lap. She hadn't even realized she was crying.

"Shit," Parker exclaimed, noticing her tears. "Don't cry. I'm really sorry. I promise I won't do it again. And I'll make it up to you. I'll even let you win at Mario Kart."

Sunny laughed through her tears. "I can whip you at Mario Kart without any help, thank you very much." She swiped at her eyes. "It's not you. I don't know what it is. Maybe I'm just tired and overwhelmed. So much has happened today."

"Wanna talk about it?"

She shook her head. "I think I just need to rest. Can I come over later? And you can tell me all about the rest of the party last night."

Parker smiled. "For sure. It was epic. Remind me to tell you about how Rooster was completely tanked and yeeted himself off the roof of the old mill. Classic." He shook his head, laughing.

"He threw himself off the roof? Is he okay?" Sunny asked, alarmed. Rooster, whose real name was Donald Johnson, was the rowdiest of their classmates, always pushing the limits and getting into trouble.

Of course, he'd been on the roof of a dilapidated old building. Typical.

"Totally fine," Parker answered. "He landed in the water. But it was still super high up. I have no idea how he didn't hurt himself. 'God has a special providence for fools.'"

Shaking her head in laughter, Sunny admitted, "I have no clue what movie that quote is from."

"Not from a movie," Parker said. "I actually have no idea who said it. I just heard it once, and it stuck with me. Seems appropriate for Rooster. He literally does the craziest stuff and never gets hurt."

Sunny chuckled and rose from the bed, turning back towards Parker. "Thanks for making me laugh."

Parker stood and gave a little curtsy. "Happy to oblige," he said and headed for the door.

"Oh, and Parker?"

"Yeah?"

"You ever pretend to be me again, and I'll make you eat pistachio ice cream every night for a month."

Parker gulped, turning slightly green. "Noted."

As Sunny drifted off to sleep, she was vaguely aware of her phone buzzing, but her head felt too heavy to lift. She slept fitfully and dreamt of her mother. They were seated at a table in a small cafe, just like the kind they used to frequent for family breakfasts on Sunday mornings when she was a child. A greasy spoon, her dad used to call it, but Sunny had been too young to know what that meant.

Seated across from her, Sunny's mother looked as though she'd been frozen in time. She wore a yellow and white flowered sundress that Sunny remembered only from pictures, and her hair was long like it had been when Sunny was born. But none of that seemed odd to Sunny at the moment. Everything was perfectly, blissfully normal. It was just another mother-daughter breakfast.

Sunny's mother was checking out the menu, chatting about something and laughing, but Sunny couldn't quite make out the words she was saying. Her mouth kept moving, but the sounds didn't reach Sunny's ears. This didn't seem odd to Sunny though, just pleasant, like a warm hum flowing through her body. It didn't really matter that she couldn't hear her mother. They were together and having fun. Sunny was happy. She felt safe. As her mom continued to speak, Sunny glanced around the restaurant. Her eyes snagged on a figure in a black shirt and jeans, and she blinked as she recognized him. Across the room was Zeke, cleaning the dishes off of a table on the other side of the restaurant.

Sometimes, in dreams, there's a moment where the dreamer just knows something in their soul, something that isn't true in real life, but it's true in the dream. And it just seems right. She didn't question it. She didn't even wonder about it. She just knew. The minute she'd recognized Zeke, she'd felt the warmth bloom in her stomach and she knew that Zeke was her boyfriend. *This is the perfect time to introduce him to my mom,* she thought as she tried to catch his eye by waving her hand in the air. But he continued to bus tables without glancing up.

Suddenly, there were empty dishes in front of them, and the meal was over. As her mom paid the bill, Sunny became more and more anxious. Her frustration grew. She still hadn't been able to catch Zeke's eye. Finally, as Sunny's agitation reached its breaking point, he glanced up. She began desperately waving her arms, rising from the table in an effort to be seen. He spotted her, and a warm smile quickly spread across his face. She exhaled as she felt relief flood her body. She looked back towards the table to tell her mother that she wanted to introduce her to someone important, but her mom was already walking away from the table, away from Sunny. Glancing over her shoulder, her mom waved at her to follow. But she continued to get farther and farther away. *No,* Sunny thought in dismay. She tried to call out to her mother, "Don't go! Wait!" but the words got stuck in her throat. Panic set in. She looked back and forth from Zeke to her mother. She was frozen in one spot between them. Zeke was coming over and she wanted to wait for him, but her mother was leaving and she wanted to follow. She felt an impending sense of desperation, as though she shouldn't let her mother out of her sight, but she didn't know why. She tried to call out again, "Wait, Mom!" But it was too late. Sunny blinked, and her mother was gone.

Sunny woke up to tears drenching her cheeks and pillow. She rolled to her side and curled into a ball, but nothing could dull the ache in her heart as she mourned the loss of her mother all over again.

Chapter 22

Zeke found himself wishing his father would yell at him. Yelling would have been easier to take. Yelling would have shown Zeke that his father still cared, even a little bit. Instead, all Zeke got from his father was stone-faced commands.

"Your flight is booked. Your community service hours are done, so you're leaving tomorrow. Period."

Alan Crawford stood a few inches over six feet tall, with a spine like steel and short gray hair to match. He was a trim man, always wearing expensive suits, nothing too flashy. His cuff links and watches were understated, elegant. He came from money, but he didn't flaunt it. His demeanor was reserved, calculating. He observed first and spoke second. There was rarely a sentence that crossed his lips that hadn't been thoughtfully planned out in advance. All things that served him well in the courtroom. But all things that frustrated Zeke to no end.

Zeke was old enough to remember a time when his dad wasn't like this, back before their mom got sick, when his dad was full of smiles and laughter. He wore jeans and sweaters, his light brown hair longer and a little unkempt. He took them on family outings to the park and pushed them on the merry-go-round. They played card games as a family in the evenings after supper, and they were happy.

As Zeke stood opposite his father with the austere desk in between them, he wished he could see some glimpse of the man his father used to be. But that man was gone. He hadn't disappeared all at once. It had happened gradually, slowly. In the same way that cancer had eaten away at his mother's strength and vitality, her death had eaten away at Zeke's dad. Until there was nothing left. No warmth, no compassion, no love. At least not any that Zeke could see.

Mr. Crawford continued, "Mark is expecting you. You'll live with them. He has plenty of extra rooms at his place in London. He got you an internship at his company. It will build your resume while I work to have your record expunged and your admission to Notre Dame reinstated."

"I'm not going to London, Dad. And I'm not going back to Notre Dame." Zeke spoke firmly, though his insides squirmed a bit. He wasn't afraid of his father exactly. But Alan Crawford, the lawyer, had such a commanding presence that it was hard not to be intimidated.

"Why on earth not?"

Zeke's face heated under his father's intense scrutiny. This must be what it felt like to sit on the witness stand of the courtroom under Alan Crawford's cross-examination.

"I..." Zeke hesitated, wondering if he should share his feelings with his father. Before he could talk himself out of it, he continued, "I hated it there. I was miserable."

"Everyone is miserable their first year of college, Ezekiel," he said impatiently. "You don't have any friends yet. Everything is new and unfamiliar. You would have found your footing, eventually. You will find your footing once I get you back in. But first things first. We'll get you to London, and then I'll sort this mess out."

"You're not listening to me. I'm not going."

His father leveled a stern glare in his direction. He'd clearly had enough. "You will. Or you won't have a trust fund when you turn twenty-five. And with no college degree, how would you live? Don't be stupid, son. You need college and your trust fund to build a life for yourself."

Zeke wanted to tell his dad to keep the stupid trust fund, that money wasn't important to him, but he remained silent. It was a lie. In reality, he had been kicked out of college, and without a college degree, he really did worry that he would need that money to live. He had no marketable skills. That money was a safety net, and he wasn't quite ready to give it up. Plus, he knew that Mr. Montgomery was still planning to talk to his dad, and he was holding out hope that it would work. But Zeke knew that if his father pushed him, he would do it. He would give all that money up if he had to.

"I don't want to move to London. My life is here. My brother is here." Zeke's voice turned pleading. He thought about mentioning Sunny, but he didn't think that particular argument would sway his father. It wasn't that his father didn't love Sunny. He did. But he wasn't an emotional person, so Zeke spilling his guts about how much he cared for Sunny wasn't going to be the argument that convinced his dad to let him stay.

Mr. Crawford remained calm. "You should have thought of that before you threw it all away by acting irresponsibly. Drinking and driving. Then staying out all night with Sunny, not a care in the world for the parents that were worried about you both. You haven't demonstrated that you are capable of making sound decisions. Now is the time to face the consequences of your actions."

Zeke argued, "This isn't a consequence of my actions. I've already dealt with my consequences. I've apologized. I've done my community service. Why are you still punishing me?"

"This isn't a punishment, Zeke. You will understand when you are older. This is what it means to be a father, to take care of your family. I'm not punishing you. I'm giving you a new opportunity. You'll thank me for this one day."

Zeke walked over to the window and gazed out across the yard. The grass was green and lush, the trees swaying in the breeze. He struggled to remain calm, to find a way to get his point across, to think of a way to break through his father's icy shell. He said quietly, still facing the window, "Mom would never have let you do this."

He heard his father walk up beside him, and he turned to face him. Was he imaging things, or did a hint of sadness cross his dad's face? His father's eyes looked almost haunted. The look was gone in a moment, and Zeke couldn't be sure. For the first time in a long time, Zeke thought that maybe the dad from his childhood was still in there somewhere.

"Your mother is gone, Zeke. And I've done the best I could to raise you boys and give you every opportunity in life."

Frustrated, Zeke realized the conversation was going nowhere. He strode over to the door, opened it, and said, "That's the difference between you and me, Dad. I never wanted opportunities. I just wanted you to love me."

He walked out of the room, leaving his father speechless and staring after him.

After her tears had dried, creating salty tracks on her cheeks, Sunny arose from her bed and hopped into the shower. The hot water felt amazing, but she couldn't shake the feeling of melancholy that had hung over her since her dream about her mother. She was still feeling nervous and excited about Zeke, but everything else was overwhelming. Having finally been admitted to MIT, Zeke possibly having to leave, not knowing if her dad was going to punish her for being out all night, the dream about her mother. It was all too much. Her chest ached. Was it possible to feel joy and sadness at the same time? Sunny thought it must be, because she certainly felt that way.

She tried to organize all of the thoughts floating around in her head. Her mind kept drifting to the moment she'd opened the letter from MIT. At first, she'd felt this fleeting moment of excitement and pride. She'd gotten in! Exactly like her mom and dad had wanted. She was good enough, after all. But that moment had been too short-lived. A knot in her stomach and a feeling of dread quickly replaced it. Now that she was rested and alone in her room, she had time to think about what the feeling meant.

Before she was officially admitted, going to college was just some fictional story in her head, something her dad talked about for years. She never even thought to question it. It was a given, preordained. Now it was real. Now it was happening. And now she had to face the questions she'd been wrestling with ever since she and Zeke had been baking cookies in his kitchen, and he asked her about her reasons for going to MIT.

She didn't want to think about it, but she had to. Why did she want to go to MIT? Was it just because of her mom and dad, or was there something there for her too? She didn't know. There were other questions floating around in her head too. What kind of life did she want for herself? Who did she want to be? Sunny needed to figure all of it out. Not her father's idea of what her life should look like. Not what her mother wanted for her. But just her. What did Sunny want for herself?

She didn't have a lot of time. College was only a couple of months away.

As she toweled off her hair and picked out a sunshine yellow crop top and white shorts, she mulled over these impossible questions. Suddenly, she recalled hearing her phone buzz as she'd been drifting off to sleep. She tossed the towel on her bed and reached for her phone.

She had missed a call from Zeke. Her stomach lurched. She quickly dialed him back.

No answer.

Sunny texted Parker next.

Sunny: *You home?*

Parker: *Yep come on over*

Sunny: *I have to talk to my dad first. Then I'll come over...if I'm not grounded for life.*

Sunny paused. It felt weird asking Parker about Zeke now that Zeke and Sunny were more than just friends. It felt like spying, like an intrusion. Not to mention that Parker had no clue about any of it. But she needed to know.

Sunny: *Is Zeke home? Is he in trouble?*

Parker replied with a shoulder shrug emoji. Sunny let out a frustrated sigh. Emojis were so unhelpful. And this one in particular wasn't telling her much. She felt like it would be weird to pepper Parker with more questions, so she tucked her phone into the waistband of her pocketless shorts and headed downstairs to find her dad. She needed to find out how much trouble she was in.

Sunny found her dad in his home office, head bent towards his computer. His reading glasses were on, and he looked absorbed in whatever was on his computer screen.

"Dad?" Sunny stood in the doorway. "Can we talk?"

Sunny's dad took off his glasses and sat back in his chair. "Sure, honey," he said, motioning for her to come in and sit on the brown leather couch next to his desk. "I wanted to talk to you too. Both about last night, and..." he gestured to his computer, "the list of things we need to do in order to get you registered for classes."

As Sunny settled herself on the couch and pulled her legs up under her, her dad asked, "Did you sleep okay?"

Sunny forced a smile. "Yeah." She paused, debating whether or not she should mention her dream. She wanted to share it with her dad, but she didn't want to make him feel sad. Ultimately, her need to share it with him won out. "I dreamed about mom."

"Did you?" her dad asked, surprised. A sad smile crossed his lips, and his eyes glossed over as his thoughts traveled back into the past.

Nodding, Sunny added. "She was wearing that yellow and white sundress she used to love. Remember it?"

Now it was her father's turn to nod. He gestured to Sunny's outfit with the hand still holding his glasses. "Is that why you chose those colors today?"

Sunny looked down at herself, surprised. She hadn't realized she'd dressed herself in the same colors as her mom's favorite dress. She shrugged. "I guess maybe it is."

"Yellow was one of her favorite colors, you know. That, and gray, just like your bedroom."

"I know."

They both fell silent, lost in their own memories. Sunny thought about how vivid the dream had been, her mom walking away from her and then disappearing. She swallowed back tears and forced herself to think about what she'd come here to ask her dad.

"Dad?" Sunny interrupted his reverie.

He blinked as though he'd just woken up from a dream. "Yes," he said, looking slightly dazed.

"Am I, like, grounded or something?"

Mr. Montgomery sighed and shook his head. "I've thought about this a lot, Addison. You're an adult now. I just can't see grounding you when you're about to leave for college and can go anywhere you want and stay out as late as you want to. I don't even really care that you stayed out all night. It's not about that. It's that you weren't responsible enough to call me and let me know. I've never been that worried in my entire life."

Sunny felt herself shrink into the couch, guilt gnawing at her insides.

Her dad continued, "That said, it was one mistake. And I believe you when you say it won't happen again. So, no, you aren't grounded."

Nodding somberly, Sunny said, "Thank you. I promise it won't happen again."

"I know. Now about college..." her dad said, turning to his computer and putting his glasses back on.

"Before we talk about that, can I ask you something else?"

"Of course."

Sunny hesitated. She wanted to know more about Zeke's relationship with his dad, but she wasn't sure how her dad would react. She felt embarrassed to be asking him about Zeke now that he knew they were kind of dating. "It's about Mr. Crawford...and Zeke." Sunny forced the question out, "Why does he hate Zeke so much?"

"Oh, Sunny. He doesn't hate him. You have to understand. It isn't really about Zeke at all. I never knew Alan before Jane died, but he's talked about her a little here and there. He loved her a great deal. And I know he loves those boys. But when she got sick...Zeke had to grow up very quickly, Addison. And Alan..."

Her dad paused, collecting his thoughts. "You know I have a lot of respect for Alan, but I can't say I agree with how he's dealt with things. Losing his wife was extremely traumatic. He wasn't really able to recover. He closed himself off. I think he pushed his grief down and buried it, rather than dealing with it. See, it's never really been about Zeke at all. I think Alan is trying to protect himself."

Confused, Sunny cocked her head to the side and asked, "Protect himself from what?"

"From being hurt like that again. From the pain of losing someone he loves. If he keeps those boys at arm's length, I believe he thinks it won't hurt as much if he loses them."

"But that makes no sense. It's selfish. And he's missed out on so much." Sunny leaned forward and tucked her hands under her knees. "I don't understand how you can be friends with him."

Frank sighed and rubbed a hand across his forehead. "I know you don't, and honestly, sometimes I don't either. He isn't an easy person to be friends with. But he needs me." Frank paused. "Do you remember how Alan and I met? You were pretty young yet."

After thinking for a moment, Sunny nodded. "It was a support group or something, right?"

Her dad answered, "Yes, I met Alan at a meeting for widowers. Kind of a place where we could all come together and talk about our grief. Alan only came once. I'd been going there nearly a year at that point." He smiled, remembering, "I think someone forced him to go, because he clearly hated it. He looked so miserable and out of place. We were all in jeans, and there he sat in his fancy suit. I saw him try to leave when we stood up for a break, and I cornered him before he could get away. I don't even know why. He just looked like he needed a friend. We talked a bit. I basically forced him to exchange contact info with me. You know this already, but Alan isn't really interested in sharing his feelings with others, so that support group was pretty much his worst nightmare. When he didn't show up at that next meeting, I just felt like something wasn't right. I called him, but he didn't answer, and I knew he had kids, so I got worried."

He had never shared this story with Sunny before, and she leaned in, listening intently as her father continued, "Well, I just showed up at his house with takeout. When I rang the doorbell, he answered in his bathrobe. He was a mess, both inside and out. I knew because I'd been there. I know how it feels to suddenly be...all alone. To lose your partner in life, the person you were supposed to grow old with." Mr. Montgomery cleared his throat and studied his hands. Sunny thought about how alone he must have felt. And now she was growing up and leaving for college. She didn't like thinking about him at home all alone, without anyone.

Sunny reached out to grab her dad's hand, and she squeezed it in comfort. He smiled up at her and returned her squeeze. Then he said, "He's so calm and reserved now, you'd never know it from looking at him, but Alan was really hurting. I just walked right in and started setting up the food I'd brought." He looked up at Sunny and laughed. "Their house was so fancy. I don't even know if he'd ever eaten KFC before that day. But I didn't give him any choice. And the boys devoured that chicken like little wolverines. I got him to open up a little that day, and that's when we made plans to meet up the next Sunday for golfing and introduce you kids. From then on, I just kept making plans for us every Sunday. At first, he acted like he didn't want to meet up or said he had too much work, but in the end, he always agreed. He always answered the phone when I called, always answered the door when I knocked. He didn't have to. But he did. See, that's the thing about some people. They may not act like they need you, but they do."

Sunny released her dad's hand and stood to pace in front of his desk. "I wish... I wish he would open up and talk to Zeke and Parker more. I think they both need him more than they let on."

"People don't change overnight, honey. And he may never be the kind of dad the boys want him to be. But I still believe he's a good father, even if he isn't always the best at showing how much he cares."

The question still tugged at Sunny's heart, so she had to ask. "Do you think you'll be able to convince him to let Zeke stay?"

Her dad gave her a sad smile. "I don't know, Sunny, but I promised you I would try. I called him earlier, and I'm going over there tonight."

Letting out a breath she hadn't known she'd been holding, Sunny relaxed and stopped pacing. She trusted her dad to help with this. He knew Zeke's dad better than anybody. It was their best chance.

Her dad raised an eyebrow at her. "Now, any more questions about Zeke, or can we talk about college?"

She could hear the excitement in his voice. Her stomach dropped in return. She didn't want to talk about college. She didn't want to pick out classes, didn't want to talk about shopping for her dorm room. None of it excited her the way it should.

She hedged, "I guess so. But I haven't had time to read the whole letter yet. Maybe we should talk more after I've read through everything they sent."

Her dad waved away her arguments. "I read the whole thing. We have to go online, create an account, accept the admission, and send a deposit. Then there's a bunch of things we need to do around housing and classes."

Sunny wanted to curl up into a ball just thinking about the laundry list of items they needed to do in order to complete her registration. She started edging towards the door. "Well, I promised Parker I would come over and talk with him." And she wanted to see Zeke, but she left those words unsaid. She knew her dad wouldn't like it if he thought she was prioritizing a boy over college.

Narrowing his eyes, her dad looked at her and asked, "I thought you were excited to start planning with me?"

"I am, I am," she assured him, lying through her teeth. She felt a wave of guilt, but pushed it away. She needed time to figure out how she felt about college, and she wasn't ready to talk with her dad about it yet. "I just have a lot on my mind. Can't we please just talk about it tomorrow?" She was almost to the doorway. So close to freedom.

Her dad frowned. "Sunny, you don't have a lot of time here. They admitted you later than other students, so we have to get this done."

Frustrated by her dad's pushing, Sunny snapped back, "Dad, I know. I still have time. I'll do it tomorrow." She immediately felt terrible about snapping at him and added, "I know you're worried about me. But I have to do this on my own. I'm not a little girl anymore. Let me handle this."

Sighing and looking weary, her dad replied, "I'm trying, Sunny. I really am."

Swamped by feelings of guilt, Sunny immediately walked over, leaned down, and gave him a kiss on his cheek. "I know you are, Dad. I love you."

Her dad chuckled and relented, "Go. Have fun. We'll talk tomorrow."

A smile broke across Sunny's face at his words. "Thanks, Dad! Love you!" she shouted as she bounded from the room on her way to the Crawford house.

Chapter 23

Sunny sat on the stairs at the Crawford house, her legs scrunched up to her chest. Her chin rested on her knees. Parker was crouched behind her, hands on the bars of the railing, peering through as though he was in jail.

They were eavesdropping.

She'd gone over to see Parker as soon as she finished talking with her dad. He'd told her all about the party last night, and she'd filled him in on her conflicted feelings about college. She also filled him in on her and Zeke. The conversation was much less eventful than she had anticipated.

"Don't you have anything to say about Zeke and me?" Sunny asked.

Parker shook his head. "Nah."

"But you literally have opinions about everything. How can you not have an opinion on this? He's your brother."

"Hey, not my business. I'm not the one who's gotta kiss him. People like different things. I don't love broccoli, but you do, Sunshine. Love who you wanna love."

"I mean, I don't... We're not... I'm not in..." Sunny sputtered.

Parker raised an eyebrow, and Sunny stopped talking.

Parker nodded. "Okay, good talk," he said before changing the subject back to the next clue he was planning to release in a couple of days.

She felt a lot better tonight. Parker had been really understanding about Zeke and about her lack of excitement over college. It felt good to confide in someone. She wanted to share her feelings with Zeke too, but she hadn't seen him anywhere. He hadn't returned her call from earlier. She texted him once, but he didn't reply. She was beginning to worry. Maybe he was really in trouble with his dad. Maybe he was regretting last night. The longer she spent away from him, the more insecure she became.

When the doorbell rang, signaling her dad's arrival, Parker suggested they eavesdrop. Sunny felt a twinge of uncertainty but agreed anyway. She knew it was wrong. But she didn't care. This was too important. Zeke's future was on the line, and she felt like their future was on the line with it.

Frank and Alan immediately headed into Alan's office. The door was cracked open, conveniently enough that Sunny and Parker could just make out what they were saying. Though Sunny couldn't see them, she knew from the clink of glasses that they were getting ready to have a drink. It was always whiskey with those two. Surprisingly, even though the Crawfords had plenty of money, it wasn't even fancy whiskey. Alan never made a fuss about what kind of whiskey they drank. It made her wonder if, underneath his fancy exterior, he wasn't really as pretentious as he acted.

"Did you even go in to work today at all?" Sunny heard her father ask.

"No," Alan said, giving a tired sigh. "You?"

"No," her dad said, chuckling. "These kids are wearing me out, Alan."

"I agree."

There was silence. The only sound Sunny could hear was the clink of ice in glasses and the whiskey pouring.

"Thanks for having me over," Frank said. "I wanted to talk to you about something." He paused, and Sunny heard the squeak of leather. She imagined her dad was settling himself on the leather sofa. "Did you know that Zeke and Sunny are...dating? Or whatever the hell they call it these days?"

Sunny heard Mr. Crawford answer, "I figured. You don't stay out all night if there isn't something going on." There was a pause before he continued, "I can't even believe I'm going to ask this, but do you think they're...being safe? I mean, you said we needed to talk. You're not about to tell me I'm going to be a grandpa, are you?"

There was a muffled hiss of laughter from Parker behind her.

Oh my god. Sunny wanted to shrivel up and die of embarrassment. Her face felt hot. She sat ramrod straight, avoiding Parker's eyes. She couldn't believe their parents were talking about their sex life. Or lack of one, not that they knew that. She knew she shouldn't be listening to this, but she had to know if her dad was going to be able to convince Zeke's dad to let him stay. So she stayed put.

Her dad nearly choked on his whiskey. She heard him cough and sputter. "No. I... I mean... I think... I don't think they're... doing that..." Her dad gave up. He was clearly not prepared to talk about his daughter having sex. Sunny was relieved. She was barely prepared to think about it herself, much less listen to her dad talk about it. Everything with her and Zeke was still so new.

Alan spoke next. "Well, I can't say I'm unhappy they are together. Sunny is a smart girl. She's ambitious, and she's a good influence on Zeke."

"I feel the same about Zeke. He's made a few mistakes, but he's responsible and kind. I know he'll treat Sunny well, and I can't ask for more than that." Sunny cheered inwardly at her dad's comments.

"I appreciate that, Frank, but I'm not so sure," Alan responded, sounding skeptical. "Zeke's been making some poor decisions of late... Don't get me wrong, I don't think it has anything to do with Sunny. I'm not sure what's happening, honestly. I feel like I don't even know him anymore. All he does is argue with me. When he was five, he used to stand in the living room, banging on his toy piano and singing off-key Christmas songs in the middle of July. Somewhere between there and here, I lost him."

Sunny heard her dad reassure Alan. "He's not lost. He's a good kid who just needs a little help right now. Everybody needs a little help now and again."

"That's why I'm sending him to London. My brother will help him get a job, help him get something good on his resume. Meanwhile, I'll get him back into Notre Dame. Or another school. I'll figure it out."

Sunny's dad cleared his throat. She could tell he was gearing up. "Are you sure your brother is the help Zeke needs? This is actually what I came over here to talk with you about. You know I don't like to meddle in your affairs, but this one time, I'm going to ask you to reconsider. It's not just because it means a lot to Sunny and she wants Zeke to stay. It's because I care a lot about your kids, Alan. And your boys, they love you. I can see it. And they love each other. I think they need each other. And they need you. Don't tear your family apart, not right now. Parker's about to leave for college. They have so little time left to just be here with us. Life will pull all of us apart soon enough. They'll have jobs. They'll live somewhere else. We'll never see them. Our houses will be empty. The house will be clean all the time. It will be miserable."

Sunny heard one of the men give a deep chuckle. She thought it didn't sound exactly like her dad, but she never really heard Mr. Crawford laugh before. He said, "Speaking of clean houses, you know what I found when I came home yesterday evening? The house looked crazy. There were photos up everywhere. Plastered all over the wall, in every room of the house. All of Zeke's old awards from his piano competitions… they nearly filled the china hutch in the dining room." His voice seemed warmer than before. Sunny glanced over at Parker. He released his hold on the railings to give her two thumbs up and a broad smile. She smiled in return.

"I've never heard Zeke play piano before. I didn't realize he had so many awards."

Mr. Crawford's voice filled with pride. "He was a sight to see, tiny little head bent over the piano, fingers furiously moving across the keys. My wife taught him, you know." He cleared his throat. Sunny realized that she'd never really seen this side of Mr. Crawford before. Proud father. She glanced at Parker. He seemed solemn, lost in thought. She couldn't read what he was thinking.

Mr. Crawford continued, "Anyway, when I saw all that stuff out everywhere, I went to look for the boys. I couldn't find Zeke, but I found Parker, and he admitted he put that stuff up. He said he wanted to remind me of the time when I was proud of Zeke. Ridiculous plan. Creative, but ridiculous. A bunch of photos won't change my mind."

"You have my daughter to thank for that ridiculous plan, I believe. They were trying to convince you to let Zeke stay."

"Well, they clearly went to a lot of work."

"Our children are a force to be reckoned with, Alan."

There was silence except for the clinking of ice. Sunny tensed.

Her dad broke the silence with a quiet question. Sunny had to strain to hear it. "Why are you so set on sending him away, Alan?"

She heard Mr. Crawford sigh, and when he spoke, he sounded weary. "I don't even know anymore, to be honest, Frank. At first, I thought it would be a good idea. But when Zeke argued, I put my foot down. I still think it's a good plan. But I can't tell if I'm doing it for him anymore or to prove that he still has to do what I say. At this point, it might just be a battle of wills... Does that make me a terrible father?"

"No. It makes you a normal one," Sunny heard her dad laugh. "All our kids do in their teenage years is test their limits. It's like a rite of passage." Her dad's voice turned serious. "But you have a choice right now, Alan. You can choose to listen to your son, who is saying he wants to spend time with you and his brother here. Or you can push him away and maybe lose him forever."

"Well, when you put it that way, is it even really a choice?" Sunny thought she detected a hint of a smile in Mr. Crawford's voice as he said it. He sighed and continued, "All right, all right, you've convinced me. I'll tell Zeke I scrapped the London plan."

She heard her dad reply, "You won't regret this, Alan," as her eyes flew to Parker's in triumph. Zeke could stay! They both stood and quietly pantomimed dance moves in celebration. Her heart felt lighter than it had been in a long time.

Suddenly, Sunny was distracted by a noise she couldn't place. She looked at Parker to see if he'd heard it, but he just continued dancing silently, his eyes closed as he flossed. Sunny rolled her eyes. She hated the floss.

There it was again. It was so quiet that she could barely make it out. Was the television on in Parker's bedroom? No, it wasn't coming from upstairs.

"You hear that?" Sunny whispered to Parker, pointing to her ear.

Parker shook his head, and then paused and cocked his head to the side, listening. Light dawned, and he smiled in recognition.

"Zeke," Parker whispered, pointing down the hall. He pantomimed playing the piano. Of course, the sound was the piano. It was so faint, she could barely make it out.

She pointed to herself and then down the hall, letting Parker know she was going to find Zeke. Now that she knew Zeke could stay, she had to tell him. Also, she really just wanted to see him. They hadn't talked since this morning, and she had a lot to say. Parker nodded and pointed upstairs to his bedroom.

Sunny waved goodbye to Parker and tiptoed down the hall to the music room, careful not to be seen by Mr. Crawford and her dad.

Zeke sat alone at the piano in the music room. He had no idea how long he'd been there, frozen, staring at the keys, wishing for inspiration to strike. He was thinking about his dad, his mom, Sunny, everything. His whole life, or at least since his mom died, he'd been busy trying to keep things together. Keep Mom's memory alive. Keep Parker out of trouble. Keep himself on the path his father set for him. Now it felt like everything was slipping out of his control. It wasn't a comfortable feeling, and he didn't know how to fix it.

He placed his fingers on the keys and played a few chords. It felt both unfamiliar and familiar at the same time. Part of him felt like he'd never stopped playing. He struck a few more chords. The music hummed inside his body. But his fingers were slow and awkward as they moved over the keys, testing out an old familiar melody. He dropped his hands in the middle of Bach's Minuet in G after he missed a few notes that used to come so naturally to him.

When Sunny found him, he was still seated on the piano bench, hands clenched on the bench beside him. He looked a little sad, a little lost. It tugged at Sunny's heart.

She slipped her shoes off at the doorway and padded over to stand next to him. He didn't look up. Something about his somber demeanor and the quietness of the music room made Sunny remain silent. But he didn't tell her to leave, so she sat down next to him.

She stole a peek at his face, still looking down at the piano keys like he was looking for something he was missing. "Will you play something for me?" she asked quietly. She had so much to tell him, but now that she was here, she couldn't deny that she wanted to hear him play more than anything else. She hadn't heard him play in so long.

Zeke looked up at her then, surprised. He didn't know what he'd expected her to say, but it wasn't that. She smiled a hopeful smile. He didn't return it, but his face softened. He couldn't deny her, even with his clunky, out-of-practice fingers. He would do the best he could.

His hands hovered over the keyboard as he considered his options. Something simple, he thought. Maybe a little slower to give himself time to remember the chords. Hopefully, she would forgive his mistakes.

And then he played.

As the first notes of Debussy's Clair de Lune filled the music room, slow and romantic, a shiver went down Sunny's spine. It sounded like a poem, but without words. She always loved this song, and Zeke played it beautifully, hauntingly. She closed her eyes as she listened.

When the last notes faded away to silence, she opened her eyes to find Zeke staring at her, a smile playing around his lips. He leaned forward and pressed a soft kiss to her lips.

"That was beautiful," she breathed, although the words didn't seem to do it justice.

"Thank you," he answered, smiling at her. "The kiss or the song?"

She slapped at his arm playfully, laughing. "I meant the song, but now that you mention it, that kiss wasn't bad either."

"Not bad?" Zeke said, pretending to be offended. "I'll show you not bad."

This time, their kiss was slower, longer, deeper. When they parted, both were out of breath.

"Why don't you play anymore?" Sunny asked breathlessly. "I mean, you're really talented. Like, a sick amount of talent. I'm not an expert, but even I can tell how good you are."

"I don't know," Zeke hedged. He separated himself from Sunny, stood, and stretched, his shirt riding up and giving Sunny a glimpse of his tan stomach. This time Sunny didn't look away. Now that she knew he liked her, she felt braver, more in control. She turned and straddled the piano bench, facing him and savoring the view.

Zeke didn't seem to notice. "I'm really not that good anymore. I used to be, but...I guess after my mom died, my heart just wasn't in it anymore. She was always there with me, teaching me and encouraging me. When I came in here after she died..." his voice trailed off, and he paused to compose himself. It was painful even to remember those days after she'd passed away. He'd come into the music room and cried nearly every day, head bent over the keyboard, wishing he could just see her, hug her one more time. He swallowed. "It just hurt too much, I guess. Eventually I just quit. I didn't feel happy when I played anymore. All I felt was emptiness. Like, an emptiness so big, it felt like it would swallow me whole."

Sunny felt her eyes well up, and she blinked quickly, trying to fend the tears off. She knew that empty feeling in her soul, because it was the same feeling she'd had when she'd realized her mother was never coming back. She remembered laying on her bed, staring up at her ceiling late at night, wishing to see her mother's face one last time. A few tears slipped out, despite her best efforts to keep them at bay. She swiped them away quickly, hoping Zeke wouldn't notice.

He did, but he remained silent. He was too busy trying to keep his own tears at bay. It felt nice that Sunny understood exactly what he meant. Not everyone understood what it was like to lose a mom. But Sunny did.

She cleared her throat. "What about now?"

"Huh?"

"What did you feel when you played for me just now?"

The question surprised Zeke, and his face showed it. He fumbled for an answer, thinking back to the song he'd just finished playing. "I don't know, I... I guess it felt kind of good. Like stretching a muscle that has been sitting still for a long time. And watching your face as I played, well, that was..." He smiled.

Sunny smiled in return. She stood, walking over to him. "Was what?" she prompted.

How could he convey all the different ways he felt looking at her? She'd had her eyes closed, her face tipped upwards, a smile on her lips, slightly swaying to the music. He'd felt desire. He'd felt in awe of her beauty and her kindness. He'd felt lucky that she liked him. He felt peaceful as his fingers floated over the keys. And he'd felt proud. That he could play something that would give her that soft smile. Well, that was just... "Amazing," Zeke finished, wrapping his arms around Sunny as she got closer.

She wound her arms around his neck in return. "So, not empty?"

"No, definitely not empty."

"So...," she continued, "Maybe you want to start playing again? It'd be a shame to keep this talent of yours from the rest of the world," she joked. But in all reality, she was serious. Zeke was good, and he clearly loved playing, even if he didn't realize it yet. Maybe he could get that feeling back again.

"Maybe," he answered. "But for now, I have other things on my mind," he said, lowering his head to hers. This kiss was more urgent and heated than the others. Hungry. Demanding. They matched each other in intensity. Zeke's lips kissed a trail down the curve of her chin to her neck.

Suddenly, Sunny's brain reminded her that she had news for Zeke. "Oh," she gasped. "I almost forgot! You get to stay." Her voice was breathless.

"What?" Zeke said, raising his head, eyes looking dazed. He'd been very focused on other things.

Sunny reveled in the fact that she'd made him look that way. "My dad talked to your dad. Just now. You get to stay."

Zeke gave a whoop and spun her around in a circle. "Addison Rose. Why didn't you tell me that earlier?"

Sunny laughed as he set her down on her feet again, feeling like the music room was still spinning a little. "I'm sorry. I got distracted. But you have to promise to act surprised when your dad tells you. We were eavesdropping."

"We?"

"Parker and I."

"Of course. Is there anything else you need to tell me about? You're here, so you're obviously not grounded, right?"

She shook her head. "Nope. My dad was actually surprisingly chill about it all. Not what I expected." Her voice dropped a bit as she shared her last bit of news. "But there is one more thing I need to tell you. I got in. To MIT."

This one didn't earn a whoop from Zeke. Sensing her change in tone, he looked at her questioningly. "You don't seem happy about that."

Sunny frowned and began pacing the music room. "It's not that I'm not happy, exactly. I was happy when I found out. For a second. Until I actually thought about going. And it's your fault, actually!" She spun toward him and pointed a finger. "I was super ready to go to college before you started asking me all those questions about why I wanted to go. And I can't answer them, because I don't know if I actually want to go or not. And now my dad wants to register and pay the deposit, and it all feels like it's happening too quickly... But what will I even do with my life if I don't go to MIT? I have no plan B." She turned away from Zeke, raising a hand to her mouth to chew on her thumbnail.

Zeke walked up behind her and wrapped his powerful arms around her. His fingers brushed her bare stomach below her crop top, and she felt her skin heat. She relaxed against him, sinking into his warmth. He leaned down and said softly, "Well, congratulations either way. It's a huge accomplishment. You should be proud."

"I am," she said begrudgingly.

Zeke could sense the war within her. "So, what are you going to do?" he asked.

She sighed. "I don't know."

"Well, that's okay," he answered. "You aren't leaving for college tomorrow. We have plenty of time to figure it out. Together." He spun her around quickly, and she let out a burst of laughter. She threw her arms around his neck and pulled him down for another kiss.

She knew he was right. They had weeks before she would have to leave for college. There was plenty of time to figure it out later. For now, all she wanted to think about was Zeke.

Chapter 24

After Sunny had left to find Zeke, Parker headed to his room. As he walked down the hallway, he passed Zeke's bedroom door. He thought about his brother, who had been there for him all his life. He had missed Zeke when he was at Notre Dame, and he felt relieved that Zeke would still be nearby, at least for a little while longer. Even though he was leaving for Tisch soon, Parker wasn't ready to say goodbye quite yet.

Parker had a lot more parties planned for the remaining clues. Plus, his birthday party was coming up too. It would all be more fun with Zeke there. As long as Zeke could chill out long enough to enjoy it.

Parker didn't always act grateful on the outside, but deep down, he appreciated that Zeke always had his back. He was a great big brother. That was why Parker had never understood why his dad was so hard on Zeke. He wasn't a bad person. He was kind. He got good grades. He didn't beat up on Parker like some other older brothers did. He always took care of Parker, no matter what. His dad should have been proud of him. So why was he so harsh and distant?

When Parker got to his bedroom, he flopped down on the couch. He was filled with a restless energy as he thought about all the things he still had planned for this summer. He reached for a game controller, but his heart wasn't really in it. After getting killed a handful of times for some noob mistakes, he threw down the controller in frustration. His mind kept drifting to the next clue he needed to release. He was aiming for Friday night, so he still had a few days to plan. He got up and headed over to his desk to make a list of all the things he needed to get ready. Making lists helped calm down the endless riot of thoughts running through his brain.

As he reached for the notepad he'd been using to jot down his plans for the clues, he saw the stack of papers on his desk for Tisch. He paused, his thoughts changing direction. He'd already registered for classes, paid his deposit, and signed up for housing, so he was all set to go. But it felt a little different now. He was still reeling a little from Sunny's admission earlier that she wasn't sure she wanted to go to MIT. It was supposed to be both of them, heading off to college together. He knew he was going to miss her when he left, but he'd mentally prepared himself for that. They weren't going to the same school, but they were still supposed to be doing this whole college thing together.

He'd even mapped out the distance between their locations. They were three hours and thirty minutes away from each other by car, one hour by plane. He knew they could still video chat during the week and then see each other on weekends. But if she stayed in Minnesota? He'd only get to see her once or twice a year when he flew home for the holidays. Maybe the summer too, but that was only if he didn't take any summer classes. Or what if she went somewhere else entirely? What if she moved to California or Alaska or somewhere equally far away? It felt weird to think about being all alone out on the east coast.

The thought of being so far apart from everyone he loved made his chest tighten. He'd never really been that alone before. He'd always had Zeke or Sunny to watch out for him. What if he couldn't survive without them? What if he couldn't make any new friends? What if he hated Tisch? He was spiraling. Forcing a deep breath, he reminded himself that he wanted Sunny to be happy. If MIT wasn't right for her, of course, he would support her. For a hot second, he even thought about staying in Minnesota with her, but he quickly discarded that idea. Working in the movie industry was his dream, and he knew Tisch would open doors for him.

Suddenly, inspiration struck. He opened his desk drawer and pulled out a red leather-bound notebook. Many years ago, he'd started jotting down all his movie ideas in a journal. Sometimes it was just a thought, a few sentences of a plot, maybe a snappy line that had popped into his head. Other times it was pages of a fully developed screenplay. And when he filled his first journal up, he bought another one. And another. And another. Now his desk drawers were full of notebooks brimming with movie ideas. He'd never told Zeke or his dad about them. Only Sunny knew. But he'd definitely never let her read them. No way. It was too embarrassing. Too personal, even for his best friend. What if they were no good? Even while he worried his scribbles were nothing special, still he dreamed of the day he could turn his ideas into reality.

Opening the red notebook, he turned to a blank page and scrawled, "Young girl torn between going off to an ivy league college and staying in her Midwestern home town - what will she choose?"

Sunny's conundrum was certainly a problem for her, but it would also make a great movie one day. He paused, contemplating the addition of some fiction to make it a bit more interesting. He wrote, "Maybe her love interest is dying and she doesn't want to leave him." After all, Parker thought, real life was a little too boring for the movies. A dying love interest was sure to tug at the heartstrings of the audience. It needed more drama in order to make an Academy Award winner. Parker liked to dream big.

With that idea jotted down, Parker slammed the notebook shut and slid it back into the drawer. He picked up the notepad from his desk again and turned his attention to the clues he needed to plan. He had all ten clues written out with notes about each one. Mika had helped him make the list and figure out some details. He crossed off the first and second clues because those were done. Now that they were in a rhythm of releasing the clues every few days, he wanted to outline a timeline. With eight clues left, if he released one to two per week over the next six weeks, that would mean releasing the final clue during the last week of July. That was perfect timing. Some kids started leaving for college in early August if they played sports, and he wanted this all wrapped up before people started heading out.

He needed to work around his birthday party, though. His birthday was June 28, which happened to be next Friday. He loved it when his birthday fell on the weekend. It was the ideal time for a sick birthday party. His dad had agreed to a band, catering, the complete package. But most importantly, his dad had agreed to disappear for the night. Completely gone, out of the house. Parker would have the gift of privacy. The best birthday present his dad could have given him. He was a little surprised that his dad agreed, especially considering everything that had been happening lately, but he didn't question it. He just promised no drugs, no alcohol, like his father requested, and got started planning.

With all this party planning, Parker was getting a lot of experience at organizing things. If his movie career ever fell through, he could practically go into business as a party planner. Parker felt a sting of guilt as he remembered that he still hadn't figured out what to do about the cost of the last two parties. The charges were sitting there on his dad's credit card bill like a ticking time bomb, waiting for his dad to discover them the next time he looked at his statement. Parker's mind spun, trying to find a way out.

What if he just told his dad about it? Parker sighed in frustration. No, that wouldn't work. His dad would probably cancel his birthday party as punishment. Better to wait until his birthday party was done so his dad couldn't take that away from him. Then Parker could come clean and figure out some way to make it up to his dad. Besides, he had some time yet before his dad's credit card bill arrived. Thankfully, his dad still got a paper bill in the mail. Parker had made fun of him before, calling him a "boomer," but now he was grateful for his dad's dedication to good old-fashioned paper and ink.

Parker made a vow to himself to scale back for the rest of the parties. He knew he was already going to be in hot water with his dad, and he didn't want to make anything worse. And besides, he didn't really need to make a ton of fuss about the upcoming clues. There was already a lot of buzz on social media, and all the kids in town were talking about it. All he really needed was to release a clue, and he knew people would show up, regardless of whether or not there was a party. They were invested now. They all wanted to see who would win.

He read through the list in his notebook and thought about his plan. His next clue was going to lead everyone to the abandoned airport outside of town on Friday night. Back in the '80s, there had been a small charter plane company that had attempted to build a business running regular flights directly to Las Vegas, but it had died after just two years of operating.

Since then, the land sat empty, desolate and decaying. Consisting of a single airstrip and a rundown one-story building, it was home to a broken-down prop plane, white paint scratched and rusted. There was even a small air traffic control tower. It had two large bay windows at the top, both of them broken out. They looked like vacant eyes, staring out over the airstrip. Parker and Mika used the scenery at the old airport as inspiration for the clue.

> *I have eyes but can't see.*
> *I have wings but can't fly.*
> *I live where no one lives.*
> *I wither in loneliness.*

It was off the beaten path, so it was the perfect place to gather. Parker planned to release the clue at eleven p.m., giving people until midnight to get there. There was a large parking lot right next to the building. He figured he could haul some wood and make a giant bonfire in the middle of it. Then he would blast some tunes from his Bluetooth speaker. That's really all he needed to make a party. Most of their classmates had been bringing their own booze to each clue party anyway, so they would do the rest.

With that decided, Parker turned his attention to the fourth clue.

I am a beginning, a middle, and an end.
Children enter, but children never leave.
Some love me. Some hate me.
I am a ghost of my former self.

He hoped the clue would lead everyone to the old Catholic school on the edge of town. Mika told him that it had stopped operating around the 1960's. It sat empty now, directly next to one of the oldest graveyards in the town. That was creepy enough, but people also said it was haunted by the nuns who used to punish the children who went to school there. Mika told Parker about the history of the old building, and she'd rambled on about how some kids had to work on their family farms, come to school, and then go back to work when they were done. Parker found all of that pretty boring, so he hadn't been paying much attention. For his part, he thought it was the perfect place to creep people out. They had to keep the game exciting, after all.

For that clue, a bonfire wouldn't work. The old building was brick and wood, rotting and dry. It would go up in a ball of flames. He needed a plan for what to do there. And it had to be cheap, because he had vowed not to use his dad's money for this anymore. Suddenly, Parker snapped his fingers. He knew just what to do. He scribbled some notes on his notepad.

With that decided, Parker tossed the notebook on the desk and headed back over to the couch to game. His mind was clear, so it was the perfect time to annihilate some zombies.

Chapter 25

S unny lay sprawled on the newly purchased couch in the music
room. She was on her stomach, her feet crossed in the air behind
her, her laptop open in front of her. The only sound in the room was
Zeke's melodic practicing of the piano punctuated by the click-clack
of her keyboard whenever he paused.

It was Friday, June 28. Parker's birthday and the day of his
long-awaited eighteenth birthday extravaganza. Parker was practically bouncing off the walls in anticipation. Sunny was excited too,
although not truly about the party itself. She was excited for Parker
to open his presents. Both the picture album that she and Zeke had
made, and also the individual present she'd gotten him. It was a new
journal for his story ideas, but this one was special, made specifically
for screenwriters. There were sections with tips for writing screen-
plays, encouraging quotes from famous screenwriters and directors,
story prompts, and blank pages for filling in story ideas. She couldn't
wait for him to see it.

While Parker and Sunny were amped up for the birthday celebrations, Zeke didn't seem to be paying much attention to the festivities.
His community service hours were complete, so that weight lifted off
his shoulders. Now, he was a man obsessed. For the entire past week,
he spent all of his free time holed up in the music room. Sunny joined

him whenever she could, happy to see his musical fervor. Watching him play was magical. He was so alive, so expressive. She couldn't remember ever seeing him this passionate about something. And even though she wasn't sure how it was possible, his dedication made him even more attractive.

And while Zeke was practicing away, Sunny took the opportunity to hang out nearby and work on her new app. She'd been making great progress mapping out the workflow for her idea about a tuition donation app. And bonus, she got to do it all while spending time with, and sometimes ogling, Zeke. If there also happened to be plenty of break times for snacks and kissing and other things... well, then, that was just fine by her.

The fact that Zeke was playing piano again had not escaped the notice of Mr. Crawford. He seemed to approve of both the music and the fact that Zeke and Sunny were spending time together. On Sunday, when they'd been standing by the clubhouse waiting for their tee time, Mr. Crawford had commented on how much time they'd been spending in the music room.

"You've been working hard on your music this week, haven't you, son?"

Zeke nodded and told him about the progress he was making. He flexed his fingers. "I need to get the dexterity back in my fingers, so I've been looking online for exercises and drills."

Mr. Crawford nodded approvingly and patted Zeke's shoulder.

Sunny made an offhand joke about how sore she was from sitting in the chairs while Zeke practiced. Mr. Crawford frowned, and Sunny worried she'd offended him. But the very next day, to her surprise, a brand new couch had been delivered. And it wasn't one of those fancy ones that would match the chairs already in place and be horribly stiff and uncomfortable. It was a giant, squishy, buttery soft, brown leather couch. When Sunny sat down, she swore she was sitting on a cloud.

A feeling of warmth spread through her as she realized that Mr. Crawford had bought the couch just for her because he wanted her to be comfortable. It was the sweetest thing he had ever done for her in all the time she'd known him. His demeanor was still stiff when he spoke to her or the boys. It seemed to her that he wore his coldness almost like a jacket that was too tight. He just couldn't seem to shake it off. But she felt like she could practically see him trying to change since he'd had that talk with her dad. And that gave her hope for the future.

Meanwhile, over the course of the past week, Sunny had somehow managed to distance herself even further from her own dad. She hadn't meant to. She loved her dad. But she had pushed the decision about MIT to the farthest reaches of her mind. She was determined not to think about it yet. And in order to do that, she needed to avoid her father at all costs. College was all her dad ever wanted to talk about anymore. Every time he spotted her, it was MIT this and MIT that. When he caught her as she was trying to tiptoe up to her room in the evening, he started in with a litany of helpful tips for freshman that he'd read about in some article online. As he tried to shove eggs onto her plate in the morning, he reminded her about the registration deadline and questions about the sample class schedules he'd slipped under her door.

She knew he meant well, and she knew she was frustrating him. But she couldn't bring herself to face his questions head-on. The thought hovered in her mind each time they spoke. *I don't want to go to MIT, Dad.* But the words never passed her lips. Partly because she was afraid, and partly because she wasn't positive it was what she really wanted. All hell would break loose if she spoke those words. And there was no way she could figure out what she really wanted for herself if her dad was freaking out. So she stayed silent. And she hid. Like a coward.

"Got time for a break?"

Zeke's words snapped Sunny back to the moment. She turned to see him twisted around on the piano bench, looking at her with a hopeful expression and a warm smile.

She sat up and eyed him with playful skepticism. "What kind of break are you proposing?" she asked.

"Oh, the kind where we are doing something a lot more fun than this stuff," he said, gesturing vaguely to her computer and the piano. Warmth spread throughout her body at his words.

"Does it involve food?" she asked, still playing.

Zeke laughed. "It could. If you wanted it to. I mean, I'm game. As long as it involves you and me. And being a helluva lot closer to each other than we are right now."

Sunny tried to hide the smile that threatened to spill across her face at his words. She still marveled at the fact that, after all this time of trying to hide her own feelings, he actually liked her back. But she still wasn't ready to let him know how much he affected her. Couldn't let him think he had too much power over her. "I don't know," she said, feigning indecision. She glanced down to check her fingernails, trying to look slightly bored. "I might need some convincing..." She peeked up at him from under her lashes.

Zeke stood and sauntered over to her. "Some convincing, huh? I think I can manage that." He gently grabbed her hands and tugged her to her feet, encircling her waist with his arms and pulling her close. She envied the way he seemed to show his feelings so easily, so confidently. He leaned down and nuzzled her neck.

Sunny felt a delicious tingle run down her spine. She sighed and sank into him. The game was over, and she didn't mind showing her hand now. She turned her head and pressed her lips to his. The kiss was gentle at first, then grew more heated.

Despite frequent make-out sessions over the past week, they hadn't crossed the line. She wasn't quite ready to have sex, and Zeke was still uncertain where her comfort level was, so he never pushed. Sunny appreciated that. Almost as much as she appreciated the heavenly way he was massaging her back with his magical hands as he rained kisses down the side of her neck. She shivered in response.

Zeke walked Sunny back towards the couch and they fell backwards, laughing in between kisses. A tangle of arms and limbs, they both sobered as Zeke looked down into Sunny's eyes. "I can't believe you're here with me," he breathed.

Sunny traced a finger down the side of his face. She was embarrassed to admit she felt the same way, but she pushed herself to answer, "Same," before angling her face up for another kiss.

Zeke's hands moved under her t-shirt, lifting it up and over her head, and she did the same for his. His kisses drifted down, over her collarbone, lower to hover just over the top of her breast. Sunny closed her eyes, reveling in the feeling.

The door burst open, and Parker flew in.

"Yo, yo, yo, it's party ti... oh my god, my eyes! My eyes!"

"Parker!" Zeke and Sunny both shouted, scrambling for their missing clothes.

Parker stood with his hands covering his eyes. "Cover yourselves, for the love of God, people!" he shouted.

Sunny grunted in frustration as she threw her shirt over her head. She checked to make sure Zeke was covered up and answered, "You can uncover your eyes now, Parker. We're decent."

"That is a matter of opinion." Parker wise-cracked. "If you were really decent, I wouldn't have walked in on..." he gestured to the couch and mock shuddered, "That whole business."

"Why are you bursting in here, anyway? The door was shut!" Sunny shot back. Zeke busied himself with straightening his already-straight shirt, avoiding everyone's eyes, and remaining silent.

"Well, this is a public place, Addison," Parker answered. His tone was snarky but not mean, and she could tell he was joking. "If you are going to be doing... things... then you should find a private location." He paused, eyeballing the couch. "I can never sit on the couch again, thank you very much."

Sunny rolled her eyes and laughed. "You're being high-key dramatic right now, Parker. Why are you even in here?"

"A very important reason," he said in a serious tone. He took a deep breath as though beginning a monologue. "It's my birthday, you know."

"We know," Sunny and Zeke interrupted in unison.

"And I can't have a party without my two bestest buds by my side. Yet you two were nowhere to be found. So I just came to tell you to get your butts out there. People are gonna be here any minute! It's time to party!"

"Okay, okay," Zeke said, "Give us five minutes." He walked forward, waving his hands to herd Parker towards the door.

"Five minutes. You promise?" Parker asked hopefully, looking around Zeke to Sunny for confirmation.

"We promise," Sunny assured him.

"Okay," Parker said begrudgingly as he headed out the door. Zeke turned and walked back to Sunny's side.

Parker popped his head back in. "Just so you know, I can't unsee the things I've seen today," Parker said with mock sadness. "I want you to think about that. You guys may have ruined sex for me forever. I hope you can live with yourselves!" he shouted gleefully as he withdrew his head from the doorway and slammed the door behind him.

With that, Sunny rolled her eyes at the closed door and turned to Zeke.

"Well, that wasn't as bad as it could have been," Zeke said, smiling wryly.

Sunny grinned as Zeke pulled her back to him for another kiss.

While Zeke and Sunny had been canoodling together in the music room all week, Parker had kept busy. He hung out with Mika, worked on some new screenplay ideas, watched movies, and released two more clues. Clue number three was released a week ago exactly, and the fourth clue was released on Tuesday. The respective parties had been epic, as Parker had hoped.

Everyone loved the bonfire at the airport for the third clue. The party raged until four a.m., though Zeke and Sunny had disappeared together long before that. Based on what he'd just seen in the music room, he didn't want to think about where they'd gone. It's not that he minded that they were together. In fact, he was glad that they were both happy. But he still didn't want to know what they did behind closed doors.

Somehow, the party at the school for the fourth clue made all the other parties look tame in comparison. Parker didn't want to have a bonfire there because of the fire hazard, so he'd contacted one of their classmates, Ramesh. Ramesh had already been knocked out of the bet at the first clue because he'd been at work and unable to leave. But more importantly, Ramesh's parents ran a party rental store. Parker asked him what kind of supplies they might be able to borrow for the night. Turns out there's not a lot of call for party supplies on a Tuesday, so Ramesh really pulled through. There were spotlights in a variety of colors, spinning disco lights mounted on poles, and string lights they hung on the trees surrounding the building. He even brought a full sound system for music and a pop-up photo booth with crazy props like fake mustaches and hats.

And best of all, it was free. Parker felt proud he'd pulled it off without needing to dip into his dad's credit card again. The parties and the bet were all their classmates were talking about on social media. As a result, the competition was getting heated. They were down to only sixty-seven people left in the competition. There had been 116 people left after clue number three. But the fourth clue had turned out to be incredibly difficult and had knocked nearly fifty people out in one shot. Parker hadn't expected that. With six clues left to go and only sixty-seven people, would anyone even make it to the end?

Much to Parker's chagrin, the remaining players were extremely focused on winning. They were getting creative in tracking Parker's movements. Some were even forming alliances to help each other get to the end. Marcus and Victoria were still in the bet, and they'd band-ed together with a few other friends, agreeing to share information and split the winnings.

Unexpectedly, the class salutatorian, second in graduating class rank only to Mika, formed a partnership with one of their classmates who had barely even graduated. Megan was quiet, studious, shy. She could often be found with her nose in a book or raising her hand to answer every single one of the teacher's questions. Tyler was the exact opposite. Loud and boisterous, he was prone to arguing with teachers instead of answering their questions. He could often be found tinkering in the school shop when he was supposed to be in biology class. It was an odd mix, but Parker could only surmise that they must each see value in the other. Why else would they pair up?

Regardless of how the partnerships came about, people seemed to think teaming up was a strategy to help them make it to the end. The last clue had scared people, because it had left so many people stumped and knocked out of the game. They were getting desperate. Ten grand was a lot of cash. Some needed the money for college. Some just plain needed it.

The result of all that fervor was that Parker was feeling like a fugitive. He found himself paranoid, checking his rearview mirror to make sure he wasn't being followed, ducking behind buildings to make himself harder to follow. With $10,000 on the line, he should have expected this. And he did, to some extent. Just not exactly to this insane level. It was a reminder to never underestimate the lengths that teenagers would go to when motivated. Especially teenagers in the summer with too much free time on their hands.

The bet had even gained the attention of others in town. The chatter was making Parker nervous. He knew he should have expected it, but he hadn't really considered that their classmates would tell other people about it. It wasn't that he needed it to be kept a secret, exactly. He just didn't want his dad to find out about any of it. Because if his dad found out about the bet, chances are, he would start asking questions about the prize money. And Parker wasn't ready to answer questions about that. Even though it was technically Parker's money, he knew his dad wouldn't approve.

The pressure was getting to be a lot, and Parker was relieved to have a night off. One whole night where it wasn't about the bet. Everyone already knew where he was, so he didn't have to hide his movements. He'd made an announcement on the app last night saying there would be no clue released today because of his birthday. As soon as he sent it, he felt relief course through his body. He was having fun with the game, but that didn't mean it wasn't stressful. Parker was looking forward to just enjoying himself tonight.

Chapter 26

"So, you and Zeke, huh?"

Sunny looked up at the slightly nasal tone of Victoria. She stood before her, having snuck up while Sunny was looking down at her phone, waiting for Zeke to return from the bathroom. Victoria was dressed to kill in a short black dress that left one shoulder bare and black stilettos that must have been four inches high. In stark contrast, Sunny wore a loose-fitting blush-colored tank top with spaghetti straps. It was silky and had a thick band of sheer fabric running along the v-shaped neckline, making it the perfect mix of sweet and sexy. Preferring comfort over all else, she paired the shirt with dark-colored skinny jeans and black and white Converse Chucks. She felt slightly frumpy next to Victoria, but reminded herself that she wouldn't have wanted to teeter around on sore feet all night. Her clothing choices were infinitely more comfortable.

"Um, yeah," Sunny answered. Having run out of things to say, she waited.

"So, how'd that happen?" Victoria pressed. She leaned forward, like a cat about to pounce on its prey. Her face appeared open and eager, but Sunny sensed that there was a more sinister intention under the surface of her question. She was digging for dirt.

Sunny wanted to exit this conversation, so she searched for Parker or Zeke, hoping to find an excuse to leave. "Oh, I don't know..." she hedged. "Some things are just meant to be." She attempted a casual laugh, but it came off sounding like a crazed giggle. She continued to search the crowd behind Victoria.

Victoria snorted in derision, and Sunny's eyes flew to her face. But Victoria's face was a mask of politeness. She almost thought she imagined the snort. Almost.

"So, where is your devoted boyfriend? Hasn't disappeared already, has he?" She clucked her tongue in sympathy.

"Just the restroom. He'll be back," Sunny answered, not sure why she was engaging but unable to stop. Why didn't she just walk away? Victoria's snort and fake tone made her angry. "You know what it's like with a boyfriend. Can't be by each other's sides twenty-four seven."

Victoria's eyes flashed, and her mouth drew into a thin line. Sunny suddenly remembered that Victoria had never had a boyfriend, at least not one that she knew of. Crap. She hadn't meant to be cruel.

Victoria's tone was sickly sweet, but her words popped out like bullets. "Of course. I'm just so happy for you two. You finally got what you wanted after all those years of waiting." She drawled out the word "all" in a way that irked Sunny.

"Yes, I did," said Zeke. "She was worth the wait."

Neither of the girls had seen Zeke approach. Victoria started in surprise. He wrapped his arm around Sunny from behind and pulled her towards him, planting a kiss on her cheek. She smiled up at him warmly, thankful for the distraction. This conversation needed to end.

Zeke continued, speaking to Victoria directly, "I've been in love with Sunny since we were kids. I'm lucky she finally agreed to give me a chance."

Victoria tittered in something resembling a laugh, but it didn't come out exactly right. Her cheeks flushed. She was clearly embarrassed, maybe even angry. Sunny felt terrible. She hadn't meant to be mean with her crack about having a boyfriend. Struggling to change the subject and make it up to Victoria, she cast her mind across all the possible things she could talk about.

"I heard you got into Cornell, Victoria. Congratulations! You worked really hard for that, and you deserve it." And she meant it. She didn't like Victoria, but she could still be kind. Plus, Victoria was smart and would likely do well at college. If she could just be nice long enough to make some friends.

Victoria tossed her hair over her shoulder, clearly trying to regain her composure. "Thanks," she said, looking slightly surprised at Sunny's kind words. "I leave at the end of August."

"Are you living in the dorms?"

Victoria nodded. Happy with the change in subject to an area where she excelled, she asked, "What about you? I think Parker said MIT, right?"

Sunny hesitated, but she felt Zeke's arm around her give a little squeeze of support. She nodded. "Yeah. Can't wait," she said, but her heart wasn't in it.

Having apparently realized she would not accomplish anything else standing here and talking to Zeke and Sunny, Victoria opted to make her exit. "That's great! Oh, there's Gabe over there. Gotta run. I'll catch you both later!"

And with that, she was gone, leaving a trail of sickly sweet perfume that Sunny couldn't identify.

She turned to look at Zeke. "Well, that was... interesting."

Zeke smiled wryly. "It always is with Victoria, isn't it?" His question needed no reply.

"So, what's next?" Sunny asked.

"Wanna go sit around the campfire?"

Sunny nodded. "S'mores?" she asked hopefully. The sour note left behind by her encounter with Victoria lifted at the thought of the ooey-gooey chocolaty goodness.

"Of course," Zeke answered, as if there were no other viable option. "Is it even a campfire without s'mores?"

They turned and walked hand in hand towards the kitchen in search of supplies.

What Zeke and Sunny saw when they arrived in the kitchen stopped them in their tracks. It looked like a liquor store had moved in. There were bottles in all shapes and sizes of every kind of liquor imaginable lining the countertop. Sunny had never even heard of some brands. Red plastic cups littered the counter. There was a line of people they didn't even recognize mixing drinks, laughing, and chattering. At the end of the kitchen island stood a giant keg with a crowd clustered around it.

Sunny looked over at Zeke to gauge his reaction. Though she was slightly surprised at the sheer volume, she wasn't really shocked to see booze at the party. That was pretty typical high school crap. She didn't normally partake, mostly because she didn't want to be caught doing something stupid that might give people a reason to make fun of her later. She preferred to have one drink at most and then stay sober enough to be in complete control of herself. But she knew alcohol was a hot button for Zeke ever since the accident.

His jaw tightened, and he leveled a gaze at her. "Where's Parker?" he asked, his voice eerily calm.

Sunny winced, knowing whatever came next was going to be so much less fun than a bonfire and s'mores. She considered playing dumb but figured that he was bound to find Parker eventually. So she told the truth. "Last I saw him, he was out by the pool."

Zeke turned on his heel and headed out the French doors towards the pool, Sunny hot on his trail.

There was a sea of people, both in the water and standing around the edges of the pool. Sunny spotted Parker over by the outdoor kitchen area. He was chatting with a couple of their classmates while simultaneously stacking empty cups and plates together and tossing them into a nearby trash can. Sunny saw some of Zeke's frustration drain away when he saw that Parker was actually cleaning up. Sunny threw up a silent prayer that Parker was doing something productive. That was bound to go a little way to cool Zeke's anger.

"Parker?" he said, more kindly than Sunny expected. She blew out a relieved breath. At least this didn't seem like it would be as bad as she thought when they first saw the alcohol in the kitchen.

"Hey, bro," Parker answered, trotting over to Zeke. "What's shakin'?"

"Have you been in the kitchen lately?"

Parker shook his head, a questioning look on his face. "Nah, I've been running around most of the night, chatting, making sure nothing gets broken, you know the drill." He smiled, extending his arms outward with a flourish. "The host never rests. Why?"

Zeke nodded, accepting Parker's answer at face value. He seemed to relax now that he knew Parker wasn't aware of what was going on. "There's a lot of booze in there. A lot. You promised Dad no drinking."

"Shit," Parker said. He ran a hand through his hair. Sunny stifled a laugh because she'd seen that same motion from Zeke whenever he was stressing about something. She'd always thought that Zeke and Parker were polar opposites, but they were more alike than she'd ever realized.

Zeke seemed to have calmed down completely now that he knew Parker was truly unaware of the booze. "I'll take care of it," Zeke sighed. Sunny could almost hear the words he left unspoken. *Another mess to clean up.* He turned away, looking resigned, and headed back into the house.

Parker started to nod, but as he gazed at his brother's retreating form and noticed the tension in his shoulders, he stopped. "Nah, wait," he called, halting Zeke in his tracks. Zeke turned around to face him, surprised. Parker continued, "I got this, Zeke. It's my party, my problem. I'll take care of it."

The party was over. Parker considered that he should feel more disappointed that he had to end it early, but he really didn't feel sad at all. The only people he really wanted to spend his birthday with were Zeke, Sunny, and Mika, anyway. And they'd all hung back after everyone else cleared out.

All four of them were clustered around the kitchen island. A giant birthday cake sat untouched on the counter in front of them. It was covered in thick white frosting and a shower of sprinkles that would make a five-year-old little girl squeal in delight. Marta's handiwork. She knew Parker loved sprinkles. The bright orange lettering declared, "Happy Birthday, Parker!" The still unlit candles, eighteen of them, of course, sat in perfectly straight rows. It was enough cake to feed an army. Or about one hundred of their closest friends. The friends that had just departed. They were going to be eating leftover cake for weeks after this. Sunny was already looking forward to it.

"How'd you get everyone out of here so fast, Parker?" Zeke asked.

"Easy." He smiled and waggled his eyebrows, rubbing his hands together like a cartoon villain. "I released the fifth clue."

Sunny's jaw nearly hit the floor. Her eyes widened in surprise. Since her phone had been on silent all night, she hadn't noticed any alerts from the app. "But Parker, you lied! You told everyone you wouldn't release a clue on your birthday."

"Ahhh, my dear Sunshine," he said, wagging his finger at her. "You underestimate me. I didn't lie. It's after midnight. I said I wouldn't release a clue *on* my birthday. I never said I wouldn't release one on the day *after* my birthday. In my defense, the players really should have anticipated a twist like this. It is a game, after all. Expect the unexpected, you know?"

Zeke let out a bark of laughter. He put his hand on top of Parker's head and ruffled his hair playfully. Parker ducked away from his hand, laughing.

"Gotta hand it to you, Parks," Zeke said. "That's one quick way to clear out a party."

Mika didn't look surprised. She must have realized where everyone was going. Sunny wondered if she'd gotten the alert on her phone or if Parker had talked with her about it beforehand. Sunny hadn't even known what was happening. It was sudden, like a tsunami. One minute people were hanging around, and then suddenly everyone had just started heading for the door. A few of them had grabbed bottles of booze on their way out, but they still had a mess of random bottles and other trash to clean up in the kitchen.

Still confused, Sunny continued her line of questioning. "I thought you weren't releasing the next clue until next Friday. Doesn't this mess with your timeline?"

"Timeline shmimeline," Parker rhymed and waved her questions away. He didn't seem upset by the change in plans. "What was I supposed to do? Stand up and just politely ask everyone to please stop drinking because I promised my dad? Grab the drinks out of their hands? They would have just laughed at me, maybe posted a video of me online and made fun of me until kingdom come. Talking wasn't going to fix this. So if I couldn't take the booze out of the party, I took the party out of the booze. Or something like that..." Parker paused, frowning as he tried to work out what he'd just said. He shrugged, continuing, "Anyway, I had to clear everyone out fast. I could kick everyone out, but that would take a little while. Not to mention, it would be majorly uncool. Again, trying to avoid a viral video of me being majorly uncool. This was way easier. Did you see how fast everyone jetted outta here? No one expected it. And now we have plenty of time to clean the place up before my dad gets home tomorrow."

Sunny frowned, her mind still churning. "Wait, don't you have to go there? To the location. Like, to meet everyone?"

"Nah," Parker waved a hand, dismissing her concern. He pointed a finger at Sunny. "Your app works perfectly. They can all use the check-in feature when they get there, and I'm sure they'll keep the party going there without me. They took most of the booze with them," he said, gesturing around the room. "The app will tell me who is still in the bet. I don't even have to be there."

Zeke looked skeptical. "Are you sure? You were having so much fun seeing who wins and all that."

Parker nodded. "There's still five more clues to go. Plenty of time." He truly didn't seem bothered. "Plus, I'd rather just hang out with you guys, anyway."

"Awww," Sunny said, tossing an arm around Parker and giving him a half-hug. Releasing him, she looked up at him, a question in her eyes. "So, what was the fifth clue?"

Parker looked over at Mika and grinned. "You want to tell them?"

Leaning close over the counter as though she were telling them a secret, Mika smiled. They all leaned in to hear. In a dramatic voice, she uttered the fifth clue.

In a forest, dark and deep,
The path has a secret to keep.
Move carefully, follow along,
Find the secret, and you'll belong.

Sunny and Zeke looked at each other, both trying to decipher the clue.

"Forest, secret, move...," Sunny mused privately while Zeke cocked his head to the side, considering.

"I don't know, the apple orchard?" Sunny guessed.

"Nope," Mika and Parker answered in unison, looking at each other and grinning. They enjoyed the fact that the clue had stumped them.

"You make paper out of trees and books have secrets in them. Well, stories, but they are kind of like secrets if you haven't read them yet. So, maybe the library?" Zeke tossed out.

"Nuh-uh," Parker said, triumphant.

Sunny tapped her finger against her lips while Zeke stared at the counter, both silently working through the clue.

"I give up," Sunny finally said, throwing her hands up in the air. "I'm usually so good at riddles, but I have no idea!"

"Me too," Zeke added, shaking his head in defeat.

"The center of that old straw bale maze at Hawthorne Farm. You know, the one where they do the haunted house thing every fall? Turns out the guy who built it left all the straw bales up at the end of the season, and they are all still there. The whole maze, just sitting there, unused. It's way far away from his property, so he won't hear a thing."

"Oh my gosh," Sunny exclaimed, slapping her palm against her forehead. "Of course! That was always your favorite place to go at Halloween when we were younger. It's surrounded by trees; hence, the forest. Then the path, follow along, like you are following the maze... that's perfect! I can't believe I didn't think of it."

Mika added, "And they don't just have to solve the clue. They have to get to the center of the maze. Since we were going to release the clue this week and the maze is all shut down until fall anyway, we actually already placed all the signs a few days ago. So when people pull up, the signs will tell them they have to get to the center before they can check in on the app. We figured since it was the fifth clue, we could add a little extra challenge to it. They're going to have to work for the ten grand." She smiled.

Parker gave her a high five.

"I love it," said Sunny. "It's genius."

"Okay, okay, enough flattery. My ego will not fit inside this house if you keep going," he said. He clapped his hands together. "Let's cut this cake and then clean this place up, people. We've got work to do."

"Wait, wait, wait!" Sunny exclaimed, running from the room. Everyone stared after her in confusion. She quickly returned with two wrapped presents. "We can't forget the presents!"

"Sweet!" Parker said, eyeing the presents and rubbing his hands together. "I love presents!"

Sunny held them just out of reach. "You can open them *after* you blow out your candles." She set them down on the counter next to the cake.

Parker groaned. "Fine, you big party pooper," he said, earning a laugh from everyone except Sunny, who gave him a mock glare.

After Parker blew out the candles, Sunny handed him the present she had gotten for him. He opened it quickly, ripping the neon green wrapping paper and tossing it aside. Just as she'd hoped, his eyes lit up when he saw the journal. He thumbed through it, stopping to read a quote aloud from the famous director James Cameron.

Parker read, "'Pick up a camera. Shoot something. No matter how small, no matter how cheesy, no matter whether your friends and your sister star in it. Put your name on it as director. Now you're a director.'" A look of wonder crossed his face, followed by a small smile. "It's that easy, huh?"

"Well, if James Cameron said it, it has to be true," Zeke said, nodding solemnly.

Parker nodded slowly in return, considering his words. "Thank you, Sunny," he said, giving her a hug.

"You're so welcome," she answered, warmed by Parker's reaction. "You're going to make movies one day, Parker. And I can't wait to watch them."

Parker wished he had Sunny's confidence. He had so many stories he wanted to tell. But so far, all he'd been doing was writing them down. Would he ever get there, to the point where he was actually making them? It seemed so far away. He cleared his throat, suddenly desperate to change the subject. "On to the next one," he said, reaching for the other present.

It was Zeke's present. The photo album. Which was kind of also from Sunny too. Tearing into the wrapping paper, Parker exclaimed, "Aw, sweet! Is this us?" He laid the album on the table, and all four of them clustered around it as he turned pages. They laughed and reminisced as they paged through it. Parker had to explain some of the funny photos to Mika, like the one where Parker's face was frowning at the camera, covered with whipping cream and crumbs, holding a fifty-dollar bill. Some of the whipping cream was dripping down onto his blue t-shirt. He was about thirteen or fourteen in the photo. He'd lost a bet to Zeke that day.

They'd been at the Crawford house watching the yearly fourth of July hot dog eating contest, and Parker had bet that Joey Chestnut would win again. He'd won the last eight years in a row, and Parker had been so certain he couldn't lose. But he did lose that year. And Parker's penance was to pay his brother fifty bucks. He had the money, but Parker hadn't wanted to accept defeat. So he'd doubled down and bet Zeke that he could eat ten hot dogs in ten minutes. After all, Joey Chestnut had just eaten sixty. If he could eat that many, surely Parker could eat ten. If he won, he got to keep his fifty bucks. But if he lost, he had to pay Zeke the fifty and take a pie to the face. Turned out, Parker couldn't eat ten hot dogs in ten minutes. In fact, he couldn't even eat seven. He puked into a bush in the backyard after downing only six hot dogs. After Parker's stomach calmed down, Zeke had gotten to smack him in the face with a banana cream pie, and Sunny had documented it all on camera.

Mika laughed as they all recounted the story to her, and Parker continued paging through the album. When he got to the last page, Parker smiled and brushed away a fake tear, declaring, "This is the best birthday ever." He enveloped Sunny and Zeke in a giant hug.

"I have something for you too," Mika said hesitantly, tucking a strand of hair behind her ear, as though embarrassed to intrude on their moment. She was still an outsider to their little group for as much time as they'd spent together this summer. She produced a small box from the pocket of her dress. "I know I don't know you as well as Sunny and Zeke," she said, gesturing to them both, "but I hope you like it."

Touched, Parker reached for the small box. "Wow, you didn't have to do that. I mean, it's really nice of you. Thanks." A month ago, Parker would have been through the moon, thinking this meant Mika was in love with him. But now he saw it for what it was. Just a really kind gesture of friendship. And he was grateful to have her friendship.

Inside was a key chain. It was a small replica of Mjolnir, Thor's hammer, about the length of Parker's thumb. "I know you love all the Marvel movies. It's for your new apartment key when you move to New York," Mika explained, babbling a bit as she anxiously watched him pick it up from the box and show Zeke and Sunny. "Or your car, whatever. I mean, what do you get for the guy who has everything?" She laughed, gesturing around her.

"Mjolnir!" Sunny exclaimed, clapping her hands in delight. She loved the Marvel movies as much as Parker did.

"Sweet!" he declared. "I love it!"

"That's the right thing, isn't it? The hammer that you can only pick up if you're worthy?" Mika asked, chewing on a fingernail.

Parker nodded enthusiastically, and Mika visibly relaxed. "Thank goodness. I remembered you telling me about it, but I've never seen the movies, so I wasn't sure... I just thought... well, I saw it, and I thought of you," she paused, as though she was debating if she should continue. "I know you're nervous about how competitive the movie industry is. I thought maybe it would remind you that you're worthy too."

Parker swallowed, his throat bobbing. Mika's words meant a lot to him. She was absolutely correct. He was constantly looking at his journals, wondering if his story ideas were good enough, original enough. It was the reason he hadn't actually written a screenplay or attempted to make a movie yet. Deep down, he didn't believe he was enough. He kept waiting. Waiting for college where he could learn more, waiting for the day when he might be ready. But would that day ever come if he never started?

His voice thick with emotion, Parker enveloped all three of them in a hug. "This really *is* the best birthday ever!"

Chapter 27

"You're not going golfing with the Crawfords tomorrow," Frank Montgomery announced the next day. His voice brooked no argument. It was nearly noon, and they were seated at the kitchen table.

Having gotten home well after four in the morning, Sunny had slept in. It wasn't just the late night that left dark circles under her eyes and a slight headache playing around the edges of her brain. She'd also slept poorly, tossing and turning. Her mind simply wouldn't stop churning. Parker had called last night the "best birthday ever." It made Sunny's heart squeeze in her chest. He was so happy. So happy and so blissfully unaware that both Sunny and Zeke were keeping a secret from him. The secret of what had really happened the night of the accident. Sunny had tried to push the knowledge from her mind every day since she'd learned the truth. The accident was over. Zeke had served his community service. What good would it do for anyone to dredge it all up again? But yet, it still felt wrong. She knew Zeke felt like he was protecting Parker. But Sunny didn't feel that way. She just felt like she was lying, and seeing Parker so happy last night made her feel worse. The feeling of guilt was taking its toll.

Although it was nearly lunchtime when she drug herself out of bed, she'd still arisen to the smell of frying bacon. Her mood should have improved at awakening to find herself being served a full breakfast. But, instead, it turned even more sour. She didn't want breakfast. Why didn't her dad understand that? She was tired. She was cranky. She was lying to her best friend. She didn't know what to do about MIT. Nothing felt right today, and everything grated on her nerves. And now, her dad was telling her she wasn't even going to get to go golfing tomorrow like she wanted.

Sunny froze at her dad's words, a piece of buttered toast halfway to her mouth. "Wait, what? Why?" Sunny whined, despite her father's austere tone. Her first thought was that Mr. Crawford had found out about the drinking at the party, and they were all in trouble. Her heart hammered in her chest as she waited for her dad's reply.

"There's an advisor from MIT in town for an event tonight, and she's flying back tomorrow afternoon. I've arranged for you to have brunch with her at the clubhouse before she leaves. She's going to give you some advice on what classes you need to take."

Sunny let out a breath. Whew. They weren't in trouble after all. After stuffing themselves full of cake, the four of them had scoured the entire house for signs of alcohol and removed everything they found. Despite the thorough cleaning, she was still afraid they missed something.

Her fear was replaced with frustration and disappointment over having to miss golfing. Even in her current crabby state, she had been looking forward to the golf game tomorrow. Parker bet her that she couldn't out-drive him on hole six, which was one of the most difficult holes on the entire course. The fairway curved sharply to the left, so golfers had to make a choice; use two hits to go down the fairway or use one hit to go over the trees straight up to the green. Sunny typically chose the fairway, the safe route. Parker always went for the green. All or nothing. Sometimes he made it; sometimes he ended up in the rough. Sunny was tired of playing it safe. Tomorrow she was planning to shoot directly for the green. But not if she couldn't play.

Sunny searched her mind, trying to find an argument to get her out of the meeting. She didn't know what to do about MIT yet, and she didn't want to talk about that with anyone, much less an advisor for the school. "But I don't have any questions. I already got in. I just have to register for classes. It's not that big of a deal." Sunny couldn't stop the petulant tone from creeping into her voice. She knew her dad could hear it too.

Her father sighed and pushed his glasses up on his nose. "And what classes are you going to register for?" He raised an eyebrow at her and waited for an answer that he knew would not come.

The truth was, Sunny had no idea. She hadn't even glanced at the class schedules her dad had been waving in front of her for the past week. Pushing her plate away, she slumped back in her chair, remaining silent. She looked down at her hands, trying to figure out what to say.

Her dad's voice turned patient and kind as he said, "Addison, I don't know what's going on with you. This is what you wanted. This is what you've worked for. But ever since getting in, you won't even talk to me." He hesitated, as though unsure if he should ask his next question. "Is this about Zeke?"

Sunny's eyes flew to meet her father's. "No!" she protested, nearly shouting. He looked skeptical. She didn't want her dad to blame Zeke for this. She willed herself to calm down and lowered her voice. "Just because I have a boyfriend now doesn't mean everything is about him."

Alan raised his hands, placating her. "Okay, okay. I get it. It's just that..." he paused before continuing, "I remember what it was like to be young and in a new relationship. You were so excited about MIT before Zeke came home. And now, whenever I talk to you about leaving for college, you push me away. It's only natural that I might conclude he has something to do with your change of heart."

Sunny said nothing. She hadn't been truly excited about MIT even before Zeke came home, but she had never been honest with her dad about that. She worried that if she told him, it would break his heart. And she wouldn't be able to undo it. She knew she needed to say something, to answer him in some way. But her mind quickly churned through the options and discarded them all. Nothing would make this better. She simply didn't know what she wanted. And her skin itched at the pressure she felt to provide an answer. In the end, she said nothing.

Frustration evident on his face, her father rose from the table. He grabbed the dirty dishes off the table and set them roughly in the sink. They clattered but didn't break. Resigned, her father said, "Fine. You won't talk to me. Maybe you'll talk to her. You're going to that meeting tomorrow. Period."

Sunny's mood was much improved the next day when she found herself at the clubhouse to meet the advisor from MIT. To her credit, the advisor had greeted Sunny with an unexpected warmth that made her feel immediately guilty that she hadn't wanted to come. As she squeezed Sunny's hand, she introduced herself as Anita Walker and insisted that Sunny call her Ani. She was a short woman, middle-aged, with brown hair cut into a chic bob. Her black dress pants and black polo shirt with the MIT logo on the upper left side were the perfect combination of business and casual. Ani either didn't notice Sunny's initial hesitancy or she chose to ignore it, for which Sunny was grateful.

Pushing her glasses up on her nose, Ani ushered Sunny over to a small table for two beside a giant open window. The scent of fresh-cut grass wafted in on the breeze, and every once in a while the gentle thwack of a golf ball could be heard. It was peaceful, and Sunny felt herself relaxing. The tension in her shoulders dropped away as Ani chattered away about her flight and how beautiful Minnesota was in the summer. Sunny murmured her agreement, happy to let Ani take the lead on the conversation as she settled into her seat.

The restaurant was large and spacious. Having eaten there often with the Crawford family over the years, she felt right at home. She loved the linen tablecloths, the fancy china, the rich food. She already knew what she would order. Their Monte Cristo was her favorite dish. A delicious cross between French toast and grilled ham and cheese accompanied by sweet berry jam. It hit all the sweet and savory notes that she loved. Even though she resisted meeting with Ani, she had been looking forward to that sandwich since her dad told her where they would be having brunch.

After the confrontation with her dad yesterday, Sunny had trudged over to the Crawford house and spent the better part of the afternoon lounging at the pool with Zeke and Parker. She'd pouted a little, but the sun and Zeke's kisses had improved her mood. They had talked about going out to a party Marcus was hosting, but Parker didn't want to deal with all the questions from people about the bet, so ultimately, they just stayed in. Sunny didn't mind. She didn't really feel like partying or chatting with people, anyway. They would just ask her about her plans for fall, if she had a roommate, what classes she was taking. All questions she didn't have an answer to.

"It's so unfair," she had lamented to Zeke and Parker as they sprawled on the pool lounge chairs, drying in the sun after a dip in the pool. "Do you think there's a chance of a blizzard by tomorrow morning?" Sunny asked the boys hopefully. "A good one, that snows everyone in for days? Then I won't have to meet with the lady from MIT and I won't have to deal with my future plans." Sunny paused and reconsidered before adding, "Or my lack of future plans, I guess."

Zeke merely cocked an eyebrow at her. It was clear he didn't think a snowstorm in ninety degree weather was likely.

Parker snorted. "Oh, sure. Yep, there's about as much chance of a blizzard as there is of Olivia Munn walking through that door right now." He pulled his shades down on his nose and peered towards the doorway into the house. Seeing nothing, he popped his shades back up on his nose and leaned back, folding his arms behind his head. "Nope, no Olivia Munn. Guess you're shit out of luck, Sunshine."

Sunny groaned, closing her eyes against the bright sunlight. "I guess I'll just pray that something happens to get me out of this." She was getting into the uncomfortable habit of just ignoring her problems, hoping they would disappear before she had to deal with them. The feeling didn't sit well with her, and she knew the clock was ticking. She was going to have to decide what to do. Soon.

"Welp," Parker said, sitting up and slapping his knees. "I gotta hit the head and get some snacks." He headed into the house, calling out, "I won't be back for ten full minutes. Set a timer. I don't want to see anything gross when I come back."

Sunny threw up a middle finger at him, simultaneously yelling, "Bring me some cheese puffs, please!"

"Ten-four," Parker yelled in return, and then he was gone.

Standing up, Zeke grabbed Sunny's hands and pulled her to her feet. Releasing her hands, he hooked his thumbs in the side strings of her bikini bottoms and gently pulled her closer. His fingers felt gloriously warm on her bare skin. The heat radiated through her.

"Finally," he breathed, dropping his head to her shoulder, where he planted a soft kiss. She tilted her head back to give him better access as he rained kisses across her throat. She sighed in contentment, relaxing into his touch. He continued his trail of kisses up and finally captured her mouth with his. The kiss was almost lazy at first, as though they had all the time in the world to savor each other. As Sunny buried her fingers in Zeke's hair and pulled him closer, a sense of urgency fueled their kisses. His tongue tangled with hers. One arm wrapped like steel around her, drawing her even closer. His other hand blazed a path towards her breast, kneading gently when it arrived.

It was Sunny who pulled away first, but both were panting with desire.

"Parker will be back soon," she whispered. Standing up on her tiptoes, she leaned forward with a soft kiss. One. Two. Three. A promise that there was more to come later.

Zeke nodded. He reached out and brushed a strand of hair from Sunny's eyes. When he spoke, his words were quiet and steady. "You're amazing. Did you know that?" Sunny smiled, her eyes casting downward. Compliments made her nervous. She never knew what to say in return. Saying "thank you" made it seem like she agreed when she really didn't. She didn't feel very amazing. She was terrified of everything, from disappointing her father to losing Zeke. Zeke grabbed her chin gently, lifting, drawing her eyes back to his. "I'm serious. I'm still in shock that you picked me. You are the smartest person I've ever met. I know you'll figure this college thing out."

He took a deep breath before continuing, "But maybe, just maybe, your dad is right. Maybe you don't have to figure it out alone. Talking about it with me and Parker isn't helping. Not talking to your dad isn't helping. Maybe this meeting tomorrow will spark something in your head or your heart, and everything will just become clear. It can't hurt to spend an hour with her. Isn't it worth it if it might help?"

Sunny fell asleep that night thinking about his words. One hour out of her day. That wasn't so much to ask. And now that she was seated across from Ani, she wondered if this had been the opportunity she'd needed to bust out of her cycle of procrastination.

After they placed their orders for food, Sunny relaxed into the conversation with Ani. Though she didn't want to admit it, her dad had been right. Sunny had needed to talk to someone. Ani was full of information about the college, and she answered all of her questions openly.

"What happens if I don't like my classes? Can I switch?" Sunny asked.

Ani smiled, nodding. "Absolutely. You have different requirements you have to meet in order to graduate, but you'll work together with an advisor to make a plan that works for you. Most advisors will have you pick alternate classes each semester too, so if you end up needing to switch or not being able to get into the one you want, you'll still have plenty of options."

As Ani spoke, out of the corner of her eye, Sunny noticed movement outside the window. Not wanting to seem rude as Ani continued to describe the registration process, she turned her head slightly to see what was going on. About ten yards away, half hidden by a giant pine tree, she saw arms waving frantically.

Oh no.

It was Parker, a giant smile spread across his face.

Her eyes widened, and she immediately looked back at Ani to see if the woman had noticed anything amiss. Thankfully, Ani was still explaining how the course selection process worked and appeared completely unaware. Parker was far enough to the side that he must be out of her field of view.

Sunny murmured "Uh-huh," as though she was still listening as her eyes dodged back to Parker. He began jumping up and down. He definitely wanted to get Sunny's attention. She panicked, her breath speeding up. Her pulse pounded. She took a sip of water, her mouth suddenly dry. What was he doing? And where was Zeke? They were supposed to be golfing together. More importantly, how could she get him to go away before Ani saw him? The last thing she needed was Ani going back to MIT and telling them to revoke Sunny's admission because she was unsuitable and also a complete nut job.

Meanwhile, Ani looked down and took a sip of her latte. Taking the opportunity, Sunny frantically tried to wave Parker away with her left arm. As Ani looked up, Sunny dropped her arm to her head and smiled innocently, pretending as though she'd been smoothing her ponytail. Thankfully, Ani didn't notice anything unusual.

"How is your latte?" Sunny asked, changing the subject to buy herself some time to think.

"Oh, it's wonderful. You were right to recommend it. I don't know how they make it, but it's the best I've ever tasted," Ani exclaimed.

Having realized that he achieved his goal of getting Sunny's attention, Parker's movements shifted. He stopped jumping and waving and was making motions with his hands that Sunny couldn't decipher out of the corner of her eye. She was going to need to look at him again. But to do that, she needed to distract Ani.

"Ani," Sunny began. "You've been really helpful. Do you happen to have any materials with you that I could look at? Something with details about classes or anything like that? Maybe in your car or something?"

"Oh, yes, actually, I do." Ani said, beaming and setting down her coffee cup. "I have a bunch of things right here in my briefcase for you. Your father said you were interested in a few different majors, so I brought along some options for you to look at. Sample course schedules, things like that. Just let me..." she trailed off as she bent down and dug in her bag on the floor next to her chair.

Sunny took the opportunity to study Parker. He was repeating a few motions, seemingly in a loop. He pointed at Sunny, then pointed at himself. Next he held up his hands in a jazz hands motion. Then he pointed at Sunny again.

Sunny attempted to decipher while shooting Parker a confused look.

You. Me. Jazz hands. You.

She was completely lost. What on earth was he trying to say? She shook her head at him, her face a mask of confusion. She threw her arms up as she gave up and turned back towards Ani.

Ani plopped a large stack of papers on the table. The top sheet wafted into the air and drifted off to the side, landing on the window ledge beside her. Ani made a move to reach for it, which would have put her in direct line of sight with Parker's crazy pantomime.

"No!" Sunny shouted. Ani started at Sunny's emphatic tone and looked at her, blinking in surprise.

"Sorry," Sunny continued more quietly. "Let me get that for you." Sunny reached across and snatched the paper up before Ani could even turn her head in that direction.

Vowing to ignore Parker, Sunny asked Ani to explain the sample course schedules. Perhaps if Sunny had stopped to think about what typically happens when one ignores Parker, she might have been more prepared for what came next.

Just as they were about to dive into Ani's stack of paperwork, their food arrived. Ani set the papers aside to make room for the food. Sunny smeared the berry jam onto her sandwich and dug in. Despite her reservations about coming to the meeting, she found herself trusting Ani. That trust made her brave enough to tackle the hardest question of all.

"How do you know if someone is right for college?"

Tilting her head to study Sunny, Ani's face took on a sympathetic look. She paused, her pancakes poised on her fork on their way to her mouth. Her voice took on a soothing tone as she said, "You aren't the first person to have doubts, Sunny. College is a big transition. And the truth is, not everyone does well their first year. Some students take a while to adjust. Others... well, others find that it just isn't the right time or the right school for them. Everyone is unique." She paused, studying Sunny silently before continuing, "Can I ask you a question in return?"

Uncertain of what Ani would ask but willing to take the risk, Sunny nodded.

"Your dad said you've been putting off your registration. That you haven't wanted to talk with him about college. Are you having doubts about going to college?"

Worrying her lip between her teeth, Sunny wondered how much to reveal. If she told Ani she was having doubts about all of it, would she tell her dad?

As though she sensed her hesitation, Ani added, "Just so you know, nothing you say here will be shared with the college or with your father. I'm here to help you. In whatever capacity that may be. I can't help you if you don't tell me what's going on."

Sunny nodded, feeling relieved. Just as she opened her mouth to speak, to admit to Ani that she didn't think college was right for her, a waiter hustled over to the table. He addressed Ani.

"Are you Ms. Walker?"

"Yes, I am." she answered, a question in her eyes.

"You have a phone call at the clubhouse front desk."

"I do?" she asked, glancing at her cell phone on the table. "That's so strange... I don't have any missed calls. Who would even know to call me here?" She wondered aloud.

Sunny shook her head, equally confused.

"He didn't say his name." The waiter motioned for Ani to follow him as she arose from the table.

"I'm so sorry about this, Sunny. I'll just be a minute," she said before hurrying after the waiter.

Suddenly, Parker's head popped into the window.

"What are you doing here?" Sunny hissed, glancing behind her to make sure Ani was gone.

Looking back towards where Ani had disappeared after the waiter, Sunny saw the waiter standing there. He quickly gave her a thumbs up and a smile. She turned back to Parker, confused, and saw him return the waiter's thumbs up.

Of course. Sunny nearly slapped her palm against her forehead. The phone call. It was all one of Parker's schemes.

"Did you just Ferris Bueller me?"

Parker beamed. "Yep. Well, I mean, no. Not exactly. I didn't pretend to be looking for Abe Froman, the sausage king of Chicago," he explained, laughing. "But I did make Toby fake a phone call to your advisor lady."

"Toby?"

"Your waiter. Don't you know him?"

Sunny shook her head, indicating that she did not.

"Super chill dude. You'd like him. Anyway, he was happy to help rescue you."

"Parker," Sunny said, a warning note in her voice. "I don't need rescuing."

"But you said you wanted a blizzard! I'm your blizzard!"

This time, Sunny really did slap a hand against her forehead. She measured her words, frustrated, but knowing Parker's heart was in the right place, as it always was. "Parker, that's really sweet of you, but I changed my mind. I actually want her advice. Now get out of here before she comes back and finds out you prank called her!" She shoved at his shoulders, trying to get him to leave.

A panting Zeke ran up to the window. Sunny's heart gave a little leap when she saw him, just as it always did.

Zeke looked annoyed, bent over, hands resting above his knees as he caught his breath. "Parker, what the hell," He looked at Sunny and straightened up, pointing his arm out to the golf course as he explained, "He abandoned me out on hole seven. Took the cart and just bolted. I had to run the entire way back and look all over before I found him."

"Well, you found him," Sunny said, annoyance clear in her voice. "He was trying to save me from the MIT advisor." She put air quotes around the word "save" and rolled her eyes.

Zeke shook his head. "Come on, Parker, let's get out of here. Sunny can take care of herself. Right?" He looked at Sunny for confirmation. She nodded. He put a hand on Parker's shoulder, guiding him away.

As they walked away, Zeke turned around, continuing to walk backwards as they headed back towards the golf course. "Hey," he yelled to Sunny. "Just so you know, you look beautiful today!"

Sunny blushed at his words. She hoped he couldn't see the pink on her cheeks that she knew must be there.

The table jolted as Ani set her phone down and settled into her chair. Oh no. How much had she heard? Sunny steeled herself for the recrimination she expected to come.

"Was that your boyfriend?" Ani asked, smiling knowingly.

Sunny stammered, "Oh, um, yes. He just popped over to say hi. How was your phone call? Is everything okay?" She smiled too brightly.

"Very strange," Ani said. "When I got there, there was no one on the line. But the waiter kept insisting that there had been a man on the phone. So, I called my husband and my father from my cell phone, but neither of them had called me." She shrugged. "I guess it could have been someone from work, but I can't think of anyone. If it was an emergency, they'll call back."

"That's so weird," Sunny agreed, feeling ashamed of lying, especially to someone as kind as Ani.

"Well, back to our discussion," Anita said, determined to get back to the topic at hand. "You were about to answer my question. Are you having doubts about college?"

This was it. This was Sunny's chance to be honest, to confess her doubts about going to college and get advice from someone who was objective. She was finally ready to open up. Sunny took a deep breath and dove in.

Chapter 28

L ater that day, Parker lay on his bed, staring up at the ceiling, his hands clasped behind his head. After golfing, he'd retreated to his room, somewhat aimless. He had nothing he had to do that day, so he thought about what he would pack when he moved to college. He would need all the normal stuff, like towels and sheets and a couch, of course, but he'd also need stuff to decorate his room too. Zeke's birthday present had inspired him. He had loved looking at all those old photographs, so he was planning to loft his bed and cover the ceiling in photographs from their childhood. That way, whenever he went to sleep, he could remember all the good times. He was a little worried about being lonely away at school. The thought of being able to look up and see all his friends and family gave him some comfort.

With that decided, Parker sat up and reached for his phone. He needed to pick a date to release the next clue. He'd been thinking about the Fourth of July, since most people would be around that day anyway, but he wasn't quite sure. Mika always gave brilliant advice. And Parker liked the way she didn't tell him what to do. She asked questions and helped him talk it out. So he texted her.

Parker: *Question - better to send clue on 4th or different day*

As he waited for a reply, Parker thought about how much had changed since the beginning of the summer. In May, he'd been absolutely obsessed with convincing Mika to love him. He would have been terrified to send her a text and probably would have chickened out entirely. But things were different now. He liked Mika, but she was right. They were better as friends.

His phone gave a ding as Mika's reply arrived.

Mika: *Hmmm. If you release it on the 4th, people might be busy. Isn't there already a party at the beach that night? And the fireworks! Do you think people will want to miss the fireworks?*

Parker: *damn thats right*

Parker: *day before or after?*

Mika didn't respond immediately, so Parker stood and walked over to his desk. There was a new idea for a movie tickling inside his brain. A story about a young boy who discovers that his dad has a secret identity as a super villain. The entire story would be from the boy's perspective, and by the end, he would convince his dad to become a hero instead. Parker pulled out the journal that Sunny had gotten him for his birthday. He flipped it open. The blank first page stared back at him. Full of promise, full of possibility. It was pristine. Nothing he could possibly write would do it justice. He wasn't good enough to write in this journal yet. He tossed it back onto the desk and pulled out one of his old, worn notebooks, flipping to a blank page at the back.

He scribbled some ideas for a while until his phone alerted him to Mika's reply.

Mika: *What's the rush? I mean, it's up to you. But you've only got 5 clues left and all of July, right? Is there a reason you need to send it now?*

Parker: *no reason just bored i guess*

Mika: *LOL. Read a book then. :)*

Mika: *What about Saturday night? Seems like you have plenty of time. Maybe waiting will build up some buzz from the players? They will be dying to get the next clue!*

Parker nodded to himself. That made sense. He'd jumped the gun on the last clue. He hadn't meant to release it that early. So they had time. He replied to Mika that Saturday was the plan and went back to writing.

He lost track of time as he buried himself in outlining the story he envisioned. Hours later, the sun had set and his stomach was grumbling. He headed downstairs for a snack and heard the sounds of music drifting softly from the music room. He couldn't make out the tune, but he wasn't a classical music expert, so he probably wouldn't have known the song, anyway. If Zeke was playing musical scores from movies, now that would be a different story. Flipping on the TV in the kitchen, he dug in the fridge and grabbed the box of leftover pizza. The weather man was giving the forecast for the week, sunny and hot. Perfect Fourth of July weather.

He threw a couple of slices onto a plate and tossed it in the microwave.

The phone on the counter rang just as he'd pulled the plate out of the microwave and brought a slice of lukewarm pizza to his lips. Parker wrinkled his nose at the phone and took a bite. No one ever called the landline. It was really only there for emergencies.

He reached for it, pizza still in hand. Picking the handset up, Parker answered "Yello?" through a mouthful of pizza.

"Hello, is this Parker Crawford?" a brisk feminine voice asked. Parker swallowed his bite of pizza. Who would call the landline for him? Weird.

"You got me. Who's asking?"

"Oh, wonderful! This is Sara Ross from Channel Four news. I'm wondering if I could get a comment from you on this new app I keep hearing all the kids talking about these days. I hear your name coming up a lot from people I've been interviewing. It seems you're running some kind of contest with your classmates? I'd love to hear more about that. Would you be open to a few questions?"

Parker was shocked into silence.

"Mr. Crawford? Are you there?"

Parker gulped.

"No comment." No comment? Sunny would laugh if she heard him utter those words. When had Parker ever had nothing to say? But this was one time that he definitely did not want to go on record.

"But if you could just spare a minute…"

Parker quickly set down the handset, feeling shell-shocked. He thought that the last news story about the app had been it. That was all. Things would just blow over. Why did this reporter want to cover the story again? If his dad caught wind of this, he was dead meat.

Parker tossed the rest of his pizza in the trash, his appetite gone. A small knot had formed in his stomach. He didn't like the feeling. He was in trouble. Needing some help from Sunny and Zeke, Parker headed to the music room.

Sunny lay cradled in Zeke's arms in the music room. Zeke had just finished practicing a piece composed by Rachmaninoff when he was just nineteen years old. Sunny wasn't a music aficionado, but she couldn't imagine writing something that beautiful and complex at that age. Zeke's fingers had flown over the keys as he played. It wasn't perfect. At one point, he slapped his hands down on the knees in frustration when he couldn't get the fingering just right. But at the pace he was practicing, she knew he would get there.

She'd quietly walked over to where Zeke sat on the bench, head hunched over in concentration. She leaned down and kissed the back of his neck gently, her hands resting on his tense shoulders. As she continued laying soft kisses across his skin, she felt the tension sink out of his body. He turned, capturing her mouth with his, and they'd quickly ended up on the couch, wrapped in each other's arms. Sunny thought that was likely in their top ten best make-out sessions ever. Not that she was keeping score. Okay, maybe she was keeping score a little.

She sighed in contentment, twirling her fingertips up and down Zeke's arm.

"What's wrong?" he asked.

"Nothing at all. That was a happy sigh." She paused, worrying her bottom lip as she contemplated whether to share her innermost thoughts. She still felt a little unsure around Zeke, as though he might suddenly announce one day he no longer liked her. And the longer they were together, the more she realized how painful that would be. But she was in it now. There was no going back. "I was thinking that I wished things could be like this forever. You. Me. Lazy summer days. Beautiful music." Zeke reached for her hand and twined their fingers together. "No future to worry about. Just us."

Zeke kissed the top of her head. "That sounds amazing. But the future is coming whether we like it or not."

Sunny groaned and buried her face in Zeke's chest. "Don't say that," she said, her words muffled by Zeke's shirt.

"Things can't stay like this forever, Addison. We've got to grow up sometime."

His words raised her hackles. Annoyed at his insinuation that she was acting like a child, she slipped out of his arms and stood beside the couch, looking down at him.

"I know that, Ezekiel." It was petty to use his full name just to get back at him for bursting her bubble, but they knew how to push each other's buttons. "I'm just saying, I wish we could freeze time. I know that's not real. It's just... things are so good now. And who knows what's going to happen this fall? Parker's the only one that actually has a plan. You and I? Where will we be?" Her voice turned pleading. She left an unspoken question hanging in the air. *Will we still be together?*

Zeke raised himself up to a sitting position, looking a little resigned as he faced a serious discussion that he hadn't anticipated moments ago. "I can't answer that, Sunny. I don't know what I'm going to do. My dad still wants me to live with my uncle. But I... I've been thinking more about playing piano. Now that I've started playing again, I don't want to stop. But I don't know what that means for me." He shook his head. "I just don't know," he repeated.

Sunny looked down at the ground and shifted her weight from side to side. His words didn't answer her real question. They didn't give her any clues as to what her place was in his future. Did she even have a place at all? Was he even considering her in his decision? Because she was thinking about him. He was practically all she was thinking about lately. Would they still be together if she went to MIT? Would they still be together if she didn't go to MIT? He wasn't the reason she was struggling with her decision, but their future was definitely on her mind. It stung to hear that it didn't seem to be on his. She stayed silent.

Zeke stood so close to Sunny he could reach out and touch her. But he didn't. "And what about your future? Did your talk with that lady this morning help you decide?"

"I don't know..." It was as though the air had been sucked out of the room. Sunny suddenly needed some space, room to breathe. She turned and paced the length of the room. "Ani was really nice, super helpful. I told her I learn more from actually trying things than from sitting in a classroom. She understood. I guess there are a lot of chances for experimentation at MIT. She talked about the clubs I can join. Some students even start businesses when they are in college. She said I could build apps on the side while going to class if that was what I wanted. I mean, that all sounds great. I just... I think I just need more time. It's not even July yet."

"July starts tomorrow," Zeke countered. "I think you're running out of time."

"I still have time," Sunny snapped, turning back to face him from across the room.

Zeke gesturing widely with his arms. "And what are you going to tell your dad while you take all this time? He's been hounding you for an answer every day. You think he's suddenly just going to stop asking you to pick out your classes and your dorm room and buy supplies and all that? Isn't your tuition payment due soon? Can he even get a refund if you don't go? Don't you think you owe it to him to be honest?"

Sunny felt her face heat. She didn't like that Zeke was shining a light on the fact that she hadn't been entirely truthful with her father and that she might cost him serious money because of her delay. She already felt guilty enough on her own without him throwing it in her face. "You're lecturing *me* about honesty?" she scoffed. "How about you point that finger right back at yourself? Are you being honest with your dad? Are you being honest with Parker?"

"That's different," Zeke defended himself.

"It absolutely is not. A lie is a lie. And you're living one right now. And you're forcing me to live one too. Do you think it's easy for me to see Parker every day, knowing that he has no idea what really happened? So don't act all innocent when you're lying too."

Zeke shook his head. "The difference is, my lie helps people. Yours doesn't. You're hurting your dad by not being honest with him."

"No way. Your lie hurts people too. You are hurting yourself by not being honest with your dad and your brother. You got kicked out of school, for chrissake. How is that not hurting anyone?" She threw up her hands in frustration.

Zeke stabbed a finger towards his chest. "I did that for my family. For Parker. It was worth the sacrifice to protect him."

"He doesn't need your protection! When are you going to realize that?" Sunny folded her arms in front of her chest and added defensively, "And I'm going to talk to my dad, eventually. When I'm ready. What about you? When does it end? Or are you just planning on lying forever?"

Zeke's face took on a stony expression, and he crossed his arms in front of his chest in a mirror of Sunny's stance. Her jaw dropped in shock as realization dawned. "Oh my god. You *are* planning on lying forever, aren't you? You have no intention of ever telling them the truth." She shook her head. "I can't believe you're judging me. You really think what I'm doing is worse than what you are doing." She let out a bark of frustrated laughter. "What you're doing is so much worse. I'm not even lying, exactly. I just haven't talked to my dad yet because I don't know what I want to do. I'm going to talk with him." At Zeke's skeptical look, she reiterated, "I will. It's just... it's a lot of pressure, you know. "

Immediately, Zeke's face turned thunderous. He took two measured steps towards her and then stopped. His voice was quiet, almost deadly. "You think I don't know about pressure? Did you seriously just say that to me? I basically had to raise my little brother. My life is nothing *but* pressure."

Sunny was too pissed to see the reason in his words. "You don't understand. I'm trying to live up to everything my mom wanted for me before she died."

Zeke let out a bark of incredulous laughter. "And what the hell do you think I'm trying to do?"

Sunny couldn't rein in the anger, couldn't admit that she saw the similarities between their two situations. Both of them were living up to the expectations of a mother who had died so long ago. But she didn't know how to stop. She was pissed off, and even though she knew he didn't deserve it, Zeke was going to bear the brunt of that. Her voice raised. "I don't know, control everything and everyone? Martyr yourself? Run Parker's life forever?"

"Oh my god, you are un-fucking-believable!" Zeke shouted.

"Me? I'm unbelievable? You're lying to Parker!" Sunny shouted back.

"And you're lying to yourself!" Zeke exclaimed. Attempting to get a handle on his emotions, he stopped and closed his eyes. He lowered his voice and opened his eyes, his gaze steady on Sunny. He looked sad, a little defeated. "This is getting us nowhere. We're just going round and round. I can't do this anymore. "

In an instant, her anger transformed into pain. These were the words she'd always feared. Was this it? Were they done? Her throat tightened as she fought back tears. She would not show him how much his words hurt. A mask of indifference slipped across her face. Her voice turned icy. "Well, thank you for letting me know," she said in a forced, polite tone. "If that's how you feel, that's fine with me. Let's just break up and be done with all of this."

"Wait, what? That's not what I said," Zeke protested. "I meant—"

"No, I heard you," Sunny interrupted. "You can't do this anymore. So fine. We won't." Sunny paused while Zeke appeared to fumble with his words. She weighed whether or not to continue. Ultimately, she had to know. She looked into his eyes and forged ahead. "I didn't factor into your future plans at all, did I? You were so busy throwing away your entire life for Parker that you didn't even stop to consider what that meant for our future. For you and me."

Zeke shook his head at her, disappointment evident on his face. "Don't do that. Don't twist things around. That decision was made before you and I were..." he waved a hand and trailed off.

Sunny hated the pleading tone her voice took on as she asked, "So what? People change their minds all the time. You can still undo this, tell Parker the truth, get your life back." If he did that, she could stop lying to her best friend. They could stop arguing and get back to where they were before. She left those words unspoken.

Zeke shook his head. "You just don't get it. There's no going back. I can't just tell the judge I lied, and he magically wipes my record clean. It doesn't work that way. Life is complicated, Addison. When are you going to grow up and realize that not everything is as simple as you think it is?"

"Wow," Sunny blinked, anger and hurt flashing through her. "I can't believe you. You self-righteous asshole. You think lying to your family makes you a grown-up? Newsflash. It doesn't. It just makes you a liar," she shot back as she stalked over to the door.

"Well, at least I'm not a coward," he fired back.

Sunny whirled to face him, her eyes wide. "A coward? How am I a coward?"

Stabbing a finger towards her, Zeke said, "You know in your heart what you want to do. You've known for months. You're just too afraid to tell your dad."

"That's not true at all. I really don't know. It's a huge decision. A life-altering one. And apparently I made the gigantic mistake of thinking you cared enough about me to help me figure it out. Don't worry. I won't make that mistake ever again. We're done." She turned on her heel to leave the room.

Zeke swiped his hands through his hair, making it stand on end. He called after her as she walked away, "Fine by me! Go to college, don't go to college. I don't give a shit anymore. But do it because it's what you want to do, not because it's what your mother wanted for you ten goddamn years ago!"

The sound of the slamming door was her only response.

Feeling the impending doom of his father finding out about the bet, Parker hummed the Star War's Imperial March as he walked down the hallway to the music room. He heard the shouts as he neared the door and twirled on his heel, back the way he came, never breaking the pattern of his humming. Nope, not interested in getting in the middle of that argument. Sunny and Zeke could really get going sometimes, and he had his own problems to deal with today.

Suddenly, he picked his name out of the shouts. He stopped humming. The knot of dread that had already been forming in his stomach grew into a pit. He quickly checked both directions down the hallway before creeping closer to the door and pressing his ear up against it.

"You're lying to Parker!" he heard Sunny shout.

Parker jumped back as though shocked. Zeke was lying to him? And Sunny knew about it? She sounded pissed. Maybe she'd just found out, and that's why they were fighting.

What was Zeke lying about?

Parker pressed his ear to the door again, but their voices had dropped and he couldn't make anything out. He quieted his breathing and strained to hear, but it was useless. The soundproofing in the room was too good. He was going to need a tool to help him hear through the door. He headed to the kitchen to get an empty water glass.

As he opened the cupboard door, he heard a door slam. He froze. That sounded like the music room door. Another door slamming, this one the exterior door to the house. Clearly, one of them had left. But which one?

Parker heard the faint tones of the piano, this time stomping out a thundering melody that Parker couldn't place. The tones were dark and heavy and fast-paced, and even through the soundproofing, Parker could tell it was the music of anger. Zeke was obviously pissed off.

As much as it was killing him, now was not the time to ask Zeke what he was lying about. His brother wasn't talkative on a good day, much less when he was angry about something. No. This was going to require Parker to take a different route. Sunny was an easier mark. He'd start with her. They never kept secrets from each other, so she would definitely tell him what was going on.

The phone call from the reporter forgotten, Parker headed for the door.

Sunny stomped away from the Crawford house and headed toward home. Her feet moved like lightning. She was fuming.

She heard Parker before she saw him. It wasn't the slapping of his Adidas slides on the concrete sidewalk that alerted her to his presence. It was the distinctive whistle to get her attention. He could whistle louder than anyone else she knew.

She was in no mood to talk, but she slowed to a stop, anyway. It wasn't Parker's fault that she and Zeke had fought. Well, in a way, it was, because he'd been the one drinking and driving. She was still mad at him about that. But he was completely in the dark about all of it, so she pasted a smile on her face and turned to face him.

"What's up?" she asked, that stupid fake smile still upon her face. She prayed her best friend wouldn't be able to tell how upset she really was.

Parker stopped dead when he saw her smiling. He frowned, his face a mask of confusion.

"What's up with me? Nothing. I came to see what's up with you. You stormed out of the house in a hot second. What's going on? Spill it."

Busted. She hadn't anticipated that he'd heard her slamming doors as she exited. Her mind spun to think up a lie quick enough, but she had no time. She stuck as close to the truth as possible. "Oh, that? Just a fight with Zeke. No big deal."

Parker nodded slowly. "Are you okay? Wanna talk about it? You guys haven't fought in a long time."

Sunny felt the smiling mask drop from her face. "I know."

She looked down at her hands, and Parker wrapped an arm around her in a side hug as they began walking towards her house again. They fell into step beside each other.

"So what happened?"

She could do this. She could be truthful with Parker and just omit some details. "Oh, you know how we get sometimes. We just butt heads. He is so damn certain he's right all the time!"

"Truer words were never spoken," Parker said in solidarity. "It's a good thing you don't *also* have that same problem. Otherwise, you two might fight all the time... oh, wait!" he mocked.

"Shut up," Sunny said with no force behind the words. She gave him a half-smile to let him know she was joking.

"Shutting up," Parker said, mimicking closing a zipper across his mouth.

They walked in silence. When they neared Sunny's driveway, she took a deep breath. "I think that was it for us. We broke up."

"I'm sorry, Sun. Are you sure? I thought you guys were the real deal."

"Me too. I guess we were both wrong."

"What was the fight about?" When Sunny hesitated, Parker continued quickly, "You don't have to tell me if you don't want to. I just thought maybe you wanted to talk about it."

She decided to share as much as she could. "It's just... I don't know what I'm doing this fall, and Zeke thinks I'm running out of time to decide. He wants me to talk to my dad, and he just doesn't understand that I'm not ready to do that yet. He's so pushy sometimes!"

"Sooooo pushy," Parker nodded in solidarity. "So, you weren't fighting about anything that had to do with me?"

A fake laugh she didn't recognize tittered from her lips. Had he overheard their fight? "Who, you? No, no. Of course not! Not a chance. My gosh, why would you even think that?" *Stop protesting,* her brain told her.

"No reason," he replied easily. Sunny relaxed. He continued, "I'm just like the third wheel, always hanging around. So I thought maybe I was getting in the way or something. You can tell me, you know. I would totally understand. No hard feelings."

This was something Sunny could be completely honest about. "Parker," she said, putting a hand on his arm. "You are not in the way at all. You could never be in the way."

"Oh, good," he said, though he didn't sound relieved. In fact, Sunny thought he sounded disappointed. Had he wanted her to say he was in the way? But that didn't make any sense.

"Do you want to come inside and hang?" Sunny asked. She was really only asking to be polite. In truth, she wanted to go into her room and listen to sad music while she cried into her ice cream. Parker would just crack jokes and try to make her laugh to cheer her up. That's what he always did when she was sad. She usually appreciated it, but not today. Not this time. This time, she wanted to wallow in her misery alone.

Parker shook his head, frowning. "Nah, I better get back. I'll text you later. Okay?"

She nodded and turned to head into the house. There was a tub of chocolate fudge brownie ice cream with her name on it.

Chapter 29

Sunny had always been certain that Valentine's Day was the worst day of the year to be single. It turned out that she was wrong. Being single on the Fourth of July was infinitely worse.

First, Valentine's Day was in the winter. In Minnesota, that meant it was freezing outside. A person could hide in their house at night, avoiding all the couples out to dinner celebrating, and no one would even notice. For Sunny, she had always felt a little pang of loneliness on Valentine's Day, but she'd never been truly alone because she had Parker. A friend wasn't quite the same, but it sure helped.

Being single on the Fourth of July was different. It was summer, and it was hot. Everyone was at the lake. And everyone was coupled up. Or maybe it was just Sunny's broken heart making it feel that way. Either way, everywhere she looked, she saw love. Marcus was making out with some girl Sunny had never seen before. Megan and Tyler, who had teamed up to win the bet, had apparently realized they made a perfect team in other ways too. They were wrapped in each other's arms beside the fire, making googly eyes at each other. They looked blissfully happy. Graham was holding hands with Piper Albert, a quiet girl from their school who was a grade below them. Sunny actually felt a little happy for a second when she saw that. She was glad that Graham had found someone. He was a really nice guy.

Even though she was happy for him, she was still a little jealous of how in love they seemed.

Even Victoria had found someone. Sunny almost choked when she saw her. She didn't recognize the guy Victoria was with. They were walking down the beach together, her arm slung casually through his. They looked comfortable, relaxed. For once, she wasn't wearing a skin-tight dress and high heels. She was barefoot, wearing a tie-dyed flowing dress, her hair down in waves. She looked as un-Victoria-like as Sunny had ever seen her. He said something, and she laughed, her head thrown back. It was a genuine laugh, not one of her fake ones when she knew people were watching. She seemed so happy. What had happened to everyone this summer?

Adding to Sunny's misery was the fact that Parker had been too busy to hang out most of the week. The only time they'd gotten together was to go to the opening of *Spider-man: Far From Home*. Not even the amazing movie and the mouth-watering popcorn had lifted Sunny's mood. And she hadn't even seen Parker the entire rest of the week, so Sunny felt well and truly alone for the first time in a long time. And it hurt. Much worse than being single on Valentine's Day.

When she'd arrived at the beach party, she aimlessly drifted from group to group, always at the fringes of the conversation. She laughed when someone made a joke, and she nodded at all the right places in the conversation. Someone offered her a beer at one point. She accepted it, but she never took a sip. It really just gave her something to do with her hands. She prayed she didn't look as pathetic as she felt. She texted Parker, but he didn't reply.

Once the sun set, everyone clustered around the fire even though it was still plenty warm without it. Sunny felt as though she were a ghost, as though she wasn't really there. She set her untouched beer down on a hunk of wood that had been repurposed as a bench. As she drifted over to the shoreline, she checked her phone again. No missed messages or calls.

She plunked down on the sand, far enough away from the water's edge that she wouldn't get wet from the waves gently breaking on the shore. There were always a lot of boats out on the Fourth of July, and tonight was no different. She watched their lights in the distance. She imagined what it would have been like to be out on one of those boats, snuggled up in Zeke's arms. They could have watched the fireworks together, wrapped in a blanket to keep out the mosquitoes. She would have liked that.

A tear spilled down her cheek, and she angrily swiped it away. She didn't want to cry anymore. She'd had the entire week to mourn the loss of their relationship and stew over their fight, though it wasn't as if she'd done nothing all week. Needing the distraction, she'd spent most of her waking hours on her trusty computer. It had shocked her to see that the app had over 800,000 downloads. She couldn't imagine that many people wanting to use something she'd created. But with that many downloads came a ton of reviews. No one had found anything awful, thank goodness. But there were a couple of bug reports and some new feature requests she wanted to address. She'd bounced between fixes and enhancements of the Bet app and working on her new app idea, the one that would match donors up directly with students who needed help with their tuition. She didn't know much about scholarships or donations, so much of her time was spent just outlining her idea and researching. There were a lot of rules about donations, taxes, and scholarships that she would need to navigate if she wanted to get this idea off the ground. It felt good to think about making something that would help somebody. And it was a welcome distraction from thinking about Zeke.

She must have picked up her phone to message him a thousand times, even going so far as to draft a text a few times. She knew she owed him an apology. But she hadn't been able to send the messages. Why was it so hard to reach out to him? The things he'd said about her mother hurt. She couldn't believe he didn't understand. Of all the people that should know how important it was to honor her mother's memory, she would have thought Zeke would get it. She felt betrayed.

Zeke hadn't messaged her either. Sunny knew she had been cruel during their fight, but Zeke had been too. He was always the mature one. Why hadn't he extended an olive branch? Even though it was over between them, she couldn't imagine not talking to him ever again. After all, they had to see each other every Sunday. She was best friends with his brother. They couldn't avoid each other forever. Sunny knew if he apologized first, she could find the strength to get the words out too. And then maybe everything would be okay again. Maybe she wouldn't feel this incredible weight pushing down on her chest every time she thought of him.

Sighing, Sunny looked back towards the fire pit. Parker was there now, laughing with Mika. Why hadn't he texted her? She stood, dusting the sand off of her backside, and headed back to the fire. She surreptitiously dabbed at her eyes to make sure her makeup wasn't smudged from her tears.

"Hey," Sunny said tentatively as she approached. Parker had been so distant all week, and she felt awkward in his presence for the first time in a long time.

"Hey, Sunny," Parker answered mildly, not a hint of anything amiss on his face.

Mika greeted Sunny with a warm hug. "How are you?" she asked with a sympathetic look. Sunny had texted Mika to fill her in on the breakup. They had exchanged a few text messages, but they hadn't talked much since.

Sunny waved her hand dismissively. "Oh, you know, I'm fine. People break up all the time, right? No biggie."

Parker raised his eyebrows, but said nothing.

Turning to Parker, Sunny asked somewhat nervously, "Why didn't you text me?"

He patted his pockets dramatically. "I'm flying analog tonight. My phone died, so I left it at home on the charger. I hate having it with me lately, anyway. Everyone is texting me constantly for hints about the next clue. It's insane."

"Oh," Sunny replied. She struggled as she considered what to say next. She couldn't help but feel like something was off between them. But maybe it was just her. Everything felt off to her right now.

Mika filled the silence with a question of her own. "Have you seen Zeke since... you know?"

Sunny shook her head. "No. I wasn't sure if he'd be here tonight." She surveyed the party, but she didn't see him anywhere.

Parker took a sip of his soda and said, "He's out of town. New York, I think? Took off right after your fight to meet up with some college friends."

Sunny's jaw dropped. All this time, she'd pictured Zeke holed up in his house much like she was in hers. It was why she'd avoided going over there all week. She never considered that he was out partying with his friends this entire time.

"Why didn't you tell me?" Sunny accused.

Parker shrugged. "You didn't ask."

Mika swatted his arm. "That's such a boy thing to say. Of course, you should have told her."

"Sorry," Parker said, shrugging again. His tone didn't seem sorry.

Sunny had refused to ask Parker what Zeke was doing all week, because that just seemed desperate and needy. In fact, on the few occasions she and Parker had spoken in the past week, she'd avoided the topic of Zeke completely. Suddenly, she was furious. Not at Parker. Not at herself. At Zeke. He was out having the time of his life while she was home, miserable and hurting. She'd sat there, thinking about texting him, thinking about apologizing. And there he was, living it up in New York City.

Well, no more of that. If Zeke was having a great time, then so could she. Resolved, Sunny squared her shoulders and said, "Well, I don't know about you two, but I could use a drink."

Raising his eyebrows, Parker asked, "A drink drink? Like a real one?"

Sunny tossed her arms up in the air. "Why not? A drink or two isn't going to hurt me."

Parker grabbed her arm, concern evident on his face. "But you hardly ever drink."

"I know, but that's not, like, because I morally object to it or anything. I just don't like to feel out of control. But I think, under the circumstances, a drink to relax is definitely in order. It's no big deal. Just one drink." Thinking back to the accident, she hastily added, "For me and Mika, I mean. You are our designated driver. Zero drinks for you."

Before Parker could respond, Sunny grabbed Mika's hand and dragged her over to the makeshift bar set up on the tailgate of someone's pickup truck.

It turned out that Sunny was proven wrong twice in two days. Not only was being single on the Fourth of July worse than being single on Valentine's Day, but being single the day after the Fourth of July when she had too much to drink and drunk-texted her ex was even worse than worse.

Her head was pounding. She resisted the urge to vomit as she lay in bed and checked her phone for the fiftieth time that morning. No reply from Zeke. Maybe he hadn't seen her message. She wished there was a way to recall the text.

It was so simple. Just four little words. Four awful little words. Four cruel little words. And one embarrassing typo.

Sunny: *I donut love you*

She'd meant to send "I don't love you," and she would bet that Zeke would know what she meant. Last night, one drink had turned into two, then three, then who knows how many. Sunny had been angry. As she drank, the anger melted away. Soon she was having fun. She laughed. She danced. At one point everyone started singing along to "American Pie." Their voices were raised in unison, and they were swaying arm in arm together around the firepit. It was magical. But that's when the sadness kicked in.

She pictured Zeke partying the night away with his college friends. He was moving on. And she was still stuck. Hung up on him. In love with him. Suddenly, she knew she had to prove to him that she was over it. She wanted him to know that she was moving on as well. So she sent that awful text. And as much as she wanted to take it back, she couldn't.

She rolled over to her side, pulling her pillow over her head to block out the light. Her dad had tried to call her down to breakfast earlier, but she'd waved him away with a groan. He'd given her a stern look. He knew what hungover looked like. But she must have looked miserable enough because he didn't yell or berate her. He just brought her a glass of water and two ibuprofen, sighing in disappointment as he set them down. She wasn't sure which was worse, the hangover or her dad's disappointment. Her head throbbed as she chugged the water. Scratch that. It was the hangover. The hangover was definitely worse.

Her phone dinged too loudly for her aching head. It was a text message alert. Hangover momentarily forgotten, Sunny tossed the pillow aside and snatched at her phone. She felt relief when she saw it was only Parker. She wasn't ready to hear what Zeke had to say in reply to her horrible text yet.

Parker: *U alive*

Sunny: *Could you text more quietly please?*

Parker: *This was u last nite*

Parker sent a gif of a Kristen Wiig standing in the aisle of an airplane with the caption "I'm ready to party."

Sunny: *Bridesmaids. Stop texting me. I need to go puke now.*

Parker: *For real*

Sunny: *No. But I'd probably feel better if I did.*

Parker: *Sleep it off*

Parker: *Call me later*

Sunny: *K*

Sunny set her phone down again and threw an arm over her face. She thought about the text she'd sent to Zeke again, and shame washed over her anew. Why hadn't Parker or Mika taken her phone away from her last night? Why had she drank so much? As she drifted off to a fitful sleep, she swore an oath never to drink again.

When Sunny awoke several hours later, to her surprise, she didn't feel like she was dying. After chugging another glass of water and taking a shower, she threw on her baggiest athletic shorts and t-shirt, knowing she looked like hell and not caring in the slightest. She checked her phone, but there was still no reply from Zeke. She wondered if he just didn't care enough to reply or if she'd upset him that badly. Either way, it wasn't good.

When she made her way downstairs, she found her dad napping in his recliner, a thick book about World War II spread open in his chest. He gave a soft snore. Not wanting to wake him and face a lecture, she tiptoed into the kitchen and scrawled a note, telling him she went to Parker's. Now that she knew Zeke was out of town, she felt safe heading over there. Not really hungry, but knowing she needed something in her stomach, she grabbed a handful of crackers from the cupboard. She choked down a few on her walk over to the Crawford house.

"Hey," Parker greeted her at the front door with a worried look. "Feeling better?" He'd forced her to drink a lot of water at the end of the night, but he'd still known she would be hungover today.

"Yeah. Kinda. But I used all my energy to get over here. I need to lie down."

Parker noticed she was white as a sheet. As they headed up to his bedroom, he joked, "Don't barf on the floor. Marta's off today. And I am *not* cleaning up your puke."

Sunny nodded. Talking made her feel worse. She dropped onto the couch in Parker's room, stuffing a throw pillow under her head. "Ugh, I feel like death."

"You look like death."

"Thanks," Sunny answered dryly.

"I hate to say it, but I told you to stop after the first drink. And the second. And the thi..." And he really had. Even though he knew she and Zeke were lying to him about something, and even though it had been driving him nuts all week trying to figure out what, he still took care of her. Of course he did. Sunny was his best friend. No matter what.

"Please. Don't remind me," Sunny interrupted, holding up a hand weakly.

Parker gave a chuckle. "Okay, I won't talk about the drinks. But can we *please* talk about your sweet dance moves?" Sunny groaned and closed her eyes. Parker continued, "I mean, seriously. The robot. The sprinkler. The shopping cart?" He ticked them off on his fingers. "But my personal favorite was that weird little head bob you were doing all night. It was very *A Night at the Roxbury*. Tres chic."

Eyes still closed, Sunny snatched the pillow out from under her head and chucked it at him, missing completely. Parker barked out a laugh.

"Do you think anyone noticed?" she asked, her voice hopeful.

Parker considered telling her yes just to mess with her some more, but she looked so miserable, he couldn't do it. "Nah." Parker waved a hand dismissively. "Everyone was hammered. Well, not me. Or Mika. But everyone else. And you didn't do anything too bad. It could have been worse. You could have been like Caleb." Caleb was a classmate of theirs. Sunny didn't know him well, but he was tall and lean and friendly with everyone. He played basketball and baseball. Sports weren't really Sunny and Parker's scene, which is probably why they hadn't crossed paths a lot.

"What happened to Caleb?" she asked, eyes still closed. It was far too bright in Parker's room. And she was trying to move as little as possible. When she didn't move, she could almost pretend she felt okay.

"You didn't see it? It was awful. Okay, so, he brought some chick from another school. I don't know her. Anyway, they got into this raging fight in front of everyone. She stormed off, and he drank. A lot. By the end of the night, he snuggled up on the beach with a blanket, and someone drew dicks all over his face with a marker. One of his friends put a stop to it all, but it was too late. There are photos. He'll never live it down."

"No way! That's horrible." As awful as she felt, Sunny felt a burst of relief that nothing like that had happened to her. Thank goodness Parker had watched over her. She was lucky to have him in her corner. She'd missed him this past week. Cracking an eye open, she looked over at him and asked, "What were you doing all week, anyway? I barely saw you."

Parker's eyes shifted away. The truth was that he'd been avoiding her all week. She was lying to him or maybe covering for something his brother was lying about. He wasn't exactly sure. But every time she had texted him, he'd felt betrayed and angry. Part of him wanted to call her out on it right now. But the other part wished she would just tell him the truth on her own.

So he hedged. "Who, me?" He looked almost guilty, Sunny thought.

"No, the Pope," Sunny deadpanned, sitting up to study him. Something was going on, but she wasn't sure what. "Of course I mean you. I barely saw you this past week. Were you busy with the next clue or what?"

Parker glanced at his desk and then moved over to sit in the window seat, facing Sunny. Sassy, who had already been sitting there in a puddle of sunshine, meowed in warning. Parker was invading her space. He gave her a gentle pat on the head.

Parker considered how much to tell Sunny. When Parker had left Sunny at her house after her fight with Zeke, he'd been filled with questions. He didn't think Sunny had lied to him exactly. What she said sounded true, and Parker knew her better than anybody. But he was pretty sure she wasn't telling him the whole truth. He headed home to confront his brother, but by the time he got there, Zeke was gone. He immediately texted Zeke, telling him he wanted to talk with him, but Zeke only replied that he had left to visit some friends in New York for the week and they could talk when he got back. Parker had considered calling him, demanding answers. But his feelings were hurt. That, and he didn't want to admit he was eavesdropping on their fight. So he waited. And avoided Sunny. And wondered. Why were they lying to him? Did they think he couldn't handle the truth? He was tired of everyone always shutting him out of things, trying to shield him. He wasn't a child anymore. Couldn't they see that?

And even as he wondered why, he knew that wasn't the real question he should be asking. There was another question he was grappling with. What, exactly, were they lying about?

"Parker?" Sunny asked, jolting him out of his reverie.

She was looking at him expectantly, but he couldn't remember what she'd asked. "Sorry, what?"

Frowning, Sunny repeated, "I asked what you were doing all week. Were you working on the next clues?"

"Yeah, a little, off and on. And writing some stories." It was the truth. He had done both over the past week. He continued quickly, steering the conversation away from himself. "Speaking of the bet, there's something I need to tell you."

Unsatisfied with his answer, she opted to let it go, because his tone sounded serious. "What is it?"

"You know how the news picked up the story about the bet a while back? Well, a reporter called here asking to interview me."

"She called you too? What did you say?" Sunny's eyes widened in surprise.

Parker shook his head, confused. "I said no comment, of course. Wait, what do you mean 'too'? She called the house phone last weekend, but I forgot to mention it because of your fight with Zeke.

Did she call you too?" Parker omitted the part about him actually forgetting because he'd been shocked to learn that they were lying to him.

Sunny nodded. "She called and talked to my dad. He told her we would be in touch if I wanted to be interviewed. Of course I said no way. I can't do an interview. I wouldn't even know what to say. It would be a disaster. She never bothered us again after that."

Parker let out a breath. "I hope that's the end of it then. If she does an article on the bet, I'm screwed. Dad would find out about the money, and I'd be dead meat."

Sunny opened her mouth to tell Parker he should just be honest with his dad, and then she snapped it shut, feeling like a hypocrite. Who was she to preach about honesty? She was currently lying to both Parker *and* her dad. She sank back onto the couch as she mulled that thought over.

She sighed. "When did life get so complicated?"

Parker answered, "I think it's called being an adult."

"Well, it sucks."

Now it was Parker's turn to sigh. "Agreed." He paused and then continued, "For what it's worth, I think you could handle an interview. I mean, I'm glad you didn't do it, because my dad would kill me and all... but I think you'd be pretty great at it, actually. You don't give yourself enough credit."

Sunny's eyes closed for a moment, and she took a deep breath. It almost physically hurt to endure his kindness when she was keeping something so important from him. She managed to keep her voice steady as she replied, "Thanks, Parker. That's really nice of you to say."

And even though Sunny and Parker were only a few feet apart, they had never felt so distant from each other.

Chapter 30

You'll have to be sneaky. Don't make a peep.
I'm filled with things that you cannot keep.
Come on down. Borrow a line.
Just make sure you get here in time.

Reading the clue aloud, Sunny wrinkled her nose as she thought about it. She and Parker were seated at her kitchen table, and he had shown her the yet-to-be-released clue on his phone.

Sunny had left Parker's house yesterday feeling pretty crappy, both mentally and physically. Then she'd gone home only to endure an uncharacteristically brief lecture from her father about drinking and taking care of her health. He seemed a little distracted and doled out no punishment. Sunny wasn't sure whether that was because being hungover was punishment enough or because she was an adult now. Either way, she was grateful.

This morning, when she woke up, her body felt back to normal, thank goodness. She'd showered, put on a white tank top and jean shorts, and even applied a little makeup. It was amazing how good it felt to *not* be hungover.

Parker texted her to come over, but with no idea when Zeke was due to return home, Sunny took the chicken's route and convinced Parker to come over to her house instead. Her dad seemed elated, since they never hung out at the Montgomery house. He took the opportunity to dig out every snack in the house and display them all on the kitchen table. Then he disappeared into his office, giving them plenty of privacy. As he left, Sunny thought to herself that she really did have the best dad in the universe. She made a mental note to give him a hug later and turned her attention to Parker and the next clue.

"Can't keep... down... time..." she mused. Parker looked at her expectantly as she continued muttering under her breath, "Borrow a line? Don't make a peep. Somewhere quiet." After a moment, she snapped her fingers and pointed at Parker triumphantly. "The library!"

Parker whooped, indicating she was correct. He reached across the table and ruffled her hair, saying proudly, "I knew you could do it."

Sunny's hair was up in a ponytail as usual, and his ruffling had caused her hair to stick out at odd angles. He knew she hated when he messed up her hair. She pulled out the ponytail holder and smoothed her hair, sweeping it back up into a messy bun this time. She gave him the evil eye, which he laughed off. Things seemed a little more comfortable between them today. Not much, but a little. It was as if they'd both agreed to just focus on the next clue and ignore whatever else was happening in their heads. For Sunny, that meant attempting to stop agonizing over Zeke. For Parker, that meant trying to stop wondering what Zeke and Sunny were lying to him about. He'd come up with some pretty creative scenarios over the past week. Zeke was adopted. Parker was adopted. Zeke was moving to Antarctica. Zeke was secretly dying of cancer. That one made Parker's heart squeeze in his chest, so he discarded that thought pretty quickly. But he was putting all of those crazy ideas aside for now to focus on the bet.

As Sunny fixed her hair, Parker announced, "I'm releasing the clue at five o'clock tonight. The library closes at six on Saturdays, so anyone who doesn't make it in time won't be allowed in."

"But how can you have a party in the library? Especially if it's closing?"

The library was one of the oldest buildings in the city, and Sunny was sure that's why Parker and Mika had chosen that location to be one of the clue destinations. It had giant stone columns out front, shiny marble floors inside, and smelled exactly like a library should smell. Dry, slightly woody, a hint of must. There were heavy wooden tables in the center for reading and tall stacks of books lining the periphery of the space. Those stacks had seemed endless when she was a child. Sunny hadn't been there in years, but she'd bet money that it still looked and smelled the same. The atmosphere wasn't exactly party-central. Not to mention the whole thing about having to be quiet.

"No party this time," Parker declared, opening a bag of gummy bears. "This whole thing," he waved his hand and continued, "all the parties at every clue... It got a little out of hand. I vowed a while ago, no more spending money, no more big parties. At least not parties thrown by me, I mean. This is just solving the clue. Plain and simple." He popped a couple of gummy bears into his mouth.

"But what about your epic summer adventure? Your last hurrah before college?"

Parker waved his arms, looking around. "What do you call everything we've been doing all summer? We've had our epic adventure, Sunshine." He sighed. "Truthfully, I'm a little adventured-out. I kinda just want to chill for the rest of the summer. Sometimes you just have to let things go."

"Wow. You? Chill? Let things go? That's a very un-Parker-like thing to say," she responded with a laugh.

Parker bristled at her words. "People change, alright?"

Realizing she'd hurt his feelings, Sunny tried to backpedal. He wasn't normally this defensive. "I wasn't trying to be mean. I just never thought I'd hear you say that. You never give up on anything. You are always the king of crazy schemes." She smiled at him, trying to smooth things over. "I love your crazy schemes."

He nodded, appeased.

Sunny scrambled for something to say to get their conversation back on an even keel. "Is Mika meeting us there tonight?"

"Yep," Parker replied. "She's helping her mom with something, so she won't be there right away, but she promised to get there before the time runs out."

"And how many people are left in the bet?" Sunny asked. Though she'd been busy working on enhancements for the app all week, she hadn't actually logged in to check the totals of Parker's bet.

"Fifty-six fabulous contestants!" Parker said in his best imitation of a television announcer voice.

Her voice skeptical, Sunny said, "I don't know, Parker. You're bringing fifty-six people to the library? That's kind of a lot."

He reached over and patted her on the head, careful not to muss her hair this time. "You worry too much, Sunshine. It'll be fine." Then he shoved a handful of gummy bears into his mouth, smiling as he chewed.

Turns out you can't keep a bunch of eighteen-year-olds from partying. Even at a library.

"The librarians must be going out of their minds with all these people," Sunny whispered to Parker and Mika. Parker looked around wide-eyed. There were easily a hundred people in the library. They were clustered around in groups, milling around the tables and bookshelves. Some people were whispering. Others were looking around. More than a few were sneaking drinks from water bottles. Parker would bet money that it wasn't water inside those bottles. No one was even attempting to look at the books. It was clear they were all here for the bet.

With only fifty-six people left in the bet, these couldn't all be players. Most had to be on-lookers, just here to see who was still in the game.

Checking first to see if any librarians were nearby, Sunny whispered, "How do all these people know where to go? The only people who get sent the clue are the ones still in the bet."

Parker gave her the side-eye. "Everything is available on the Internet, Sunshine. After I release a clue, players have been posting it on their socials. Some people have been commenting on their posts to help them solve it."

Sunny frowned. "Isn't that cheating?"

Parker shrugged. "I never made a rule that people couldn't help each other. And the people who were already knocked out of the bet have been picking sides. There's Team Marcus," Parker pointed at Marcus across the room, standing in the largest circle of people. "It goes without saying that he's got the most support. He's in an alliance with a bunch of people, including Victoria. Oh, and there's Team Ashlyn. I don't actually know who she's working with, but I know a lot of people are commenting on her posts, trying to help her win. And then there's Team Randy," he said, pointing to Randy Johnson. He was short, thin as a rail, and appeared as though he was trying to lick a table. Randy then laughed and high-fived a guy standing next to him. "As far as I can tell, Randy is the only one on Team Randy," Parker added dryly. Sunny snorted in laughter.

"I'm Team Megler," Mika announced proudly. Parker and Sunny looked at her blankly. "You know, Megan and Tyler!"

"Ohhhhh," Parker and Sunny said in unison, as understanding dawned.

Mika sighed, a dreamy look on her face. "I love a good romance."

Parker tapped a finger on his lips, thoughtful. "I'd have gone with Tygan personally. Sounds more fierce."

Three more people raced into the library, skidding to a stop as they tapped furiously on their phones, checking in on the app. There were only five minutes left. Yasmin, Blake, and Skye had made it in time. "Yes!" shouted Yasmin, arms in the air.

"Shhhhhhhh!" someone whispered sternly. Sunny assumed it was a librarian, but she couldn't see much over the sea of people in the room.

A voice came over a loudspeaker. "The library is closing in five minutes. The library is closing in five minutes."

Everyone anxiously turned towards the door, watching for more players.

Mika whispered to Parker, "How many people are we waiting for?"

Parker consulted his phone. "Fifty-two people have checked in out of fifty-six. Only four left."

"Looks like this clue wasn't too hard for people," Mika commented.

Parker frowned. "Do you think we made it too easy?"

"No," Mika replied. "I think you have to have a mix of easy and hard. Otherwise, people wouldn't want to keep playing. Too many hard clues and people would give up. Sprinkling in some easier clues makes it seem like they could win, so they keep trying."

"Three minutes to go," whispered Sunny.

The silence stretched as everyone continued to stare at the door. Mika turned to Parker and Sunny and whispered, "Did you know that books are constantly decomposing?" Sunny gave Mika an alarmed look. Mika nodded in confirmation and continued, "Yup. That's why libraries smell the way they do. The paper in the books is releasing chemicals into the air."

Sunny wrinkled her nose. "From rotting?"

"Yup."

"So when I hold a book in my hands..." Sunny's voice trailed off.

"Technically, you're not just holding paper," Mika said with a wicked smile on her face. "You're holding *decomposing* paper."

Parker shuddered in mock horror. "Well, I could have gone my entire life without that fun fact, so thanks for that."

Mika smiled warmly, her eyes crinkling in laughter at Parker's discomfort. "You're welcome."

"One min—" Sunny was cut off by the sound of the door flying open and slamming into the wall behind it. It was Steve Balfour. He threw his hands in the air and brought them down to his pelvis in a sharp motion, shouting, "Suck it, Crawford!" The entire crowd roared in celebration.

The clock turned to six p.m.

There were officially fifty-three people left in the bet.

At the ruckus, multiple librarians appeared, frowns on their faces. They announced that the library was closed, yelling to be heard over the din. The cheering toned down a notch at that, and the librarians herded everyone towards the door. Sunny was impressed by how efficient they were.

"After-party at my house!" Steve shouted, and the cheering renewed.

As they were being ushered outside, Parker kept getting pulled away by various people who wanted to talk to him. His popularity even seemed to eclipse Marcus', at least for the moment. Sunny took the opportunity to grab Mika's arm and pull her off to the side. She'd been dying to tell Mika about the text she'd sent to Zeke. She already told Parker about it earlier today, but he hadn't said much. He hadn't even laughed at her typo, which she thought was strange. She needed to get the perspective of someone more objective.

"I drunk-texted Zeke on the Fourth of July." Sunny covered her face with her hands.

Mika shrieked, earning a shush from the eagle-eyed librarian who was still busy trying to herd a group of their classmates out the center doorway. "You what?" she asked.

"I drunk-texted him," Sunny whispered furiously. "I texted him that I don't love him, but I misspelled 'don't' and wrote 'donut' by mistake."

Mika's jaw dropped open. "You donut love him? You *donut* love him?" Her face started to break into a grin, and she clamped a hand over her mouth to stop it. "I'm so sorry," she said, her voice muffled through her fingers. "I'm so, so sorry. It's not funny. It's really not." A giggle escaped. Then another.

Sunny felt laughter bubble up inside her. She felt awful, but even she had to admit, it was funny. Soon, both Sunny and Mika were doubled over in laughter, clutching their sides as they tried to catch a breath.

Extricating himself from a group of players who were quizzing him on the next clue, Parker loped over to Sunny and Mika. He stopped short when he saw their faces. "What's so funny?" he asked.

"I *donut* know," answered Mika, launching another fit of giggles from both girls.

"Seriously, though. What am I supposed to do?" Sunny directed her question to Mika. All three of them had moved outside. They were standing on the sidewalk in front of the library. Most of the crowd had dissipated, but there were still a few stragglers milling about.

Mika cocked her head, considering. "Well, did he text you back?"

"No. Nothing," Sunny replied.

"And you haven't texted him anything since?" Mika pressed.

Sunny shook her head.

"Maybe he didn't get it," Parker interjected.

"Maybe," Sunny agreed hopefully.

"Maybe he's just waiting so he can talk to you in person when he gets home," Mika suggested.

"Maybe," Sunny replied and then continued, "or maybe he hates me and is too angry to even text back. Or maybe he is having so much fun in New York that he doesn't even give a shit about me. Or maybe he's blocked me from his phone and his life and I'll never see him again!"

Parker and Mika exchanged looks.

"What?" Sunny demanded.

"You're spiraling," Parker said firmly. "Let's get you out of here."

"I don't want to go to the after-party," Sunny said petulantly. "I've had enough parties for a while."

Parker waggled his eyebrows and said, "Don't worry. That's not where we're going."

"It's not?" Mika asked, surprised. She'd just assumed that's where they were headed. That's where everyone was going.

"Nope," Parker answered. "We're going to the movies."

Sunny's face lit up while Mika groaned.

Clapping her hands together in excitement, Sunny confirmed, "Like the movie movies? At the actual theater?"

"Yep!" Parker held a hand up expectantly.

Sunny gave him a high-five, yelling, "Yay!"

Sliding her feet towards the parking lot, Mika said, "Maybe I'll just head home."

"Nooooo. Come on, lady," Sunny said, throwing her arm around Mika before she could escape. "You'll love it. I promise."

Mika looked uncertain, but she didn't flee.

Sunny turned to Parker, her arm still keeping Mika firmly in place. "What are we going to go see? Oh, can we see *Crawl*? Can we? Pretty please?" Sunny loved cheesy horror movies.

Parker shook his head. "It's not out yet, so no."

Sunny stuck out her lower lip.

"*Midsommar* is out and the reviews are stellar," Parker offered.

Sunny gave Parker a stare that wasn't quite a glare, but it was close. "It looks boring. And weird."

"Says the girl who wanted to see *Crawl*," Parker said dryly. "Okay. How about *Toy Story 4*?"

Sunny cooed, "Awww, I love those movies."

That got Mika's attention. She said, "Wait. There's a new *Toy Story* out?"

Parker and Sunny nodded, each privately wondering if Mika lived under a rock, but neither saying a word.

"I loved those movies when I was little," Mika said, excitement lacing her words.

Parker practically jumped for joy. "I knew we'd find a movie you liked one day. Who knew it would be a children's movie? But still. It's a movie. That's what I call progress." He fanned his eyes dramatically. "I'm so happy I could cry."

Mika swatted his arm and rolled her eyes. "Ha, ha," she said sarcastically.

"Shall we?" Parker swept an arm out in front of him, and they all headed out.

Sunny thought that a little bit of childhood nostalgia might be exactly what she needed.

Chapter 31

Sunday morning dawned bright and clear, just a few wisps of white clouds floating high in the sky. Sunny dressed in white linen shorts and a navy blue polo, preparing for their two p.m. tee time that afternoon. She applied her makeup carefully. Understated and classy. She wanted to look mature. Well, not mature exactly. At least not like a total train wreck. Parker hadn't sounded exactly certain where Zeke was, so she needed to look put together in case he showed up. The moment Parker got out of the car in the parking lot, he gave a small shake of his head. He knew what she was hoping for. Zeke wasn't with them. She gave him a questioning look, and he shrugged, understanding her immediately. He clearly still had no idea when Zeke was coming home.

Though it took every bit of restraint that she had, Sunny managed to make it until hole three before she asked about Zeke. Since there were only four of them today, they were golfing together. Parker and Sunny had the golf cart, while their dads were walking, clubs slung over their shoulders. Despite the unseasonably hot summer, the grass on the course was lush, deep green, and well-maintained.

As they waited to tee off, she casually asked Mr. Crawford about Zeke. At least, she hoped it was casual. Parker gave her a side-eye, so she wasn't sure she was fooling anyone about how invested she was in the answer.

"So, where's Zeke today?" she said, taking a swig from her water bottle.

Mr. Crawford was mid-practice swing. He straightened and looked up at Sunny, his eyebrows raised in surprise. "He didn't tell you? I just assumed—" he broke off, clearing his throat.

Sunny shook her head. Her heart sped up, and she felt nervous under his watchful gaze. It was clear that Mr. Crawford didn't know what had happened between Zeke and Sunny. She'd briefly filled her dad in about the break-up, leaving out nearly all the details about what had actually happened. She'd assumed Zeke or Parker had done the same with their dad. But apparently not. She shouldn't be surprised, with how little time they spent with him. Sundays were really the only day of the week that they even saw Mr. Crawford.

Mr. Crawford's eyes tracked over towards Parker. A slight frown crossed his face. "You either?"

Parker answered, annoyance clear on his face, "Nope. You know Zeke. He's not exactly Mr. Communication." He slapped a ball into the ball washer and thumped it up and down angrily.

"Hmmm. I guess that's true. He is fairly reserved. Well, he's out in New York." He turned to address Sunny's dad. "Remember how I told you about his old piano playing days? He's really been getting into it again. Sunny knows," he said, waving towards her. "Anyway, he came to me last weekend, and all but demanded that I put him on a plane immediately to wherever his old piano instructor was so that he could work with him again."

He continued, his gaze turning back to Sunny, "I was so damn happy to see how passionate he was about it. That spark of ambition... Well, I haven't seen it in years, not since Jane died. I got him on the first plane out of MSP." He paused. It seemed like Sunny could almost see the wheels turning in his brain as he considered the urgency of Zeke's request. "Come to think of it, I was pretty surprised that he wanted to leave, especially after all of you kids worked so hard to convince me to let him stay."

Now it was Sunny's dad who spoke up. He cleared his throat before explaining, "They broke up, Alan. Last weekend."

Understanding dawned on Mr. Crawford's face. "Ahhhh. It all makes sense now. A broken heart is a powerful motive."

"I'm not sure his heart was exactly broken," Sunny said weakly. As much as she wanted to believe Zeke still cared for her, she doubted it.

Her heart warmed a little when Mr. Crawford returned, "I wouldn't be too sure about that, Sunny."

She looked down at the grass, suddenly embarrassed.

Mr. Crawford turned back to her dad. "Long story short, turns out that Alessandro was in New York, so that's where Zeke is now. It's a sort of... tryout."

"A tryout for what?" Sunny couldn't stop herself from asking. She cocked her head to the side in confusion.

"To see if Alessandro will consider working with him again."

Sunny bit her lip. What an amazing opportunity for Zeke. She imagined him in New York, sitting at a grand piano in a giant auditorium. He had left without telling either of them where he was going. It was understandable why he'd run away from Sunny, but why was he shutting Parker out?

"He's staying with some friends from college while he's out there," Mr. Crawford added.

So Zeke hadn't lied about that. But he'd left out a sizeable chunk of information.

"When will he be home?" Parker asked.

Sighing, Mr. Crawford dabbed at his face with a small golf towel. It was hot again today, and everyone was glistening with sweat. "I don't know. Alessandro emails me a progress report daily. But Zeke has to prove himself after quitting so many years ago. Alessandro was furious about how Zeke wasted his talent. You have to understand, Alessandro is..." Mr. Crawford waved his arm in the air, searching for the correct word, "mercurial. He's the best in the business, so he can afford to be. He tells me he will know when he knows. Zeke knows that he only has one shot at this, and he can't mess it up. So it could be tomorrow, or it could be a few weeks or even longer." Mr. Crawford shrugged, unconcerned. "I don't care how long it takes."

"But what about Notre Dame?" Sunny asked.

He waved a hand dismissively. "I know I wanted to get him back in there, but that was when he had no direction, no focus. Zeke is really talented. I don't care what he does, as long as he does *something*."

The other golfers ahead of them had cleared the hill, so it was their turn to tee off. As soon as his dad stepped up to hit, Parker turned to Sunny and whispered, "Why didn't Zeke just tell me he was practicing with Alessandro?"

Mr. Crawford hit a beautiful line drive straight down the fairway as usual.

Sunny shook her head as she watched her dad step up to tee off next. "I don't know. I mean, I know why he didn't tell me, since we aren't exactly on speaking terms. But it makes no sense why he wouldn't tell you."

"He never tells me anything." Parker kicked at a patch of grass, his brow furrowed.

Sunny paused, looking at him carefully. "What do you mean?"

Her dad's shot landed his ball right next to Mr. Crawford, in the middle of the fairway.

"Nothing. Forget it." It was his turn to hit. Parker marched over to the tee, thunked down his tee and ball, and whacked it as hard as he could. It was an awful hit, heading deep into the rough on the right side of the fairway. "Dammit!" he swore loudly.

Sunny frowned.

As he stepped to the side of the tee box and walked towards the rough to search for his ball, Sunny made her way over to the women's tee box to hit. She pondered Parker's words as she lined up her shot. As Sunny teed off, her ball flying high and straight, she couldn't shake the feeling that something wasn't quite right with Parker.

"Would you mind switching up, Parker?" Mr. Montgomery asked politely, approaching the golf cart. He gestured from himself to Parker and back again.

"Sure," Parker agreed, hopping off of the passenger seat and un-latching his clubs from the back end. He slung his clubs over his shoulder and trudged off down the fairway in search of his ball. They were on the eighth hole, and Parker's game hadn't improved much.

"What's up, Dad?" Sunny asked as he sat down next to her on the cart. Her body tensed. She'd successfully avoided talking with her father about college for a while. As much as she hated to admit it, she knew Zeke was right. She needed to make a decision. It wasn't fair to her dad to keep him in the dark. And it wasn't fair to herself to live with this uncertainty. But she still wasn't ready to talk with him about it.

She wasn't sure what she was waiting for. It wasn't like she thought some sign from heaven was going to come down and show her what she should do. But somewhere in her heart, she held onto this silly hope that one day the decision would be clear, that it would just come to her somehow. Perhaps she would see something that would trigger her brain, and she would just suddenly *know* where she belonged. Her head was so filled with conflicting thoughts, all the pros and cons of going to MIT, all the possibilities of what she could do with her life, what happened with Zeke. It was a jumble in there. Pure chaos. She was pretty sure there wasn't a single coherent thought rattling around in that brain of hers.

How was she ever supposed to decide what to do?

Her dad shifted his weight, trying to get comfortable on the seat of the golf cart. "Oh, nothing in particular, honey. I just wanted to spend a little time with you."

Sunny eyed him suspiciously, unconvinced. "You never golf with me. And you hate riding in the cart. What gives?" She shifted her hands to the wheel, preparing to drive, but she paused, waiting for her dad to explain.

"Okay, okay." He held his hands up in defense, trying to prove his innocent intentions. "You've just been a little down lately, and I wanted to check in with you, make sure you're okay and everything." He paused, as though he was considering whether he should continue. "You know you can talk to me. I don't want to pry, but you can tell me what happened with Zeke. I was trying to let you work through it on your own because it seemed like you didn't want my help, but you just haven't been yourself for a week now. I just need you to know I'm here for you. Okay?"

Nodding, Sunny blew out a breath in relief. He just wanted to talk about Zeke. That wasn't exactly a topic she wanted to discuss with her father either, but she preferred it to a conversation about college. She stepped on the gas pedal, and the cart puttered away towards her ball. She had made a decent shot. Her ball was up on the green nearby her dad's, so they had a short drive in front of them.

Maybe it would feel good to talk about it, cathartic or something. She took a deep breath. "I ruined everything with Zeke," she said. "We got in a fight. It doesn't matter what it was about. It was stupid."

Her dad nodded, remaining silent as she vented.

"Things just got out of hand. And then, before I even knew what happened, we were breaking up. I didn't even realize it was happening. One minute, we were so happy, and then it was all over." She held her breath, wondering if she should speak the words that had been rattling around in her brain the last few weeks. "I really loved him, Dad. I still love him. But it doesn't matter now. It's over. I messed up." She swiped furiously at the tears clouding her eyes, trying to see since she was driving.

He put an arm around her as they headed down the cart path. When he spoke, it was soft, consoling. "I know it feels like you ruined everything. I've had fights like that too." He rubbed his hand up and down her arm, comforting her as she struggled to stop her tears. She thought she was all cried out, but apparently not.

"Can you try to remember something for me? It's something your mother once told me when we had a fight."

Sunny sniffled. "Yeah," she said pitifully.

"Relationships are not eggs," he said.

Sunny looked at her dad in confusion. "Huh?" she replied.

He repeated, more firmly this time, "Relationships are not eggs." He continued to explain, "Eggs are fragile, right? If you drop an egg on the floor, it's basically ruined and you can't use it anymore."

"Yeah?"

"I want you to remember that relationships aren't like that. It's nearly impossible to ruin relationships beyond repair. People are always growing and learning and evolving. You can't put a broken egg back together, but you can put a broken relationship back together."

"But how?" Sunny asked. She didn't think her relationship with Zeke could ever recover from their fight.

"Forgiveness. It's such a simple answer, but it's really hard to do. If you can forgive him and he can forgive you, this doesn't have to be the end."

Sunny mulled his words over in her head as they pulled up near the green. They parked, and Sunny brushed the remaining tears out of her eyes as she hopped out and grabbed her putter. Parker and Mr. Crawford were still down on the fairway. They had each found their ball and were readying to hit up to the green.

Mr. Montgomery and Sunny stood to the side, out of the way of Parker and Mr. Crawford's golf balls as they soared up to the green. Maybe it was the quiet, maybe it was just because her dad had offered to listen, but for whatever reason, Sunny felt compelled to speak.

She leaned on her putter. "Dad?"

"Yeah?"

"Thank you," she said.

His eyebrows raised. He was clearly caught off guard. It was a surprise, but not an unpleasant one. A soft smile spread across his face. "Well, you're welcome, honey, but thanks for what?"

She looked down at the ground, embarrassed. She felt her eyes welling up again, and she opened them wide to keep the tears from falling again. "Everything," she said around the lump in her throat. She swallowed. "Everything. You're the best dad I ever could have asked for. You're always taking care of me, even when I don't want you to. And I know it wasn't easy to do it alone, without Mom." She almost choked on the word, but she pressed on. "You've always been there for me, and I... I haven't always been very nice to you. I know I've been frustrating, and I just... Well, I love you," she ended simply, unsure of what else to say to express what he meant to her.

She couldn't be sure, but she thought her dad's eyes got a bit watery too. "I love you too, sweetie."

He walked over to her and enveloped her in a hug. It felt so good to be hugged, safe and comforted like she had been as a child. She squeezed him back, squishing her eyes shut and relishing the feeling of love that washed over her.

Pulling back, he marveled, "You have so much of your mother in you. I'm so amazed when I look at you, how strong and confident and smart you are. I couldn't be more proud of the woman you've become."

"Thanks, Dad," Sunny said, feeling slightly self-conscious under his praise. She swiped at her face, drying the fresh tears that had spilled over at her dad's kind words.

Parker approached tentatively. It was clear he didn't want to interrupt, but they had to putt out because there were more golfers coming up the fairway behind them. "Everything alright over here?"

Sunny nodded. "Everything is perfect."

And for the first time in a long time, Sunny's heart felt lighter.

Chapter 32

Monday came and went, but there was still no sign of Zeke. Then Tuesday, then Wednesday, and so on. All week, Sunny waited for Parker to text her that Zeke was home. She was beginning to wonder if Zeke was coming back at all. She wasn't brave enough to text him again, and he never did reply to her drunken text, nor any of Parker's texts to him. The days stretched on endlessly, despite the fact that Sunny was keeping plenty busy working on her apps. Parker was busy too, so they barely saw each other. A few months ago, that would have been unthinkable to Sunny. But things were so different now.

Even though it was already eight p.m on Friday night, it was still light out. Sunny loved the long days that came with summertime in Minnesota. Parker had released the seventh clue, and Sunny was getting ready to head to the clue location, a graveyard on the west end of town. She was both scared and excited that Parker had chosen such a creepy location. She loved horror movies, but she didn't exactly want to be *in* one.

It was still eighty degrees outside, so she donned a simple yellow t-shirt with a wide neck that hung off one shoulder and jean shorts. Dropping a kiss on her dad's cheek and telling him she'd been back later, she snatched the keys from the counter and headed out.

When she arrived, she was surprised to find that there weren't many people there yet. At least, not when compared to previous clues. She did a quick count in her head and came up with only about thirty people. Parker had released the clue forty minutes prior, so there were only twenty minutes left.

The crowd was all gathered to the side of the graveyard. No one wanted to walk or stand on top of anyone's grave. She didn't know if it was respect or fear, but regardless, she was glad.

Parker and Mika were right smack in the middle of the crowd, being bombarded with questions. Both looked a little overwhelmed by all the attention. Mika looked beautiful in a black halter top romper. Meanwhile, Parker was the king of casual in his gray t-shirt and neon orange athletic shorts. Sunny approached them, grabbing their hands and dragging them to the edge of the crowd. "Where is everyone? Did you scare everyone away with your location choice?"

Parker rubbed his hands together, gleeful. "This clue was harder. There's only eleven players here so far. It's going to be interesting!"

A petite, brown-haired young woman approached them. "The latest clue was absolute fire," she exclaimed. She was dressed in a soft pink blouse with white piping and light-colored jeans, her feet clad in light brown leather ankle boots. Her hair fell in immaculate waves, and her makeup was impeccable. She couldn't have been more than a few years older than Sunny, but her demeanor gave the impression that she was much older.

"Glad you liked it," Parker answered. He turned to give Sunny a quizzical look. He clearly didn't know this woman either.

"Liked it?" She smiled warmly. "It was inspired." She proceeded to recite the seventh clue from memory.

> *Secrets bloom, ripe and red,*
> *And drip like blood upon your head.*
> *Underneath the blood, we sleep.*
> *Our names and ages, you shall keep.*

She continued, "I got the fact that it was a graveyard right away from the tone and the reference to sleeping. But it took me a while to puzzle through which one. It was the words 'red' and 'blood' that gave it away. It's a reference to the trees that surround this particular graveyard, right? Red chokecherry trees. No other graveyard had them."

Parker affirmed her correct guess with a nod of his head.

The woman stuck out a hand. "Sara Ross. Channel Four News."

Sunny reached out to shake it, surprised to see that the reporter who had called them on the phone a few weeks ago was so young. "I'm Sunny," she replied.

"Oh, I know. And you must be Parker?" Sara offered a hand to Parker, who shook it. "And you're Mika, right?"

"How did you know who we were?" Mika asked while she shook Sara's hand.

Leaning in, Sara answered rather conspiratorially, "Well, I knew all your names from interviewing your classmates about the bet. As far as your faces, that's a little journalism trick. Libraries archive all kinds of information. Did you know that?" She didn't wait for an answer before continuing. "The library here in town keeps a copy of every single yearbook from Cloud Lake High School. When I can't find photos of people on social media or through an online search, I go analog and start looking up yearbooks."

"I didn't know that," said Sunny.

"That's... creepy," said Parker.

Sara leveled an assessing gaze at the trio. "Information about you three was pretty sparse on social media, I have to say. That's not typical of teens your age."

Sunny shrugged and replied, "Yeah. We use it, but none of us really post much. I don't want a record out there of every dumb thing I did when I was young."

Parker chimed in next. "I'm not giving anyone that much information about me. Big brother and all." He nodded solemnly.

Sara blinked, as though she was not quite sure what to make of Parker's comment. She quickly recovered and turned expectantly to Mika, awaiting the reason she wasn't active on social media. Mika looked back and forth between everyone and held up her hands defensively. "I just prefer books."

Nodding, Sara smiled. "Now that, I can understand. I love to read too. I mean, obviously. After all, I *am* a journalist." She laughed and then continued, switching gears. "Listen, I know you don't want to be interviewed, but I just had to come here and plead my case in person. This story is fascinating, and I'm going to write it. I prefer to do that with your input. It will be more accurate and give me a chance to dig deep and talk about the motivations behind this game you all are playing. I want to hear the authentic story directly from you." She paused, taking a deep breath. "That's my preference, as I said... But I'll write it without you if I have to."

"You know, you've done something amazing here," Sara said, gesturing around at the crowd.

Sunny looked around, wondering what Sara was referring to. She had done nothing amazing that she was aware of. "I have?"

They moved to sit down on a bench off to the side of the cemetery. It was a little quieter there. There were more players arriving and only about ten minutes left before time ran out. After Sunny agreed to speak with Sara, Mika and Parker had wandered away, giving them some privacy.

Laughing, Sara nodded. "Oh my gosh, yes. I don't think you realize how remarkable it is. It's not just about the app you built, although that is nothing short of amazing at your age. It's also about how it's bringing people together in the physical world."

Shaking her head, Sunny disagreed, "But that's not my app that's doing that. That's all Parker. It's his bet."

"Yes and no," Sara replied. "I mean, yeah, it's his bet. I get that. But your app bridges the world of the digital with the physical. Make a bet in the app, but the bet happens in real life. Real people, interacting with each other, having fun. I love it. And my audience is gonna eat this story up."

"Do you really think people will care? It's such a little thing. It's not like it's going to help people or change the world or anything."

"Oh, sweetie," Sara patted her arm. It should have sounded condescending, and coming from anyone else, it might have. But it just sounded kind, like an older sister giving advice. "You aren't giving yourself enough credit. Someone wise once told me it's the little things that can change the world."

Sunny stayed silent, contemplating Sara's words.

Pulling out her cell phone, Sara asked if she could record their conversation. Sunny hesitated, unsure. Recording felt so... permanent.

Sara assured her, "I don't post this anywhere. It's just for me so I don't have to write notes while you talk. I find that writing notes changes the flow of our conversation."

Something about Sara put Sunny at ease. She trusted her. She hoped her trust wasn't misplaced. "Sure," Sunny agreed. "You can record it, I guess."

When Sara told them she was writing the story with or without them, Mika, Parker, and Sunny had all looked at each other, silently debating. Sunny realized that if the story was going to be out there either way, she at least wanted a chance to tell her side of it. She was the first to agree to the interview. She wasn't sure what the other two would do.

Tapping the record app on her phone, Sara began. "I already know a little about Bet and how it works, but let's go backwards in time a bit. What was the inspiration behind the app, if I may ask?"

Sunny felt sheepish as she thought of all the silly bets she and Parker had shared over the years. It felt a little... immature. But Sunny pressed on, explaining, "Well, growing up, Parker and I and his brother all used to make bets with each other. Silly stuff, like who could hit a golf ball the farthest. We were very competitive. We used to keep track of every win and loss on a giant chalkboard. When I started getting into computers, I knew there was a better way. When I first built the app, it was just for us. But then Parker had this idea to launch it to the world. So I rebuilt the entire thing from the ground up, and the rest is history." She glossed over the part about Parker wanting to use the app to win over Mika. That felt too personal, and she knew it would embarrass Parker if she shared it.

"That's an amazing story. A childhood game turned into all of this." She swept an arm out. "You and Parker have been friends a long time, then?"

"Best friends. We've pretty much been inseparable since we met when we were eleven years old." Sunny felt the smile slip on her face. Inseparable until recently, that is...

Sara was listening intently but didn't seem to notice the change in Sunny's expression. "So, that's how Bet got its start. But how about you?"

Oh no. Sunny didn't mind talking about the app, but she really didn't want to share any personal information. Wrinkling her nose, she asked, "Do we have to talk about me? I mean, my life is so boring. I'm sure no one wants to read about that."

Laughing, Sara said, "You'd be surprised. I think people would love to hear about the real person behind the app. But I can tell you're uncomfortable talking about yourself. That's totally normal. Let's put a pin in that question for now, and we can focus on something else. We'll come back to you later."

Sunny let out a breath she didn't realize she'd been holding. She smiled and tossed out a relieved, "Thanks."

Sara switched up her line of questioning. "Your app is obviously a tremendous success. You have over a million downloads last time I checked. And it's still available for free. Have you thought about monetizing it? Ad revenue, add-on features?"

Sunny nodded. "I actually have an update ready to roll out next week. I'm just putting the finishing touches on it. It's important to me to keep the basic function free for everyone to use, but some people have asked for more advanced features. I've bundled all of those together, and I'm planning to allow people to subscribe monthly." She rushed to explain, "It's not like I want to overcharge people or anything. I just thought that maybe, if people want to use the advanced features, they could pay a dollar or two a month to access them."

"That's a great idea. Lots of apps follow that model." Sara nodded. "Don't feel one bit bad about charging. You worked hard on this app, and you will have to keep working hard to add content and continue to grow it. You deserve to be compensated for your efforts."

Encouraged, Sunny explained, "It's essential that everyone be able to use the basic features of Bet for free. I built it for fun, after all. But it would be nice if I had a little funding for my time."

"Perfectly understandable." Sara waved an arm as though she was brushing away Sunny's concerns.

Sunny felt relieved. She'd been feeling a little guilty about wanting to charge for a set of advanced features, so Sara's reassurance meant a lot to her.

"So tell me," Sara leaned in, "what are you working on next?"

Sunny hesitated, a slow smile spreading across her face as she thought about how excited she was about the new app she was creating to help students find funding for college. She didn't answer.

"Come on," Sara persisted. "A sharp young woman like yourself? You've got to have another app in the works. You do, don't you?"

Sunny smiled and knotted her hands together in front of herself. She wasn't embarrassed exactly, but she was reluctant to talk about it. She didn't want to jinx anything. At the same time, she was really proud of the idea and kind of wanted to share it with Sara. "Well, I do, but it's not quite ready yet."

Sara continued to prod. "Would you be willing to tell me about it?"

So Sunny did.

Chapter 33

Sunny had been refreshing the web browser on her computer for the past ten minutes. Sara had said the article would be released online at nine o'clock Tuesday morning. Naturally, Sunny had started refreshing her screen early, just in case. But it was now 9:04 a.m. and nothing had changed as far as Sunny could tell.

9:05 a.m.

Refresh again.

Sunny gasped. There it was!

Recent high school graduate Addison Montgomery turns a childhood game into a viral sensation.

That was her! A viral sensation? Sunny wasn't sure about that. Her app had over one million installations now, and it was growing every day. But she still didn't feel like she'd gone viral. She wasn't famous or anything.

It felt surreal to see her name in print. She thought the article was going to be about the app, not so much about her. As she read, she prayed Sara had said only positive things about both her and the app. Her fears were for nothing. Sara had been complimentary and kind, thank goodness. Sunny heaved a sigh of relief. Then she read a paragraph that made her heart jump into her throat.

Addison's long-time friend, Parker Crawford, is currently running a bet that's causing quite a stir among the recent Cloud Lake High School graduates. With a prize of $10,000 on the line, Crawford is leading his former classmates on a sort of scavenger hunt all over the town of Cloud Lake.

Parker had asked Sara to keep out the terms of the bet. He hadn't gone into detail about why, but he had said that it was private, and he would appreciate if it wasn't part of the story. Sara had listened, but she had been noncommittal. She said she would think about it, but that she had to follow where the story led her. Apparently, the story led her to the $10,000 prize and Parker's name in print.

If his dad read this, he was dead meat. She grabbed her phone and called instead of texting. This was too important to wait for him to reply over text.

She skipped past the greeting when he answered. "Did you read it yet?" she asked, her voice urgent.

She could hear the grimace in his voice. "I'm almost done. Hang on."

She paused to let him finish.

"Well, shit," he said. She heard his laptop slam shut.

"Do you think your dad will see it?" she asked.

"I don't know," Parker replied. He sighed, and she could imagine him pacing his room in frustration. "He doesn't exactly read news on the Internet. Or watch TV, for that matter. But chances are that someone will see it and tell him. My name is right there in print."

"You have to tell him, Parker."

"I know," he answered, his tone resigned. "Can you come over?"

"On my way."

Parker and Sunny were sitting out by the pool. To the casual observer, it looked like they were chatting, sipping some fruit smoothie concoction that Marta had made for them, and enjoying the sunshine. But in reality, they were strategizing. They hadn't even bothered to don their swimsuits, despite the ninety degree weather.

"I've laid it all out here, and I think it can work," Parker said, holding up a pad of paper. This plan had been marinating in his head for a while, and the article had spurred him into finally taking some action. "I have to tell my dad the truth about the money. I know I can't avoid it any longer. But I can't just come at him with what I did and expect him to be okay with it. And he won't care why I did it. He'll think my reasons were stupid and immature. I have to tell him my plan to pay him back."

He turned the notepad around for Sunny to see. He pointed at each item with a pen as he explained. "Step One, I tell him that I owe him some money on his credit card for some expenses this summer. Step Two, I tell him that I'm sorry, and I'll pay him back monthly because I got a job."

"You got a job?" Sunny blinked in shock.

"Yep."

"When? Where? How? Why didn't you tell me?" The questions popped out of her mouth. His admission completely floored her. Parker had never had a job, and he certainly had never expressed a desire to get one. But Parker had secretly been thinking about this for a while. He knew he had to pay his dad back somehow, and all the money he had came from his dad. So the only proper way to remedy the situation was to earn some money. He'd spent hours combing the Internet for jobs. There were a lot of jobs available, but unfortunately for Parker, he had virtually no marketable skills having never been employed before. Then he'd gotten the idea to search on Tisch's website, and that's when he found it. The perfect job.

Parker shrugged off Sunny's questions. Why didn't he tell her? The truth was, he was a little bitter that she was keeping secrets from him. Okay, a lot bitter. So he just hadn't felt like being around her lately. He kept trying to drop hints so that she'd open up, but she never did. Add to that, he was worried he wouldn't get the job, anyway.

"I didn't tell you because I was worried I wouldn't get it. I knew I had to pay my dad back somehow, so I applied to work in the video production studio when I get to college. They hire a bunch of students every fall. Sometimes they film live events; sometimes they make short movies or videos. I'm not really qualified since I have zero actual experience, and they must have a million applicants, so I figured I had no chance. But we did a phone interview a few days ago, and they offered me one of the positions."

"That's badass, Parker!"

"I know!" he exclaimed. Then he continued down his list, tapping off the items. "So, they will pay me $13 per hour, and I can work twenty hours per week. After I take off taxes, I figure I'll have $150 a week. Dad's paying my tuition, room, and meal fees, so I won't have any other expenses to pay. That means that I can pay my dad back with all the money I earn. So about $600 a month. It'll take me a while, but I'll pay him back, eventually."

Sunny interjected, "And bonus, you have your first actual job in video production. This is an amazing opportunity!"

"I know," Parker agreed.

"So that covers the credit card bill, but what about the $10,000 prize? Won't he be mad you used your savings for that?"

Parker had an answer for that already. "Probably. That's the last item on the list. After I pay him back, I will keep working, and all my earnings would go back into that savings account. I figure if I tell him that, maybe he won't be so pissed."

Sunny thought that was a good plan. "Do you think he will listen to you?"

"I don't know. I have to try. It's my only hope at this point. I mean, he's literally gonna blow his top. We might actually see his head explode. But he has to give me some credit for trying, right?"

Nodding, Sunny marveled at Parker's plan and his attitude. "You've really changed this summer, Parker. And I mean that in a good way. You're still you, but... you're more. You're... all grown up."

Parker ducked his head, hiding whatever expression was on his face. He wasn't embarrassed, exactly. He just didn't know how to respond to her praise. He knew he was different. He could feel it. For so long, everyone had been taking care of him. And it was so easy to let them. But this felt better. He was proud of the fact that he had gotten a job. And he felt more confident, like he knew he was ready to go to college, ready to tackle hard things on his own.

"I'm really excited about this job."

"I'm happy for you, P," Sunny gushed.

"It's a chance to pay my dad back for the mess I made this summer. But it's not just that. It's a chance to start living my dream. I didn't really realize it, Sunny. Not until you got me that journal for my birthday. But I've been sitting around, writing down stories, just waiting for the day when I could go away and make great movies. But there's nothing holding me back. I can make movies now if I want to. They may not be good ones. But they would be mine."

"Well, yeah," she replied, as though he was the biggest idiot on the planet for not believing in himself. "You can do anything you set your mind to. Did you not know that?"

Parker stood and paced the edge of the pool. "No, I think I knew. But I think I was just scared that my ideas weren't good, that I didn't know enough, that I wouldn't be good enough. I convinced myself that I had to wait for my life to start. I had to go to college, learn about film-making, and then I could do it. Reading those quotes from those directors in that journal from you... those guys actually went out and did it. They made movies. Some bad ones, some great ones. It doesn't matter. They didn't wait for someone to tell them they were ready. They just did it. I think I'm realizing that I'll never be ready. It's my dream, and I just need to step up and live it. Don't get me wrong. I still have a lot to learn. But I can start now. I don't have to wait. The truth is, the only thing holding me back is... me."

Sunny sat at the edge of the pool, dangling her feet in the water. The cool water felt refreshing in the midday heat. She kicked her feet back and forth. She loved to watch the ripples of the waves as they glittered in the bright sunshine. Parker was inside getting some lunch from Marta, and she relished the moment alone to think.

Parker was growing and changing. Zeke was off pursuing his dream of playing piano. But Sunny still felt stuck. She didn't want to be stuck anymore. She wanted to move forward too. As she looked out across the water, she decided she wasn't going to MIT in the fall. It wasn't the lightning strike of suddenly *knowing* that she wanted. This was different. It was something intentional. It was a choice. Her choice.

As she sat there, she said goodbye to the vision of herself sitting in a dorm room surrounded by books. She said goodbye to the idea of walking the halls that her mother once walked. She said goodbye to college parties and football games and everything that went with it. She felt the sadness of never getting to have those experiences. But she also felt relief too. None of that was what she truly wanted.

A feeling of comfort washed over her.

When Parker returned, he dipped his feet in the water beside her, offering her a peanut butter and jelly sandwich from the plate he held. She shook her head, declining. It was one of her favorites. Marta used a special homemade lingonberry jam that was the perfect balance of sour and sweet. Maybe it was the heat, or maybe it was all the emotion she was feeling today, but the thought of eating just wasn't appealing.

She tucked her hands under her knees and announced quietly, "I'm not going to MIT in the fall."

Parker sighed and took a bite of his sandwich. "I know," he said through a mouthful of food.

She looked at him sharply. "What do you mean, you know?"

He shrugged. "I think if you'd been going, you would have decided that a long time ago. It was the easy decision. I think you were never going. It just took you a while to realize it." He took another bite, chewing, a contemplative look on his face.

Sunny felt her ire rise at his words. "Well, oh wise one, if you already knew that, why the hell didn't you tell me?"

He swallowed his bite of food and then replied, "Just like you couldn't tell me to just nut up and make movies. Sometimes we have to sort stuff out on our own. It's not like I could just tell you what to do. It had to be your own decision. You know what happens when someone tries to tell you what to do? You get mad, and you yell, and it never ends well. For anyone."

She sighed. She did hate to be told what to do. "You're probably right."

He angled a skeptical look at her. "Probably?"

"Okay," she reluctantly agreed, laughing. "Definitely. You're definitely right."

Parker shoved the rest of the sandwich in his mouth and chewed thoughtfully. "So, college dropout, what's next for you?" he asked when he'd finished.

"Am I actually a dropout if I never got started?"

"Oh, I'm most definitely calling you that regardless," Parker said in mock seriousness.

Sunny felt her smile die on her lips. She gave a half-hearted shrug and looked out across the water. "What comes next is the part I haven't quite figured out yet."

Setting his plate down, he threw an arm around her. "That's okay. You'll figure it out, eventually. You are easily the smartest person I've ever met. And," he added jovially, "you can always sleep on my dorm room floor if you're broke."

Sunny suddenly felt a lump form in her throat. Parker was being so supportive. And he had no idea she was lying to him about the accident. Or maybe he did. She didn't know what was going on anymore. But what she did know was that she couldn't stand lying for one second longer.

"Parker?"

"Yup?" he replied, dropping his arm from around her shoulders and going to work on the other half of his sandwich.

"I have to tell you something." He chewed, waiting. Sunny took a deep breath. She had to tread carefully. "I've been keeping something from you." She continued in a rush, "And I feel awful about it. But it's not my information to share. I need you to know that I'm so sorry. I'm sorry that I didn't tell you sooner, and I'm sorry, but I can't tell you what it is. It's not my secret to tell." Tears formed in Sunny's eyes, but she didn't let them fall. She didn't want to break Zeke's trust, but she also had to stay true to herself. And she just knew she couldn't be stuck in the middle of this anymore.

"Yeah," Parker said. "I know."

Sunny's eyes widened and her jaw went slack in surprise. Parker admitted, "I overheard some of your fight with my brother. A tiny bit. Nothing helpful," he grimaced. "Just enough to know Zeke's lying to me about something."

"Parker..." Sunny began, but Parker held up his hand, silencing her.

"I am not asking you to tell me what he's lying about. Okay. Wait. I am asking you to tell me. It's been driving me nuts. What's the secret?" he demanded.

"Parker," Sunny said firmly. "I can't tell you. I'm sorry, but I can't break Zeke's confidence. At least not anymore than I have already. You need to talk to him."

"Okay," Parker said, acquiescing. "You're right. That's for me and Zeke to discuss. I've been trying to get ahold of him, but he won't return my calls or texts. I guess it has to wait until he gets home."

Sunny nodded, relieved that he wasn't pressing her to reveal Zeke's secret.

Parker said, "You really hurt me, though, Sunny. It's been really hard these past few weeks. It's no fun being lied to. Especially not by my best friend."

The tears that had been forming in Sunny's eyes threatened to spill over. "I'm so sorry, Parker. I know I was wrong not to tell you. I feel awful."

"Can you just tell me... is it bad? Like," he gulped, looking pained, "is Zeke dying?"

Sunny started. It never occurred to her that Parker's mind would go there, but after losing his mother, it made sense that he would go to the worst possible scenario. "Oh my gosh, no. It's nothing like that. Everyone is fine. No one is dying," she said emphatically.

Parker blew out a breath. That fear had been weighing on him for weeks. After losing his mother, he couldn't handle losing Zeke too. Even if he was mad at Zeke for lying, he still loved him. He would always be his brother.

Parker threw an arm around Sunny again and hugged her close. "It's okay, Sunshine. I forgive you."

It was Sunny's turn to blow out a relieved breath.

Parker continued, his voice taking on a mock serious tone, "Just don't ever lie to me again, or you'll find a severed horse head in your bed."

Sunny laughed, dashing the tears from her eyes. It was at that moment she knew that she and Parker would be just fine.

Chapter 34

"Sunny, telephone," Mr. Montgomery called.

"Who even calls a landline, anyway?" Sunny grumbled as she trudged into the kitchen and grabbed the phone from her dad's hand.

She was feeling a touch grumpy today. It was Wednesday morning, the day after her and Parker's talk. He was planning to tell his dad last night after Mr. Crawford got home from work, but she hadn't heard from him yet. She was worried. They were supposed to be releasing clue number eight today, but what if Mr. Crawford flipped out and the bet was canceled? She'd feel better after she heard from Parker.

"Who calls a landline?" her dad parroted. "Normal people, that's who. It's still a telephone, you know."

Sunny rolled her eyes but tossed her dad a smile to soften it.

"Hello?"

"Hello. Is this Addison Montgomery?"

"Yes, this is she." She gave her dad a side-eye as he stood watching her with interest. He quickly busied himself tidying up the kitchen, pretending he wasn't listening to her every word.

"Hi, Addison. I'm so glad I was able to reach you. I'm calling today because we saw an article about you online. My name is Katia

Winters, and I work at a company called Ultra Apps. We're based out of the Twin Cities. I'm not sure if you've heard of us?"

"I'm sorry, no."

"That's okay. We are kind of new to this space. We're constantly looking for new talent to help grow our team, and you caught my eye. The initiative you showed by developing Bet, well, it's very impressive. We'd love it if you would come in and speak with us about a job."

"Oh, wow. I mean, that's really nice of you... But I don't have a degree or anything. I mean, I'm sure I'm not qualified."

Katia chuckled. "We don't have a degree requirement for our entry-level app developer jobs. And I can assure you, from what I've seen looking at Bet, you are more than qualified. Some of our developers who start have never even made a single app before. We provide on-the-job training, mentoring, everything you need to get started."

"That sounds amazing."

"Yes, I have a feeling you might be a perfect fit. If you would come in and meet with us, I can give you all the details."

"Wow. I mean, yes. Yes. I would love to meet with you."

"Great! Are you free tomorrow? I know that seems fast, but we like to move quickly here. The app development market is extremely competitive. And we have a project list a mile long."

"Sure, tomorrow works."

"Great. I'm going to have my assistant follow up with you to set up a specific time and give you directions to our office. Her name is Emily, and she'll be calling you later today. Sound good?"

"Yes, absolutely. Thank you so much!"

"You're welcome. I look forward to seeing you soon."

Shell-shocked, Sunny hung up the phone and turned to her dad.

"I have a job interview. Tomorrow."

A look of confusion crossed her dad's face. "A job interview? Where? I didn't know you applied anywhere."

"I didn't apply. They saw the app I built and liked it. It's an app development company. In the Cities. I can't believe it! They want to meet with me about an entry-level app developer position. This is amazing!"

Her dad looked at her, his expression unreadable. "That is wonderful, honey. Congratulations."

"Your voice says congratulations, but your face says something different."

He shook his head and gave her an encouraging smile. "I'm happy for you. I really am. I'm proud of you too. This is an amazing opportunity, and I am not surprised that someone recognized your talent. I just... what does this mean for MIT?"

Sunny looked down at her hands, twisted together in a knot. "Dad, we need to talk about MIT."

Taking a deep breath, Sunny sat down at the table. It was time. She needed to be honest with him. The call from Katie had sparked something inside her, some excitement that she'd never felt when she thought about attending MIT.

"Oh, thank goodness, honey," her father said, sitting down next to her at the table. He covered her hand with his own.

She wrinkled her nose in confusion. "What do you mean?"

"I've been waiting for you to talk with me. I've known for a while that something wasn't quite right."

Sunny nodded, confirming his suspicions. She was surprised, but she supposed she shouldn't be. Her dad often knew what she was thinking before she did. She explained, "Going to MIT just doesn't feel like the right fit for me."

Her dad nodded. "I figured you had changed your mind. You kept hedging about registering. But I wanted to give you some space to work things out on your own. I kept waiting for you to talk to me about it. Why did you wait so long?"

"It was your dream. And Mom's. I didn't want to disappoint you."

"Oh honey, you could never do that. Your mother wanted what's best for you. I do too."

Sunny hesitated. She was almost afraid to say the next words, even though she'd been thinking them for a long time. "I felt like saying no to MIT was like saying goodbye to her memory."

Her father nodded in understanding.

"I miss mom," she whispered. At those words, her face crumpled.

"Oh, honey," her dad said, enveloping her in a hug. After a few moments, he pulled back and smoothed her hair away from her face. "Me too. I miss her every day. But you have to know how proud of you she would be. She wouldn't care if you were at MIT or not. She would just want you to be happy."

Sniffling, Sunny reached for a napkin and wiped her eyes.

"I'm so sorry for how I acted, Sunny, putting so much pressure on you about college. I just wanted you to open up to me. I know I pushed you into applying to MIT. I think I held on to your mom's memory too long, just like you did. When your mom died, I..." he paused, resting his hands on the table and taking a deep breath. Sunny saw tears glistening in his eyes. "I didn't know how to take care of you without her. But I know she wouldn't have wanted you to have any regrets."

Sunny laid her hand on top of his. "Dad," she said, "the only thing I'll regret is if I go to college just because you want me to. I can't live my life for either of you anymore."

With that, he let out a little sob and pulled her close in a bear hug. "I never meant to make you feel like your job was to please me or live up to your mother's expectations. I'm sorry. We wanted you to be strong, to be independent and confident. You are. You always will be. I want you to be true to everything we raised you to be."

"Thank you, Dad. I promise, I will be."

He paused. "You can't live your life for her. Or me. It's time to let go."

Sunny nodded. "I know MIT meant everything to you and Mom but it's just not me."

"I've come to terms with that over the summer, as I realized you were less than enthusiastic whenever we talked about leaving for college. And I need you to know that I fully support you. But I would be remiss if I didn't ask you one last time. Are you certain you want to give it up? It's MIT. It's an amazing opportunity."

"You're right. It is an amazing opportunity. And it was Mom's dream." She felt a tear slip down her cheek. "And it was yours too. But it's not my dream. So it's time to let it go."

"I understand. I want you to do what's right for you, Sunny. I can't say I feel completely comfortable with the idea of forgoing college. You know my thoughts on how important it is to continue to educate yourself. Will you explore one thing for me? Well, not for me, really. For yourself."

"What is it?" Sunny said, afraid to commit before she knew what he was asking.

"Will you reach out to MIT and see what other options they have?" Sunny opened her mouth to argue, but her dad held his hands up, halting her. "I know you don't want to do traditional college. But sometimes colleges will let you do an independent study or even design your own course or major. The point is, you still have a lot to learn, and even if you aren't going to college full-time, I still want to see you dedicating yourself to something that helps you grow. Colleges are doing a lot more flexible learning experiences than they were in the past. If MIT agreed to let you design your own course and you could do that on your own time, at your own pace, while working, don't you think that would be a worthwhile endeavor?"

Sunny had to admit, she loved the idea. She hadn't even known that was an option. Just because she didn't want to sit in a classroom didn't mean she wasn't still eager to learn. She just had a different idea of how she wanted to learn. She nodded in agreement.

She realized how lucky she was that her dad had accepted her decision so readily. "Dad?"

"Yeah?"

"I know I don't say it enough, but you're the best dad I could have ever asked for. I miss mom, but I didn't, like, miss out on anything. Because of you."

Her dad blinked back tears and glanced away. He choked out, "Thank you for telling me that." He patted her arm. "I will always support you, honey. Always."

"Dad," Sunny said, feeling a compulsion to defend her decision. She appreciated that he was supporting her. It was probably too much to ask for, but she didn't just want his support. She also wanted him to believe she was making the right choice. "I know this sounds dumb, but you know how Parker and I are always making bets?"

"Yeah?" he answered.

"Well, I usually win those bets. I'm smart. And a hard worker. And I'm not a child anymore. In fact, I'm going to make a bet right now. But I'm not betting against anyone. I'm betting on me. I bet that I can succeed at this. I can do it. I know I can. I'll put everything I have into winning."

Sunny's dad narrowed his eyes at her. "Addison, life isn't a game."

"That's what I don't think you understand! These bets aren't games, Dad. Some of them are for fun, sure. But the whole point of a bet is that you have to do something or else you face the consequences. You know I've always faced my punishment if I've lost a bet. No matter how bad. These bets have taught me responsibility. I want you to know that I understand the consequences of my actions. I know what it means to turn down MIT. I'm betting I can succeed. If I don't, I'll face the consequences. I might be broke, poor, living on the streets, eating out of dumpsters..."

Holding up his hands in surrender, her dad chuckled, "Okay, okay. There's no need to be dramatic. You won't be eating out of dumpsters." He smiled, relenting. "I would toss some food out on the front porch for you every once in a while."

Sunny leaned over the table and wrapped her arms around him, pressing her face into his chest like she used to when she was just a young girl. "I know you would, Dad," she said into his shirt, her voice muffled. "But you won't have to. I'm betting on myself. And I'm going to win this one."

She felt him press a soft kiss into her hair, just like he used to do when she was little. And she heard her dad say softly, "I bet you will, honey. I bet you will."

Grabbing her phone off the counter, Sunny headed to her room, texting while she walked. The conversation with her dad had shaken something free, almost like a snake shedding its skin. She felt optimistic, light, as though anything was possible. She had to tell Parker about it all.

Sunny: *Did you talk to your dad yet?? Call me asap. I have a job interview!*

A few seconds later, her phone rang.

"Sorry," Parker said, yawning over the phone. He sounded hoarse, like he hadn't used his voice yet that morning. "Dad and I were up late talking, so I slept in. You got an interview? I'm so confused. How did that happen?"

Sunny's excitement bubbled over. Even though she wanted to hear how it went with Parker's dad, she couldn't stop herself from sharing her news first. She bounded up the stairs as she spoke. "It was the weirdest thing. I got a call from this company out of the cities, Ultra Apps. They saw the article and liked my app, and now they want to hire me. I have an interview tomorrow!"

"Whoa. That's sick!"

"I know! I can't believe it. It's like everything is coming together. And I told my dad I'm not going to MIT." She put her phone on speaker and flopped into bed, laying on her back. She rested the phone on her chest as she spoke. "The timing just felt right to tell him now that I have an interview and a potential plan for what to do instead. I got off the phone, and I just knew. I had to tell him."

"Did he freak out?"

"No. He's actually pretty okay with it all. Not thrilled, but okay. I think mostly because I have a job interview. If I had no plans, I think he'd be spiraling a lot more." She paused and turned the conversation back to Parker. "What about you? Did your dad freak out?"

Parker thought back to last night. His dad had gotten home late as usual, well after ten p.m. Parker had been waiting in the kitchen, sitting at the island counter writing in his notebook. He knew his dad would eat something before going to bed, and he wanted to catch him. He needed to talk to him because he knew it was only a matter of time before his dad would find out about the article and the bet. Parker had really been living on borrowed time all along. At least he had a plan, and he was ready. When his dad entered the kitchen, Parker began to go through his prepared list of items one by one, just like he'd practiced with Sunny.

After he finished item one on the list, telling his dad that he'd spent a tiny bit too much on his credit card, his dad interrupted.

"Parker?" he asked, drawing out his son's name, his voice low and demanding. "How much did you spend?"

"I'll get to that in a minute. Just—"

Interrupting, Mr. Crawford folded his arms in front of him and barked out, "Parker! I don't think you understand the seriousness of what you've done. My credit card is not your personal piggy bank. I gave that to you for emergencies. Were you having an emergency?" he said, although he was well aware it was not an emergency.

"Well, no... but I—"

His dad held up a hand, effectively cutting him off. "You still haven't answered my original question. How much money?" He drew the question out slowly, emphasizing his frustration.

Parker hesitated. This wasn't going how he pictured it. He'd had a plan, but he felt like it was already off the rails. If he told his dad the number, he was sure to explode. But his dad was like a bulldog when he wanted a question answered, so Parker knew he couldn't avoid it. "About four thousand dollars."

And then his dad exploded.

"Four thousand dollars? Are you joking? You had better be joking, Parker Lincoln Crawford."

Parker winced and remained silent. He slumped down in his chair and inspected his hands, interlaced on his lap.

"How could you be so irresponsible? I thought I raised you better than this. What on earth could you have even spent four thousand dollars on? I give you everything you could possibly need. Maybe that's the problem. I've given you boys too much. I've given you more than you need, and you simply don't—"

Tuning out, Parker scoffed inwardly. He'd given them everything? Sure, his dad had given them clothes and food and an expensive home and every physical thing their heart desired. But he'd never given them the one thing they truly needed — his time. His dad was still lecturing, his arms clasped in front of him. He was in lawyer mode. Parker focused on the words he was saying.

"—time you learned a lesson. Ezekiel learned a valuable lesson after the accident when he had to do his community service, and now he's dedicating himself to piano. Maybe I need to teach you a lesson too. Maybe you need to learn what it's like to fend for yourself, without my money to support you. I've enabled you for far too long. Well, it ends now—"

His frustration mounting, Parker burst out, "Dad, will you just let me talk?" He felt like stomping out of the room but refrained. He knew it would make him look like a petulant child to leave in the middle of an argument. Dammit, he'd had a plan. He was trying to prove to his dad that he could take responsibility for his actions. And here he was, being reduced to feeling like a child again.

"Fine," his dad relented, but his stance remained firm, resolute. "What do you have to say for yourself?"

Parker took a deep breath. "I want to tell you my plan to repay you."

That stopped his dad in his tracks. Mr. Crawford was in the middle of a fabulous lecture, and he hadn't been done yet. Parker could tell by the way his brow was furrowed and his hands were still clasped in front of him. Lawyer mode. But at Parker's words, he froze and blinked in surprise. "You have a plan to repay me?"

Parker nodded emphatically. "It's why I didn't tell you right away. I knew it was irresponsible of me, so I immediately stopped spending and started working on a plan." Well, it hadn't been exactly immediately, but it had been mostly immediately.

"Okay," his dad said, temporarily disarmed. It clearly wasn't what he'd expected. Mr. Crawford spread his arms wide. "I'm all ears. What is this plan?"

So Parker outlined his plan to get a job and make payments until his debt was paid off. To his dad's credit, he only interrupted a few times to ask clarifying questions. Parker was about to reveal that he'd also used his savings for the grand prize of the class bet. But he stopped. His dad had nearly cut his head off when he owed him four thousand dollars. What would he say about Parker being frivolous with ten thousand?

It was then that Parker made two decisions. One, he was going to tell his dad about the ten thousand dollars, even if it meant his dad was going to blow his top. And two, he was thoroughly and completely done with secrets. This summer, too many people were keeping too many secrets. They never ended well, and people always got hurt. He was going to put an end to all these secrets, once and for all.

"Hello? Earth to Parker? How'd it go with your dad?" Sunny broke into Parker's reverie.

"Terrible. I told him about the credit card bill and he yelled. Then I told him about my job, and he calmed down."

"Oh, that's good," Sunny interjected.

Parker continued. "For about five minutes. Then I told him about the ten thousand dollar grand prize, and he yelled some more. Louder. Longer. There was a lot of yelling, Sunny. Blah, blah, blah, irresponsible. Blah, blah, blah, need to learn a lesson. It was brutal. I definitely have to pay all of it back with my job. He cut up my emergency credit card, and he told me I basically have zero access to money until I've 'earned back his trust.' I'm not cut off, exactly. But he has to approve all purchases, and he made it *very* clear that he's not approving anything but necessities. Considering I owe him a butt-ton of money and all, at least he didn't murder me or ship me off to military school."

"Parker, you're eighteen. He can't ship you anywhere."

"Have you met my father? I should introduce you sometime. He's loads of fun," Parker said, his tone dry.

Ignoring his sarcasm, Sunny comforted him. "I'm so sorry. But don't you feel a little better now that he knows?"

"Actually, I do. Even though it sucks that he's pissed, at least it's over with."

"Me too," Sunny agreed. "I'm glad I told my dad too."

"You know what the worst part was, Sunny?"

"What?"

"He asked me why. Why did I spend the money? Why did I use my savings for the bet? Why did I even come up with the bet in the first place? Just why."

"Did you tell him it was for Mika?"

Parker was silent for a few seconds on the other side of the line. He felt oddly choked up. Was it really for Mika? "I couldn't answer him. I told him I didn't know. I think he was more pissed that I didn't know why I had done it than the fact that I did it."

Sunny waited for him to continue. She had wondered why Parker had done it. At first, she'd believed him when he said it was in order to get Mika to notice him. But it was an awful lot of work to go to for a girl. And he'd moved on from her so quickly. Was that the real reason? When he said nothing else, she asked gently, "Why do you think you did it, Parker?"

He sighed. "I don't know, Sunny. I've thought about it and thought about it since he asked me. I barely slept last night. I know I said it was all about Mika, but... I don't think it was. Not deep down."

"So what was it?" she pressed.

"At first I thought it was just boredom, or maybe wanting that last taste of childhood fun before college. But honestly, I think I wanted my dad to notice me. And I hate how cliché that sounds. Instead of just talking to my dad, I basically tried to sabotage myself so he would be forced to interact with me. I think I wanted a reaction. Any reaction. But it's weird because I didn't want to get in trouble. I was terrified of it, actually. As pathetic as this sounds, I think I just wanted his attention. And before you say anything, yes, I know that makes me sound like a damn toddler. But it is what it is."

Mulling that over, Sunny summarized, "So instead of doing this epic adventure for a girl, you actually did it for your dad?"

"I think I did," He gave a wry laugh. "How messed up is that?"

"It's not messed up," Sunny defended. "Your dad is never around. I totally get it."

Parker was grateful that Sunny had understood. "Thanks for not thinking I'm crazy."

"Hold on, hold on. I never said you weren't crazy," Sunny joked.

"Ha, ha," Parker said, his tone mocking. "Can we please change the subject now?"

Sunny still had questions, but she set those aside for now. Parker was clearly tired of talking about it. "You still releasing the clue today?" she asked.

"Oh yeah. And now that my dad's aware of everything, I intend to enjoy the hell outta the rest of this game. Thank god he didn't make me call off the bet. He said I need to honor my commitments. That, and we'd be in legal trouble if we offered people ten grand and then rescinded the offer." Parker gritted his teeth, remembering that part of the conversation. "So I'm definitely releasing the next clue today. It's like a giant weight is lifted."

"Same. The only dark shadow hanging over me right now is what happened with Zeke."

"Same," Parker echoed.

Picturing Zeke, Sunny's heart gave a little dip. It still hurt to think about how they'd left things. "Any word yet?"

"No," Parker replied. He could hear in her voice how much the question meant to her. "You'll be the first to know when I hear," he assured her.

Sunny nodded, even though Parker couldn't see her. "Remind me," she stated, desperate to distract her mind. "Where's the location for the clue this time?"

"This one is the barbershop on the corner of Main and 2nd Avenue."

"I don't think you ever told me the clue."

Parker recited it for Sunny:

> *When you are here, you're not a stranger.*
> *There's brush but no forest.*
> *There's blades but no danger.*
> *When times were dry, you'd come at night.*
> *Stop on down, the time is right.*

"Oh, you did tell me this one," Sunny recalled, though it made little sense to her at the time. "I still don't get it, though. Why a barbershop? And what's with the 'times were dry' reference?"

Parker knew this clue would be hard for people to figure out unless they did some research. He explained, "It's actually super cool. This barbershop is historically significant. At least that's what Mika says. There used to be a speakeasy in the basement of this particular barbershop during the prohibition. Let's just say a lot of people got a lot of haircuts back when booze was banned..."

Sunny laughed, imagining men heading into the barbershop for a haircut every day just to sneak a drink.

Parker continued, "People will likely get the reference to a haircut place first, but they will need to figure out which one. There's a dozen within city limits alone. They won't figure out which one to go to without deciphering the rest."

Blowing out a breath, Sunny pronounced, "This will be a tough one. And how many people are left?"

"Only thirty-eight. It's really getting down there. And the rest of the clues are no joke. It's gonna get tougher from here on out. 'We're in the endgame now,'" he quoted in a deep, dramatic voice.

"Ha! I know this one!" Sunny yelled. She thumped her arms on the bed in triumph. "*Avengers: Infinity War.*"

She could hear the smile in Parker's voice. "Yeah, figured you'd get that one."

Sunny picked her phone up and checked the time. It was just after eleven a.m. "So, what time are you heading there?"

"Well, that's actually an interesting story..." Parker trailed off.

"Well?" Sunny prompted, rolling her eyes. She hated when Parker paused for dramatic effect. He really was going to make a great movie director one day.

"Okay. You know how people have been following me around, trying to get hints about where to go?"

Of course she knew. People were hounding Parker all the time now. They were getting more desperate as they got closer to the end. "Yep," Sunny acknowledged.

"Well, it turns out people have been snapping pictures of me or my car and posting it on social with the hashtag 'Parker patrol' in order to track my whereabouts."

Sunny sat up, and her jaw dropped. The lengths people would go to for ten grand were unreal. "No way!" she exclaimed. "That's such an invasion of privacy!"

"I know," Parker agreed. It made him feel skeeved out that his face was up on the Internet for everyone to see. In multiple pictures. He didn't even look good in some of them. One picture appeared to have caught him mid-sneeze, his face all squinched up, his head thrown back. And it was just out there. Forever. When he was a famous director and someone searched for his name on the Internet, that photo would still be there. Parker shuddered in mock horror. "But I brought this on myself, I guess. I just didn't expect the players to get this rabid about it."

Sunny hadn't expected it either. She was eternally grateful that she was just the person behind the curtain. No one was tracking her movements, thank goodness. "No kidding. So, what are you going to do?"

"So glad you asked, Sunshine. I kinda got this sick idea to lead people on a wild goose chase."

"Parker!" Sunny quickly admonished. "Isn't that kind of like cheating?"

"No more than what they're doing! And it's not even cheating, really. I don't have to be at the clue location, and I never really said I would be. I didn't go that night of my birthday, and everything worked out fine. Really, they are the ones that are cheating by tracking me instead of solving the clue. I did say they had to solve the clues to win the money. So, actually, I'm just encouraging them to follow the rules."

"By punishing those that don't follow the rules," Sunny finished for him.

Parker thought Sunny had summed that up nicely. "Mika and I talked about it. She's going to wear a hoodie and cap and drive my car around town, parking at random places. Meanwhile, I'm going to let myself be seen and photographed in a variety of public places. We are going to confuse people so much that they'll be forced into solving the clue because they can't figure it out any other way."

Sunny sagged against the headboard of her bed. Leave it to Parker to make sure that cheaters never win.

"It's genius, P."

"Whaaaat? Doth mine ears deceive me? Did you just call me a genius?" he asked dramatically. "Hang on. Can you just give me a minute to turn on the recording feature on my phone and then repeat that? Slowly and loudly, please. I need to document this monumental occasion."

Sunny's annoyed reply wasn't something Parker wanted to record for posterity.

Chapter 35

Parker: *Zeke home call u morning*

Sunny stared at the text message, wondering what to do. Having just woken up, her brain felt sluggish, like it wasn't quite catching on to what was happening. The text must have arrived overnight while she was asleep. She checked the time of arrival.

1:03 a.m.

Zeke was back. Her stomach fluttered as her nerves awakened. She felt a sense of comfort, as though nothing had been quite right while he was gone. It was the oddest thing, but accompanying that sense of comfort was a sense of unease over what she would say when she saw him.

It was Saturday morning, and they would all be golfing together tomorrow. No way to avoid him. Sunny thought about telling her dad she was sick, but as nervous as she was to see Zeke, she also desperately wanted to see him at the same time. Her emotions were all muddled up in her head and her heart. Fear and excitement. Love and anger. Sadness and joy. Regret and longing.

She checked the time. 9:15 a.m. It wasn't too early to text Parker back. And she didn't care if she woke him up, anyway. She needed answers, and she didn't care how desperate she sounded.

Sunny: *Did you talk to him yet???!!!!*

She had a ton of questions for Parker, but she held them all back. How did Zeke act when he got home? Was he still mad? Why had he ghosted all of them while he was gone? Had he asked Parker about Sunny at all? Did he say anything about her drunk text? How did things go with Alessandro?

The questions fluttered around in her brain. She couldn't focus. She needed to make her apologies to Zeke, but she was having trouble figuring out what to say when everything was such a mess in her head.

At the same time, she didn't want to wait any longer before apologizing. She felt a sense of urgency. Before they went golfing tomorrow, she needed to talk to him. She couldn't handle seeing him for the first time when her dad and Mr. Crawford were there. She needed to get ready before she headed over to the Crawford house. Better to catch Zeke off guard, get her apologies out, and then run home to hide. But she needed to look her best first.

She carefully applied her makeup and combed her hair. It snaked down her back, curling slightly at the ends. She knew it looked good, so she left it down, even though she desperately wanted to throw it up in a ponytail because of the heat. She grabbed a short, flowy blue skirt and a white crop top. None of it was her typical Saturday morning attire. She wasn't normally a vain person, but she was just vain enough to want Zeke to see what he was missing out on.

All week, she had been more attentive than usual to her appearance, just on the off chance that Zeke came home. She felt like her body had been on high alert, constantly watching for any sign of him. He'd shown up at a few of the previous clue locations, so when Parker had released the eighth clue, she headed to the barbershop, hopeful he would materialize. As Parker and Mika led players on a wild goose chase around town, Sunny had sat on a park bench across the street, watching to see who showed up. And secretly hoping to see Zeke. She knew it was a long shot, but she couldn't stop herself from hoping. But he never came.

At the end of the hour, there were only eighteen contestants remaining in the bet. Sunny saw some familiar faces. Tyler and Megan were still in. Mika would be happy. She was still rooting for Team Megler. Some alliances must have broken up because Victoria made it in time, but Marcus didn't. Apparently, now that they were getting down to the end, it was every person for themselves.

Parker was releasing clue number nine this evening, and Sunny wondered how many people would make it to the final round. Now that Zeke was back, would he come tonight? The thought was even more motivation to go see him now so she wouldn't awkwardly run into him later.

Her phone, still set to silent, vibrated on the nightstand. Parker had texted back.

Parker: *not yet*

Well, that was cryptic. And very strange. Parker had been positively dying to talk to Zeke for the past few weeks. She would have thought he would have accosted Zeke and interrogated him the minute he got home. She slipped on some navy ballet flats and headed out the door, on the way to talk to Zeke and now Parker too.

What was going on?

Sunny stared at the two white bedroom doors, both closed. Zeke's and Parker's. Zeke. Parker. Which door should she open? Who should she talk to?

Marta had let her in the house, informing her that both boys were up in their bedrooms. She'd quietly ascended the steps, debating who to speak to first. She wanted to know why Parker hadn't spoken to Zeke yet, but she also needed to apologize to Zeke.

She leaned her back against the wall, facing the two white doors and contemplating her options.

If Sunny chose Zeke, she would have to deal with the embarrassment of facing him after that drunken text and all the awful things she said before he left. Not to mention the somersaults he caused in her stomach. What had she been thinking? She couldn't talk to him. She didn't even know what she was going to say yet.

If she chose Parker, she was only doing it to delay the inevitable. Yes, she would find out why he hadn't talked to Zeke yet, but she didn't really need to know that right this second. Parker's door was the coward's way out.

So Sunny simply stood there. Staring at two doors. Wondering which one to enter.

Zeke or Parker. Zeke or Parker.

Who was she? Was she brave or was she a coward?

She took a deep breath and a step forward.

She made a choice.

As Sunny knocked, her stomach was a bundle of knots. She knew what she needed to do. Giving herself a pep talk, she told herself to be brave. She needed to apologize to Zeke for her behavior. She just didn't know how he would react. Would he forgive her, she wondered, or would he still be angry? She tried to envision the scene. She pictured Zeke sweeping her into his arms and telling her he loved her. It was too much to hope for, so she instead pictured him yelling at her, telling her he didn't forgive her. That was the worst-case scenario. She knew Zeke. He wouldn't be mean. At least, she hoped not.

No one answered. Was he not there, or had she knocked too quietly? She found her breath quickening. She tried to slow down and take deep breaths. The last thing she needed was to be panting like a dog in his doorway. Marta had said Zeke was in his room, so she figured Zeke would answer. She took another deep breath, closed her eyes, and knocked again, louder this time. This time, Zeke opened the door. Their eyes met. His face was blank, revealing nothing. Sunny would give anything to know what he was thinking at that moment.

Zeke propped the door open with one hand and leaned one shoulder on the door frame. "What's up?" he said, his manner reserved. She hadn't expected things to be normal between them, but it still hurt to be greeted this way, as though she was a stranger, as though they hadn't spent part of the summer wrapped in each other's arms.

Sunny began. "Can we talk for a minute?"

Zeke shrugged. "Sure." He didn't invite her inside his bedroom. She was glad. It was too intimate, held too many memories. She glanced past him to the rumpled sheets on his bed, and she remembered a time when she'd joined him there. No one had been home. She remembered the feel of his lips on her neck. His fingers lightly grazing her thigh, inching higher. His skin, satiny smooth under her fingertips as she traced them up and down his back. The urgency as their kisses grew in intensity. How much she wanted to —

Sunny shook off the memory and fought against the urge to fan herself. She suddenly felt overheated. Zeke was looking at her expectantly. Her confidence already waning, Sunny continued in a rush, "I know we haven't talked in a while, but I needed to..." She paused, collecting her thoughts, and began again, "I needed you to know a couple of things."

"Okay." He wasn't making this easy for her.

"First, that stupid app Parker made me create actually got me a job offer. I'm going to work in app development. A company in the Cities offered me a full-time job. I'm going to build apps for a living." She gave a wry laugh before continuing, still marveling at her luck. "Can you believe it?"

His lips raised into a sad half-smile. The first hint of emotion from him. He answered, "Of course I can believe it. That sounds perfect for you." As quickly as it had arrived, the smile disappeared.

Sunny nodded and swallowed. She wiped her sweaty palms on the sides of her skirt. "Thanks."

"What about school?"

Giving a tight shrug, Sunny answered, "Traditional school just wasn't for me. At least not right now. I emailed MIT to see if I could still do an independent study remotely or take a class here or there. I'm waiting to hear what they say." She twisted her fingers together. Her whole body felt like it was on high alert, waiting for some sign from Zeke that he still felt something for her. But to her disappointment, none came.

Zeke dropped his gaze, his eyes focused on the floor in front of Sunny.

Sunny continued, "And that brings me to the second thing I wanted to tell you. I told my dad. I told him all of it."

Zeke remained quiet. His eyes stayed on the ground as he nodded.

Sunny knew she needed to say more. "You were right."

Zeke looked up at her words. His eyes locked on to hers.

She continued, "That's the third thing I needed to tell you. You told me that I needed to talk to my dad, and you were right. I'm glad I did it. It wasn't easy, and he's not thrilled. But he's not exactly pissed either. He's somewhere in between, I guess. And he understands. I feel better that it's out in the open, at least. We'll get through it."

Zeke nodded again. "I'm glad." His tone was somber.

Sunny's heart sank. She'd hoped that when she told him, maybe he'd tell her how much he missed her. Maybe he'd smile at her the way he used to. Maybe he'd say they could try again. But he didn't. He didn't say anything at all.

Annoyed at herself that she'd gotten her hopes up even though she tried not to, she continued, "And that brings me to the fourth thing. I wanted to say I'm sorry. I never meant for us to fight. I never meant to say all those awful things. I never meant to text—" She halted. He'd never replied to her text. There was still a chance he didn't see it. "Did you get my text?"

"I don't have my phone anymore," he replied, shaking his head. "Alessandro threw it away after I got there. He said it was a distraction. I had to prove that I was dedicated. He's a little nuts sometimes." He rolled his eyes in exasperation.

Sunny nodded. Mr. Crawford had mentioned Alessandro's eccentricities. She couldn't believe he had thrown Zeke's phone away, but she guessed Alessandro knew that the cost of the phone wasn't an issue for Zeke's family.

Zeke continued, "One wrong move, and he would have shipped me back home. The rule was, no communication, no devices. I mean, I guess it worked because he agreed to tutor me."

Sunny was happy to hear that Zeke was getting what he wanted, to work with Alessandro again. But even more than that, she was unbelievably relieved to hear that Zeke hadn't seen her text. "That's wonderful, Zeke. I'm so happy for you." She pictured Zeke in New York with Alessandro and Parker nearby at Tisch. They would be together... without her.

She couldn't dwell on that. She needed to say what she came here to say. "Well, anyway, I just wanted to say... I just... Well, I'm sorry. About all of it." Her words came off a little more defensive than she'd intended.

"I know," Zeke answered, "and I'm sorry too. For everything." His words weren't defensive at all. They were sad, almost resigned. They had a finality to them that caused Sunny's heart to squeeze painfully in her chest.

It was Sunny's turn to nod. She was sorry. He was sorry. She'd been stewing about their fight for so long. It should have felt good to hear him apologize, to have this settled. But his words weren't quite what she wanted to hear. He was so calm, so distant. The warmth she'd seen from him this summer was gone. It really was over, she realized with a start. Suddenly, she knew she needed to leave, or she was going to break down in tears right in front of him.

"Okay. Bye," she choked out. She didn't wait to hear if he replied.

She whirled away from Zeke and dashed down the hallway, praying she could get out of there before the tears began to fall. There was nothing left to say.

Chapter 36

H ours later, Sunny found herself in a small circle with Parker, Mika, and, of all people, Victoria and her new boyfriend, Liam, at a party in the middle of a field. Parker had released the ninth clue at nine p.m. In true Parker style, he had chosen the timing because he thought it was sort of poetic. The clue pointed to the water tower in the heart of town. Old and rusty, it was no longer in use. It was perched there more for its historical charm than anything else. Buildings surrounded it, so there was nowhere for people to gather. As players and onlookers arrived, they milled around on the sidewalk, spilling onto the street until a car would drive by and honk in annoyance. It was only a matter of time before the cops showed up. A bunch of teenagers partying in the street wasn't exactly subtle.

As soon as the time expired, Parker announced that there were ten people left in the bet, and then Caleb shouted that everyone should head over to "The Back Forty" for a party. He added that he had a couple of kegs waiting, and that was all anyone needed to hear in order to tear out. The Back Forty was their nickname for a chunk of field in the middle of nowhere owned by Caleb's family. They had all partied there off and on over the years. To get there, they had to drive down a long gravel road, which meant it was isolated enough that it never got busted. There were rumors that cops weren't allowed on private property without a warrant, so it was safe, but Sunny was pretty sure that was a myth.

As they headed to the car, Parker remarked privately to Sunny and Mika that Caleb was just trying to make everyone forget about the photos of him drunk on the beach, with penises drawn on his face. Sunny thought Caleb's plan to redeem himself was solid. People loved a good party, and they loved free beer even more.

Sunny rode to the party with Parker and Mika, after which she somehow found herself in a circle of people that included Victoria and Liam. Liam was from Montana, only in town for the summer, and staying at his family's lake cabin nearby. It surprised her that Victoria was dating him. He was a fairly normal looking guy, medium height, brown hair, easy on the eyes. But he had to be one of the absolute kindest people Sunny had ever met. He was warm and friendly and only had nice things to say to everyone. If Sunny had thought of Victoria as the evil queen, he was the charming prince.

No one was more shocked than Sunny to learn that she was actually having a great time talking to them. Victoria hadn't made a single snide remark. In fact, she seemed calm, at ease in her own skin in a way that Sunny had never seen before. Sunny didn't know what had happened to Victoria these past few weeks, but she was here for it. She liked this new version.

"Earth to Sunny?" Parker snapped his fingers in front of her face.

Sunny swatted them away and offered an annoyed, "What?"

"I asked you what you wanted me to ask Marta to make for brunch in the morning."

Sunny frowned. They usually only did brunch in the winter when they couldn't golf. "Brunch?" she questioned. "Why aren't we golfing?"

"Oh, we're not going golfing tomorrow," Parker said with a smile. "Didn't your dad tell you?"

"We're not?" Sunny asked, confused. This sounded like one of Parker's schemes. "No. He didn't say anything." She checked her phone, but there was no text from him.

"No golf. Brunch. At our house." Parker rubbed his hands together. "I can't wait."

Parker loved brunch more than golfing. He loved to eat. But even so, his enthusiasm seemed a little extra. "Because of the food?" Sunny prompted, suspicious.

"Oh yeah, definitely that," Parker agreed easily. Then he added, "And other things."

"Parker?" Sunny said in a chastising tone.

Laughing, Parker exclaimed, "You know, the way you said my name sounded just like my dad. I don't think I like it. It always sounds so disapproving."

"Parker!" Sunny barked, trying to direct his attention back to the topic at hand. "What are you planning? This isn't another one of your crazy schemes, is it?"

"For once, it's not, Sunny. I promise. Well, it might be a scheme, but this isn't crazy. I asked our dads to do brunch this week instead of golf. Just trust me. This is actually one of the most mature things I've ever done."

Trust wasn't something Sunny gave easily, but if there was one person in the world who she gave it to, it was Parker. So she shut her mouth.

Well, at the very least, it was sure to be an interesting brunch.

She tossed her hair over her shoulder and scanned the party, looking to see who had arrived. It was pretty dark, but there was a bonfire and some floodlights set up, illuminating most of the area. Suddenly, her eyes landed on Zeke on the other side of the bonfire. She hadn't even known he was there. Someone must have told him there was a party out here. Word tended to spread in small towns like theirs.

He looked up, and their eyes locked. There was an intensity there that took her breath away. She saw a flash of something else. Sadness, maybe? But then it was gone, like a shutter had closed. He looked so normal, she almost thought she'd imagined what she first saw. Almost.

Sunny looked away, unable to bear it any longer.

Victoria laid a hand on Sunny's arm. "Are you okay?" she asked.

A few weeks ago, Sunny would have scoffed at the question, looking for signs that Victoria was trying to make fun of her or prey on Sunny's moment of weakness. But now she could see nothing but actual concern in Victoria's eyes. It was... nice.

"I'm fine," Sunny said unconvincingly.

Victoria smiled sadly as though she knew exactly what Sunny was going through. She patted her arm kindly and said, "For what it's worth, he looks just as miserable as you."

Sunny looked up, surprised. She hadn't thought Zeke looked miserable at all.

Victoria saw her surprise and explained, "Oh, he hides it well. I'll give him that. But I can tell. I'm pretty good at sensing what's underneath."

Sunny knew she was. It's how Victoria had always found her targets when she was shooting barbs at people. She was incredibly insightful. Weaknesses were her specialty. She could see what people were trying to hide. So when Victoria said that she saw something in Zeke, Sunny considered her words carefully.

Parker spotted his brother and yelled, "Yo, Ezekiel!"

Zeke waved reluctantly, realizing that he couldn't ignore his brother. He trudged over to the group. Victoria slid closer to Liam, making room for Zeke in the circle. Right beside Sunny. That sneaky, wonderful little witch. Sunny was both grateful to her and annoyed at the same time.

Zeke accidentally jostled her as he came to a stop in the circle. "I'm sorry," he said politely.

"I'm sorry," Sunny said at the same time.

They both laughed awkwardly.

"We seem to be apologizing to each other a lot lately," Zeke said.

"Well, it's better than arguing." Why had she said that? Was she trying to pick a fight?

But Zeke just murmured his agreement.

They were a mere inches away from each other. The party was getting packed, and people were pressing in on their circle, trying to get closer to the fire as the temperature dropped a bit. Sunny could feel the heat radiating off of Zeke's arm, and she forced herself not to lean into it. Oh, she desperately wanted to lean into him. It was almost instinctive. But she resisted.

Sunny caught her breath. She could smell his cologne, hear the deep rumble of his voice as he answered a question that Victoria asked him. Sunny wasn't even trying to pay attention to the conversation anymore. She was wholly focused on Zeke.

Parker said something to Mika, and everyone laughed. Sunny realized she better join the conversation before someone realized how distracted she was by Zeke.

When Liam mentioned he was attending the University of Montana in the fall, Sunny jumped in.

"What are you planning to major in?" she asked. There. That was normal, right?

Liam replied, "Business. They have a great program there. I don't really know what I want to do, so business seemed like a good place to start, you know?"

Sunny nodded.

"And where do you go to college, Zeke?" Liam asked.

Everyone froze. Liam seemed oblivious to the tension he'd caused.

Zeke cleared his throat before replying, "I'm actually not in college right now. I'm studying piano under an Italian pianist."

Everyone except Liam let out a breath at his response.

"That's badass," Liam said, nodding his head. "So, are you going to perform or what?"

Zeke nodded in return. "Hopefully, someday."

"Definitely someday," Sunny declared before she could stop herself.

Zeke turned to look at her, surprised. He clearly hadn't expected her to say something so supportive, especially after all that had gone on. The conversation continued on as Victoria asked Mika about her college plans and Mika responded.

Meanwhile, for Sunny, the world seemed to have faded away. There was only her and Zeke. Zeke was still turned towards her, his eyes drinking her in. His gaze dropped to her mouth. Sunny licked her lips self-consciously. She saw something dark flicker in his eyes.

"Zeke," she began. She didn't even know what she was going to say, so she stopped. His eyes flew up to meet hers, as though he'd been caught doing something he shouldn't.

Someone jostled them from behind, and Zeke grabbed her around her waist to keep her from falling.

His hands felt hot where they touched her bare skin below her crop top. She thought she'd never feel his touch on her skin again. She was secretly glad she'd chosen to wear it.

"Addison," he said, his voice low and urgent. It might have been her imagination, but she thought she felt his fingers tighten as he said her name.

"Yes?" she answered breathlessly.

There had to be a reason he was still looking at her like that, still holding on to her. Some part of him must still want her. Or maybe he still loved her. Maybe it wasn't too late for them.

"Yo, Crawford!" a voice yelled.

Sunny jumped, springing away from Zeke.

It was immediately clear that the voice was directed at Parker, not Zeke, as Parker turned and gave the guy some weird bro handshake that Sunny had never seen before. She turned back to Zeke, but the look on his face was completely different. It wasn't cold, exactly, just distant. Like they were strangers.

"Was there something you wanted to say?" she asked him.

Zeke merely shook his head.

It was too late. The moment was lost.

It turned out that Victoria was right. Zeke was miserable. And he'd been mostly miserable since the moment he and Sunny had argued. He couldn't be completely miserable, because he'd spent the weeks playing the piano, and there had been moments of joy. But not one second had passed that he hadn't regretted all the horrible things he said and the way they'd left things. As he lay in bed, one arm propped behind his head, staring at the ceiling, he thought back to earlier that day.

Seeing Sunny again, both at his house and at the party, it had been all he could do to keep himself from begging her to take him back. He'd been so angry when they fought, and she walked out of the music room. He belted out the 3rd movement of Beethoven's Moonlight Sonata, a part that he'd always found particularly angry sounding. The 3rd movement was supposed to range in volume from soft to *fortissimo*. As he played, Zeke knew that Alessandro would most certainly have yelled at him because he was all *fortissimo*. It seemed to fit his mood, but it offered no comfort. His fingers stumbled and tripped. This wasn't even the hardest piece he'd ever played. He just couldn't play as well as he wanted to, and that added to his mounting frustration. He wished Alessandro was there to tell him what to do. His former tutor was slightly crazy, but he knew what Zeke needed to learn, and he knew how to teach him. He hadn't been a patient teacher, but he had pushed Zeke to be his best. Practicing alone simply wasn't getting him where he wanted to go. He swept out an arm across the top of the piano, scattering the sheets of music that rested on the music desk. As he watched the pages float to the floor, it came to him. Why couldn't he work with Alessandro again? Nothing was stopping him now. Sure, they had parted ways. But what if he could convince him to tutor him again? Zeke had no college prospects, no real future to look forward to, at least not career-wise. What if playing the piano could be his future?

He stood up, shocked by how much sense it made. All he had to do was convince his father, and it astounded him how readily his dad agreed. Zeke was on a first-class flight to New York within a matter of hours. It was all so easy. Zeke's dad had tried to make arrangements to have Zeke stay at a hotel, but Zeke didn't want to stay all alone. It felt too depressing. He had a couple of college friends from New York that were home for the summer. They weren't close friends, but close enough that a quick text message to them, and he had a couch to bunk on while he was there. As his flight taxied to the runway, Zeke had been assaulted with guilt over leaving Sunny after their fight, but part of him was excited too. This was the first thing of his own that he'd had to look forward to since getting kicked out of college, and it felt good to have a purpose.

When Zeke's plane touched down in New York, he headed straight to Alessandro's apartment. Alessandro had laid down the rules in short order. Eight hours of sleep a night, no drinking, no girls, and no electronics of any kind. Period. He plucked Zeke's phone straight from his hand. Zeke didn't dare protest. He needed to pass this test. He needed Alessandro to work with him. Thankfully, when he landed, he'd sent Parker a text message telling him he was with friends in New York. He felt a stab of remorse that he hadn't texted Sunny, but what would he say? He was still pissed at her for being so obstinate, and he wasn't quite ready to say he was sorry for the words he'd spoken. And she'd been very clear that she was done with him anyway, so maybe she didn't even want to hear from him. Either way, he knew Parker would tell her where he was.

The weeks in New York had flown by. Zeke was playing the piano every day. And not just playing. He was living it. If Zeke imagined what it was like to be in the military, he imagined it was a lot like this. Alessandro was rigid. He was demanding. Zeke was exhausted. He was alive. And he loved every minute.

He was so immersed in improving his skills, so focused, he really only had time to think about Sunny in the down times. Even then, he tried to push her out of his mind. He wanted to focus. There was so much on the line. He wanted Alessandro to agree to work with him again. His whole future was riding on this.

It was at night, when Zeke was drifting off to sleep, that he pictured Sunny, her long blonde hair, her green eyes looking up at him. He could almost feel her arms around him. The memory was so real that it hurt. He knew in his heart that he'd said things he shouldn't have. He was sorry for that. But Sunny was being so stubborn. Couldn't she see that he couldn't ever tell Parker or his dad about the accident? It was done. He was moving on. In fact, he was better off. He was happier here, playing the piano, than he'd ever been at Notre Dame.

But as certain as he was that things were better, he was starting to doubt that he'd done the right thing in covering for Parker. He'd protected Parker for so long. Zeke didn't know exactly how much money Parker had wasted on this stupid bet game, but he knew enough to understand that their dad was going to be pissed when he found out. Parker couldn't keep going through life without realizing there were consequences for his actions. What if all the help he'd been providing to Parker had actually enabled him to continue being irresponsible?

But what if he let go and something terrible happened? Parker hadn't been seriously injured in the accident, but he could have been. If Zeke had been more careful, there wouldn't have been an accident at all. If Zeke wasn't there to protect Parker, who would? Mr. Crawford was so absent, Zeke knew it wouldn't be him. Part of Zeke was tired of always having to be the parent that his dad wasn't. Maybe he was holding on too tightly. But he couldn't seem to let go.

Chapter 37

W hen Sunny sat down at brunch the next morning, she could never have envisioned the shit show that was about to occur. Brunch began as normal. They were using the formal dining room at the Crawford house. As far as Sunny knew, they had only ever used it for brunches like these. She was seated next to Parker with Zeke across from them, Mr. Montgomery and Mr. Crawford at either end of the long mahogany dining table.

It was exactly like the brunches they had growing up, except for one thing. One very significant thing. Zeke and Sunny had since dated and broken up. Both of them were trying to act as normally as possible. But that made it worse. Sunny felt as though everything had shifted since the last time they'd all had brunch together. She felt off-kilter, uneasy.

All awkwardness aside, the meal started off fairly well, with their dads discussing golf, as they usually did, Parker chiming in occasionally. Sunny picked at her food, hyperaware of every move Zeke made across the table from her. She felt like a taut wire, ready to break at any moment. Zeke remained silent, shoveling food into his face as though he were trying to be done as quickly as possible.

"I don't know what we'll do this September, Alan." Mr. Montgomery waved his arm around the table. "With all these kids gone, it'll be just you and me golfing alone."

"We may have to make some more friends, Frank," Mr. Crawford joked.

Mr. Montgomery chuckled. "Sundays will certainly look different around here with all of our kids all grown up."

"Have you picked out your classes yet, Sunny?" Mr. Crawford asked. Or accused. It was hard to tell with Mr. Crawford. Whenever he asked a question, Sunny inevitably felt like she was the defendant in one of the trials he was prosecuting. He wasn't being mean. He was just so direct.

Sunny's eyes shot to her dad. "Um, I'm not going. To college," she added, her voice growing stronger with each word. "I got a job working for a company in the Twin Cities." She gave a lopsided smile and returned her eyes to her plate self-consciously. Her choice didn't embarrass her, but she was worried Mr. Crawford would judge her.

"A job?" Mr. Crawford asked, leaning back in his chair. "That's impressive for someone your age. When do you start?"

Sunny looked up at him, surprised. His comment was so... kind. He was a lawyer and had gone to college for practically a hundred years, so clearly, he valued education. Emboldened by his support, she explained, "They wanted me to start right away, but I convinced them to give me four weeks. I wanted to enjoy my last summer of freedom." She tucked a strand of hair behind her ear. She felt a tad bit guilty that she hadn't started right away, as though it made her less dedicated. But she'd thought about it, and she had the rest of her life to work. She only had one summer left where she could just relax. It was important to her.

Her dad beamed and said proudly, "You would have been proud of her negotiation skills, Alan. She not only got a higher salary than they offered, she also managed to get them to wait for her."

"Smart woman," Mr. Crawford said, taking a drink of coffee.

His praise made Sunny blush. She had never learned how to take compliments gracefully.

Parker, noticing Sunny's discomfort at being the center of attention, interjected, "Zeke, are you all packed for your flight, you international man of mystery?"

Zeke's eyes shot to Parker's face, bearing a distinct look of betrayal at his question.

Meanwhile, Sunny's eyes had flown from her plate to Zeke's face. "International?" Sunny said before she could stop herself.

Zeke gave Parker a glare before he looked towards Sunny, his face softening as he said, "Alessandro agreed to train me."

"Yeah, you told me that," Sunny said, confusion clear on her face.

"In Italy. I leave in a week." Zeke added.

"Oh," was all Sunny could think to say. In Italy. At least when she had pictured him in New York, she had the hope that she'd see him occasionally when she flew out to see Parker or when they came home for the holidays. But Italy? Would he ever come home to visit? Would she ever see him again?

"Thanks a lot, Parker," Zeke said, his tone gruff. "I hadn't exactly had a chance to talk about it yet."

"Sorry," Parker said. But Parker did not look sorry. "I just think that maybe we should all be *honest* with each other."

Oh no. Sunny recognized the spark in Parker's eyes. Everyone else at the table was still eating and hadn't noticed anything amiss. Parker pulled his napkin off of his lap and laid it down on the table. He pushed back from his chair and stood. He cleared his throat, clearly gearing up for something.

That's when the brunch went off the rails.

"I have something I want to say."

"Oh no," Sunny murmured under her breath.

"I suppose you're all wondering why I gathered you here today. It's time we brought to an end certain... secrets we've been keeping."

This speech was sounding vaguely familiar to Sunny. His tone was formal, reserved, as though he was making a rehearsed speech. She suddenly remembered where she'd heard something oddly similar. "Parker, have you been watching *Clue* lately?"

"That's neither here nor there, Sunshine," he answered, deflecting her question with a wave of his hand before continuing smoothly, "We are all adults here. But more importantly, we're family. And family doesn't keep secrets from family. I'm tired of it. It's not healthy, and it needs to end. Now, you all know that I've told my dad," he gestured to his father, "that I was keeping a secret from him about spending money I shouldn't have. I have felt an immense sense of relief now that I've unburdened myself. Some others in this room have been keeping secrets too. And we are going to get all of them out today."

He looked pointedly at Zeke as he said the last sentence.

There was absolute silence in the room.

Mr. Montgomery looked thoroughly confused, and something else Sunny couldn't place. Was he worried? Mr. Crawford had furrowed his brow and looked as though he was trying to work out a puzzle.

Zeke's eyes shot from Parker to Sunny, and they were filled with betrayal.

"What did you tell him?" Zeke accused Sunny.

"Nothing," Sunny defended herself. That wasn't exactly true, but technically, she hadn't told Parker anything that he hadn't already known. "This is between you and Parker, not me."

Zeke clearly didn't believe her because he was still glowering at her. He pushed his chair back from the table but remained seated. "I can't believe you. You promised me. But of course, you always know better, don't you?" It wasn't really a question. It was an insult, and he hurled it at her. Her chest hurt with the force of his accusation. He didn't trust her. But what got under her skin was the accusation that she always knew better, like she was some know-it-all. She felt her face heat as she grew angry.

Narrowing her eyes, "What exactly do you mean by that?"

Mr. Montgomery tried to intervene at that point. "Now, now, kids—"

Zeke shrugged, completely cutting off Sunny's dad. "Nothing. Just that you think you are always right, don't you? You always know best. Honesty is the best policy for everyone. Except yourself."

"Are you kidding me right now?" Sunny burst out. After all that time she'd spent apologizing, it was like it never even happened. "I literally told you yesterday that you were right, and I said I was sorry. I knew that I should have been honest with my dad about not wanting to go to college. How dare you accuse me of ratting you out to Parker? And after you were keeping Italy a secret?"

Zeke flushed with guilt at her accusation, but his expression remained stony.

"Sunny, hold—" her dad tried to interject again. But they were too far gone to stop.

Zeke interrupted him. "Oh yeah? How'd he find out, then?" he asked Sunny.

"Find out what?" Mr. Crawford interjected, but no one acknowledged him.

"He overheard us fighting about it the day you left, you absolute hypocrite." Sunny was full-on yelling now.

Mr. Crawford turned to Mr. Montgomery. "For Pete's sake, are we invisible right now?"

Sunny's dad shrugged, clearly unsure of whether he should let this play out or try harder to stop it.

"Ah, there's the Sunny and Zeke I remember. Just like the good old days," Parker said jovially. Then his tone sobered, and he put his hands out, trying to calm them down. "Guys, we are supposed to be talking out our issues, not arguing. This isn't helping anything."

Both Sunny and Zeke swiveled their glare from each other to Parker.

"Shut up, Parker." Sunny and Zeke barked at the same time.

Now there was something they could both agree on.

"That's quite enough," Mr. Montgomery said loudly, holding up his hands for a ceasefire. "Why doesn't everyone calm down and explain what the hell is going on here? I feel like you all are flying down the freeway, and Alan and I are stuck over here on the entrance ramp."

"Why don't you tell them, Zeke?" Sunny said, petulantly crossing her arms in front of herself.

"I *donut* know, Sunny. Why don't you tell them since you're the expert on honesty?"

Sunny gasped, rising from her chair.

Realizing that Sunny was about to fly off the handle, Parker's eyes shifted from side to side as he muttered, "Uh oh..." under his breath. Things were not going exactly how he'd planned.

Balling up her white linen napkin, Sunny threw it at Zeke. It hit him square in the stomach. He caught it easily. She pointed a finger at him. "I *knew* you saw my text! Liar!"

"Actually," Zeke corrected her with an air of self-righteousness, "I didn't see your text." He pointed at Parker. "Parker told me."

Parker was casually backing away from the table towards the exit. He froze when Sunny swiveled to look at him and admonished, "Parker!"

He threw up his hands, giving up. "See? This is exactly why I wanted us to hash all this out all together. There are *too many secrets*. I can't be expected to remember who knows what. It's too much!" He pointed at Sunny. "And that text was funny. Admit it."

"I admit nothing." Sunny stated emphatically.

"That's my girl," Mr. Crawford smiled, cutting into his steak and shoving a bite into his mouth. As a lawyer, he always appreciated when people knew when to keep their mouths shut. And he'd clearly given up trying to figure out what was going on. He was just going to continue eating and observing, and eventually it would all come together. It always did. Mr. Montgomery snorted in what might have been a laugh.

All eyes turned to look at them both, as though they've forgotten their parents were even in the room.

Mr. Montgomery cleared his throat self-consciously. "Well, Alan, perhaps should we finish the rest of our food in the kitchen?" he asked, attempting to escape. "I don't know what purpose we're really serving here. It seems as though the kids have things to discuss." He waved his hands and raised his eyebrows as to emphasize the word "things."

"No," said Parker. "You both need to be here for this. I told you. I'm tired of everyone keeping secrets. This is what we're here for. Well, not this," he said, waving an arm around. "This was a little extra. I just wanted to get everyone on the same page so that we could all start fresh with a clean slate. And Zeke is going to tell us all of his secrets now."

Zeke folded his arms in front of him.

"All. Of. Them." Parker repeated emphatically.

Sunny was in full agreement with Parker. The lying and secrets needed to end. But she had calmed down slightly too. She looked over at Zeke, in a defensive stance, his arms folded across his chest. He looked a little like a cornered animal searching for escape. She sympathized, because she didn't love being ambushed, either. Feeling a bit guilty for her part in all of this, she tried to soften her tone. "Zeke?"

He spared her a glance. At least it wasn't a glare this time.

Giving him what she hoped was a sympathetic look, she asked, "Don't you think it's time?"

As their eyes held for a beat, then another, her breath caught at the haunted look in his eyes. He knew he was trapped. She could see it in his eyes. There was no way he could keep this secret any longer. He sighed deeply, unfolded his arms, and relented. "Fine."

He paused, framing his words carefully, and then he looked direct-ly at Parker. He held Parker's gaze and said in a sorrowful tone, "I wasn't driving the night of the car accident."

Parker's brain went into overdrive. That was Zeke's secret? But that was great. No drunk driving. Zeke could get his record cleared. He could go back to college if he wanted... but wait... if Zeke wasn't driving... A light bulb clicked on. Sunny saw it in Parker's face as soon as he realized the implications of Zeke's words.

Before anyone could speak, Mr. Crawford rose from his chair so quickly that it tipped over. Sassy, who had been asleep under the table this entire time, awakened and tore out of the room at the crash. He roared, "What the hell do you mean, you weren't driving? Do you know what I had to go through to convince the judge to give you a lighter sentence? The prosecutor wanted jail time, Zeke. And you got kicked out of college! Why on earth would you lie about something like that? Why did I go through all that work if you didn't even commit a crime?"

Zeke remained silent, enduring his father's wrath. His eyes re-mained fixed on Parker. He was searching for something, checking to make sure Parker was all right.

It was Parker who answered Mr. Crawford, speaking slowly and quietly as he realized the truth of what had happened and what Zeke had sacrificed for him. "Because *I* committed the crime." He turned back to Zeke. "Didn't I?"

Zeke nodded, confirming what Parker already knew. His eyes nev-er left Parker's face.

Mr. Crawford was beyond frustrated. "What the hell does that mean?"

"I was driving the night of the accident," Parker said the words he'd been thinking out loud. It all made sense now, why he was injured and Zeke wasn't. He still didn't remember a lick of it, but it made sense. He'd been angry and driven away, stranding Zeke. And Zeke had taken the fall for all of it. Floored by the admission, Parker collapsed back down into his chair.

"What? Why?" said Mr. Crawford. "Why would you lie? Why would you do that?"

Zeke stood, facing his father this time. "Are you kidding me?" he scoffed. "Why would I lie? 'Take care of your brother, Zeke.' 'Don't let your brother get hurt, Zeke.' 'Be responsible, Zeke,'" he mimicked. "What did you expect me to do? It was my job to take care of him. It's always been my job to take care of him. And I failed." His voice broke.

"You didn't fail, Zeke," Sunny said, inserting herself into the conversation. She was tired of the unfair way everything fell on Zeke's shoulders. And if he wouldn't stand up for himself, Sunny was going to do it for him. "It isn't your job to take care of the world. You never should have been put in that position as a child."

Mr. Crawford defended himself, "I never raised you to lie, Ezekiel."

"You never raised me at all," Zeke tossed out, his anger palpable. "You were never here. I raised myself, and I raised Parker." He threw out a hand, gesturing to Parker, still sitting dumbfounded in his chair. "And I did the best I could. I'm sorry that I fucked it all up." He hurled his apology at his dad like a javelin.

Knowing it wasn't her place but unable to stop herself, Sunny broke in, "You didn't fuck anything up. You did a great job, Zeke. You're an amazing brother to Parker. You're an amazing friend to me. But it's not the same as when we were kids. Parker is not fragile," she said, jabbing a thumb at Parker. "I am not fragile," she continued, pointing to herself. "We aren't going to break. You don't have to keep secrets from us. You don't have to clean up our messes. You don't have to protect us anymore."

"But what if I'm not there and something happens?" The words poured out of Zeke as he looked from Sunny to Parker and then back to his dad. "Parker could have died in that accident. Died. Do you understand that? And it was my fault. I wasn't watching close enough. I didn't take care of him." He threw his arms to the sky in frustration. "None of you understand what's at stake here. All it takes is one thing to go wrong, and he's gone forever." His eyes flew back to Sunny and Parker as repeated. "*Forever*. And I can't lose—"

He stopped, his voice breaking. He ran his hands through his hair as he tried to gain control of his emotions.

Zeke's words triggered something in Mr. Crawford. Parker and Sunny may not have understood why Zeke was so protective, but Mr. Crawford suddenly did. He knew exactly what was happening. He couldn't believe he'd been so blind. It was so clear now. This wasn't about Parker and Sunny at all. This was about Zeke. And his mom.

"You can't lose your brother too." Mr. Crawford finished for him. "That's what you were going to say, wasn't it?"

Zeke nodded, and his dad continued, "Zeke, you couldn't have stopped your mother from dying. It wasn't your fault," Mr. Crawford said in a voice that was more gentle than any voice the boys had heard him use before. He couldn't believe he hadn't put the pieces together earlier. Zeke was terrified of losing Parker and Sunny like he'd lost his mother. His heart ached at the realization of what his son had been going through alone. He continued, "You can't protect everyone you love."

"I know that," Zeke defended.

"Do you?" his dad asked softly.

Understanding finally dawned on Sunny. Ever since his mom had died, Zeke had taken charge, tried to control everything. She always thought he was bossy, a control freak, overprotective. But that wasn't the real reason. He hadn't been able to prevent his mom's death, and he was so afraid of losing anyone else that he loved. He'd grabbed on with both hands and wouldn't let go. It wasn't because he was trying to run the show or even because he didn't trust them. It was fear.

"I don't know how I didn't see it earlier. I've been so absent," Mr. Crawford mused, almost to himself. "Jane would be so disappointed in me, in what I've done to our boys..." He ran a hand down his face as he wrestled with his emotions.

Sunny's dad spoke up, "Now, Alan, you can't blame yourself. I know as well as anyone, losing someone you love is one of the hardest things a person ever has to go through."

Realizing that Parker was being uncharacteristically quiet, Sunny glanced over at him. He still looked shell-shocked.

Meanwhile, Mr. Crawford was ramping up for one of his famous lectures. This time, it was directed at himself. He thumped his fist on the table, and everyone jumped. "I damn well will blame myself. There's no one else *to* blame. I am the parent. It was my job to see what was going on. It was my job to be here, to take care of them. If I hadn't shut down after Jane died..." his voice broke. He collected himself and continued more calmly, "This is no one's fault but my own. I haven't been here for my boys. I... I was so afraid of losing someone else that I loved. I shut everyone out. I've hurt everyone. And I failed you both." His eyes filled with tears as he looked from Parker to Zeke.

Privately, Sunny agreed with him, but she had enough sense to remain silent. Her admonition wasn't necessary right now. He was blaming himself quite enough. As well he should, she thought. He had failed his boys. He had abandoned them when they needed him most, isolated himself in a cave of his own grief. But she could see how much pain the realization was causing him, and she felt a pang of sympathy for him. After all, she knew what it was like to lose someone who was your entire heart and soul.

Zeke and Parker were stunned into silence. Well, Parker had already been stunned by the realization that he had been driving drunk, but he was doubly stunned to see his dad be so vulnerable.

The silence stretched.

Unable to bear the tension any longer, Mr. Montgomery cleared his throat. "Well, I don't know if this is exactly what you'd intended, Parker, but it is clear that our families have some work to do in the honesty department. And as ill-timed as this may be, I have something I need to get off of my chest. I too haven't been entirely honest this summer. And I think it's time to get it all out on the table. I've been... well, I am seeing someone. Well, sort of. Maybe. I think."

"Ah ha!" Parker yelled triumphantly to no one in particular, awakening from his stunned trance. "You see? Secrets! Everyone is keeping them. Even those we least suspect!"

Sunny felt the blood drain from her face. Parker took one look at her, and his expression sobered.

"But I don't understand... How? When?" Sunny asked. The questions poured out of her. "Who is she?"

Hurt coursed through her at the idea that her father had kept something so important from her. And a little sliver of something else. Anger on behalf of her mother. He was betraying her memory. And he hadn't even had the decency to tell Sunny about it.

Mr. Montgomery nodded, understanding her need for more information. He ticked each mundane detail off on his fingers. "Um, I met her at work. Her name is Catherine. She teaches creative writing, and she's really nice. She asked me to get some coffee, and I said yes." He looked at Sunny apologetically. "I'm sorry, honey. I thought it was just a colleague thing, but then it became a weekly thing... and then, one day she reached for my hand, and I pulled back. But then... Well, I realized that I'd actually wanted to hold her hand, which surprised me—"

"Stop!" Sunny yelled, not wanting to hear anymore. She thumped back into her chair with a thud, stricken. He had been lying to her. She thought back over the summer. Her dad had been leaving her alone more often than usual. She'd been so caught up in her own stuff, she hadn't even realized why. She thought perhaps he was just letting go. And he was. But he wasn't just letting go of her. He was letting go of her mother too. He had been busy living his own life.

Tears filled her eyes, and she tried to will them away. Sunny knew she should understand. She'd been keeping her own secrets this summer, after all. Shouldn't she be happy for him? She should congratulate him, ask to meet her or do something, anything, that showed her support. But she simply couldn't. Not yet.

Her dad came over and tried to put his hand on her shoulder, but she pulled away. "I'm sorry I didn't tell you about it, Addison. I wasn't sure there was anything to tell, and then, suddenly, there was. But I didn't know how."

"That doesn't give you an excuse to lie about it." Sunny knew she shouldn't say it, but it came out anyway. She stormed towards the door but was halted by her dad's stern voice.

"Now, you get back here, young lady, and you listen up. I'm only human, and I'm not proud of keeping this from you. But I'll thank you to remember that you've made some mistakes too," he admonished. "And you," he said, turning to Parker. "And you," he said, turning to Zeke. "And you," he said, finally turning to Mr. Crawford. "We've all made mistakes. Every one of us. What Parker did here today was a noble cause. He is trying to clear the air. Now," he said, pausing, "does anyone have anything else they need to get off their chest?"

Silence.

Sunny squirmed in her seat. She kept her gaze on the floor, holding herself back from sneaking a peek at Zeke. The only secret she was keeping now was about her feelings for him. But he didn't return those. He'd made it clear they were done. And he was leaving for Italy in a few days, so she wasn't about to bring that up now.

No one spoke up.

"Okay, then," Mr. Montgomery continued, taking charge of the situation. "Here's what's going to happen. We have learned a lot this morning. We're not done talking yet. But I think it best we all take some time alone to think. I'm giving everyone one hour."

Chapter 38

Sunny knocked on the door to Parker's bedroom.

"What?" came the sullen reply.

It was all the permission she needed to open the door. Poking her head inside, she said, "Can I take my alone time with you?" She stuck out her lower lip, begging.

Parker smiled and waved her over to the bed. "Always," he said. He was lying on his back, staring up at the ceiling. He had repainted it again. There were swirls of different shades of blue like one would find in the ocean, ranging from deep blue to Caribbean blue and everything in between. There were little white bubbles and a giant shadow of a shark, making it look like they were on the bottom of the ocean, staring up through the water. Sunny realized she didn't even know when Parker had painted it. They'd grown apart this summer. Not necessarily in a bad way though. They were each a little bit more of their own person and a little bit less dependent on each other. She knew when he left for college, they would both be okay on their own.

She plopped beside him on the bed and leaned her head on his arm. "This is amazing, Parker. How did you paint this?"

Shrugging off her praise, he answered, "I found something on Pinterest and kind of copied it."

"It's beautiful."

They were both silent for a while.

"Do you want to talk about it?" Sunny eventually asked.

"Yes. No. I don't know. I'm trying to put it all into perspective. 'Strikes and gutters, ups and downs.'"

"Ugh. *The Big Lebowski*," she guessed, punching his arm softly. She hated that movie. For some reason, Parker adored it. He'd made her watch it at least a dozen times. She tried to see it through Parker's eyes, but she couldn't get past her perception of Lebowski as lazy.

"Lebowski is the GOAT. You know it's true," Parker said, laughing. "He's full of life lessons."

She shook her head. "He's full of something..." she said. "And anyway, what do you mean?"

He drummed his fingers across his chest. "It's not every day a man finds out he drove a car drunk and his brother took the fall for him. But on the upside, I'm alive, we're all finally being honest with each other, and my dad seems to be genuinely sorry for ignoring us for the past seven years. So, yeah. Ups and downs," he repeated.

"Yeah," Sunny agreed. "I have to say, you're handling it amazingly well, all things considered." She peeked at him out of the corner of her eye.

"Oh, that's on the outside," he said blithely. "Inside, it's more like..." he trailed off and waved his hand around. "I don't know. I can't think of a movie reference that symbolizes the chaos that's going on inside my head right now. That's how fried my brain is."

Sunny understood. Her brain felt like it was on overload too. "What are you going to do?" she asked.

"Do? I don't know. What can I do? Go to the police and tell them the truth? Try to get Zeke's record cleared and mine... dirtied? I don't really know how this works."

"You know who will know how this works?" Sunny asked pointedly.

"Don't say my dad. Don't say my dad," Parker chanted.

Sunny laughed. "Well, you literally have a legal expert in your own house."

Sighing, Parker acquiesced. He hopped off the bed and began pacing the room, suddenly filled with restless energy. "I know. I just... He's still mad at me over the whole money thing, and now I was the one drunk driving. At least before, I felt like the heat was evenly spread between me and Zeke. Now it turns out that I'm a bad seed. Just me."

"You're not a bad seed, Parker." She rose onto her side and propped her head in her hand.

He continued as though she hadn't spoken. "And the worst part is that I can't even be mad at Zeke for lying to me, because he was actually trying to save me. And he did. Tisch could have revoked my admission if they found out. I could have been a college dropout before I even dropped in. So what am I supposed to say to him? Thanks for lying? Thanks for saving my ass again?"

"I don't think you're *supposed* to say anything, Parker. I think you just say whatever you feel."

Parker sat down on the bed next to Sunny.

"Speaking of what's next, what are *you* going to do?" he asked.

Sunny felt tears fill her eyes as she considered his question. She couldn't answer as she tried to fight them off. She didn't know if he was asking about Zeke or her father, so she deliberately chose to focus on the situation with her dad. "Well, I guess I'm going to ask to meet my dad's new girlfriend," she said, her voice all squeaky as tears spilled over and dripped down her face.

"Oh, Sunny," Parker said, leaning forward to give her a hug. "I'm sorry. I didn't mean to make you cry."

"It's fine," she insisted through her tears. "I'm happy for him. I really am."

"Yeah," Parker said, leaning back to look at her face and nodding solemnly. "You seem real happy."

Sunny laughed through her tears. "I am. I promise," she sat up and swiped at her eyes. "I just... I guess a small part of me feels like he's betraying my mom. And I know I need to get over it, and I know it's not realistic, and I know that he's been all alone for so many years.

I'm letting go of this dream she had for me, and now he's letting go of her too. It's a lot all at once. I wasn't ready for it."

"Are you mad he didn't tell you?"

She cocked her head to the side and considered his question. "I was at first. But now? I'm shocked. Maybe a little annoyed?" She paused. "But it's not like they were dating, dating. And I totally get wanting to keep things to yourself when you don't know what's happening in a relationship. I didn't tell him about Zeke right away either, because I didn't think it was real. I mean, I get it."

Parker nodded. "But you know, when I asked what you were going to do, that wasn't really what I meant. I was asking what you were going to do about Z—"

"I know what you were asking," she interrupted. "There's nothing to do. We broke up. He's leaving. Period. The End."

Parker just looked at her expectantly.

She jutted her chin out defensively. "What?"

"Nothing, I guess," he replied, checking his phone. He slapped his knees and stood. "Well, our hour is up. Let's go talk it out with Zeke and our dads."

"Ugh, do we have to?" Sunny whined, even though she knew he was right. She stood and trudged to the door.

Parker took a deep breath and began, "We are gathered here today—"

Four sets of eyes swiveled towards him. "Parker," four voices groaned simultaneously, cutting him off.

"Okay, okay," he said sheepishly, holding up his hands in surrender. "I was just trying to make it more interesting," he grumbled to Sunny. She nodded, patting his shoulder in sympathy.

They were assembled in the kitchen. Zeke, Parker, and Sunny were seated in the chairs on one side of the island, while their dads stood across from them.

Mr. Montgomery kicked everything off. "Here's the deal. Everyone is going to speak their piece. We're going to talk through our issues, and then we're all going to move on. Together. Got it?"

There were nods all around.

He continued, "I'll go first." He turned to Sunny, his expression contrite. "I'm sorry that I wasn't honest about dating Catherine." He paused, searching Sunny's face to see how his words were received. Sunny tried to tamp down the emotions swirling inside her. "I felt like I was betraying your mother, and I wasn't at a place where I knew how to discuss that with you yet. I was scared that I would hurt you. But that's no excuse," he said, holding up a hand in apology. "I shouldn't have done it. I promise not to keep things from you in the future."

Sunny blinked away tears. She didn't know what to say. She truly wasn't mad, at least not anymore. It gave her a funny feeling in her gut when she thought about her dad dating someone, but she knew she just needed time to come to terms with all the changes. "It's okay, Dad. I get why you didn't tell me. And I... I'm happy for you. Really. You deserve to be happy."

"Thank you, sweetie," he said, stepping around the island to wrap her in a hug. When they separated, they both dabbed their eyes.

Mr. Crawford cleared his throat. "I guess I'll go next." His eyes darted back and forth from Zeke to Parker. "Boys, I realize now that I haven't been there for you. I used my own pain after your mother died to hide away, and I hurt you both. I'm so sorry. More than you could possibly know." Sunny couldn't be sure, but she thought his eyes were turning misty. She'd seen him get emotional in the past, but only from anger, usually at something the boys had done wrong. She'd never seen this softer side of him before. She liked it. He continued, "I know you are both adults, and you're leaving the house soon. I can't change the past, but I can make you a promise for the future. I want to change. I want to be there for you both. I know I can be a better father."

Parker stood and rounded the corner of the island, throwing himself into his dad's arms. He'd missed his dad so much. For Parker, it was easy to forgive, because he wanted nothing more than to have his dad back. "Ooof," Mr. Crawford grunted with the force of it but then wrapped his arms around Parker in return.

"I'm sorry too, Dad," came the muffled voice of Parker as he continued to squeeze his dad. "I made some major mistakes, but I promise never to do anything wrong ever again."

Mr. Crawford pulled back and looked into Parker's face. He said dryly, "You might be setting yourself up for failure there, son. After all, everyone makes mistakes. How about you just try your best, and I'll try to be more forgiving if you make a mistake? How does that sound?"

"Deal," replied Parker.

As Parker headed back over to his seat, Mr. Crawford added, "And I already called out of work tomorrow. You two boys will be sitting down with me to discuss how to handle the accident. I need to think about how to approach this. It's not a simple matter to unwind this. Frankly, I don't even think we can at this point. I doubt the police would listen. We've got no proof of what happened and no reason for anyone to believe that Parker was actually driving. But regardless of what happens with the legal side of this, there's going to be some ramifications for you, Parker."

Parker froze, his body tense. "Am I going to lose Tisch, Dad?"

"Not if I can help it. But the fact remains that you boys have gotten yourselves into a fine mess. Zeke perjured himself, and I need to think about the best way to handle that. Perjury isn't like a drunk driving charge. It stays with you in a different way, follows you your whole life. I've got some work to do on all of this tomorrow."

Parker sunk down in his chair. "I'm so sorry you have to go through all that work."

"Me too," added Zeke, looking chagrined. And he was sorry. He had only meant to protect Parker. He hadn't meant to cause this mess, nor make his dad clean it up.

Mr. Crawford declared, "Owning up to one's mistakes is the mark of a fine man. That's something my father used to say to me. I can't say I'm pleased with the mistakes you've made, either of you. But I'm proud of the way you're facing the consequences of your actions now. You will make amends in some way, Parker."

"I will, Dad," Parker said.

Parker nudged Zeke with his elbow. "Zeke?" he said expectantly, angling his head over to his dad.

There was a long pause as Zeke tried to figure out what to say. He was so angry with his dad that he wasn't sure he would ever be able to fully forgive him. He couldn't just give him a hug the way Parker had. The words his dad had said didn't make years of pain and isolation fade away. He finally spoke, forcing out the words. "I'm angry at you, Dad," Zeke admitted. "And I don't know what to do about it. You say you're sorry, and that's great. I've waited years for you to say these things. But you abandoned us after Mom died. I was just a little kid. I felt so alone." Zeke stopped, his voice thick with emotion. He didn't know if he could speak anymore without crying, and he was doing everything he could to hold it together.

Sunny had to blink away tears as she felt her heart swell at the thought of the day she'd met Zeke at the golf course. So quiet and reserved. He'd taken care of Parker that day and every day since. Her heart broke for that little boy who missed out on just being a kid.

Taking a breath, Zeke continued, "I missed her just as much as you did. Parker did too. But I didn't get to be sad. There was no comfort for me. I didn't get to be a kid anymore. It wasn't just Mom that died. You left too. And my entire childhood was over, just like that. I had to take care of Parker. It wasn't fair." He knew the words sounded whiny, but he didn't care. It was how he felt. It wasn't fair that his dad had left him to pick up the pieces of their family.

"You're right, son. It wasn't fair. I know that the words don't mean much, but I'm sorry. I didn't realize what I was doing to you. If I had...well, there's no sense in dwelling on what I might have done. I failed you. End of story. I had no idea what was going on with you.

Or Parker. I wasn't there for you. But I can be there for you now. If you'll let me." He looked so forlorn. Zeke had been keeping a shield up, scared to hope that maybe his father could be the dad he needed again. He felt that shield slip a little.

"I can't just suddenly forget everything," he said. He wasn't sure who he was reminding, himself or his dad.

"I'm not asking you to," Mr. Crawford said, shaking his head. "I'm asking you to give me a chance."

It was a reasonable ask. And Zeke wanted so badly to believe his dad. He had desperately wished to have him back in his life, and here it was, looking him in the face. He couldn't deny him. Nodding slowly, he answered, "I'll try. I'll try to give you a chance."

"That's all I can ask," his dad replied, giving Zeke a half-smile.

"I have something to say," Parker said, raising his hand.

"Parker, you don't have to raise your hand," Sunny said, rolling her eyes.

Parker cleared his throat and looked at Zeke. "Zeke, I understand why you did what you did. I know you did it to protect me. The fact is, you've been protecting me in one way or another since Mom died. I'm sorry for being so irresponsible sometimes."

Parker continued, rubbing his sweaty palms on his jeans. "And I want to say thank you. Thank you for being there for me when Mom died, for being the only one who understood that I couldn't look at her at the funeral, and for taking me to her grave weeks later when I was finally ready to say goodbye." Parker's voice cracked, but he continued, "Thank you for being the best big brother anyone can ask for. Thank you for making me peanut butter sandwiches when I was hungry before bed. Thank you for coming into my room when I had a nightmare and making me laugh with your terrible alligator shadow puppets. Thank you for being my best friend."

Sunny had been watching Parker, but sneaking glances at Zeke. His eyes were welling up.

Parker continued, "And there's just one last thing I wanted to say. You can stop now. You can stop thinking it's your job to protect everyone in the world. I know the pressure you feel, the responsibility to keep everyone safe, but it's not your job to keep everyone safe. Not me and not Sunny."

Parker paused dramatically. "Fly free, my little butterfly. Soar like a—"

"Parker, that's enough." Sunny sing-songed, trying to rein him back in.

"Oh yeah. Um, in conclusion, I love you. Now go get yourself a life of your own." Parker smiled to soften his words.

"I don't know what to say to that," Zeke said, running a hand through his hair. "I just..." He swooped over to hug Parker, clapping him on the back. "Thanks, bro. I love you too."

He pulled away, knowing he owed Parker an apology in return. "And I'm sorry I lied about the accident. I really thought I was doing the best thing for you."

"I know you did," Parker agreed.

"I promise to let go," Zeke said. He looked back and forth from Parker to Sunny. "Okay?"

Parker nodded. Sunny nodded too, although she wasn't sure she liked the sound of that. She had been begging him to stop trying to boss them around. But when he said he would let go of her, why did it sound so final? And why did her heart clench at his words?

Zeke looked back at Parker and clapped a hand on his shoulder. "But I'll always be here if you need anything at all. Got it?"

Parker nodded again. Sunny could tell that he was trying not to cry.

Mr. Crawford cleared his throat. He clapped his hands and rubbed them together. "Okay. I think that's everybody. Is there anything else that anyone needs to say?"

Parker looked at Sunny, and she busied herself looking at the ground. She was not dealing with anything related to her and Zeke. Not today.

Parker looked at Zeke, who also mysteriously avoided his gaze.

"Apparently not," said Parker, disappointed.

Chapter 39

"Come on, come on, come on," Parker grumbled. "Finish already. I have to ask you something! I've been waiting all morning." His voice turned whiny, like a child begging for a toy.

Sunny shrugged and replied, "Parker, it's ten a.m. That's hardly all morning. But ask away. I can listen and work at the same time. It's called multi-tasking." It was Thursday, four days after "The Great Brunch Fight," as Parker was calling it. She was seated at the island in the Crawford kitchen. Her head was bent over her laptop, and she was working on her new app.

The French doors leading to the pool were wide open. The fresh morning air wafted into the kitchen, and the birds were singing. Parker was in a great mood. "Okay. Here's the deal. We're releasing the last clue tonight, and it's the perfect time to have a party."

Sunny stopped typing and looked up at him, surprised. "I thought you were done with parties? You were all 'I've already had my epic adventure' and everything."

"I know, I know. But that was before. Now, everything's out in the open. I feel free, relaxed, even." Sunny knew exactly how Parker felt. She hadn't realized how all these secrets this summer had been throwing a shadow over everything. But Parker had seen it. He knew they had to come out, and he'd forced them all to face them head-on.

Sunny knew Parker still thought of himself as irresponsible, but she'd seen such a change in him this summer. She'd seen one in herself too. And it was all for the better.

Parker continued, "There's ten people left in the bet, and there's going to be a winner tonight. Or maybe multiple winners. I don't know. But either way, don't you think it deserves a party?"

He paused and held up his hands to ward off the argument from Sunny that he knew must be coming. "Stop. Don't say it."

"I have to say it. Did you forget that you are grounded right now? No car, no phone, no computer, no movies, no gaming, no fun of any kind. Remember?" Sunny had thought it sounded harsh at the time. But Mr. Crawford said that Parker had to face consequences for his actions. He had met with a friend of his, a retired police chief, to ask his advice on how to handle things. The police chief had confirmed his suspicions. They had no evidence to show that Parker was really driving, and Zeke was not. In short, no one would believe them. Zeke was already convicted, and he'd served his sentence, so as far as the police and the prosecutor were concerned, they'd caught the offender and he'd been punished. Case closed. Even if Mr. Crawford could get someone to believe them, Zeke would face new charges of perjury, and Parker would face drinking and driving charges. The prosecutor would likely want to try Parker as an adult since he was so close to turning eighteen at the time of the accident, which would mean a harsher sentence, as well as a greater likelihood that Tisch would find out and rescind Parker's admission. It was lose-lose.

It felt awful, but Mr. Crawford concluded that there was nothing to be done from a legal aspect, no way to unwind the mess the boys had created. So he was employing old-school punishment methods for Parker. In addition to the grounding and the no fun rule, he was assigning Parker community service, the same number of hours that Zeke was forced to fulfill. For his part, Parker was glad to do it. He felt like he deserved the punishment, and it made him feel better to be productive. He was filling his hours at the local retirement center, and it turned out he had a knack for making the residents laugh. Seeing the smiles on their faces made him feel as though he was contributing to something good.

"I am not allowed any fun. That is true. However, I got special permission from Dad when he doled out the punishment to see the last clue through to the end. He agreed that I needed to see the bet through because I made a commitment. So I have a free pass for tonight, and I intend to make the most of it. I won't get to do a single other fun thing before I leave for Tisch. This is officially the last party of the summer for me. Plus, it's like a going-away party for Zeke since he flies out in the morning."

Sunny's stomach twisted at the mention of Zeke leaving for Italy in the morning. The corners of her mouth drooped down. She hadn't seen much of him all week. Parker said he was packing and practicing. Alessandro had set out a rigid practice schedule for Zeke, and he was following it to the letter.

"Don't worry," Parker continued, misunderstanding the look on her face. "I'm not spending any money on this party. And it will not be here at the house. It's going to be at the final location. And you're definitely coming."

"I don't know, Parker. I don't really feel like partying, personally." She couldn't stop thinking about Zeke leaving. She pictured him on the airplane, getting further and further away. Her heart squeezed.

He paused and looked down at her, as serious as she'd ever seen him. "We're doing it."

"No." Sunny shook her head emphatically. She didn't want to talk to people and act all cheerful when she was so miserable on the inside. She also didn't want to see Zeke. He clearly had moved on, but she hadn't, and she was embarrassed. What if he saw her face and knew she was still hung up on him? At this point, she just wanted to move on. Seeing him again was too hard.

Parker smiled and opened his arms to encase Sunny in a hug. "It's happening, Sunny Bun."

"I said no!" Sunny insisted.

Parker unleashed his failure-proof tactic. Tickles. Sunny could never resist.

Through her increasing giggles, Sunny shouted, "Okay, okay! Uncle! Party. Fine. I'll come. Ugh."

"YES!" shouted Parker triumphantly as he released her.

"This party is gonna be lit," Parker said, as he turned and walked out of the open doors onto the patio. Sunny turned her attention back to her computer. He raised his arms in the air and hollered into his backyard, "This party is gonna be litter than lit!" He paused and turned around, looking at Sunny questioningly.

"Litter?" he mused over his shoulder. "Is 'litter' a word? I mean, I know 'litter' is a word. But in this context, is it 'litter' or 'more lit'?"

Sunny answered without looking up from her laptop. "More lit."

Parker turned back towards the balcony railing. "This party is gonna be more lit than lit!" he shouted.

He turned around again, frowning at Sunny. "Still not right..."

Still head down, focused on her work, Sunny replied, "Lit AF."

"Yeeeees!" Parker nodded and hollered one last time, "This party is gonna be lit AF!"

Seek and seek and ye shall find,
The thing that some would leave behind.
Many will thrive when one gets burned.
Knowledge gained is knowledge earned.
Listen well, and you will hear.
Your prize is waiting. The end is near.

"It's a good clue," Sunny marveled to Mika as they stood together, surveying Zeke and Parker's work. "I couldn't solve it, no matter how hard I tried. Parker had to tell me the location."

"I know! It's great, isn't it? I don't think all ten people will make it. There's no way. I mean, they have to figure out that they are looking for the site of the original Blackwater Courthouse. It was built in the 1800s before they renamed the town Cloud Lake, but it burned down in 1908."

"Why didn't they rebuild the courthouse here?" Sunny asked. She looked around the conservatory where they stood. It was a beautiful structure made of steel and glass. Large, with a high ceiling, it could easily fit a couple hundred people if the party grew as large as Parker expected. The soft evening light shone through the glass ceiling. There were flowers and vines everywhere and a large, round reflecting pool in the middle of the room. Parker and Zeke were busy hanging twinkle lights all around the edges of the space. Parker was releasing the clue at ten p.m., and he'd muttered something about "ambiance" and "setting the mood" when he'd dragged all the Christmas lights out of their basement earlier that day.

Sunny watched their progress as Mika answered her question. "Businesses had kind of built up really close around it, and there wasn't enough space to rebuild as big as they wanted to. So they moved it to where it is now, and then the town kind of sprung up over there, and this area died off. The surrounding businesses slowly closed down or moved, and this place was just sitting here vacant for years until someone bought it and built the Greenwood Conservatory."

Mika was growing more animated by the minute. "It is actually really interesting. There was a boom of florists and horticulturists in Minnesota around the 1913 time frame because the Society of American Foresters hosted a national convention in the Twin Cities." She paused and smiled sheepishly, realizing she was probably boring Sunny. "Sorry. I get carried away sometimes."

Sunny smiled, throwing an arm around Mika affectionately. "No, it's fine. It was interesting. I never knew any of that. And I think that's why I couldn't figure out the clue. There was the reference to both growing and burning, which was so confusing."

Mika added, "And we used the word 'hear' like how you hear a case in a courthouse. That was Parker's idea. That's why I don't think many people will find this place. It's going to take not just deciphering the clue, but some real historical digging to figure this one out. And they only have an hour."

"So what if no one shows up?"

"Well, then Parker wins, I guess?" Mika shrugged. "He did bet they couldn't make it to the end, after all. Hey, Parker," Mika said, hollering over to him. He was across the pool from them, still lining up the twinkle lights, dressed casually in a red polo and khaki shorts. Zeke was on the other end, high on a ladder, trying to attach one end of the light string to a post with zip ties. Mika continued, "If no one shows up, this is going to be one small party!"

"Nah," Parker replied, shaking his head. "When the clock runs out, I'll push a message out to all the players using Sunny's app and tell them where to go. This party is happening." He did a little dance, dropping the lights in the process.

"Hey!" Zeke yelled, as he tried to hold on to his end.

"Sorry," sing-songed Parker, reaching down to pick the lights back up.

Since Zeke's back was to her, Sunny was free to admire the view without him being aware of it. Her gaze zeroed in on his arms, reaching to hang the lights, his muscles accentuated by his black t-shirt. His shirt pulled up as he stretched farther, drawing her eyes to the gap of skin between his shirt and shorts. Her gaze drifted lower... Suddenly, her mouth turned dry, and she gulped. It was unfair that he could look this good when they'd broken up. He should be as miserable as she was.

For her part, she looked tired, and she knew it. She did her best to cover the bags under her eyes with makeup. Overcompensating, she'd dressed in a short black miniskirt and a sequined black tank top. It was the opposite of what she normally wore, but it made her feel slightly better to be dressed up. And seeing Zeke's eyes travel down her body when she'd arrived made it worth it. It was likely that no one even noticed how tired she was, but she felt it. She hadn't been sleeping well lately. It wasn't all about Zeke. She was also getting nervous about starting her new job and thinking about all the things she needed to do to prepare. But if she was honest with herself, Zeke took up far more of her brain power than he should, considering they weren't together anymore.

Mika nudged Sunny and winked. She had caught where Sunny's eyes traveled. Busted.

Gesturing to Zeke, Mika whispered, "Have you talked to him yet? About how you feel?"

Sunny rolled her eyes. Why wouldn't people stop asking her that? "Nope. You and Parker must be in cahoots because he's asked me the same thing nearly every day this week. It's over. He's leaving. You guys need to give it up."

"Never," whispered Mika.

"What are you two whispering about over there?" Parker yelled. "Are you talking about my amazing muscles?" he asked, flexing his arms and dropping the lights again.

"Parker!" Zeke barked, frustrated. "Come on, man."

"Whoops," Parker returned, sheepishly picking up the lights again. They had one last string left to hang.

Sunny ignored Parker's question. "How did you get permission to use this place for the party?" Please lord, she hoped he had permission, and they weren't trespassing. She reminded herself that Parker had grown up over the summer.

Parker finished securing the end of the lights, and Zeke stepped down off the ladder. Dusting his hands off on his pants, Parker replied, "Actually, that was all Dad. He knows the guy who owns this place and called in a favor. I guess he owed my dad big time for some legal help a few years ago. And it turns out the guy has a soft spot for, like, treasure hunts and stuff, because he thought the whole idea of his place being the answer to a clue was amazing. Dad swore him to secrecy about the location. We are under strict instructions to clean everything in the morning, and Dad said I'm on the hook for any damages. I'll be watching everyone like a hawk tonight."

True to his word, Parker watched carefully all night. Sunny, Mika, and Zeke all helped, and they managed to keep things fairly contained. The biggest mess was due to some prankster who brought a bunch of gold glitter bombs to the party and passed them out. They were long tubes filled with gold glitter, and when the cap was pulled off, glitter shot out everywhere. Every time someone would set one off, people would scream and cheer. Just when Parker thought he'd confiscated them all, another cheer would go up and glitter would rain down, sparkling in the twinkle lights.

There were a few hundred people at the party by midnight, but that was a complete turnaround from where they'd been earlier in the evening. Parker had released the clue at ten p.m. As Mika suspected, it had been incredibly difficult. With about ten minutes left in the bet, there was still no one there. Mika and Sunny were scrolling through cute cat videos on their phones. Meanwhile, Zeke and Parker were fussing with the music system they'd set up, trying to pick a playlist that would set the party mood. Parker started to think that he was going to be able to keep his ten grand after all. But it wasn't to be.

The clock ticked down. With three minutes left on the timer, two players came flying into the conservatory. They ran towards Parker, yelling, "We're here!" They both scrambled to check in on their phones before the time expired. It was Team Megler, as Mika called them. Megan and Tyler.

Parker, Zeke, Mika, and Sunny all rushed over to congratulate them. They were excitedly talking at the same time, hugging and laughing. Parker wasn't even sad about giving up the money. It had been the plan all along, after all, and it felt good to see Megan and Tyler so excited. They'd earned it.

As the time continued to wind down, it was clear that no one else had solved the clue. The timer rang, signaling that the time had expired. Megan and Tyler won. They would split the winnings equally between them. Parker immediately sent out a message via the app announcing the winners and inviting everyone to the location for a party. Within ten minutes, Marcus had posted the party location to his social, and people began showing up. Soon they were pouring in the door.

Hours later, Megan and Tyler were still celebrating, wrapped in each other's arms. Sunny looked over at them, envious but happy for them. If not for Parker's crazy bet, they may never have found each other. The music thumped. There was dancing. There was laughter. It truly was the epic party Parker had desired, the perfect way to cap off the bet. All night, people approached him. They asked him if he was sorry he lost, what he had planned next, and a million other questions. He was a celebrity, and he was in his element.

Through significant effort, Sunny and Zeke had avoided speaking directly to each other for most of the night. Without meaning to, Sunny's mind tracked Zeke's movements throughout the party. Unbeknownst to her, Zeke did the same. When a brunette wearing a tiny crocheted top held together with one lone string ran her hand along Zeke's arm, Sunny's blood boiled. When Graham stopped to give Sunny a hug and held her close for a moment too long, Zeke's hands clenched into fists. But neither spoke to the other.

Until Parker intervened.

It was a little after one a.m. when Parker shoved Mika's car keys into Sunny's hand and sent her out to get the rest of the snacks from the trunk. When she arrived, she found Zeke leaning against the trunk of the red Malibu, arms crossed over his chest.

"Fancy meeting you here," she said, striving for a casual tone even though her stomach flipped over at the sight of him. He looked so casual standing there, but there was something about his stance, some tension that demonstrated he wasn't quite as comfortable as he appeared.

Zeke gave her a half-smile. "I can't say I'm surprised. Parker has been hounding me all week to talk to you."

She tossed him a sympathetic look, knowing exactly how he felt. "Same. It figures he would find a way to get us alone."

"Typical," Zeke agreed easily.

Walking over to him, Sunny stuck the keys in the trunk lock and twisted, trying to lift the lid. Nothing happened. She twisted it back and then to the right again. Nothing. She jiggled the key and tried again.

"Want some help?" Zeke asked, stepping up behind her.

Sunny could feel the heat from his body, and she took a deep breath, trying to steady herself. "I can do it," she responded, irritated. She wasn't sure if she was more annoyed at the trunk, Zeke, or herself for her reaction to Zeke's nearness.

"I know you can," Zeke said, his voice betraying his frustration at her refusal. "Just let me help."

"I don't need your help," Sunny said through gritted teeth, pushing with all her might. *Click.* The trunk opened. She blew a wisp of hair out of her eyes. "See?" she said.

"I see," Zeke said, holding up his hands in defense. "I was just trying to help."

"I thought you were done trying to save me," Sunny said, turning to face him. She was sandwiched between him and the trunk of the car. It was closer than she liked, but not close enough at the same time. Her body wanted to lean into his, and she had to hold herself back.

"I'm trying." He smiled sadly.

Sunny bobbed her head in response.

Neither made any move to get the snacks.

Her heartbeat sped up as he reached forward and tucked a dangling strand of hair behind her ear. "It's a hard habit to break, I guess," he admitted ruefully.

Her breath caught. She bit her lower lip, trying to conceal the effect he was having on her. His gaze dropped to her lips. His eyes were unreadable, but he leaned towards her. His hand moved to her waist, almost as though he couldn't stop himself from touching her. It was then that she knew he still wanted her.

Emboldened by that knowledge, she leaned up on her tiptoes and drew his head down to hers. The kiss felt familiar and new at the same time. Maybe it was because they had both grown up over the past few weeks. Maybe it was because he was leaving tomorrow.

But Sunny didn't stop to think about any of that. Zeke deepened the kiss, and Sunny matched him. He broke away to burn a trail of kisses down the side of her neck. She sighed, clinging to him. But he was still leaving tomorrow. Holding him now, she knew she didn't want to be apart from him. She loved him. She pulled back, but Zeke held on. He folded her into a hug, burying his face in her hair.

"I'm going to miss you," Zeke murmured into her hair.

The kiss and his comment gave Sunny the encouragement she needed. "What if," she began hopefully and then halted. Zeke pulled back to look at her. "What if I came with you to Italy?" she finished.

His expression changed almost immediately. He let her go and took a step back, distancing himself physically. "You can't come with me." His statement had a finality to it. Sunny felt her stomach dip.

"Oh," Sunny said, confused. A few minutes ago, she'd been so certain that he wanted her. Had she been wrong? "Why... Why not?" she stammered. And hated herself for sounding so vulnerable. But she had to know. She took a step forward and placed her hands on his chest, pleading.

Zeke shook his head and placed his hands over Sunny's, removing them from his chest and backing away further. "I'm sorry," he said, his expression turning stony. "I don't want you to come with me. This was a lot of fun." He turned away. "But that's all. I never asked you to come with me."

Sunny froze. She couldn't believe what she was hearing. How could she have been so stupid? He never said he loved her. He never said he wanted her to go with him. She just assumed. She assumed just because he kissed her.

Suddenly, Sunny was furious. At him and at herself.

"So that's all this was to you? Fun? I thought you cared about me." The betrayal she felt leaked out into her voice, and her face twisted in pain. Her brain told her to walk away, to save herself from this embarrassment. But she couldn't do it. She had to know.

He took a step forward but stopped. His eyes begged her to understand. "I do care about you. You're my brother's best friend. You're my friend."

It was all she could do to stop herself from gasping. It was as though a knife had twisted in her gut. His brother's best friend? His friend? Was that all she was? The words echoed in her head over and over as she stared at Zeke. She didn't know what to say.

"I'm sorry," he said again.

Then he turned and walked away, leaving Sunny standing alone, her heart in pieces. Again.

Chapter 40

"I showered immediately when I got home, and I still found glitter in my bed when I woke up this morning." Sunny huffed as soon as she sat down on the lounge chair by the pool. The midday sun shone brightly, and she shaded her eyes with her hand as she looked over at Parker.

Parker smiled devilishly. He was lying on his own lounge chair, arm propped up behind him, sunglasses perched low on his nose. He had his swim trunks on, and he looked ready to dive into the water. "Oooh, kinky. Well, I sneezed gold glitter a half hour ago, so clearly, I win."

Sunny stuck her tongue out at him. After last night's confrontation, she was crabby. She'd even barked at her father that morning. She'd apologized immediately but still felt guilty about it. Not wanting to run into Zeke today, she'd deliberately lounged around her house this morning, feeling miserable and foolish. Parker had told her that Zeke's flight was leaving at four this afternoon, so Zeke was already on the way to the airport. As soon as she knew it was safe and she wouldn't see him, she'd thrown on a t-shirt and frayed jean shorts and ran over to the Crawford house to see Parker.

"We're gonna have our work cut out for us when we head over there later and clean," Sunny remarked. "We need a vacuum or something to suck up all the glitter."

Parker nodded. "Mika is organizing a cleaning crew, and we're meeting up there in a couple of hours. We'll have plenty of help if she has anything to say about it."

"That's really nice of her. She's amazing," Sunny remarked.

Parker smiled at her. "I think she had as much fun this summer as we did." He turned to stare out at the pool, contemplative. "I'm gonna miss this when I'm gone," Parker sighed.

"No, you're not," Sunny disagreed, a smile on her face. She knew Parker, and he wasn't the type to miss things. He was going to live in the moment and enjoy every moment of college. "You're gonna be too busy making movies to miss anything."

Recognizing the truth of her words, Parker returned, "Yeah, well, you're gonna be too busy slaving away at your new job to miss anything either!"

"I hope so," she said wistfully. She hoped she was so busy that she didn't have a spare second to think about Zeke, living in Italy. If she had to think about him laughing at a bar, surrounded by beautiful Italian women, she wouldn't be able to stand it. He would be living an entirely different life, without her in it.

Parker knew what she meant immediately. Sitting up, he gave her a concerned look. "Have you talked to him at all today?"

"No," she answered, clasping her hands in front of her. "He's not interested in me anymore. He made that very clear last night. So what's the point of talking to him?"

"Well, I hate to point out the obvious, but apparently I have to because you are so damn dense. He's completely head-over-heels in love with you, Sunshine."

"No. He's not." She shook her head.

"Yes. He is," Parker insisted.

"No. He's not," she argued. She felt a tear slip down her cheek. Not even realizing that she'd been crying, she angrily swiped it away.

"I asked him to take me with him to Italy, P. Like a total idiot. Last night at the party. And he said no. If he's so in love with me, why did he say that?" Sunny had left the party immediately after Zeke had walked away, so she hadn't told Parker what had happened until this moment.

Parker slapped his hand to his forehead in frustration. "Holy crap, Sunny. For someone so smart, you are the stupidest person I know sometimes."

Sunny laughed through her tears, rolling her eyes. "Gee, thanks."

He leaned forward and patted her arm sympathetically. "I mean that with all the love in my heart. I really do. I have to ask you this, though. In your conversations with Zeke, did you happen to mention to him that your job is remote and you can work anywhere in the world?"

Sunny's eyes widened as she thought back to all her conversations. "Well, I... I..." She couldn't believe it. She'd told her dad. She'd told Parker. Had she told Zeke? She thought everyone knew. She wasn't moving anywhere. Her plan had been to live at home with her dad until she'd saved enough money for an apartment. But Parker was right. She'd never explicitly told Zeke that she could work from anywhere in the world.

"Exactly," pronounced Parker, pointing at her. "So picture this..." He spread his arms wide as he set the scene as though it were a movie. "Zeke, the hero of our story, struggles with wanting to protect those that he loves. Sunny, our lovely heroine, has a once-in-a-lifetime job opportunity that Zeke believes is in Minneapolis. Our hero is leaving the country for an amazing opportunity, and the heroine offers to join him. Our hero thinks that means she has to give up her new job. What does our hero do?"

Sunny answered slowly, her brain churning as she thought through everything. "He tells her no."

"Why?" Parker prompted.

The answer was so obvious that Sunny couldn't believe she hadn't seen it earlier. She resisted the urge to slap her forehead as the realization struck her. "He's protecting her."

"Bingo," Parker stated, and then he prompted again, "And why?"

Sunny blinked. "Because he loves her..." she said haltingly.

"Ding, ding, ding! Correct. He said no because he's Zeke. And even when he promises he won't protect us anymore, he will not ask you to sacrifice your opportunity just to be with him."

Sunny stood up abruptly. "But I wouldn't be sacrificing anything. I can do my job in Italy. With him."

"But *he* doesn't know that, does he?" Parker pointed out, rising from the lounge chair.

Sunny stared at Parker. He was annoyingly correct sometimes.

"You really think he loves me?" She was afraid to hope.

"Duh," Parker returned.

"Oh no. He loves me... and he's leaving?"

"Took you long enough." He reached down and ruffled her hair.

"Oh my god. I've got to get to the airport!"

"No, you don't."

"Yes, I do," she said impatiently. "His flight leaves in three hours. If I leave now, I can make it there before he leaves. I have to go now. I have to see him."

He answered more firmly, "No, you don't. He's not at the airport."

That stopped Sunny in her tracks. "What?"

Parker removed his car keys from his pocket and twirled them around his fingers. "Let's go. I'll tell you in the car."

"Um, Parker, did you forget? You're grounded. And no driving."

Without missing a beat, he tossed the keys to Sunny. "Well, looks like you're on your own, then. Probably better that way, anyway. You don't need me for this."

"Where am I going? Where is Zeke?" Sunny insisted.

"He's at the lot. The one where my mom wanted to build her dream home. Remember?"

Of course, she knew what he was talking about. Luckily, she still remembered the way there.

"Why is he there, Parker? Why isn't he at the airport?"

Parker smiled mysteriously. "I'll let him tell you that."

Sunny started for the door but stopped herself. She turned around and threw her arms around Parker, squeezing tightly. "Thanks, Parker," she said.

He patted her back and released her, shoving her gently towards the French doors that would lead her out to the garage where his car was parked.

"Oh, and Sunny?" Parker asked. She paused, turning back to look at him on her way to the door. "You're perfect for each other. But you'll never survive if one of you doesn't learn how to freaking communicate."

As Sunny pulled Parker's car up next to Zeke's truck, she searched the field for Zeke. She spotted him sitting in the grass, about twenty feet from his truck, looking out over the horizon. The grass was a little more brown than the last time she'd been here. The summer heat had taken its toll.

She parked and hopped out of the car. "What are you doing out here?" she asked Zeke as she approached. He wore jeans and one of Sunny's favorite shirts, a blue v-neck shirt, the one that brought out his eyes.

"Just thinking," Zeke responded. He had been thinking, but he'd also been waiting for her. Parker had texted to tell him that Sunny was on her way. He didn't turn to face her. He couldn't quite yet. Ashamed of how he'd acted, he wanted to choose his words carefully. He kept his eyes on the field stretched out in front of him.

Sunny swallowed. Now that she was here, she didn't know what to say. She started with the obvious.

"Aren't you supposed to be getting on a flight soon?"

Zeke nodded. "I changed my ticket." He'd done more than that, but he wasn't ready to share that yet.

Sunny's breath caught. He wasn't leaving today. Parker had to be right. He did still have feelings for her. She moved to stand to the side of him, facing him, willing him to look at her. But he kept his eyes fixed on the field. "Why?"

"Why?" Zeke repeated as he pulled some grass up out of the ground and tossed it out in front of him. He cocked his head towards her and gave a lopsided smile. "Parker told me to get my head outta my ass."

Well, what Parker actually said to Zeke that morning was a lot longer and more involved. He'd definitely called him an ass, an idiot, and a few other choice words. But the moral of Parker's lecture, which frankly rivaled one of Alan Crawford's lectures, was that Zeke was a fool for leaving without telling Sunny how he felt about her.

And for once, Zeke had listened to his little brother. He'd needed to think, so he told Parker he was headed out to the lot, intending to gather his thoughts and then go talk to Sunny later today. He hadn't known that Parker would send Sunny out here, although, in retrospect, he should have anticipated it. Parker always had a plan.

"Sounds like Parker," Sunny said.

Zeke hesitated. That hadn't been an entirely truthful answer. He wasn't just here because Parker had told him to stay. He loved Sunny, and he couldn't leave things the way they ended last night. She deserved the truth. "And I stayed for you."

Sunny's heart gave a leap.

Knowing he couldn't do this halfway, Zeke continued earnestly, "I have been such an idiot. I'm sorry, Addison. You deserve so much better than how I treated you."

"You lied to me last night." It was a statement and a question, but she couldn't keep the hurt out of her voice.

"I did," Zeke said, bowing his head. He wished he hadn't said those things to her. He lay awake all night, reliving the conversation over and over. When she'd asked to go to Italy, all he could think about was what she'd be giving up. Sunny had worked all summer to find her path forward, knowing in her heart that college wasn't it. And then she found it. He saw the excitement in her eyes when she talked about this new job. She glowed every time she mentioned it. He would not let her give it up for him. So he'd pushed her away, thinking it was what was best for her. But he regretted it, and he'd told Parker as much this morning. It wasn't his decision what Sunny did with her life. She was the only one that could make that choice.

He knew he couldn't go back and change what he said last night. All he could do was try to fix it.

"You said you didn't want me to come with you," Sunny pressed. "Was that true?"

She had to hear him say it.

"No. It wasn't true." He blew out a breath, relieved to offer her the truth. "The truth is, I wanted you to come with me so much it hurt."

Sunny felt joy flow through her, accompanied by a jolt of anger. How dare he put her through this? He'd convinced her she was alone in her feelings for him. He'd made her feel like a fool. She burst out, "You had no right to push me away last night. You lied to me." Her voice got louder as she struggled to rein in her emotions. "After we just talked about honesty!"

She was full-on yelling now. "You don't get to do that. You don't get to lie to the people you love. You don't get to take our choices away from us anymore. I don't want you to go to Italy without me! Don't you realize that I would miss you? I would miss your smile, and your laugh, and the way you make me feel like I can do anything! You can't just leave me behind like that!"

Zeke stood, dusting off his backside and turning to face Sunny. He looked confused. "I'm sorry! You're shouting nice things at me, and it's really messing with me!" He was yelling now too. He stopped and groaned loudly.

Attempting to lower his voice, Zeke repeated, "You're right, and I'm sorry. I'm sorry for everything I put you through. I can't take it back, but I promise I'll do better. If you'll just give me another chance." He ran his hands through his hair in frustration, making nearly every hair stand up on its end. He looked like he'd been electrocuted. Sunny couldn't stop herself from laughing at his hair, at the whole crazy situation. Now that she knew he wanted her, she simply felt like laughing. So she did.

"And now you're laughing at me!" He raised his arms to the sky in exasperation. "What is going on? You make me crazy."

She smiled at him, shaking her head and putting it all on the table. "What's going on, Ezekiel Jefferson Crawford, is that I love you. I mean, like, I'm in love with you. And it's turning me into a crazy person." She took a step towards him, and her expression turned serious again. "Please don't go to Italy without me."

"Okay," he said agreeably. He walked towards Sunny, stopping inches away from her. The word was spoken casually, but his eyes were deadly serious.

"Okay?" she parroted, surprised it was that easy after all the arguing they'd been doing.

"Yes. Okay. I won't leave you. I promise. Cross my heart." He motioned an X across his heart.

"Just like that?" she asked skeptically, putting her hands on her hips.

Zeke grinned that cocky grin of his that made Sunny's toes curl inside her shoes. He asked, "When are you going to realize that I'll do nearly anything you ask me to do?"

She returned his grin and grabbed his shirt, tugging him closer. "And why is that?"

He leaned down and rested his forehead against hers. They both closed their eyes. Their lips were inches away from each other. "Because I love you too."

"You do?" she whispered, still scared to believe it.

He opened his eyes, pulled back, and wrapped his arms around her, pulling her closer. It felt so good to have her in his arms again. He never wanted to let go. "Don't act so surprised. You know I've had a crush on you forever."

"Do guys get crushes?" Sunny asked, raising an eyebrow at him, and wrapping her arms around his neck in return. She reveled in the feel of his body pressed against hers. She'd thought she'd lost this. "I thought that was only for girls."

"It was a very manly crush, I can assure you," he said in mock seriousness.

"Hmmm," she said, noncommittally. "So, what are we going to do about this?"

"Well, I can't speak for you because you are a total heathen and are probably going to try to jump my bones right away, but I, for one, am a total gentleman. And as a gentleman, I propose we go out. On a date. Together. In Italy."

"In Italy?" Sunny felt a smile spread across her face.

Zeke smiled. "See, I didn't just change my flight." He paused, suddenly looking a little uncertain. "I also added a second ticket. I know you have a job here, but it's not my decision to make. The ticket is yours if you still want it."

"Oh, I want it. And I'm keeping my job too." Sunny grinned triumphantly.

"How are you going to do that?" Zeke asked, confused.

"It's a remote position," she replied. "I can work from Italy."

Zeke groaned. Parker was right. He really was an idiot. He couldn't believe he had almost lost Sunny for nothing. "Why didn't you tell me that sooner?"

Instead of answering, Sunny pulled Zeke's head down to hers and kissed him with everything she had in her.

Epilogue

THREE MONTHS LATER

S unny sat on the balcony sipping a steaming cup of coffee, her laptop perched on the small round table beside her. The morning sun shone a golden light, warming her all the way to her bare toes. She could see the Duomo, which rose above the city in the distance. The bright scent of orange blossoms from a nearby garden wafted up to her nose. Florence was her favorite city in Italy so far. Lots of people raved over Venice or Rome or Milan or Naples. But for Sunny, it was Florence.

She couldn't even pinpoint what it was exactly that fascinated her so much. The city was beautiful, of course, but so were most cities in Italy. The people were friendly, but no more so than anywhere else. It was simple to navigate. The Duomo was pretty much in the center of the city, making it nearly impossible to get lost. The architecture and museums were some of the most amazing she'd ever seen. But it was more than that. It was a feeling. A peacefulness. A wonder.

She was thoroughly enjoying Italy. It probably also had something to do with the fact that she was here with Zeke. They had been in Italy for three months, and during that time, Zeke had been studying the piano under Alessandro.

Sunny was working remotely while also enrolled in an independent study course. It was perfect for her. She worked with her professor to design her own course content, and it was all self-led, exactly the way she loved to learn. Her dad was happy that she was still continuing to learn and grow. In the end, that was all he really wanted for her.

Her job was challenging, but she enjoyed digging in and solving problems. She was on a small team of programmers, led by an incredible manager. He was patient with Sunny, and he took extra time to teach her the ropes. She was new to the business world and needed that extra help. Their entire team was remote, so she wasn't the only one. One woman was working from India, one from Canada, and the rest were all living in the United States in various places. They met once a day on video chat to update each other on their progress. When she got stuck, she could call any of them. It was the perfect balance.

Familiar, warm hands grasped her shoulders. She turned her head upward to see Zeke standing behind her. He leaned down and planted a kiss on her lips. His hair was damp, and she smelled the fresh scent of his cologne, both signs he'd just gotten out of the shower. She smiled up at him. "What was that for?"

He returned her smile, moving to sit down next to her in the remaining chair on the narrow balcony. "I just felt like it."

Sunny felt giddy as she asked, "Are you heading out to meet with Alessandro today?"

"Yep. I need all the practice I can get. He just told me he wants me to perform at this event he's hosting next week. It's a charity event, but he's showcasing up-and-coming talent. I guess that's me. I'm 'up-and-coming talent.'" He sounded excited.

Sunny could hardly believe how much joy Zeke found in playing now. It was like he came alive. Where once Alessandro was disappointed in him and accused him of having no passion, now he was praising Zeke at every opportunity, calling him a genius. The transformation in Zeke was amazing.

"I'm so happy for you. You deserve this."

"Thanks. I emailed my dad about it, and he said he's going to fly out with Parker and your dad for the event."

Sunny was so excited, she shrieked. She'd been missing both Parker and her dad. Video chat was great, but it wasn't enough.

"And if it goes well, Alessandro said he thinks I can play solo concerts one day. I mean, I need to train more and get a manager and all that. But I feel like everything's finally coming together. I may never book a gig, though. So I don't want to get ahead of myself."

"Book a gig?" Sunny echoed. "You've even got the music slang down. Oh, you'll definitely book a gig. You're too talented not to."

"I don't want to get too cocky about this. There's plenty of people in the world who set out to be concert pianists and never make it. And of the ones that do, sometimes they only get paid peanuts."

"You'll make it. And you'll make money at it too. I know it."

Zeke continued to look skeptical, but Sunny was certain. So certain, in fact, that the next words that came out of her mouth were, "Wanna bet?"

Zeke cocked an eyebrow. "A bet, huh?"

Sunny smiled playfully and leaned forward. "I bet you book a gig by next summer. A paying one."

Zeke leaned forward. "And what do I get if I win?"

"My undying love and devotion."

Zeke snorted. "I already have that."

"Ugh, you know you do." Sunny tapped her finger against her lips. "Okay, okay. How about this? You can pick my flavor of gelato next time."

"No way. All the flavors of gelato are good. There's no pizza or pistachio or anything awful like what Parker forced us to eat. There are no bad ones!"

"Oh, so you want me to suffer?" Sunny feigned outrage.

"Yes," Zeke said emphatically. "Horribly. The loser of the bet has to suffer. It's a rule."

"You might as well make me go to that weird little piano museum in northern Italy that you keep yapping about, if you really want me to suffer."

Zeke snapped his fingers and said, "That's perfect."

"No," Sunny said, in mock horror. "I was joking!"

"Yes, it's perfect. I want to do it, and you don't, so that's what I get if I win."

"Fine," Sunny said petulantly, slumping back in her chair like an upset child. Then she brightened. "It's fine, actually. I'm going to win, anyway. And I better get something good when I win."

"My undying love and devotion?" Zeke said, echoing her words from earlier.

Sunny stuck her tongue out at him. Then she thought for a moment. Inspiration struck.

"If I win and you book a paying gig before June of next year, I get to make all our movie choices for an entire year."

"A whole year? No way. That's not equal to a trip to the piano museum. You pick the worst movies. I can't handle a year of rom-coms and horror movies and so-called classics." He put air quotes around the word "classics" to show his low opinion of her choice of movies. "I'll never survive. A week," Zeke countered.

"A month," Sunny fired back.

"Bet," Zeke confirmed.

Standing, Zeke held out a hand to her. She took it and used it to propel herself up and into his arms. She wrapped her arms around his neck.

He smiled. "Should we seal the deal with a kiss?"

Sunny answered him without using words. The kiss was slow and relaxed, exactly how Sunny felt standing on a balcony on a warm, sunny day in Italy.

When they parted, Zeke said, "Mmmmm, I think we should seal every bet that way."

Sunny laughed. "That can be arranged."

Zeke leaned in for another kiss. Then he pulled back and beamed, a mischievous look on his face. "Hey, Sunny?"

"What?" she replied, suspicious.

"I donut love you." His grin widened.

She laughed, slapping at his arm, still mildly embarrassed about her drunken text. "I donut love you too."

She wrapped her arms around him and pulled him in for another kiss. Zeke groaned when his phone alarm rang. He pulled away too soon for Sunny's preference and clicked the screen to silence the alarm. "I've got to go. Alessandro is waiting, and you know how impatient he is."

"Okay. Fine. Go," she said, but she didn't release him. She removed her hands from his neck and slid them down his chest. When her hands reached the bottom of his shirt, they slipped inside, fingertips trailing over his bare chest.

"Well, maybe just a few more minutes," Zeke said, lifting Sunny up easily. Her legs encircled his waist, and he carried her backwards through the French doors and into the bedroom.

They fell back onto the bed, laughing.

As he showered her with kisses, she paused and clasped her hands on either side of his face, forcing him to stop. "You're happy here, right? You don't miss home? Or Notre Dame?"

He halted and answered seriously, "I don't miss a thing except Parker and our dads. You?"

Sunny smiled. "Same."

"Not sad you didn't go to MIT? You could be sitting in your dorm room right now or getting ready to go to class or partying with your friends. Any regrets?"

"With a view like this?" She pointed out the window, but she continued looking directly at Zeke. "Not sad at all. I have everything I want. I have you. Work is amazing. I'm learning. It's exactly what I wanted, what I needed."

Zeke turned serious. "And you're okay that it's not what your mom dreamed of for you?"

She nodded, certain. "I've made my peace with it. I sometimes wonder if I would have felt closer to her if I'd have gone there. But I can't keep living in the past. My mom wasn't at MIT. She's with me, in my heart and my mind, no matter where I go." She paused. "I think my mom would be proud of me."

Zeke nodded. "Definitely," he confirmed.

Sunny continued, "At some point, we all have to grow up and make our own decisions. This isn't exactly what my mother said she wanted for me. But it's everything *I* wanted for me. And that's important."

As she tugged Zeke's head down to hers for another kiss, she realized it was true. She didn't know what tomorrow would bring, but today, she had everything she'd ever wanted.

Acknowledgments

Creating this book was a labor of love that took many years, and there are so many wonderful people who helped me along the way. I owe my deepest gratitude to them all.

A gigantic thank you to my husband for his love and support. Thank you for getting bedtime snacks for our sons while I was hunched over my keyboard writing. Thank you for never complaining about it. Thank you for putting up with the clickity-clack of my typing at midnight when inspiration struck. Thank you for only complaining about it a little. Thank you for never doubting that I could finish this.

Thank you to my two sons for testing out the clues so I could make sure they made sense. You are both excellent puzzle solvers. Thank you for your excitement to read my "About the Author" section. Authors everywhere appreciate that you care who they are.

Thank you to my mom, Linda Wagner, and my sisters, Jeanna Zunker and Kristi Smith, for being my cheerleaders, guinea pigs, and early readers. I appreciate your patience when it took weeks (or months) before any new chapters came your way. I appreciate the spelling corrections, advice on my cover, and your support. Also, I apologize for changing the story many, many, many times while you were in the middle of reading it. A special thank you to Jeanna for contributing her expert proofreading skills. She did a beautiful job, and all grammatical errors that remain are strictly my own, because I was married to a few particular style choices. Thank you to my dad, Richard Wagner, for your willingness to read even though I'm certain that teenage romance isn't your favorite topic.

This book would not have been possible without the support of my creative and talented friend, Melonie Nathe. Thank you, Melonie, for all of the hours you dedicated to me. Thank you for sharing your ideas with me, your ability to truly understand my characters and their motivations, and your insightful feedback, all of which greatly improved this book. Thank you for celebrating the completion of each chapter so joyfully. I simply would never have finished this without you.

To Michelle Pape and my entire EPG family, your support and encouragement means everything to me. Thank you for listening, providing advice, and cheering me on.

Thank you to my talented photographer, Savannah Pierson of SavvyPhotage, for taking my first-ever author photos, making the process not only painless, but fun.

To my best friends, Ashley and Angie, thank you for never doubting that I could finish this book. I am so lucky to have you in my life. I am grateful to you both for your laughter, your honesty, and your support.

I would be remiss if I didn't mention one of my professors from college for his influence on my passion for writing, Dwight Purdy. Since Dr. Purdy has passed on, I'll address this note to my dear friend, Anna. Anna, your dad was a brilliant man, an engaging professor, and an even better human being. He opened my eyes to looking at literature in a different way. He was all about heart and emotion and story-telling, and I loved that about him. He is deeply missed.

To my readers, thank you for taking a chance on a new author. It means so much to me. I've wanted to write stories since I was a little girl, and this book is the culmination of a life-long dream. I hope you enjoyed reading about Sunny, Zeke, and Parker.

About the Author

Casey Gordon lives in Minnesota with her husband and two sons. She has a fat gray cat that somehow manages to be both loving and crotchety at the same time. She firmly believes one can never own too many books, a belief that luckily her children share. In school, she often got in trouble for reading instead of paying attention to class, and she never felt one bit guilty about it. Her head is constantly filled with stories, and it was always her lifelong dream to share them with others.

Learn more about the author: https://www.caseyjgordon.com/
Photo by SavvyPhotage: https://www.savvyphotage.com/

Made in the USA
Middletown, DE
12 July 2022